MW01485551

IMAGINARIUM

THE BEST CANADIAN
SPECULATIVE WRITING

CZP

ChiZine Publications

FIRST EDITION

Imaginarium 3: The Best Canadian Speculative Writing © 2015 ChiZine Publications
Introduction © 2015 by Ian C. Esslemont
Cover artwork © 2015 by Susanne Apgar
Cover and interior design by © 2015 by Samantha Beiko

All Rights Reserved.

This book is a work of fiction. Names, characters, places, and incidents are either a product of the author's imagination or are used fictitiously. Any resemblance to actual events, locales, or persons, living or dead, is entirely coincidental.

Distributed in Canada by
HarperCollins Canada Ltd.
1995 Markham Road
Scarborough, ON M1B 5M8
Toll Free: 1-800-387-0117
e-mail: hcorder@harpercollins.com

Distributed in the U.S. by
Diamond Comic Distributors, Inc.
10150 York Road, Suite 300
Hunt Valley, MD 21030
Phone: (443) 318-8500
e-mail: books@diamondbookdistributors.com

Library and Archives Canada Cataloguing in Publication

Imaginarium : the best Canadian speculative writing.

Contents: [v. 3] 3 / edited by Sandra Kasturi and Helen Marshall ; introduction

by Ian C. Esslemont.

Issued in print and electronic formats.

ISBN 978-1-77148-199-1 (v. 3 : pbk.).--ISBN 978-1-77148-200-4 (v. 3 : pdf)

1. Speculative fiction, Canadian (English). 2. Short stories, Canadian (English).

3. Canadian fiction (English)--21st century. I. Kasturi, Sandra, 1966-, editor

II. Marshall, Helen, 1983-, editor

PS8323.S3I43 2012   C813'.08760806   C2012-904197-1

C2012-904211-0

CHIZINE PUBLICATIONS
Toronto, Canada
www.chizinepub.com
info@chizinepub.com

Edited by Sandra Kasturi & Helen Marshall
Proofread by Dominik Parisien

A **free** eBook edition is available
with the purchase of this print book.

CLEARLY PRINT YOUR NAME ABOVE IN UPPER CASE

Instructions to claim your free eBook edition:
1. Download the BitLit app for Android or iOS
2. Write your name in **UPPER CASE** on the line
3. Use the BitLit app to submit a photo
4. Download your eBook to any device

Canada Council   Conseil des arts
for the Arts   du Canada

We acknowledge the support of the Canada Council for the Arts which last year invested $20.1 million in writing and publishing throughout Canada.

ONTARIO ARTS COUNCIL
CONSEIL DES ARTS DE L'ONTARIO

an Ontario government agency
un organisme du gouvernement de l'Ontario

Published with the generous assistance of the Ontario Arts Council.

Printed in Canada

IMAGINARIUM 3

TABLE OF CONTENTS

INTRODUCTION
Once More Into the Woods

Ian C. Esslemont

While the title of this essay/rant doesn't pose a question, there is a mystery it wishes to explore and this is: Why the attraction? Why this abiding fascination with the fantastic? When the authors of literary fiction sigh with ennui within their too-familiar kitchens, their dreary work-places, and their predictably alienating urban settings, whither they? When literary genre-crossing becomes all the rage—whither these authors?

Why, to the deep dark woods where the fantasy authors play.

When a crisis of genre identity afflicts, whither the critics? To fantasy they turn. Why the attraction? Is it the woods—lovely, dark, and deep?

And when I write "fantasy" here I wish to be clear that I am not using it as reference to any one particular genre. Rather, I am referencing the deep well-spring of the fantastic which feeds a multiplicity of genres and sub-genres, and which in point of fact lies open to any author to draw upon. I make no claims to any genre definition other than the one particular guiding metaphor that I wish to explore here.

Very broadly, when literary critics and theorists turn to pinning down the differences between literary fiction and genre fiction, they often cite the usual suspects: plot convention and predictability (you know what you're getting). They also claim they will not base their comparison on the quality of the prose (since you mustn't compare apples to oranges), and yet then they promptly go on to do precisely that.

Admittedly, fantasy generally is not the home of economy of prose, nor pure elegance—though many authors operating within it can achieve such beauty—rather, fantasy is about wilderness. The tangled unknown. The potentially ominous and certainly threatening wild woods that is, of course, the imagination.

In the wilds nothing is neat. By definition you do *not* know what may lie beyond the next turn. Dare you risk becoming lost? Where lies the familiar and comforting moment of character self-realization now? Which way to the epiphany? What you thought you saw or heard just then—can you be certain of psychological realism here? Dare you enter the wild trackless woods where the fantasy writers play?

Many searching for something beyond the tired and the familiar do. Cross-genre pollination, some call it. I call it daring to set a toe into the frightening wilds.

I began this rant determined not to name names, nor drag out the usual perpetrators, however, I feel that I must—if only to confound those readers who, even now, are saying to themselves: Well! He hasn't mentioned so-and-so. . . . And so comes the litany of Michael Chabon with his Jewish enclave in Alaska, Colson Whitehead's zombie apocalypse, Jonathan Lethem, et al., Karen Russell and her vampires, and Aimee Bender's imaginings. It is also true that many of the above authors yet remain acceptable topics within literary criticism; perhaps because while they wandered a touch further into the woods to steal a few magic mushrooms, they certainly didn't linger.

The question is, then, why the appeal? Why come to fantasy?

One reason may lie in an assigned weakness that is in fact a strength. Like a sister genre (or sister non-genre, as I will argue) fantasy and so-called "historical fiction" share a certain type of definition—or lack thereof. Some critics and literary theorists assign all fiction that is "not contemporary" into a bottomless bag that they name historical fiction. Following this logic, writers are apparently only allowed to portray their contemporary moment or risk being dumped into a shameful genre ghetto—or more importantly—tossed over the walls of so-called "literary" writing. Yet just what defines contemporary? This particular year? This particular month? This particular day? More recently, however, many critics do now reluctantly acknowledge that there may be *some* merit to such "historical" authors as Pat Barker and Hilary Mantel. And yet, imagine their spluttering rage in the face of authors who actually go ahead and write whatever they damn-well please without any consideration of their precious genre definitions, such as Jim Shepard.

The die-hard defenders of the boundaries of literary fiction (and very vigilant they are), have built very tall and well-defined walls around their claimed territory. They patrol them with sharp pens and equally sharp disapproval. However, should one of them happen to raise their gaze to the forest at large, they would discover that all they have succeeded in doing is confining themselves to a very tiny, very strangled, meadow. And that surrounding them, extending beyond sight in all directions, stretch the tangled woods of possibility: the near infinity of all-that-*could*-be. The far off future; the distant past; unguessed possibilities of human social organization; utopias and dystopias; and, yes, even talking animals (George Orwell would approve).

So possessive of their small choked-off and rather inbred meadow are these critics that when a literature emerged from another tradition, one which did not share English-language tradition's biases, blinders and lacunae, and thus one that partook of the fantastic, an entirely new category had to be invented to explain away how this could be possible. And so was "magic realism" born. And so were those pesky iconoclasts— supposedly—put in their place.

It would seem that to some literary critics an expansive freedom of literary techniques is acceptable only so long as that author hails from a differing tradition. Just as, in colonial times, other cultures were the purview of anthropology—but certainly not that of the metropole.

Why then this continuing attraction of fantasy, its forms and its tropes? It might be that here one finds the deepest roots of all literature. Here, lost or hidden somewhere within the darkest grove or frond-choked pool, lie direct living fibrous connections with the first legends and stories put to scroll or stone—the very beginnings of what Western scholars name "history" itself. Here heroes battled monsters, gods walked among men and women, and an ancient king searched for immortality.

My claim then, is that it is here within the trackless wilds of fantasy that one can find *anything*. Here lie an infinity of ways to portray things. If, in fiction, one pressure is to bring the new to something old . . . then you can find just that in the woods.

And here, if you go looking with open eyes and an open creative spirit, you will always be surprised by what you discover.

ROSARY AND GOLDENSTAR
Geoff Ryman

The room was wood—floor, walls, ceiling. The doorbell clanged a second time. The servant girl Bessie finally answered it; she had been lost in the kitchen amid all the pans. She slid across the floor on slippers, not lifting her feet; she had a notion that she polished as she walked. The front door opened directly onto the night: snow. The only light was from the embers in the fireplace.

Three huge men jammed her doorway. "This be the house of Squire Digges?" the smallest of them asked; and Bessie, melting in shyness, said something like, "Cmn gud zurs."

They crowded in, stomping snow off their boots, and Bessie knelt immediately to try to mop it up with her apron. "Shoo! Shoo!" said the smaller guest, waving her away.

The Master roared; the other door creaked like boots and in streamed Squire Digges, both arms held high. "Welcome! Good Count Vesuvius! Guests! Hah hah!" Unintroduced, he began to pump their hands.

Vesuvius, the smaller man, announced in Danish that this was Squire Digges, son of Leonard and author of the lenses, then turned back and said in English that these two fine fellows were Frederik Rosenkrantz and Knud Gyldenstierne.

"We have corresponded!" said Squire Digges, still smiling and pumping. To him, the two Danes looked huge and golden-red with bronze beards and bobbed noses, and he'd already lost control of who was who. He looked sideways in pain at the Count. "You must pardon me, sirs?"

"For what?"

The Squire looked harassed and turned on the servant. "Bessie! Bessie, their coats! The door. Leave off the floor, girl!"

Vesuvius said in Danish, "*The gentleman has asked you to remove your coats at long last. For this he is sorry.*"

One of the Danes smiled, his face crinkling up like a piecrust, and he unburdened himself of what must have been a whole seal hide. He dumped it on Bessie, who could not have been more than sixteen and was small for her years. Shaking his head, Digges slammed shut the front door. Bessie, buried under furs, began to slip across the gleaming floor as if on ice.

"Bessie," said Digges in despair, then looked over his shoulder. "Be careful of the floors, Messires, she polishes them so. Good girl, not very bright." He touched Bessie's elbow and guided her toward the right door.

"*He warns us that floors are dangerous.*"

Rosenkrantz and Gyldenstierne eyed each other. "*Perhaps we fall through?*" They began to tiptoe.

Digges guided Bessie through the door, and closed it behind her. He smiled and then unsmiled when there was a loud whoop and a falling crash within.

"All's well, Bessie?"

"Aye, zur."

"We'll wait here for a moment. Uh, before we go in. The gentlemen will excuse me but I did not hear your names."

"*He's forgotten your names. These English cannot speak.*" Vesuvius smiled. "Is so easy to remember in English. This be noble Rosary and Goldenstar."

"Sirs, we are honoured. Honoured beyond measure!"

Mr. Goldenstar sniffed. "*The whole place sags and creaks. Haven't the English heard of bricks?*"

Mr. Rosary beamed and gestured at the panelling and the turd-brown floor. "House. Beautiful. Beautiful!"

Squire Digges began to talk to them as if they were children. "In. Warm!" He beat his own arms. "Warrrrrrrrrrm."

Goldenstar was a military man, and when he saw the room beyond, he gave a cry and leapt back in alarm.

It was not a dining hall but a dungeon. It had rough blocks, chains, and ankle irons that hung from the wall. "*It's a trap!*" he yelped, and clasped young Rosary to pull him back.

From behind the table a tall, lean man rose up, all in black with a skullcap and lace around his neck. *Inquisitor.*

"Oh!" laughed the Squire and touched his forehead. "No, no, no, no alarms, I beg. Hah hah! The house once belonged to Philip Henslowe; he owns the theatre out back; this is like a set from a play."

Vesuvius blinked in fury. *"This is his idea of a joke."*

"You should see the upstairs; it is full of naked Venuses!"

"I think he just said upstairs is a brothel."

Goldenstar ran his fingers over the walls. The rough stones, the iron rings and the chains had all been frescoed onto plaster. He blurted out a laugh. *"They're all mad."*

"They are all strolling players. They do nothing but go to the theatre. They pose and declaim and roar."

Digges flung out a hand toward the man in black. "Now to the business at hand. Sirs! May . . . I . . . introduce . . . Doctor John DEE!"

For the Doctor, Vesuvius had a glittery smile; but he said through his teeth, *"They mime everything."*

"Ah!" Mr. Rosary sprang forward to shake the old man's hand. He was in love, eyes alight. "Queen Elisabetta. Magus!"

Dr. John Dee rumbled, "I am called Mage, yes, but I am in fact the Advisor Philosophical to her Majesty."

Digges beamed. "His *Parallaticae commentationis* and my own *Alae seu scalae mathematicae* were printed as a pair."

Someone else attended, pale skinned, pink cheeked, and glossy from nose to balding scalp, with black eyes like currants in a bun and an expression like a barber welcoming you to his shop.

"And this example," growled Digges, putting his hand on the young man's shoulder, "will not be known to you, but we hold him in high esteem, a family friend. This is Guillermus Shakespere."

The young man presented himself. "A Rosary and a Goldenstar. These are names for poetry. Especially should one wish to contrast Religion and Philosophy."

Vesuvius's lip curled. "You mock names?"

"No no, of course not. I beg! Not that construction. It is but poetic . . . convenience. My own poor name summons up dragooned peasants shaking weapons. Or, or, an actor whose only roles are those of soldiers." The young man looked back and forth between the men, expecting laughter. They blinked and stood with their hands folded not quite into fists.

"My young friend is a reformed Papist and so thinks much on issues of religion and philosophy. As do we." Digges paused, also waiting. "Please sit, gentlemen."

Cushions, food, and wine all beckoned. Digges busied himself pouring far too much wine into tankards. Mr. Rosary hunkered down with pleasure next to Dr. Dee, and even took his hand. He then began to speak, sometimes closing his eyes. "My dear Squire Digges and honourable Doctor Dee. My relative Tycho Brahe sends his greatest respects and has entrusted us to give you this, his latest work."

He sighed and chuckled, relieved to be rid of both a small grey printed pamphlet, and his speech. Digges howled his gratitude, and read a passage aloud from the pamphlet and passed it to Dr. Dee, and pressed Rosary to pass on his thanks.

Rosary began to recite again. "I am asked by Tycho Brahe to say how impress-ed with your work. Sir. To describe the universe as infinite with mathematical argument!" His English sputtered and died. "Is a big thing. We are all so amuzed."

"Forgive me," said the young man. "Is it the universe or the argument that is infinite?"

"Guy," warned Digges in a sing-song voice. He pronounced it with a hard "G" and a long eeee.

"And is it the universe or the numbers that are amusing?"

Mr. Rosary paused, understood, and grinned. "The two. Both."

"We disagree on matters of orbitals," said Squire Digges.

Vesuvius leaned back, steepling his fingers; his nails were clean and filed. "A sun that is the circumference of Terra." He sketched with his finger a huge circle and shook his head.

Almost under his breath the young man said, "A sonne can be larger than his father."

Digges explained. "My young friend is a poet."

Vesuvius smiled. "I look forward to him entertaining us later." Then he ventriloquized in Danish, "*And until then, he might eat with the servants*."

Mr. Rosary looked too pleased to care and beamed at Digges. "You . . . have . . . lens."

Digges boomed. "Yes! Yes! On roof." He pointed. "*Stierne. Stierne*."

Rosary laughed and nodded. "Yes! *Stierne*! Star."

"Roof. We go to roof." Squire Digges mimed walking with his two fingers. Blank looks, so he wiped out his gesture with a wave.

Vesuvius translated with confidence. "*No stars tonight, too cloudy*."

"No stars," said Mr. Rosary, as if someone's cat had died.

"Yes." Digges looked confused. "*Stierne*. On roof."

Everything stalled: words, hands, mouths and feet. Nobody understood.

Young Guy made a sound like bells, many of them, as if bluebells rang. His fingers tinkled across an arch that was meant to be the Firmament. Then his two flat hands became lenses and his arms mechanical supports that squeedled as they lined up his palms.

Goldenstar gave his head an almost imperceptible shake. "*What the hell is he doing?*"

Vesuvius: "*I told you they have to mime everything.*"

"*No wonder that they are good with numbers. They can't use words!*"

"*It's why there will never be a great poet in English.*"

Rosary suddenly rocked in recognition. He too mimed the mechanical device with its lenses. He twinkled at young Guy. Young Guy twinkled back.

"Act-or," explained Digges. "Tra-la! Stage. But poet. Oh! Such good poet. New poem. *Venus and Adonis!*" He kissed the tips of his fingers. Vesuvius's eyes, heavy and unmoved, rested on his host.

"Poet. Awww," Rosary said in sympathy. "No numbers."

John Dee, back erect, sipped his wine.

Bessie entered, rattling plates and knives in terror. Goldenstar growled, and his hands rounded in the air the curvature of her buttocks. She noticed and fled, soles flapping, polishing no more.

The Squire poured more wine. "Now. I want to hear more of your great relation, Lord Tycho. I yearn to visit him. He lives on an island? Devoted to philosophy!" He pronounced the name as "Tie-koh."

Vesuvius corrected him. "Teej-hhho."

"Yes yes yes, Tycho."

"The island is called *Hven*. You should be able to remember it as it is the same word as 'haven.' It is called in Greek Uraniborg. Urania means study of stars. Perhaps you know that?"

Digges's face stiffened. "I do read Greek."

Rosary beamed at Guy. "Your name Gee. In Greek is Earth."

Guy laughed. "Is it? Heaven and Earth. And I was born Taurus." He waited for a response. "Earth sign?" He looked at them all in turn. "You are all astrologers?"

Dr. Dee said, "No."

"And your name," said Guy, turning suddenly on the translator as if pulling a blade. "You are called Vesuvius?"

"A pseudonym, Guy," said Digges. "Something to hide. *A nom de plume.*"

"What's that?"

"French," growled Vesuvius. "A language."

Rosary thought that was a signal to change languages, and certainly the subject. *"Mon cousin a un nez d'or."*

Squire Digges jumped in to translate ahead of Vesuvius. "Your cousin has a..." He faltered. "A golden nose."

Rosary pointed to his own nose. *"Oui. Il l'a perdu ça par se battre en duel."*

"In . . . a . . . duel."

Goldenstar thumped the table. "Over *matematica!*"

Squire Digges leaned back. "Now that is a good reason to lose your nose."

"Ja! Ja!" Goldenstar laughed. *"Principiis mathematicis."*

"I trust we will not come to swords," said Digges, half-laughing.

Rosary continued. *"De temps en temp il port un nez de cuivre."*

Vesuvius translated. "Sometimes the nose is made of copper."

Guy's mouth crept sideways. "He changes noses for special occasions?"

Vesuvius glared; Goldenstar prickled. "Tycho Brahe great man!"

"Evidently. To be able to afford such a handsome array of noses."

Squire Digges hummed "no" twice.

Rosary pressed on. *"Mon cousin maintain comme un animal de familier un élan."*

Vesuvius snapped back, "He also has a pet moose."

Digges coughed. "I think you'll find he means elk."

"L'élan peut danser!" Rosary looked so pleased.

Digges rattled off a translation. "The elk can dance." He paused. "I might have that wrong."

Goldenstar thought German might work better. *"Der elch ist tot."*

Digges. "The elk is dead."

"Did it die in the duel as well?" Guy's face was bland. "To lose at a stroke both your nose and your moose."

Rosary rocked with laughter. *"Ja-ha-ha. Ja! Der elch gesoffenwar von die treppen gefallen hat."*

Sweat tricked down Digges's forehead. "The elk drank too much and fell down stairs."

Guy nodded slightly to himself. "And you good men believe that the Earth goes around the sun." His smile was a grimace of incredulity and embarrassment.

Dr. Dee tapped the table. "No. Your friend Squire Digges believes the Earth goes around the sun. Our guests believe that the sun goes around the Earth, but that all the other planets revolve around those two central objects. They believe this on the evidence of measurements and numbers. This evening is a conference on numbers and their application to the ancient study of stars. Astronomy. But the term is muddled."

Guy's face folded in on itself.

"Language fails you. Thomas Digges is described as a designer of arms and an almanacker. Our Danish friends are called astrologers, I am called a mage. I call us philosophers, but our language is numbers. Numbers describe, sirrah, with more precision than all your poetry."

Shakespere bowed.

"The Queen herself believes this and thus so should you." Dee turned away from him.

"But the numbers disagree," said Shakespere.

Bessie laboured into the room backwards, bearing on a trencher a whole roast lamb. It was burnt black and smelled of soot. The company applauded nonetheless. The parsnips and turnips about it were cinders shining with fat.

Digges continued explaining. "Now, this great Tycho saw suddenly appear in the heavens. . . ."

Goldenstar punched the air and shouted over the last few words, "By eye! By eye!"

"Yes, by eye. He saw a new light in the heavens, a comet he thought, only it could not be one."

"Numbers by eye!"

"Yes, he calculated the parallax and proved it was not a comet. It was beyond the moon. A new star, he thought."

"Nova!" exclaimed Goldenstar.

"More likely to be a dying one, actually. But it was a change to the immutable sphere of the stars!"

"Oh. Interesting," said Shakespere. "Should . . . someone carve?"

"You're as slow as gravy! Guy! The sphere of the stars is supposed to be unchanging and perfect."

"Spheres, you mean the music of the spheres?"

Goldenstar bellowed. "*Ja*. It move!"

"I rather like the idea of the stars singing."

Digges's hand moved as if to music. "It means Ptolemy is wrong. It means the Church is wrong, though why Ptolemy matters to the Church I don't know. But there it was. A new light in the heavens!"

Guy's voice rose in panic. "When did this happen?"

John Dee answered him. "1572."

Shakespere began to count the years on his fingers.

John Dee's mouth twitched and he squeezed shut Shakespere's hand. "Twenty. Years. And evidently the world did not end, so it was not a portent." As he spoke, Vesuvius translated in an undertone.

Squire Digges grinned like a wolf. "There are no spheres. The planets revolve around the sun, and we are just another planet."

"Noooooooooo ho-ho!" wailed Rosary and Goldenstar.

Digges bounced up and down in his chair, still smiling. "The stars are so far away we cannot conceive the distance. All of them are bigger than the sun. The universe is infinitely large. It never ends."

The Danes laughed and waved him away. Goldenstar said, "Terra heavy. Sit in centre. Fire light. Sun go around Terra!"

"Could we begin eating?" suggested Guy.

"Terra like table. Table fly like bird? No!" One of Goldenstar's fists was matter, the other fire and spirit.

"I'll carve. Shall I carve?" No one noticed Shakespere. He stood up and sharpened the knife while the philosophers teased and bellowed. He sawed the blackened hide. "I like a nice bit of crackling." He leaned down hard on the knife and pushed; the scab broke open and a gout of blood spun out of it like a tennis ball and down Guy's doublet. The meat was raw. He regained his poise. "Shall we fall upon it with lupine grace?"

Vesuvius interpreted. "*He says you have the manners of wolves.*"

Rosary said, "Hungry like wolves."

The knife wouldn't cut. Guy began to wrestle the knuckle out of its socket. Like a thing alive, the lamb leapt free onto the floor.

"Dear, dear boy." Digges rose to his feet and scooped up the meat, and put it back on the board. "Give me the knife." He took it and began with some grace to carve. "He really is a very good poet."

"Let us hope he is that at least," said Vesuvius.

Digges paused, about to serve. "He's interested in everything. History. Ovid. Sex. And then spins it into gold."

He put a tranche onto Goldenstar's plate. Knud did not wait for the others and began to press down with his knife. The meat didn't cut. He speared it up whole and began to chaw one end of it. The fat was uncooked and tasted of human genitals; the flesh had the strength of good hemp rope. He turned the turnip over in his fingers. It looked like a lump of coal and he let it fall onto his plate. "*I suggest we sail past this food and go and see the lenses."*

Rosary tried to take a bite of the meat. *"Yes. Lenses."*

Thomas Digges's house stood three stories high, dead on Bankside opposite the spires of All Hallows the Great and All Hallows the Lesser. Just behind his house, beyond a commons, stood Henslowe's theatre, The Rose, which was why Guy was such a frequent houseguest. Digges got free tickets in the stalls as a way of apologizing for the groundlings' noise and litter and the inconvenience of Guy sleeping on his floor. Guy didn't snore but he did make noises all night as if he were caressing a woman or jumping down from trees.

No noise in February at night. The wind had dropped, and a few boats still plied across the river, lanterns glowing like planets. The low-tide mud was luminous with snow. The sky looked as if it had been scoured free of cloud.

Over his slated roof, Digges had built a platform. Its scaffolding supports had splintered; it groaned underfoot, shifting like a boat. The moon was full-faced and the stars seemed to have been flung up into the heavens, held by nets.

The cold had loosened Guy's tongue. "S-s-s-size of lenses, you look with both eyes. No squinting. C-c-can you imagine f-f-f-folk wearing them as a collar, they lift up the arms and have another set of eyes to see distant things. W-w-w-would that make them philosophers?"

"The gentlemen are acquainted with the principle, Guy." Digges was ratcheting a series of mechanical arms that supported facemask-sized rounds of glass.

"But not the wonder of it. D-do you sense wonder, Mr. Rosary?"

Rosary's red cheeks swelled. "I do not know."

"Many things I'm sure, Rosie, are comprehended by you. Are you married, perchance?"

"Geee-eee-heee," warned Digges. He bent his knees to look through the corridor of lenses and made an old-man noise.

Goldenstar answered. "Married."

"As am I. That signifies, b-b-but not much." Guy arched back around to Rosary. "Come by day the morrow and walk alongside the river with me. The churches and the boats, moorhens, the yards of stone and timber."

Vesuvius shook his head. "We have heard about you actors."

Goldenstar said, "We leave tomorrow." Rosary shrugged.

Digges stood up and presented his lenses to them. "Sirs." Vesuvius and Rosary did a little dance, holding out hands for each other, until the Count put a collegial hand on Rosary's back and pushed. Rosary crouched and stared, blinking.

Squire Digges sounded almost sad. "You see. The moon is solid too. Massy with heft."

Rosary was still. Finally he stood up, shaking his head. "That is . . ." He tried to speak with his hands, but that also failed. "Like being a sea." He looked sombre. "The stars are made of stone."

Goldenstar adopted a lunging posture as if grounding a spear against an advancing horde. "*This could get us all burnt at the stake.*"

John Dee answered in Danish. Vesuvius looked up in alarm. "*Yes, but not here, not while my Queen lives.*"

Shakespere understood the tone. "Everything is exploding, exploding all at once. When I was in Rome—it's so important to g-g-get things right, don't you think? Research is the best part of the j-job. Rome. Verona. Carthage. I was in a room with a man who was born the same year I was and his first name was the same as his last, G-G-Galileo Galilei. I told him about Thomas and he told me that he too has lenses. He told me that Jupiter has four moons and Saturn wears a rainbow hat. He is my pen pal, Galileo, I send him little things of my own, small pieces you understand—"

Vesuvius exploded. "Please you will stop prattle!" He ran a hand across his forehead. "We are meeting of great astrological minds in Europe, not prattle Italian!"

Digges placed an arm around Guy as if to warm him. Rosary phalanxed next to them as though shielding him from the wind. "Please," Rosary said to Vesuvius.

John Dee thought: People protect this man.

Guillermus Shakespere thought:

I can be in silence. My source is in silence. Words come from silence. How different they be, these Danes, one all stern and leaden, forceful with facts, the other leavening dough. Their great cousin. All by eye? Compromise by eye, just keep the sun going around the Earth, to pacify the Pope and save your necks. Respect him more if he declared for the Pope forthrightly and kept to the heavens and Earth as we knew them. Digges digs holes in heaven, excavating stars as if they were bones. Building boats of bone. He could build boxes, boxes with mirrors to look down into the heart of the sea, show us a world of narwhales, sharks, and selkies.

All chastened by Mr. Volcano. All silent now. Stare now—by eye—

you who think you see through numbers, stare at what his lenses show. New eyes to see new things.

How do rocks hang in the sky?

How will I tell my groundlings: the moon is a mountain that doesn't fall? The man with gap in his teeth; the maid with bruised cheek, the oarsman with rounded back? What can I say to them? These wonders are too high for speaking, for scrofulous London, its muddy river. Here the moon has suddenly descended onto our little eye-land. Here where the future is hidden in lenses and astrolabes. The numbers and Thomas's clanking armatures.

"Guy," says old Thomas, full of kindness. "Your turn."

I bow before the future, into the face of a new monarch of glass who overturns. I look through his eyes; see as he sees, wide and long. I blink as when I opened my eyes in a basin of milk. Dust and shadow, light and mist cross and swim and I look onto another world.

I can see so clearly that it's a ball, a globe. Its belly swells out toward me, a hint of shadow on its crescent edge.

It is as stone as any granite tor. Beige and hot in sunlight. The moon must see us laced in cloud but no clouds there, no rain, no green expanse. Nothing to shield from the shrivelling sun. No angels, nymphs, orisons, bowers, streams, butterflies, lutes. Desiccated corpses. No dogs to devour. A circle of stone. Avesbury. A graveyard. Breadcrumbs and mould.

Not man in the moon, but a skull.

Nothing for my groundlings. Or poetry.

I look on Digges's face. He stares as wide as I do; no comfort there. He touches my sleeve. "Dear Guy. Look at the stars."

He hoists the thing on some hidden bearing, and then takes each arm and gears into a new niche. The lenses rise and intersect at some new angle, and I look again, and see the stars.

Rosie was right, it is an ocean. What ship could sail there? Bejeweled fish. That swallow Earth. Carry it to God. I can see. I can see they are suns, not tiny torches, and if suns then about those too other Earths could hang. Infinite suns, infinite worlds, deeper and deeper into bosom of God, distances vast, they make us more precious because so rare and small, defenceless before all that fire.

Here is proof of church's teaching. God must love us to make any note of us when the very Earth is a mote of soot borne high on smoky gas.

My poor groundlings.

John Dee watched.

The boy pulled back from the glass, this actor-poetplaywright. Someone else for whom there is no word. In the still and icy air, tears had frozen to his cheeks. Digges gathered him in; Rosary stepped forward; Goldenstar stared astounded. Only the spy stood apart, scorn on his face.

"You are right, Squire Digges," said the boy. "It is without end. Only that would be big enough for God." He looked fallen, pale and distracted. "The cold bests me. I must away, gentlemen."

"The morrow?" Rosary asked. "We meet before we go?"

The wordsmith nodded, clasped Rosary's hand briefly and then turned and trundled down the steps. The platform shook and shuddered. Dee stood still and dark for a moment, decided, and then with a swirl, followed.

Winding down the stairwell past people-smelling bedrooms, through the dungeon of a dining room. The future that awaited them? Out into the paneled room, flickering orange.

"Young Sir! Stay!"

The boy looked embarrassed. "Nowhere else to go."

Such a poor, thin cloak. Was that the dust of Rome on it? Or only Rome wished for so hard that mind-dust fell upon it? But his eyes: full of hope, when I thought to see despair. "Young master. Have you heard of the Brotherhood of Night?"

Hope suspended like dust, only dust that could see.

"I see you have not, for which I am thankful. We are a brotherhood devoted to these new studies late from Germany and Denmark, now Austria and Italia. None of us can move, let alone publish, without suspicion. That man Vesuvius is as much spy as guide, the Pope's factotum. How, young Guillermus, would you like to see Brahe's island of philosophy, in sight of great Elsinore? Uraniborg, city of the heavens, though in fact given over to the muse of a study that has late been revived. And all this by a man with a golden nose. Would you like to see again your starry twin Galileo? See Rome, Verona, Athens? Not Carthage, not possible, don't say that in good company again. But Spain, possible now. The courtship of Great Elizabeth by Philip makes travel even there approved and safe."

"My . . . I'm an actor. I used to play women."

"You still do." Dee's grim smile lengthened. "Men like Vesuvius dismiss you. Bah! Religion is destroying itself. The Protestants prevent the old

Passion Plays, and in their stead grow you and Marlowe. You write the history of tragic kings. That has not happened since the Greeks."

Guy shook his head. "Ask Kit to do this."

He is, thought Dee, a good, faithful, fragile boy. And something in his thin shoulders tells me that he's contemplating going into Orders. That must be stopped.

Dee said aloud, "Kit draws enemies." The boy's eyes stared into his. "Men who want to kill him. They love you."

Out of cold policy, Dee took the boy into his arms and kissed him full on the lips, held him, and then pushed him back, to survey the results in the creature's eyes: yes: something soft, something steel.

Guy said, "You taste of gunpowder."

"You would still be able to write your poetry. Send it to Kit in packets to furnish out the plays. In any case he will be undone, caught up in these Watchmen unless we hide him. As you might well be undone if you stay here and miss your chance to see the world blossom. Move for us and write it down. And learn, boy, learn! See where Caesar walked; breathe the scents of Athens's forest. Go to high Elsinore."

Shakespere stood with his eyes closed. The old house crackled and turned about them. The world was breaking. "Are there tales in Denmark of tragic kings?"

Dr. Dee nodded. "And things as yet undreamt of." He took up his long staff and the black cloak that was taller than himself. He put his arm around the slender shoulders and said, "Riverwalk with me."

The door shut tight behind them, and only then did Bessie come to open it.

Outside, white carpeted everything, and Bessie stepped into the hush. Somehow it was snowing again, though the sky overhead was clear. She kicked snow off the stone step and sat down, safe and invisible. It looked as if the stars themselves were falling in flakes. The idea made her giggle. She saw thistledown: stars were made of dandelion stuff.

As so often once it starts to snow, the air felt warmer. The blanket of white would be melted by morning; if she were abed now she'd have missed it. So she warmed the stone step by sitting on it, and let the snow tingle her fingertips. She scooped up a ridge of it and tasted: cold and fresh, sweeter than well water.

She looked up, and snow streaked past her face like stars. Her stomach turned over and it felt as if she were falling upward, flying into heaven where there would be angels. She could see the angels clearly; they'd be tall and thin with white hair because they were so old, but no wrinkles, with the bodies of men and the faces of women. The thought made her giggle, for it was a bit naughty trying to picture angels. She lifted up her feet, which made her feel even more like she was flying.

An hour later and Guy came back to find her still seated on the step.

"Hello, Bessie." He dropped down next to her and held up his own pink-fingered ridge of snow. "It's like eating starlight."

She gurgled with the fun of it and grabbed her knees and grinned at him. She was missing a tooth. "Did you see the old gent'man home?"

"Aye. He wants me to go to Denmark. He'll pay."

"Oooh! You'll be off then!"

He hugged his knees too and rested his head on them, saying nothing. She nudged him. "Oh. You should go. Chance won't come again."

"I said I would think on it. He wants me to spy. Like Kit. I'd have to carry a knife."

"You should and all. Round here." She nudged him again. "Wouldn't want you hurt."

"You're a good lass, Bessie."

"Aye," wistfully, as if being good had done her no good in return. He followed her eyeline up into the heavens, that had been so dreary and cold. The light of stars sparkled in her eyes and she had a sweet face: long nosed, with a tiny mouth like a little girl, stray hair escaping her kerchief, a smudge of ash on her face. He leaned forward and kissed her.

"Hmm," she said happily and snuggled in. These were the people he wanted to make happy; give them songs, dances, young blades, fine ladies in all their brocade, and kings halfway up the stairs to God.

"What do you see when you look at stars, Bessie?"

She made a gurgling laugh from deep within. "You know when the sun shines on snow and there's bits on it? Other times it's like I've got something in my eye, like I'm crying. But right now, I'm flying through 'em. Shooting past!"

"Are you on a ship?" He glimpsed it, like the royal barge all red and gold, bearing Queen Elizabeth through the Milky Way, which wound with a silver current. Bessie sat on the figurehead, kicking her heels.

"Oh, I don't know!"

"Like Sir Walter Raleigh with a great wind filling the sails."

"That'll be it," she said and kicked her heels. She leaned forward for another kiss, and he gave it to her, and the rising of her breath felt like sails.

"Wind so strong we're lifted up from the seas, and we hang like the moon in the air." He could see the sails fill, and a storm wave that tossed them free of the sea, up into the sky, away from whatever it was held them to the Earth. "We'll land on the moon first, beaching in sand. It's always sunny there, no clouds. We'll have taken salt pork and hardtack."

"Oh no, we'll take lovely food with us. We'll have beer and cold roast beef."

"And we'll make colonies like in the Caribbean now, on Mars, and then Jupiter. They'll make rum there out of a new kind of metal. We'll go beyond to the stars."

Bessie said, "There'll be Moors on Mars."

Shakespeare blinked. She was a marvel. They all were, that's why he wrote for them. He loved them.

That old man: *like the Greeks had done,* he said. Their great new thing that he and Kit were doing. And the others, even miserable old Greene; their *Edwards* and their *Henrys.* Mad old John Dee had made them sound old-fashioned, mouldy from the grave. Bessie didn't care about the past. She was traveling to Araby on Mars.

So why write those old things from the grammar school? Write something that was part of the explosion in the world.

I need to bestir myself. I need to learn; I can turn their numbers into worlds, such as Bessie sees, where stars are not crystals, where the moon is a beach of gravel and ice.

Dee would be gone by dawn. He and the Danes were sailing. Were the Danes still in the house? If they were he could leave with them.

As if jabbed, Guy sat up. "Bessie, I'm going to go."

"I knew you would," she said, her face dim with pleasure for him.

Go to that island of philosophy, be there with Rosary; he liked Rosie, wanted to kiss him too—and Rosie could explain the numbers. Guy jittered up to his feet, slipping on the slush. He saw Fortune: a salmon shooting away under the water. He nipped forward, gave Bessie a kiss on the cheek, and ran into the house, shouting, "Squire. My good sirs!"

From inside the house came thumps and racketing and shouts, the Squire bellowing "Take this coat!" and the Danes howling with laughter. Outside, it started to snow again, drifting past Bessie's face.

Well, thought Bessie, *I never had him really.*

She was falling between stars again on a silver ship shaped like a swan with wings that whistled. They docked on a comet that was made not of fire, but ice; and they danced a jig on it and set it spinning with the lightness of their feet; and they went on until clouds of angels flew about them with voices like starlings and the voyagers wouldn't have to die because they already were in Heaven, and on the prow stood Good Queen Bess in silver armour and long red hair, but Good Queen Bess was her.

Shakespere's next play was called *A Midwinter's Nonesuch on Mars*.

NAHUALES
Silvia Moreno-Garcia

The *nahual* smiles, showing off its yellowed teeth, as it stands under the streetlamp. He wears a black leather jacket, smokes cheap cigarettes, but he is still a *nahual*. There is the whiff of mountains about him and the glint of the coyote in his eyes. I've never seen a *nahual*, but I heard of them through my great-grandmother. Old-lady stories. Folktales. The tales steer me to the other side of the street, avoiding him. He notices, the corner of his mouth twitches, but I head down the steps towards the subway.

Safe, sitting inside the orange subway car, the smell of the mountains and the *matorral* fades and I am once more in Mexico City. A boy walks down the aisle selling bubble gum. A teenager bobs his head up and down to the music from his headphones. A man reads a newspaper. Once more *nahuales* are stories, very old stories, and nothing more.

And yet I place three nails in my bag the next morning.

Three days later I step out and feel the city changing. The scent of pines and shrubs where there ought to be only smog.

I look at the homeless man sprawled in an alley and wonder if his grey shape betrays another nature.

I take the underpass to the subway, quickening my pace. When I emerge, I almost bump into him.

The *nahual* from the other night with his black jacket. He's with two others this time. They're also dressed in leather; they also smoke cheap cigarettes that stain the fingers.

The one in black smiles at me and he says something I can't make out. Maybe he's trying to put a spell on me.

I can deal with this.

I duck my head and toss the nails behind me, and they do not follow.

I turn to look at them as I reach the steps. They're laughing. It resembles the barking of wild dogs.

I place the rosemary and the knitting needles under my bed for protection. I carry nails to ward my tracks. But that doesn't make them go away. They remain there, waiting by the subway station.

In my great-grandmother's time, in her hometown, they tied a poor, bawling goat to a post to lure the *nahual*, then dropped a crucifix at its feet when it appeared. My great-grandmother shot the *nahual* in the head herself. It had killed her sister. The only thing she regretted was the bawling of the goat as the *nahual* tore its belly open.

It is impossible to attempt that these days. Where would one get a goat? How could one fire a rifle? The only rifles I've seen are in the sepia-coloured pictures of my great-grandmother's youth, she with the weapon against her shoulder, staring squarely at the camera, the corpse of the *nahual* at her feet. A dark mountain range behind. A land of forests and monsters.

I lower my head, I try to hide between the folds of my clothing and walk faster. Faster, faster. The click of my shoes against the cement. Their shadows behind me until I slip into the subway car. Until it pulls from the station and I can breathe again.

The walk from work to the subway has become unbearable. Each night they are there. Sometimes they sit, hunched down, drinking from green bottles. Other times they lean against the wall, arms crossed. But they're always there.

The nails will only do so much and I fear my method of protection might be losing its strength. Meanwhile, their grins seem to grow wider. I can almost hear the snapping of their jaws as I rush forward, trying to move as quickly as my heels will allow.

I never understand what they say to me. I don't want to understand. Garbled nonsense which might be a threat. Or an entreaty.

I take a taxi one Friday, unable to face the walk to the subway. But I can't afford one each night. Only the subway can take me to my apartment.

The *nahuales*, not content with inhabiting the outskirts of the station, have made the neighbourhood their home. Shadows and cracks appear where they have never been before, and the buildings resemble mountains. One day I fear I shall walk out the door and find myself deep in the *matorral*, the dense thickets making it impossible to make my way back.

Fear has made me look for different routes. But eventually, just like all rivers lead to the sea, I must make my way into the station. And they'll be there. It does not matter if I approach it from the north or the south, if I take the underpass, or round the streets. They find me.

They have grown brazen in their approach. No longer content to whisper and watch me, they sniff and touch a strand of hair as I walk by. Sneak a hand up my arm.

They are so close I think I see the ticks in their matted hair, which is like fur. Their eyes are narrow, opportunistic.

Their voices, as I descend into the station, bounce off the walls with vicious glee.

The rain comes and seems to flush the *nahuales* away. Once again I can walk to the station, heels splashing in the puddles.

I am relieved.

But then I spot it, gnawing at garbage: a great black dog. It growls at me. Two other dogs appear and join the black one.

I take a step back.

It takes a step forward.

I run, back through the underpass, back to the street. I take off my heels and run barefoot, nylons tearing and sweat dripping down my neck.

The pack chases me across a forest of tall pines. I wade through a stream and emerge on the other bank, until I reach the safety of a café and rush inside. I look out the window and see the dogs' eyes in the dark. They glow yellow, like the stub of a cigarette.

I hear laughter and three men walk from the shadows. The one in the black jacket opens his mouth and smoke curls out of it, like incense rising in the night. He smiles at me.

I wait for an hour before I leave the café, but I do not seed my tracks with nails.

When I get home, I climb into bed without taking my clothes off and press my bag against my chest. I think of the goat tied and bawling in the dark.

The moon shines yellow and round through the curtains. The din of traffic grows distant and the night is blacker than ink, all the city lights blotted out.

The door creaks open as a black dog nuzzles his way into my bedroom. Two other dogs pad behind him.

The black dog sniffs and approaches my bed. Its bark is close to laughter.

I draw the sharp knitting needle from my bag and grin before plunging it into his neck.

TRAP-WEED
Gemma Files

For their land-longing shall be sea-longing and their sea-longing shall be land-longing, forever.

—An old legend of the Orkneys, concerning those seals who shed their skins to become women and men.

Any selkie can be Great, if he fights for it when challenged. We are by no means a democracy.

But for myself, I did not care to, and was driven forth, into deeper waters. So I swam until my fat and fur could no longer warm me, 'til the chill had almost breached my heart. I swam 'til my lungs gave out, then sank, deep into darkness.

When I woke, I found myself aboard-ship, peltless and doubly nude. A lean man stood looking down on me, his elegant face all angles, while others watched from behind, above . . . so many, for this creaking wooden shell to carry ocean-bound in safety. I had never seen such a number before, all in one place.

(For we stay as far from human men as possible on Sule Skerry, if we can, unless our instincts drive us otherwise. We know their works.)

I was gasping, painful all over, in strange places—burnt and scraped, as though I'd been dragged over rocks. Indeed, my arm had a chunk torn from it, neat and triangular—nipped straight out at the point where it blended into shoulder, that same place I saw most mariners adorn with tattoo-work. I gaped at this a while, then tried to touch, and flinched from the sting of my own fingers' salt.

"I wouldn't do that," the man advised, without sympathy. "Call it the price of your salvation—a lesson either to keep to shallower waters or learn to hold your breath longer, when you choose not to."

Though it had been some time since I tried for human speech, I found it returned quick enough. "Where . . . am I, sir?"

And this he smiled at, grimly enough—no surprise there. Since in their hearts, most men like the pap they call courtesy, that sorry salve to their impossible pride.

"This scow of a brig's mine, by right of seizure," he replied, sweeping a contemptuous little bow. "*Bitch of Hell*, some call her, or *Salina Resurrecta*, since she's cobbled from shipwrecks. While I myself am Jerusalem Parry, captain: A pirate, as you suspect. You were *drowning*, meantime—a sorry sight, in one sea-bred. Yet Mister Dolomance here brang you up, before mortality could quite take hold entirely . . . and while I misdoubt he did you as little hurt in the performance of it as he might have, we must always recall how those he comes from are not known for their restraint, in general."

"Mister Dolomance?"

"Aye, that's he, hid over yonder, where he likes it best—you'd be dead if he hadn't found you, or if he was still able to do as he wished, instead of how I tell him to. For which you should, in either case, be suitably grateful." Fixing me with cold, pale eyes, then, like two silver pennies salt-blanched to the colour of water-cured bone turned coral: "And what are we to call *you*?"

You could not say it if you tried, I thought. But since I seemed compelled to answer, I rummaged for the last human name I'd heard—the one that boy I'd pulled from his boat's kin had called after him, its syllables dissolving down through water into meaningless sound by the time they reached the cave where my sisters kept him tethered, forcing him to sire a fresh crop of younglings. What they did with him after I never witnessed, for I was already at the sparring by then, about to choose discretion over valour, exile over family. Indeed, it only now occurred to me, I might not see them again, in his company or otherwise.

In that moment I knew myself alone, entirely, lost amongst those who normally hate and prey on us—who either club us dead to steal our skins in error, thinking us only animals, or make away with them when we're foolish enough to leave them unguarded and detain us for *their* pleasure, breeding children who will never feel at home on either sea or shore. And so, seeing no other way out, for the time being—

"You may call me Ciaran, sir," I said, at last.

To my left, I heard the thing Captain Parry called Mister Dolomance give out with a disgusted little noise from his hidey-hole—half snort, half spit—and turned, abruptly far more angry than bereft, to confront whatever creature had dragged me up onto this rotting, lurching mass of timber held together mostly by barnacles and forward motion, at the still-sore price of its snatched mouthful of flesh.

I found him squatting on the weather deck in a strange nest made from two massy coils of rope with a tarpaulin slung overtop, keeping himself moist by angling into the splash from a nearby cannon-port's mouth. Standing, he would be half as tall as Captain Parry but a good two hands broader, squat yet sleek. With doll-eyes and an almost lipless mouth hiding a serrated bear-trap bite, he sported what some sailors called "a drowned man's pallor," close-wrapped to save himself from burning in direct sunlight. It was that sea-bed dweller's skin of his, I later found out, which had left me so raw, drawing blood from frictive angles on the very briefest of contacts.

I know you now, I thought, meeting that lidless black gaze, if only for a moment; he well might mock, since his own kind were known to scorn names entirely. So the fact that he answered at all to that mockingly polite and inexact one the Captain'd applied, showed him just how puissant this man's magic must be, when reflected in "Mister Dolomance's" grudging obeyance, his infinitely resentful loyalty. Or, for that matter, the mere fact of Parry being yet alive, having not only bent this tadpole version of a Great White shark to his will, but forced it to assume a (mostly) human form, while doing so.

I have no doubt but that Mister Dolomance perceived both my terror and my pity, though his waverless glare rejected them both. And so we stood a while, locked in mutual regard: one cold-blooded, the other warm, doomed to meet for the first time in assumed shapes, confined to this creaking hulk. Me with my man-shape like a secret weakness revealed, as though I'd been forcibly shook inside-out; him with his man-shape imposed from the outside-in, never more than cruel illusion. For beneath it, he remained all rough muscle and horrid teeth, a terrible hunger, not even held together with bones.

Though we suffered the same privations, we could never be allies. I was prey to him, as much as any other thing without Captain Parry's power to protect it.

"Well, then, gentlemen," my captor told me, meanwhile, and Mister Dolomance as well—I could tell from the begrudging liquid grumble Mister Dolomance gave Parry back, by way of a reply. "Shall we retire to my cabin, and speak a bit further?"

And since there seemed no option *but* to go, I bowed my clumsy, fresh-made man-head, and went.

"I will trouble you for my skin, sir, if I may," I ventured, when the door was safely closed behind us.

By the look of his possessions and on closer examination, I gathered that Parry had once been of some quality, as humans reckon such things—regally slim, his fine hands sword-callused and ink-stained, not roughened with rope. If he went un-wigged, that seemed to be by choice; the hair thus revealed was still mostly brown, though shot through with hints of grey. There were also more books in his quarters than I had seen in my whole life, though grantedly, the sea does not treat such objects well.

But the Captain only shook his head. "No, I'll take care of that awhile yet, as I hold most of my crew's effects in trust for them. For we are none of us here entirely by choice, you see—not even me."

"Surely, though, it can matter little to you if I remain. I am no great hunter, like your . . . Mister Dolomance, there; my place is near the shore, not the open sea. And while some of my people have magic, of a sort, I am not one of them."

Parry sniffed again, prim as any cat. "I have all the magic I need already at my disposal, 'Ciaran,' and little liking for competition. You would provide me a very different service; less a tool to my hand than an object-lesson, for others."

"But what use can I possibly be of to you, bound *or* free, when you have one of the ocean's greatest nightmares sworn to your service already?"

"You undervalue your own impressiveness. My men fear me, and rightly, because I have a way with supernatural creatures, so adding a selkie to that roster cannot do me ill, even if it does me little comparative good."

Having no arguments left, I resorted to simply pointing out: "I . . . am no sailor, sir." To which Captain Parry gave merely a chilly smile, as though to say that was both of no matter, and hardly a skill requiring great genius to master.

"Oh, you'll soon learn," was all he replied, and waved me away.

Thus I found myself press-ganged, after a fashion; I betook myself to the quartermaster and begged my share of the ship's labour, setting myself to it with energy, if not much effect. Yet the crew, on the whole, were kind—perhaps because they were sorry for me, a thing so far out of its place, if not its element.

And always I could just glimpse Mister Dolomance stalking attendance, following at the Captain's heels even while his gaze roamed after me. The farther we went from land, the happier he seemed, his sharp grin less a threat than a promise. While I wished myself increasingly back with my kin, fighting for supremacy I neither craved nor thought myself fit to hold, on that bloody rock; anywhere with land and sea alike, in close enough proximity to swim between.

As my despair mounted, I prayed outright to the eel-tailed Maid of the Sea (whose teeth are fishbones and whelk-shells, whose wet breath smells only of salt, and cold, and death), though She was far more likely to answer Mister Dolomance than the likes of me. But then again, my elders had taught me his kind do not trust in invocations to free them from mishap, if their own strength proves unequal to the task. For they are a harsh people, the sleepless ever-moving ones, even to themselves—unwilling to incur debts they do not wish to pay, even to the goddess who watches over all such wrack as we, the fertile ocean's muck and cast-offs. Its children, lost at sea, or out of it.

As time wore on, meanwhile, the quartermaster grew friendly with me, giving me leave to eat raw fish from the common net, and stroking my hair as I did. "Do not be sad," he would say; "the Captain will tire of ye soon enough, like any other toy he plucks from the deep. 'Sides which, were you bound for anywhere in particular? No? Then it'll serve you just as well to stay a while wi' us; just drift along, as if current-borne. See where *that* takes you."

"Do I have a choice?" I asked him, sullen, picking bones from my flat, blunt man-teeth. Only to have him laugh aloud at my bitterness, matching it with his own.

"Do any of us?" he asked me, in return.

The answer, of course, being no. We all existed entirely subject to the Captain's whim, just as he himself was inwardly consumed by a seemingly-constant quest for novelty, sharp-panged as any mere bodily famishment. Those silver-penny eyes of his always scanning away at the horizon, seemingly incognizant of Mister Dolomance crouched like some lump of pure hatred made flesh at his side—though not so much *ignorant* of his closest companion's feelings, I eventually came to see, as simply content to ignore them.

Rumours followed Parry, as with any other fatal man, so I listened to them whenever they were offered, eager for any possibility of escape. "Captain's cursed, is what I 'eard," the second gunner said at mess, as the rum-cup was passed 'round one way, the water-cup the other. "'Twas laid on 'im 'ow 'e can't set foot on land. . . ."

The first gunner, impatient: "No, fool, for I've seen him *do* so, to his cost—it's that he can't *stay* on land, or he starts to bleed."

"Aye," the quartermaster broke in here, nodding sagely. "I was there as well, that same occasion, and saw what come out—enough t' fill a slaughterhouse trough, and him so pale t' start with! Which is why he stays afloat, these days, and sends Mister Dolomance out scoutin' for prizes instead, settin' him t' bite through anchor-ropes or gnaw holes in some other ship's side. For it's wrecks the Captain wants, as we all know, and there's no earthly reason why he should be content t' wait for 'em to happen natural . . . not when he has so many other ways to make it so."

But to what purpose? I almost asked, before thinking better of it. Answering myself, as I did, with the sudden realization: *To cobble this ship of his ever-bigger with them, of course. To grow his kingdom—or increase his prison's capacity, at the very least.*

Salina Resurrecta, Bitch of Hell; *Parry's Doom* they called it, as well, whenever they thought him too deep-engaged in his arcane business to notice. A blot of a thing, literally engorged with flotsam from every prize it took and scuttled, hull gaping open maw-like at Captain Parry's gesture to suck in whatever items he—or it?—most took a fancy to. Thus it increased in size, steadily, over the months I spent as just one more item of that literally damnable vessel's cargo—sprouted fresh decks and hulling, masts and port-holes rabbit-breeding 'til the whole ship sat taller against the waves with a veritable totem-pole of figureheads to guide it, a corpse-fed trail of destruction left behind in its ever-widening wake.

I remember the Captain standing high in the fore-deck, shaking that hex-bag he used to raise fog and draw storms out into the wind, full to its brim with less-than-sacred objects. These I saw variously, at differing times, when he would reach in and withdraw them for specific tasks: A wealth of red-gold hair, braided and knotted nine times nine (this aided in illusions); some dead babe's finger, pickled in gin (he used it as a pointer, to navigate). An eyeball carved from ivory, set with the skull and crossed bones in fine black jet, was all that was left of the *Bitch's* legendary former Captain Rusk, fashioned to replace one lost in battle and plucked from his barnacle-torn corpse after Parry had him keelhauled, scraping him dead on his own ship's bottom-side—a trophy for luck, perhaps, though Parry sometimes raised it to his ear and gave that cat's-wince smile of his, as if it whispered advice to him.

But then there was an idol of dark wood, too, so gnarled one could barely ascertain its shape and studded all over with rusted nails, staining its weathered skin like blood—who had Parry stolen *that* from, and why? Bone fragments, sea-glass, scrimshaw, plus what I took to be a serrated tooth from Mister Dolomance's smile, knocked violently free at its root. And deep down, far beyond my reach, though I caught the occasional teasing glimpse of it, now and then . . .

. . . my skin, contradictory heart of all I was, reduced to one more fetish, one more weapon in Parry's arsenal. One more tool to bend my and the shark's great Mother to his all-too-human will.

"*Who* was it cursed him, though?" I demanded, eventually, scrabbling for some sort of detail to use against Parry, some way out of this closing trap. To which the quartermaster replied, musingly—

"Now, that I can't say, young Ciaran. Only that it happened quick enough, without warning, some time after he first took the *Bitch* in mutiny, I think, and laid our old Captain down. So perhaps it was Solomon Rusk's work, not that I ever saw him do for any who rose against him with weapons other than sword and fist, previous. Still, keel-haulin' is an ill death, a singularly painful end . . . and it does give you time t' think on things, I can only s'pose, when you're down there under-hull. . . ."

"How foolish he'd been to bring Parry on, in the first place?" I suggested.

A nod. "Maybe so. Rusk took him off a Navy prize, y' see—found him down in the brig like cargo, iron-collared, and knew him a magician bound for the next port of call, to face the King's Justice: be burned alive or hanged in chains, depending on the Admiralty's fancy. Those other blue-coats who swore the ship's Articles t' keep their lives were mightily afeared of him already, sayin' how he was accused of all manner of wizardous ill-doings—necromancy and doll-makin' and catchin' gales in a sieve, the way most sailors think only women do. But Captain Rusk, he wouldn't be warned away, not once his temper was up, or his interest piqued. He'd have a man-witch at his beck and call, or know the reason why."

"Most magicians die in the uncollaring, don't they?"

"Aye, for them rigs don't have locks, just seams—the witchfinders put 'em on hot and force 'em sealed, so's they'll waste all their effort on one last spell to keep from dyin'; Captain Parry keeps his cravat high for a reason, t' hide the scars all 'round his neck. But Rusk broke it open, with his hands; he was a strong man, and always knew the trick of twistin' where a thing was weakest."

"I 'eard this tale, too," the second gunner chimed in. "'Jerusha, I'll call ye,' he said, 'seein' you owe me all.' And Parry just snapped at 'im, like they was two gents in a drawing-room: 'Sir! I have not given you permission to use me thus, familiarly!'"

"No, and he never did, did he? Though Solomon Rusk, bold bastard that he was, wasn't a one t' ever pay such niceties much mind. . . ."

So Parry had begun in servitude himself, of the same sort he practiced on Mister Dolomance and me—a slave turned slave-master who, just like the shark-were, had no sympathy for his own past weakness, let alone the weaknesses of others. I *fought free,* he might say, if questioned; *do the same, if you can . . . and if not, stop your whining.*

(Yet for such a creature to base his power in the sea, where nothing is permanent, ever . . . not the shape of land, the ebb and flow of tide, or even any clear distinction between what makes one more itself than the other. . . .)

I think you court destruction, sir, I thought, allowing myself the very faintest beginnings of hope. And would almost have risked a smile to myself, had I not been so afraid he might be watching.

On those few brief occasions when we put ashore to trade, restocking with food and weaponry, the Captain always hung back, with only Mister Dolomance (who had an instinctual distrust of anything under his feet which did not move according to the ocean's in- and out-breath) for company in his watery exile. And though other times women might come aboard, for the crew's recreation, the Captain never indulged himself, though he might have had his pick—being not only undeniably handsomer than any other man on his ship, but having far better manners.

Instead, the two of them would retire early, and I would peep in through the window's crack to discover them bent together over parchment, Mister Dolomance squeak-gurgling away in Parry's ear while his master scratched away furiously with pencil and charcoal, checking and re-checking measurements with various instrumentation. And slowly, I came to figure they must be making a map together, hopelessly impenetrable to any land-dweller's eyes: A grand survey of the ocean's most uncharted areas, from the *bottom up*.

"He seeks for a place more land than sea, yet neither," was the quartermaster's theory. "Only there might this bane of his be lifted, and he find peace, if that's indeed what he's after."

"Do you doubt it?"

"With the Captain? Where he's concerned I doubt all things, 'til I'm told otherwise. 'Tis the best policy I've found, thus far."

I glanced away, just in time to catch my fellow captive—listening too, as always—shoot me what passed for a smirk on that mask-like parody of a human face of his, as if to say: *What fools!*

Indeed, it did often seem to me the crew barely knew whereof they spoke, notwithstanding the fact they'd spent far more time under Parry's rule than I had. And one way or another, for all my researches, exactly nothing they—or I—had discovered about him could in any way free me from my situation. I remained trapped, his possession, his slave; yet still worse, for I was not even of any great interest to him, of any particular *use*.

It galled me to realize this, almost as much as it galled me to realize I cared, either way. But perhaps Captain Parry was not altogether human either—partly dragon, maybe, for his twinned love of gold and fire, his magic, his damnable arrogance; partly wolf, for his love of blood.

Or he was just a man like any other, plundering this great sea-womb and stealing its children, using power he had no right to bend our Mother herself to his selfish desires. Would that make things better, or worse?

I could not fight him, either way—not I, who had declined to fight even my own kind, against whom I might have stood some chance of success. So I must find some other, more subtle, way . . . think myself out of this trap, like the man he'd condemned me to pretend to be, instead of the seal I so heartily wished I still was.

So I thought, and thought again, and thought yet further. Until, at last—I found a way.

One night, while Mister Dolomance swam his own discomforts away in the sea below's black bosom, I threw a rope over the ship's side and shimmied far enough down to face my fears—plunged my face into the water and took a deep, drowning breath, opening my mouth wide enough to let words leak out, trusting the water to carry them to Mister Dolomance's ear-holes, translated thus into speech we might both understand.

We must work together, I told him, *to gain our freedoms.*

A gulp, and the reply came back, harsh even through silky fathoms: *Clumsy sea-cow in man-skin, born neither of one sort nor the other, you fat-greased, fleshy thing! What could you offer that I had any need of, save for enough of your meat to fill my craw, and your too-hot blood to wash it down with?*

I had expected nothing less, nothing more. Yet I spoke on, anyhow, and he . . .

. . . hard words aside, I could tell, even then: Mister Dolomance *listened*.

There was a long silence, after. So long I feared he might be swimming closer, too intent on an easy kill to truly mull my plan over.

But: *I accept,* he said, at last. Just that.

Good, I replied. And shimmied back up, before the crew might find me gone.

We did not consult long, Mister Dolomance and I, in forming our plans; I knew from the start just how ill-suited by nature he was to be anything like the planning sort. Yet it is always in their desires that men make themselves most vulnerable, and though Mister Dolomance had surely never looked to, we both understood he had already gained far more insight into our captor's yearnings than I ever would.

So—having extracted such intelligences about the hungers which drove Captain Parry as my co-conspirator was capable of giving—it fell to me, instead, to find a way to turn their direction to our mutual benefit.

It was not so much that the Captain trusted Mister Dolomance (for in truth, he trusted no one, thinking no one equal enough to him to merit such a gift). Yet, as had already become rapidly clear, he placed a quite foolish amount of trust in his dominance *over* this awful creature, whose taming-by-force formed much of his own reputation.

"I think you are not entirely honest with me, sir," I heard him say, one evening, over those charts of theirs. "Yet so long as you do what I require, I find I care little what details you may think to withhold."

A mistake, on his part. And to not consider *me*, at all, in his equations . . . this was a mistake too, though he did not know it.

Not yet.

The *Bitch* made on, leading ever-westerly, with Mister Dolomance's grumbles our pilot's only guide for navigation. Islands grew scarce, and stores likewise; the crew grew unhappy, yet loath to express it. While Captain Parry kept his face carefully schooled, with only the dullish glint in those sea-burnt eyes to indicate a growing undercurrent of excitement—until the night when I saw him stride into the mess unexpectedly and swig lit rum from the communal store along with the rest, all of them too disconcerted by far to refuse him a part in their drunkenness.

Later, his back set against the fore-deck's supplemental mast while the crew revelled down below, I watched him stare out over the topmost figurehead's shoulders at the dark billows Mister Dolomance hid in, and mutter to himself: "Hell gape to take you, Solomon Rusk, if it didn't that day, the way it should have—you had no stink of the true practitioner about you, trained or un-, that I could discern. How was I to know it hid in your blood, any more than you did, waiting for that very last breath to bring your death's vow of ruin on me to fruition?"

Here he actually paused a half-moment; I swear I saw him listen, as to an invisible companion. Then grimace at nothing and reply, pale face suddenly touched with heat—

"'Nice as a divine' . . . yes, you *would* say that. But here is truth: You took liberties with me, though I warned you not to, and this is the result. Do not think to deny it! I swore you ship-loyalty, nothing more, but you were not the sort to stint yourself and you have reaped bitter fruit from that decision since, dead man. So you may complain all you wish when drink opens my ears, but I have suffered long enough for your sins, as well as my own. I *will have my place*, got for me with the sea's help, and you—you will have nothing. Now stop your mouth, before I prison your ghost in a bottle and sink you further still; from this instant forward you may watch but not touch, not ever again, and choke on the sight."

All at once, the humid breeze seemed to turn sharp-cold, blowing in one bitter gust from where the Captain sat to where I squatted, listening; I shivered to feel it pass by, as if touched by some strange hand. Behind us, meanwhile, the quartermaster took up with a chantey tune, fellow after fellow soon joining in as a bawling round. Quickly, I recognized in it a song usually attributed to Captain Kidd, here modified to fit a different, entirely predictable personage:

. . . *oh, 'Salem Parry is my name, as I sail, as I sail,*
The root of my infame, as I sail, as I sail,
My faults I will display,

Committed day by day—
Damnation be my lot, as I sail . . .

For every legend, good or bad, warrants a song made from his exploits. But sailors are fatalists all, drowned men kept upright sheerly by luck's vagaries—and thus unlikely to stay long impressed by anything, or anyone, who claims to be able to cheat destiny forever.

. . . So we'll taken be at last, and then die, and then die,
Though we have reigned awhile, we will die—
Though we have reigned awhile,
While fortune seemed to smile,
We must have our due deserts, and still die . . .

If Parry found the implication insulting, however, he gave no sign of it; his fine-cut face stayed closed and stony, indifferent as always. And his thoughts, now he was done discoursing with Captain Rusk's ghost, remained his own.

The next day, we finally reached that place Mister Dolomance had described to me—a great knot of weed flowering up from the ocean's bottom, roots sunk two hundred feet or more, down to the darkness where blue-clear water becomes mulch-black sand. For even at its very deepest places, the sea too gives way to land, eventually.

(And might this have been the worst part of old Captain Rusk's curse, made all the more potent by his extremity—for if there were truly no place without land, how could the ocean ever be anything but a stop-gap, a salve between bleedings against pain that never fully died? Which, in turn, perhaps explained so much about Parry's manner, his stiff coldness, his constant distraction; things become clearest in hindsight, always, after the fact. *Long* after, most often.

(But since I am now coming near my own story's end, as you can no doubt tell, I judge I too may well be falling into a distraction. So I will take care to try and tell the rest of it through without embellishment, from here on.)

We nosed in slowly, seeking not to entangle ourselves, 'til the weed-forest's thickness made it impossible and we dropped anchor as best we might, hooking it in the crook where three branches grew together at the holdfast like ivy. Parry and a small party took to the boats, following Mister Dolomance, who merely gave that creaky laugh of his when Parry vented his doubts as to where, exactly, he might be leading them. For once, I felt I could tell exactly what he was saying:

If you believe me capable of deception, wizard, even when still so ensorcelled I keep this shape you've laid on me, then it is yourself you make look bad, not I.

At this, Captain Parry merely sniffed yet once more, forbearing response—haughty as the Devil himself, if with far less reason—and waved the oarsmen to their task, bidding them into the weed's heart 'til all of them were eventually lost from sight. The remaining crew stayed on deck, watching after with weapons ready, lest their master send up some sort of signal for aid. But since I knew exactly what they would find if they only went far enough, I slipped down below and performed a few small tasks, while no one else was looking.

One boat came back, the quartermaster at its helm. "Captain wants ye, Ciaran-boy, and quick-smart," he called up to me. "To 'bear witness to his triumph,' or some-such nonsense."

"Coming," I said, and was over the side a second after, not waiting on a ladder or rope; I hit the water with a splash and let the man haul me bodily aboard, all uncaring of how wet I got these ill-fitting clothes I soon expected to no longer have to wear.

The Captain's boat had moored, again by tethering itself to whatever was handy, right by a weed-clump so thoroughly knotted it had grown a sort of skin, fleshy-rough as any mushroom. A veritable floating island, such as crews tell tales of from one end of the sea to the other, never for a moment thinking to set foot upon its like in real life. And it was here that Jerusalem Parry already stood, boot-heels sunk just a bare quarter-inch into the spongey mass below; stood and swayed slightly, braced against pain, 'til he was sure no blood would come. Whereupon his bitter mouth finally stretched wide and he threw back his head to laugh, delighted as any child with the way his magic had brought him at last to that place he'd so long sought for.

"See?" he called to me, triumphant. "I stand victorious. Though Rusk stole the land from me, yet have I conquered; the sea itself delivers whatever I demand, no matter how impossible!"

"Mister Dolomance and myself, rather, to whom *you* now owe a debt of thanks."

Parry raised a brow. "Mister Dolomance has proved a treasured investment, undoubtedly," he admitted with surprising grace, "so much so I may even free him for it, one day. But you've given me little enough during your stay with my crew, aside from sullen looks and poor labour. Or am I mistaken?"

He thought to toy with me in his customary style, all aristocrat's drawl and fine vocabulary—as he'd done with Rusk, perhaps, who'd seemingly found it more attractive than I. But because I knew something the Captain did not, for once, I met his insults with a similar grin.

"As it ensues, yes," I replied. "For instead of giving, I have in fact *taken* something, without your notice."

"Explain yourself, sir."

I shrugged. "Wait, and see."

Out where weed gave way again to ocean, the *Bitch* floated low, lapped at by some gentle tidal gyre; we caught yet more music off its thronged deck, playing counterpoint to light laughter, scuffle and jesting. But all this changed a moment later, when—with a flash and muffled roar, like some cracked cannon's back-fire—its magazine, which I'd carefully set fire to before disembarking, went off, blowing her hull so far open her guts were laid bare. The mainmast went one way, the mizzenmast another, tearing wood like splintery paper; screams rose, as did smoke, and flames.

Had he been still on board, Captain Parry's magic might have turned the trick, but from here, there was no help for it: those careful bonds suturing wreck to wreck dissolved, leaving the ship itself to slide apart in chunks and sink, taking the bulk of his crew down as well.

Parry's smile became a snarl, his eyes two werewolf moons. "You flotsam scum," he called me, words ground out between his teeth like bones. "God curse the day I ever let you on my vessel."

"Yes, and that was entirely at *your* pleasure, was it not? Well, I wish you full joy of that call, just as you once wished Rusk's ghost joy of his, when you thought no one was listening . . . and joy of this new home of yours, likewise, for however long your stay on it may last."

Caught gloating as only fools do, I was so puffed with my own cleverness that I barely registered Parry's hand slipping inside his coat, though I knew what it was he kept there. But when he withdrew the hex-bag, brandishing it like a pistol, I at least knew to shy away; the boat rocked sharply, salt spray slopping in over the side, prompting the quartermaster—shook from his shocked silence, and grabbing for his oars—to swear in three separate languages.

Still: "Not so much as I wish *this* joy on *you*," Parry told me, coldly. And up-ended the whole mess into the waves between us—bottle-finger, eyeball, hair-rope, fetish, tooth and all else, useless to him in his current cheated state, except as one last weapon. Since, at the very end, yet another thing more came slipping out to feed the churn . . . my skin.

My skin.

I must confess I almost went in after it, just on the off-chance, before I recalled what lurked in wait below. But then I caught sight of Mister Dolomance, still crouched in his captor's shadow, tearing away at his own parody-of-human disguise in a paroxysm of painful delight: mouth already ripped to either earhole with new teeth sprouting up along the bottom jaw in a bloody spray, muzzle punching out triangular, while his eyes—already far too widely spaced for comfort—migrated to either side of his head, losing their minimal ability to blink entirely. Shoulders hunched and splitting down mid-line, too, as his fin's long-buried crest at last came arching up between. . . .

All your bad works brought to ruin in the same instant, I thought, staring Captain Parry down, straight in his silver-penny glare. *All you've sowed bloomed up full, sir, and ripe for reaping; well, I do hope you relish the taste of it, you sad fellow sport of unnaturalness. What little you can swallow, that is, before the end.*

Beneath the Captain's boots, the weed-island rocked and buckled, forcing him down on one knee. I watched it crack, pull apart at its weakest points, and remembered how Mister Dolomance had described the forest that supported it, where his kin (who do not of a custom flock, or even pair, at least for longer than it takes one to get a kit on another) glided so close they risked touching in order to graze the schools that fed on those mile-high weed-fronds. It was always twilight there, a purple half-night forever blood-tinged, the water itself heavy with rotting meat; a bed of infinite appetite upon which every prospective victim knew they would, at least, die full-stomached.

This was what Jerusalem Parry found himself momentarily balanced above—a chasm of open mouths, all waiting to take a bite, before what was left of him drifted to the ocean's mucky floor. Yet even as he summoned his last few shreds of power to stave that judgement off, if only for a breath, he opened himself to the surprise attack he should have *most* feared, all along: Mister Dolomance, leaping high in mid-spasm to bite deep into the Captain's unprotected nape, severing spine and the spell which kept him man-shaped alike. The shared arc of that jump threw them both sidelong, dragging Parry off-balance even as Mister Dolomance's legs shrank vestigial, once more fusing to form a tail; the weight of it put them down together with a great slap, waves gouting high, and slammed shut a blue-water door upon them both.

It was done, then—our revenge, complete—and Mister Dolomance surely got the lion's share of spoils, though *I* was the one self-condemned to live out a false man-life 'til laid in some land-bound grave. And since cowardice, at least, could never be counted amongst his sins, I somehow knew the Captain would go down fighting, to the very last . . . that image bringing me a variety of pleasure, at least, even as grief for my own losses cored my buried seal's heart.

The quartermaster pulled to with a will, meanwhile, and I took up oars as well, helping him put enough distance between us and the *Bitch*'s overthrow to make sure we were well out of range before the true frenzy began. After which we drifted, delirious with heat and fever, with hunger our only company; it occurred to me more than once, during this phase, that if I *had* managed to regain my true shape then the man I shared this boat with would have slit my throat long since, and be already picking his teeth with my bones. But thankfully, another ship picked us up before he could fully recall what lurked inside me, instead of thinking of me only as a boy—a tender thing, more his kin than not, to be protected rather than eaten.

"Ye're one of us now, son," was the last thing he spoke to me, which I know he meant kindly. Yet I just shook my head, waiting until he slept to steal what few coins he still possessed to pay my passage and roll him out through the sluices with a splash so quiet I reckon it was barely heard, either above-decks or under.

It was an impulse and no doubt an unworthy one, for I did feel bad after, if only a little while. But the feeling did not last long, confirming what I hoped was still true, even in my current skinless state: That we were *not* alike, he and I, no more than I and Mister Dolomance. That we never could be.

By ship after ship and voyage after voyage, sometimes spaced years apart, I made my long way back to the Skerry where I took up residence on the shore, gazing each day from cliffside across to the home I would never regain. I built myself a boat, and fished from it; I made myself a life, and lived it. At a midsummer dance, I told a girl my name was Ciaran, and married her. Our son became Young Ciaran, in his turn.

And then, one day, I pulled up my net to find a skin—*my* skin—inside it.

Now it is late, and the fire is almost out. In the other room, Young Ciaran and his mother lie sleeping; my tale is told, in almost every particular. So I sit here and stroke the long-lost pelt spread out upon my knees, so soft, so durable . . . barely a mark on it, though my own hide has grown rough from ill-use, and not even a tear to show where the scar I once took from Mister Dolomance's teeth should be. Indeed, it reminds me of nothing so much as its polar opposite, my former co-conspirator's skin, which—like Captain Parry himself, as one man learned, to ill-profit—could hardly stand to be touched at all, at least from some angles, without danger of wounding. Never without cost, of one sort or another.

Tonight, I think, *I will go swimming*. And I smile, even knowing what probably awaits me, out there in the dark stretch of water between beach and Sule—something cold-blooded, grown huge as a bull in its far-roaming freedom, with little about it to indicate it was ever forced to walk upright, bowing and scraping at the whim of a man whose magic kept it prisoned in a shape it never would have chosen otherwise. For unlike my own kind, Mister Dolomance was only made to be what he is, not what he could be; his sort have no use for contradiction, let alone for metaphor.

Yet we are both equally treacherous, he and I—just as our Mother the sea is, in Her changeable yet unchanging heart. We cannot be overborne even by the subtlest magics, as Jerusalem Parry learned too late; we cannot be trusted, ever, even by those who love us. And as the sea is my home, so I will be proud to die there, if I must . . . more proud than I ever would have been to die on land, had I been forced to, as for so many years I was certain I would be.

Perhaps, though . . . perhaps I *will* fight, this time, the way I declined to, so long ago. Why not? What more do I have to lose?

Little enough, in the end.

The tide turns. The fire becomes ash. I rise. And here—in silence—is where I take my leave of all you who listen, closing the circle with these words: Just as any man may seize power if he consents to pay for it, by whatever method, any selkie *may* be Great, eventually. . . .

. . . if he cares to.

A TALL GIRL
Kim Goldberg

A tall girl with long, tanned arms wanders the beach at low tide. She is wearing a loose, sleeveless dress the colour of the sky overhead. Her footprints in the wet sand stretch out behind her, comingling with shells, stones, a stray feather, bits of coloured glass buffed smooth as pebbles. The beach ahead is a blank sheet devoid of all impressions and castaways. At her hip hangs a large satchel woven from grass. The satchel's strap is slung diagonally across her lank body. As she walks, she reaches into the bag, retrieving shells, stones, a stray feather, bits of coloured glass buffed smooth as pebbles, and strews them upon the beach. Next she brings out a cool breeze and lets it go. Her loose dress begins to billow.

THE EASTHOUND
Nalo Hopkinson

Oh, Black Betty, bam-ba-lam,
Oh, Black Betty, bam-ba-lam.

"The easthound bays at night," Jolly said.

Millie shivered. Bad luck to mention the easthound, and her twin bloody well knew it. God, she shouldn't even be thinking, 'bloody'. Millie put her hands to her mouth to stopper the words in so she wouldn't say them out loud.

"Easthound?" said Max. He pulled the worn black coat closer around his body. The coat had been getting tighter around him these past few months. Everyone could see it. "Uck the fuh is that easthound shit?"

Not what; he knew damned well what it was. He was asking Jolly what the hell she was doing bringing the easthound into their game of Loup-de-lou. Millie wanted to yell at Jolly too.

Jolly barely glanced at Max. She knelt in front of the fire, staring into it, re-twisting her dreads and separating them at the scalp where they were threatening to grow together. "It's my first line," she said. "You can play or not, no skin off my teeth."

They didn't talk about skin coming off, either. Jolly should be picking someone to come up with the next line of the game. But Jolly broke the rules when she damned well pleased. Loup-de-lou was her game, after all. She'd invented it. Someone had to come up with a first line. Then they picked the next person. That person had to continue the story by beginning with the last word or two of the line the last person said. And so on until someone closed the loup by ending the story with the first word or two of the very first line.

Jolly was so thin. Millie had saved some of the chocolate bar she'd found to share with Jolly, but she knew that Jolly wouldn't take it. If you ate too much, you grew too quickly. Millie'd already eaten most of the chocolate, though. Couldn't help it. She was so hungry all the time!

Max hadn't answered Jolly. He took the bottle of vodka that Sai was holding and chugged down about a third of it. Nobody complained. That was his payment for finding the bottle in the first place. But could booze make you grow, too? Or did it keep you shrinky? Millie couldn't remember which. She fretfully watched Max's Adam's apple bob as he drank.

"The game?" Citron chirped up, reminding them. A twin of the flames of their fire danced in his green eyes. "We gonna play?"

Right. The game. Jolly bobbed her head yes. Sai, too. Millie said, "I'm in." Max sighed and shrugged his yes.

Max took up where Jolly had left off. "At night the easthound howls," he growled, "but only when there's no moon." He pointed at Citron.

A little clumsy, Millie thought, but a good second line.

Quickly, Citron picked it up with, "No moon is so bright as the easthound's eyes when it spies a plump rat on a garbage heap." He pointed at Millie.

Garbage heap? What kind of end bit was that? Didn't give her much with which to begin the new loup. Trust Citron to throw her a tough one. And that 'eyes, spies' thing, too. A rhyme in the middle, instead of at the end. Clever bastard. Thinking furiously, Millie louped, "Garbage heaps high in the . . . cities of noonless night."

Jolly said, "You're cheating. It was 'garbage heap,' not 'garbage heaps.'" She gnawed a strip from the edge of her thumbnail, blew the crescented clipping from her lips into the fire.

"Chuh." Millie made a dismissive motion with her good hand. "You just don't want to have to continue on with 'noonless night.'" Smirking, she pointed at her twin.

Jolly started in on the nail of her index finger. "And you're just not very good at this game, are you, Millie?"

"Twins, stop it," Max told them.

"I didn't start it," Jolly countered, through chewed nail bits. Millie hated to see her bite her nails, and Jolly knew it.

Jolly stood and flounced closer to the fire. Over her back she spat the phrase, "Noonless night, a rat's bright fright, and blood in the bite all delight the easthound." The final two words were the two with which they'd begun. Game over. Jolly spat out a triumphant, "Loup!" First round to Jolly.

Sai slapped the palm of her hand down on the ground between the players. "Aw, jeez, Jolly! You didn't have to end it so soon, just cause you're mad at your sister! I was working on a great loup."

"Jolly's only showing off!" Millie said. Truth was, Jolly was right. Millie really wasn't much good at Loup-de-lou. It was only a stupid game, a distraction to take their minds off hunger, off being cold and scared, off watching everybody else and yourself every waking second for signs of sprouting. But Millie didn't want to be distracted. Taking your mind off things could kill you. She was only going along with the game to show the others that she wasn't getting cranky; getting loupy.

She rubbed the end of her handless wrist. Damp was making it achy. She reached for the bottle of vodka where Max had stood it upright in the crook of his crossed legs. "Nuh-uh-uh," he chided, pulling it out of her reach and passing it to Citron, who took two pulls at the bottle and coughed.

Max said to Millie, "You don't get any treats until you start a new game."

Jolly turned back from the fire, her grinning teeth the only thing that shone in her black silhouette.

"Wasn't me who spoiled that last one," Millie grumbled. But she leaned back on the packed earth, her good forearm and the one with the missing hand both lying flush against the soil. She considered how to begin. The ground was a little warmer tonight than it had been last night. Spring was coming. Soon, there'd be wild, pungent wild leeks to pull up and eat from the riverbank. She'd been craving their taste all through this frozen winter. She'd been yearning for the sight and taste of green, growing things. Only she wouldn't eat too many of them. You couldn't ever eat your fill of anything, or that might bring out the Hound. Soon it'd be warm enough to sleep outside again. She thought of rats and garbage heaps, and slammed her mind's door shut on the picture. Millie liked sleeping with the air on her skin, even though it was dangerous out of doors. It felt more dangerous indoors, what with everybody growing up.

And then she knew how to start the loup. She said, "The river swells in May's spring tide."

Jolly strode back from the fire and took the vodka from Max. "That's a really good one." She offered the bottle to her twin.

Millie found herself smiling as she took it. Jolly was quick to speak her mind, whether scorn or praise. Millie could never stay mad at her for long. Millie drank through her smile, feeling the vodka burn its trail down. With her stump she pointed at Jolly and waited to hear how Jolly would loup-de-lou with the words "spring tide."

"The spring's May tide is deep and wide," louped Jolly. She was breaking the rules again; three words, not two, and she'd added a 'the' at the top, and changed the order around! People shouldn't change stuff, it was bad! Millie was about to protest when a quavery howl crazed the crisp night, then disappeared like a sob into silence.

"Shit!" hissed Sai. She leapt up and began kicking dirt onto the fire to douse it. The others stood too.

"Race you to the house!" yelled a gleeful Jolly, already halfway there at a run.

Barking with forced laughter, the others followed her. Millie, who was almost as quick as Jolly, reached the disintegrating cement steps of the house a split second before Jolly pushed in through the door, yelling "I win!" as loudly as she could. The others tumbled in behind Millie, shoving and giggling.

Sai hissed, "Sshh!" Loud noises weren't a good idea.

With a chuckle in her voice, Jolly replied, "Oh, chill, we're fine. Remember how Churchy used to say that loud noises chased away ghosts?"

Everyone went silent. They were probably all thinking the same thing; that maybe Churchy was a ghost now. Millie whispered, "We have to keep quiet, or the easthound will hear us."

"Bite me," said Max. "There's no such thing as an easthound." His voice was deeper than it had been last week. No use pretending. He was growing up. Millie put a bit more distance between him and her. Max really was getting too old. If he didn't do the right thing soon and leave on his own, they'd have to kick him out. Hopefully before something ugly happened.

Citron closed the door behind them. It was dark in the house. Millie tried to listen beyond the door to the outside. That had been no wolf howling, and they all knew it. She tried to rub away the pain in her wrist. "Do we have any aspirin?"

Sai replied, "I'm sorry. I took the last two yesterday."

Citron sat with a thump on the floor and started to sob. "I hate this," he said slurrily. "I'm cold and I'm scared and there's no bread left, and it smells of mildew in here—"

"You're just drunk," Millie told him.

"—and Millie's cranky all the time," Citron continued with a glare at Millie, "and Sai farts in her sleep, and Max's boots don't fit him any more. He's growing up."

"Shut up!" said Max. He grabbed Citron by the shoulders, dragged him to his feet, and started to shake him. "Shut up!" His voice broke on the "up" and ended in a little squeak. It should have been funny, but now he had Citron up against the wall and was choking him. Jolly and Sai yanked at Max's hands. They told him over and over to stop, but he wouldn't. The creepiest thing was, Citron wasn't making any sound. He couldn't. He couldn't get any air. He scrabbled at Max's hands, trying to pull them off his neck.

Millie knew she had to do something quickly. She slammed the bottle of vodka across Max's back, like christening a ship. She'd seen it on TV, when TVs still worked. When you could still plug one in and have juice flow through the wires to make funny cartoon creatures move behind the screen, and your mom wouldn't sprout in front of your eyes and eat your dad and bite your hand off.

Millie'd thought the bottle would shatter. But maybe the glass was too thick, because though it whacked Max's back with a solid thump, it didn't break. Max dropped to the floor like he'd been shot.

Jolly put her hands to her mouth. Startled at what she herself had done, Millie dropped the bottle. It exploded when it hit the floor, right near Max's head. Vodka fountained up and out, and then Max was whimpering and rolling around in the booze and broken glass. There were dark smears under him.

"Ow! Jesus! Ow!" He peered up to see who had hit him. Millie moved closer to Jolly.

"Max." Citron's voice was hoarse. He reached a hand out to Max. "Get out of the glass, dude. Can you stand up?"

Millie couldn't believe it. "Citron, he just tried to kill you!"

"I shouldn't have talked about growing up. Jolly, can you find the candles? It's dark in here. Come on, Max." Citron pulled Max to his feet.

Max came up mad. He shook broken glass off his leather jacket, and stood towering over Millie. Was his chest thicker than it had been? Was that hair shadowing his chin? Millie whimpered and cowered away. Jolly put herself between Millie and Max. "Don't be a big old bully," she said to Max. "Picking on the one-hand girl. Don't be a *dog*."

It was like a light came back on in Max's eyes. He looked at Jolly, then at Millie. "You hurt me, Millie. I wouldn't hurt you," he said to Millie. "Even if . . ."

"If . . . that thing was happening to you," Jolly interrupted him, "you wouldn't care who you were hurting. Besides, you were choking Citron, so don't give us that innocent look and go on about not hurting people."

Max's eyes welled up. They glistened in the candlelight. "I'll go," he said drunkenly. His voice sounded high, like the boy he was ceasing to be. "Soon. I'll go away. I promise."

"When?" Millie asked softly. They all heard her, though. Citron looked at her with big, wet doe eyes.

Max swallowed. "Tomorrow. No. A week."

"Three days," Jolly told him. "Two more sleeps."

Max made a small sound in his throat. He wiped his hand over his face. "Three days," he agreed. Jolly nodded, firmly.

After that, no one wanted to play Loup-de-lou any more. They didn't bother with candles. They all went to their own places, against the walls so they could keep an eye on each other. Millie and Jolly had the best place, together near the window. That way, if anything bad happened, Jolly could boost Millie out the window. There used to be a low bookcase under that window. They'd burned the wood months ago, for cooking with. The books that had been on it were piled up to one side, and Jolly'd scavenged a pile of old clothes for a bed. Jolly rummaged around under the clothes. She pulled out the gold necklace that their mom had given her for passing French. Jolly only wore it to sleep. She fumbled with the clasp, dropped the necklace, swore under her breath. She found the necklace again and put it on successfully this time. She kissed Millie on the forehead.

"Sleep tight, Mills."

Millie said, "My wrist hurts too much. Come with me tomorrow to see if the kids two streets over have any painkillers?"

"Sure, honey." Warrens kept their distance from each other, for fear of becoming targets if somebody in someone else's warren sprouted. "But try to get some sleep, okay?" Jolly lay down and was asleep almost immediately, her breathing quick and shallow.

Millie remained sitting with her back against the wall. Max lay on the other side of the room, using his coat as a blanket. Was he sleeping, or just lying there, listening?

She used to like Max. Weeks after the world had gone mad, he'd found her and Jolly hiding under the porch of somebody's house. They were dirty and hungry, and the stench of rotting meat from inside the house was drawing flies. Jolly had managed to keep Millie alive that long, but Millie was delirious with pain, and the place where her hand had been bitten off had started smelling funny. Max had brought them clean water. He'd searched and bargained with the other warrens of hiding kids until he found morphine and antibiotics for Millie. He was the one who'd told them that it looked like only adults were getting sick.

But now Millie was scared of him. She sat awake half the night, watching Max. Once, he shifted and snorted, and the hairs on Millie's arms stood on end. She shoved herself right up close against Jolly. But Max just grumbled and rolled over and kept sleeping. He didn't change. Not this time. Millie watched him a little longer, until she couldn't keep her eyes open. She curled up beside Jolly. Jolly was scrawny, her skin downy with the peach fuzz that Sai said came from starvation. Most of them had it. Nobody wanted to grow up and change, but Jolly needed to eat a little more, just a little. Millie stared into the dark and worried. She didn't know when she fell asleep. She woke when first light was making the window into a glowing blue square. She was cold. Millie reached to put her arm around Jolly. Her arm landed on wadded-up clothing with nobody in it. "She's gone," said Citron.

"Whuh?" Millie rolled over, sat up. She was still tired. "She gone to check the traps?" Jolly barely ate, but she was best at catching gamey squirrels, feral cats, and the occasional raccoon.

"I dunno. I woke up just as the door was closing behind her. She let in a draft."

Millie leapt to her feet. "It was Max! He sprouted! He ate her!"

Citron leapt up too. He pulled her into a hug. "Sh. It wasn't Max. Look, he's still sleeping."

He was. Millie could see him huddled under his coat.

"See?" said Citron. "Now hush. You're going to wake him and Sai up."

"Oh god, I was so scared for a moment."

She was lying; she never stopped being scared. She sobbed and let Citron keep hugging her, but not for long. Things could sneak up on you while you were busy making snot and getting hugs to make you feel better. Millie swallowed back the rest of her tears. She pulled out of Citron's arms. "Thanks." She went and checked beside Jolly's side of the bed. Jolly's jacket wasn't there. Neither was her penguin. Ah. "She's gone to find aspirin for me." Millie sighed with relief and guilt. "She took her penguin to trade with. That's almost her most favourite thing ever."

"Next to you, you mean."

"I suppose so. I come first, then her necklace, then the penguin." Jolly'd found the ceramic penguin a long time ago when they'd been scavenging in the wreckage of a drug store. The penguin stood on a circular base, the whole thing about ten inches tall. Its beak was broken, but when you twisted the white base, music played out of it. Jolly had kept it carefully since, wrapped in a torn blouse. She played it once a week and on special occasions. Twisted the base twice only, let the penguin do a slow turn to the few notes of tinny song. Churchy had told them that penguin was from a movie called Madagascar. She'd been old enough to remember old-time stuff like that. It was soon after that that they'd had to kill her.

Millie stared at her and Jolly's sleeping place. There was something . . . "She didn't take socks. Her feet must be freezing." She picked up the pair of socks with the fewest holes in it. "We have to go find her."

"You go," Citron replied. "It's cold out, and I want to get some more sleep."

"You know we're not supposed to go anywhere on our own!"

"Yeah, but we do. Lots of times."

"Except me. I always have someone with me."

"Right. Like that's any safer than being alone. I'm going back to bed." He yawned and turned away.

Millie fought the urge to yell at him. Instead she said, "I claim leader."

Citron stopped. "Aw, come on, Millie."

But Millie was determined. "Leader. One of us might be in danger, so I claim leader. So you have to be my follower."

He looked skywards and sighed. "Fine. Where?"

That meant she was leader. You asked the leader what to do, and the leader told you. Usually everyone asked Jolly what to do, or Max. Now that she had an excuse to go to Jolly, Millie stopped feeling as though something had gnawed away the pit of her stomach. She yanked her coat out of the pile of clothing that was her bed and shrugged it on. "Button me," she said to Citron, biting back the 'please.' Leaders didn't say please. They just gave orders. That was the right way to do it.

Citron concentrated hard on the buttons, not looking in Millie's eyes as he did them up. He started in the middle, buttoned down to the last button just below her hips, then stood up to do the buttons at her chest. He held the fabric away from her, so it wouldn't touch her body at all.

His fingers didn't touch her, but still her chest felt tingly as Citron did up the top buttons. She knew he was blushing, even though you couldn't tell on his dark face. Hers neither. If it had been Max doing this, his face would have lit up like a strawberry. They found strawberries growing sometimes, in summer.

Leaders didn't blush. Millie straightened up and looked at Citron. He had such a baby face. If he was lucky, he'd never sprout. She'd heard that some people didn't. Max said it was too soon to tell, because the pandemic had only started two years ago, but Millie liked to hope that some kids would avoid the horrible thing. No temper getting worse and worse. No changing all of a sudden into something different and scary. Millie wondered briefly what happened to the ones who didn't sprout, who just got old. Food for the easthound, probably. "Maybe we should go . . . ?" Millie began to ask, then remembered herself. Leaders didn't ask, they told. "We're going over by the grocery first," she told Citron. "Maybe she's just checking her traps."

"She took her music box to check her traps?"

"Doesn't matter. That's where we're going to go." She stuffed Jolly's socks into her coat pocket, then shoved her shoulder against the damp-swollen door and stepped out into the watery light of an early spring morning. The sun made her blink.

Citron asked, "Shouldn't we get those two to come along with us? You know, so there's more of us?"

"No," growled Millie. "Just now you wanted me to go all alone, but now you want company?"

"But who does trading this early in the morning?"

"We're not going to wake Max and Sai, okay? We'll find her ourselves!"

Citron frowned. Millie shivered. It was so cold out that her nose hairs froze together when she breathed in. Like scattered pins, tiny, shiny daggers of frost edged the sidewalk slabs and the new spring leaves of the small maple tree that grew outside their squat. Trust Jolly to make her get out of a warm bed to go looking for her on a morning like this. She picked up three solid throwing rocks. They were gritty with dirt and the cold of them burned her fingers. She stuffed them into her jacket pocket, on top of Jolly's socks. Citron had the baseball bat he carried everywhere. Millie turned up her collar and stuck her hand into her jeans pocket. "C'mon."

Jolly'd put a new batch of traps over by that old grocery store. The roof was caved in. There was no food in the grocery any more, or soap, or cough medicine. Everything had been scavenged by the nearby warrens of kids, but animals sometimes made nests and shit in the junk that was left. Jollie'd caught a dog once. A gaunt poodle with dirty, matted hair. But they didn't eat dogs, ever. You were what you ate. They'd only killed it in an orgy of fury and frustration that had swelled over them like a river.

Black Betty had a child,
Bam-ba-lam,
That child's gone wild,
Bam-ba-lam.

Really, it was Millie who'd started it, back before everything went wrong, two winters ago. They'd been at home. Jolly sitting on the living room floor that early evening, texting with her friends, occasionally giggling at something one of them said. Millie and Dad on the couch, sharing a bowl of raspberries. All of them watching some old-time cartoon movie on TV about animals that could do Kung Fu. Waiting for Mum to come home from work. Because then they would order pizza. It was pizza night. Dad getting a text message on his phone. Dad holding the phone down by his knee to make out the words, even though his eyesight was just fine, he said. Jolly watching them, waiting to hear if it was Mum, if she'd be home soon. Millie leaning closer to Dad and squinting at the tiny message in the phone's window. Mouthing the words silently. Then frowning. Saying, "Mum says she's coming home on the easthound train?" Dad falling out laughing. Eastbound, sweetie.

There hadn't been an easthound before that. It was Millie who'd called it, who'd made it be. Jolly'd told her that wasn't true, that she didn't make the pandemic just by reading a word wrong, that the world didn't work that way. But the world didn't work any more the way it used to, so what did Jolly know? Even if she was older than Millie.

Jolly and Millie's family had assigned adjectives to the girls early on in their lives. Millie was The Younger One. (By twenty-eight and three quarter minutes. The midwife had been worried that Mum would need a C-Section to get Millie out.) Jolly was The Kidder. She liked jokes and games. She'd come up with loup-de-lou to help keep Millie's mind off the agony when she'd lost her hand. Millie'd still been able to feel the missing hand there, on the end of her wrist, and pain wouldn't let her sleep or rest, and all the adults in the world were sprouting and trying to kill off the kids, and Max was making her and Jolly and Citron move to a new hiding place every few days, until he and Jolly figured out the thing about sprinkling peppermint oil to hide their scent trails so that sprouteds couldn't track them. That was back before Sai had joined them, and then Churchy. Back before Churchy had sprouted on them one night in the dark as they were all sharing half a stale bread loaf and a big litre bottle of flat cola, and Max and Citron and Sai had grabbed anything heavy or sharp they could find and whaled away at the thing that had been Churchy just seconds before, until it lay still on the ground, all pulpy and bloody. And the whole time, Jolly had stayed near still-weak Millie, brandishing a heavy frying pan and muttering, "It's okay, Mills. I won't let her get you."

The feeling was coming back, like her hand was still there. Her wrist had settled into a throbbing ache. She hoped it wasn't getting infected again.

Watchfully, they walked down their side street and turned onto the main street in the direction of the old grocery store. They walked up the middle of the empty road. That way, if a sprouted came out of one of the shops or alleyways, they might have time to see it before it attacked.

The burger place, the gas station, the little shoe repair place on the corner; Millie tried to remember what stores like that had been like before. When they'd had unbroken windows and unempty shelves. When there'd been people shopping in them and adults running them, back when adults used to be just grown-up people suspicious of packs of schoolkids in their stores, not howling, sharp-toothed child-killers with dank, stringy fur and paws instead of hands. Ravenous monsters that grew and grew so quickly that you could watch it happen, if you were stupid enough to stick around. Their teeth, hair and claws lengthened, their bodies getting bigger and heavier minute by minute, until they could no longer eat quickly enough to keep up with the growth, and they weakened and died a few days after they'd sprouted.

Jolly wasn't tending to her traps. Millie swallowed. "Okay, so we'll go check with the warren over on Patel Street. They usually have aspirin and stuff." She walked in silence, except for the worry voice in her head.

Citron said, "That tree's going to have to start over."

"What?" Millie realized she'd stopped at the traffic light out of habit, because it had gone to red. She was such an idiot. And so was Citron, for just going along with her. She started walking again. Citron tagged along, always just a little behind.

"The maple tree," he puffed. When you never had enough to eat, you got tired quickly. "The one outside our place. It put its leaves out too early, and now the frost has killed them. It'll have to start over."

"Whatever." Then she felt guilty for being so crabby with him. What could she say to make nice? "Uh, that was a nice line you made in Loup-de-lou last night. The one with eyes and spies in it."

Citron smiled at her. "Thanks. It wasn't quite right, though. Sprouteds have bleedy red eyes, not shiny ones."

"But your line wasn't about sprouteds. It was about the . . . the easthound." She looked all around and behind her. Nothing.

"Thing is," Citron replied, so quietly that Millie almost didn't hear him, "We're all the easthound."

Instantly, Millie swatted the back of his head. "Shut up!"

"Ow!"

"Just shut up! Take that back! It's not true!"

"Stop making such a racket, willya?"

"So stop being such a loser!" She was sweating in her jacket, her skinny knees trembling. So hungry all the time. So scared.

Citron's eyes widened. "Millie—!"

He was looking behind her. She turned, hand fumbling in her jacket pocket for her rocks. The sprouted bowled her over while her hand was still snagged in her pocket. Thick, curling fur and snarling teeth as long as her pinkie. It grabbed her. Its paws were like catcher's mitts with claws in them. It howled and briefly let her go. It's in pain, she thought wonderingly, even as she fought her hand out of her pocket and tried to get out from under the sprouted. All that quick growing. It must hurt them. The sprouted snapped at her face, missed. They were fast and strong when they first sprouted, but clumsy in their ever-changing bodies. The sprouted set its jaws in her chest. Through her coat and sweater, its teeth tore into her skin. Pain. Teeth sliding along her ribs. Millie tried to wrestle the head off her. She got her fingers deep into the fur around its neck.

Then an impact jerked the sprouted's head sideways. Citron and his baseball bat, screaming, "Die, die, die!" as he beat the sprouted. It leapt for him. It was already bigger. Millie rolled to her feet, looking around for anything she could use as a weapon. Citron was keeping the sprouted at bay, just barely, by swinging his bat at it. It advanced on him, howling in pain with every step forward.

Sai seemed to come out of nowhere. She had the piece of rebar she carried whenever she went out. The three of them raged at the sprouted, screaming and hitting. Millie kicked and kicked. The sprouted screamed back, in pain or fury. Its eyes were all bleedy. It swatted Citron aside, but he got up and came at it again. Finally it wasn't fighting any more. They kept hitting it until they were sure it was dead. Even after Sai and Citron had stopped, Millie stomped the sprouted. With each stomp she grunted in thick animal rage at herself for letting it sneak up on her, for leaving the warren without her knife. Out of the corner of her eye she could see a few kids that had crept out from other warrens to see what the racket was about. She didn't care. She stomped.

"Millie! Millie!" It was Citron. "It's dead!"

Millie gave the bloody lump of hair and bone and flesh one more kick, then stood panting. Just a second to catch her breath, then they could keep looking for Jolly. They couldn't stay there long. A dead sprouted could draw others. If one sprouted was bad, a feeding frenzy of them was worse.

Sai was gulping, sobbing. She looked at them with stricken eyes. "I woke up and I called to Max and he didn't answer, and when I went over and lifted his coat" —Sai burst into gusts of weeping— "there was only part of his head and one arm there. And bones. Not even much blood." Sai clutched herself and shuddered. "While we were sleeping, a sprouted came in and killed Max and ate most of him, even licked up his blood, and we didn't wake up! I thought it had eaten all of you! I thought it was coming back for me!"

Something gleamed white in the broken mess of the sprouted's corpse. Millie leaned over to see better, fighting not to gag on the smell of blood and worse. She had to crouch closer. There was lots of blood on the thing lying in the curve of the sprouted's body, but with chilly clarity, Millie recognized it. It was the circular base of Jolly's musical penguin. Millie looked over at Citron and Sai. "Run," she told them. The tears coursing down her face felt cool. Because her skin was so hot now.

"What?" asked Sai. "Why?"

Millie straightened. Her legs were shaking so much they barely held her up. That small pop she'd felt when she pulled on the sprouted's neck. "A sprouted didn't come into our squat. It was already in there." She opened her hand to show them the thing she'd pulled off the sprouted's throat in her battle with it; Jolly's gold necklace. Instinct often led sprouteds to return to where the people they loved were. Jolly had run away to protect the rest of her warren from herself. "Bloody run!" Millie yelled at them. "Go find another squat! Somewhere I won't look for you! Don't you get it? I'm her twin!"

First Citron's face then Sai's went blank with shock as they understood what Millie was saying. Citron sobbed, once. It might have been the word, "Bye." He grabbed Sai's arm. The two of them stumbled away. The other kids that had come out to gawk had disappeared back to their warrens. Millie turned her back so she couldn't see what direction Sai and Citron were moving in, but she could hear them, more keenly than she'd ever been able to hear. She could smell them. The easthound could track them. The downy starvation fuzz on Millie's arm was already coarser. The pain in her handless wrist spiked. She looked at it. It was aching because the hand was starting to grow in again. There were tiny fingers on the end of it now. And she needed to eat so badly.

When had Jolly sprouted? Probably way more than twenty-eight and three-quarters minutes ago. Citron and Sai's only chance was that Millie had always done everything later than her twin.

Still clutching Jolly's necklace, she began to run, too; in a different direction. Leeks, she told the sprouting Hound, fresh leeks. You like those, right? Not blood and still-warm, still-screaming flesh. You like leeks.

The Hound wasn't fully come into itself yet. It was almost believing her that leeks would satisfy its hunger. And it didn't understand that she couldn't swim.

You're thirsty too, right? she told it.

It was.

Faster, faster, faster, Millie sped towards the river, where the spring tide was running deep and wide.

That child's gone wild.
Oh, Black Betty, bam-ba-lam.

Loup.

THE CORRESPONDENCE BETWEEN THE GOVERNESS AND THE ATTIC

Siobhan Carroll

for Susan Gubar

OPENING

The changeling hides in the window seat. On one side of her is glass, gauzy with rain. On the other, a thick curtain. November whistles through the crack in the window frame, but she dares not move. In this house she is a creeping, persecuted thing. Best if they don't see her.

She opens the book. Reading, she knows, is dangerous: none of the books in the house are hers, nothing is hers, and the family will hold this small act against her. But reading is a better escape than none at all.

Boards creak. The changeling looks up from the book's eerie paintings. She tries to breathe without noise. But she is only a frail orphan, without friends or magic, and she is not hidden well enough.

The curtain is pulled aside. Together, you are dragged into the beginning of the story.

THE RED ROOM

For fighting back, they punish her. The orphan pounds at the door of the haunted bedroom. Her screams claw down the hallway, but no one will save her.

She dies her first death in the red room.

There will be others.

THE INTERVIEW

Afterward, the girl is interrogated, to see if she has learned her lesson:

"And what must you do to avoid hell, child?"

"I must keep in good health, and never die."

This gives the family pause. Only yesterday, the orphan shrank away from them. Now she is upright, glittering, dangerous. Death will do that to some people.

"I am not deceitful," the changeling says. "If I were, I should say I loved you. But I am glad you are no relations of mine. If anyone ever asks how you treated me, I shall say the thought of you makes me sick, and that you treated me with miserable cruelty."

This will not do.

THE SCHOOL

The family washes their hands of her in a respectable way: They send her to school. This is not a clean, well-lit institution but a prison, where unwanted children stand in rigid lines and faint from hunger. The servants bind the corpses in cheap linen and line them up in the courtyard for collection.

The changeling's fury sustains her. When the headmaster singles her out for abuse, she glares at him. She will not die, not again, not so soon.

She is befriended by Helen Burns, a girl with a saintly smile and a red cough that will martyr her before the story is even underway. Burns counsels the embrace of suffering, and dies (beautifully) to illustrate her point.

The changeling is not convinced. She scratches the walls of her prison, searching for a way out. A kind ancestral fairy drops the solution on her pillow: She will become a governess.

THORNFIELD

Jane (let's call her Jane now, everyone else does)—

Jane Errant sets out for a house called Thornfield, where she is to tutor a clockwork French girl who sings stuttering arias.

The housekeeper claims the house has no ghosts in it. The changeling chooses to believe her, although she already knows that the servants laugh too loudly and that strange footsteps sound in the attic. As she lies awake at night, the attic creeps into the governess's thoughts, just as it creeps into yours. Dreams of yellow wallpaper, and women who will not be caged.

THE CLOCKWORK GIRL

Adele, unlike Jane, is ideal.

At eight years old she is already pretty, with bright blue eyes that are empty of thought. Her golden hair falls in ringlets, and when she sings she tilts her head just so and shakes her curls as her mother taught her. She smiles frequently at men, displaying teeth that are white and straight.

If you let her, she will sing for you. She will recite poems that she doesn't understand, raising her hand in the places her mother taught her. When she has finished, she will sink into a curtsey and look up demurely through her fringe of golden hair.

In France, her audience pretended to find this sweet; the gentlemen watched her with eager eyes as she danced for them like a music-box ballerina. Afterward she was sent to sit on their knees. Sometimes in their laps.

Adele dislikes the governess's lessons, for they are full of big words and numbers that clatter noisily in her head. But she likes the governess well enough, though she is a plain, mousy thing with a thoughtful face. At eight years old, Adele already knows that women should never be thoughtful. They should be pretty and work hard to catch men's eyes and keep them.

It takes a lot of concentration not to think of the footsteps she hears in the attic, but Adele has been practising the art of thoughtlessness for a long time. Her mother began the clockwork process—to aid Adele's dancing, she said—and now Adele has almost completed it on her own. Sometimes, when the ghosts in the attic threaten to dig their way into her mind, Adele likes to think about her clockwork body, how solid it is, how quiet and regular. Her body will last forever, and unlike people, it will never abandon her.

The noise in the attic starts again, but Adele turns away. She places her hand over her heart, feeling its fleshy beats thud disgustingly against her ribcage. Soon, she thinks, her transformation will be complete. Then she will be perfect. Then she will be loved.

THE ATTIC

It is time we speak of the attic, this space around which Thornfield's stories turn. Thornfield is a fairy-tale prison, after all; its thorny walls must guard *something*. But do they guard it from the world or guard the world from it?

The changeling lies awake in her virginal governess's bed, listening to the attic. Are those footsteps she hears real, or figments of her imagination?

One night, tentatively, she writes out a note, and slips it through a crack into the attic: *Who are you?*

Excellent question. Sadly, it goes unanswered for weeks. During this time Adele lisps her lessons and the governess is bored. Idly, she plans a trip to the crossroads.

One day she finds a note pinned to her door. The pin is long and sharp; its head is red as blood. The creased paper contains a single word: *Myself.*

The governess writes a longer note, filling the margins with carefully phrased questions. She never receives an answer. The attic has already told her all she needs to know.

THE CROSSROADS

At midnight the changeling goes to the crossroads. She puts her delicate hands to the dank, pressed earth and digs a hole as deep as her forearm. She takes out the charm—a simple thing made of rags and rabbit's blood, like the ones her nurse used to make—and drops it down.

There, the changeling thinks. *Now do something.*

Nothing happens.

The changeling lets a breath out she did not know she was holding. She formed the charm to ask for a change, a breath of excitement in a life fast becoming dreary. But of course nothing will happen. Her nurse's tales were fantasy only.

Then the hair rises on the back of her arms. Her sweat crisps into cold jewels of ice and skitters to the ground. It pools around her accusingly.

Looking up, the changeling sees a lone dog rushing toward her, eyes gleaming like underwater coins. Her nurse told her stories about dogs like this, fairy guardians of solitary ways.

She feels a surge of fear. Is this another beginning for her? A rough hand come to drag her into yet another story?

The dog rushes past her. It's his master—and hers—who stops. Falls, actually, tumbling from his horse with a clatter of bones and ugly deeds. It's up to the changeling to help him to his feet again, a dark man with gloomy manners.

If he had been handsome, if he had smiled, if he had treated her kindly—this story would be different.

She is used to rudeness, and to the insults he hurls in her direction. She offers him a hand and helps lift him up, into a story she—mistakenly—believes unchanged.

THE SECOND INTERVIEW

"When you came on me in the Hay Lane last night, I thought unaccountably of fairy tales, and had half a mind to demand whether you had bewitched my horse. I am not sure yet. Who are your parents?"

The governess tells her master the truth: She has none she can remember.

"And so you were waiting for your people when you sat on that stile? Did I break through one of your rings, that you spread that damned ice on the causeway?"

The changeling feels an unaccountable chill at Rochester's words. Does he know? But see how perfectly she answers, mimicking her master's ironic tone:

"*The men in green all forsook England a hundred years ago.*"

The lie looks well on her, reflecting in the light of her preternatural eyes.

BLANCHE

A party of gentlefolk has arrived at the great house. The servants scurry through Thornfield's dark chambers, trying to scrub away layers of Gothic with harsh brown soap. The governess can think only of the woman she heard talked about: Blanche Ingram, the lady the servants say her master will marry.

On the night of the party, the governess sees her rival for the first time: a woman white as bleached marble. Blanche has an imperial air about her, the crackle of repressed power. She is careful not to touch the governess, not even with the hem of her gown.

Oddly, there is something about Blanche that reminds the changeling of herself. Ignorant of all but the most basic instincts of the fey-blooded, she cannot tell what it is. She only knows that Blanche's power is to be respected; that her anger will make itself felt even at great distances. She knows, also, that Blanche has inherited a feral cruelty that the changeling herself does not possess.

Oh, thinks the governess, as Blanche passes by. Is this the kind of woman her master likes?

The changeling has learned to love her master (poor thing). And why not? In his rough way, he has treated her kindly. At least, he has been interested in her, and to those who are used to being ignored, interest is a kindness.

Besides, Thornfield is a dreary place. There is little else for a young woman to do here but fall in love or go insane. The changeling chose the first option (she thinks). She cannot unlove him now, merely because he has ceased to notice her.

THE FORTUNE TELLER

An old gypsy is at the gate, hissing prophecies. She offers to tell everyone's fortunes, if the servants will let her cross the threshold.

The guests summon her into the hall—a stooped cipher of a woman, bundled like a leper—and give her a private room to interview them in.

One by one the gentlefolk go in, laughing. They emerge with questions gathering in the creases of their eyes. Blanche comes out and announces that she is leaving; the party has exhausted her. She asks that all due apologies be conveyed to the host.

The governess has not met Blanche's gaze until now. All night, this fine lady's eyes swept past her, but now she stares at the governess, and her eyes glitter like cold iron.

The changeling stares back, her face set. Sensing danger, she is stubborn. As Blanche turns to leave, Jane feels the same chill she did at the crossroads. *This will not go well,* she thinks, but does not know what she is afraid of.

A guest comes and touches her arm. The gypsy woman wants to see her.

THE THIRD INTERVIEW

The changeling and the gypsy woman confront each other in a flame-lit room.

"Why don't you tremble?"

"I'm not cold."

"Why don't you turn pale?"

"I'm not sick."

"Why don't you consult my art?"

"I'm not silly."

The gypsy laughs. *You are all three,* the old woman says. *Cold from want of love, sick from desire, and silly for not pursuing it.*

The changeling will say nothing to that. The flame flickers in the eye. Perhaps she already detects her master's face beneath the soot and rags. Perhaps she's already wondering what game he's playing.

WAITING

After the guests leave: silence.

The servants move about as quietly as they can, cleaning up all traces of the week of parties. The governess wonders at her master's charade, about the queer games he is playing with her and Blanche Ingram.

Her master is congratulating himself on his cleverness. He thinks he has driven Blanche off with a few well-turned prophecies. But women like Blanche have a way of making their feelings known even after your doors are barred to them, and the changeling fears that Blanche's power will not be gainsaid.

There are signs. A tree in the garden is blasted by lightning, and afterward the air around its stump smells like roses. The milk left beside the door turns sour. The clouds around Thornfield threaten rain, but no storm arrives.

The changeling can sense the magic in the air, but she has not the least idea how to turn back the curse coiling around them. Someone has set something dreadful in motion, and she does not know what to do.

It occurs to the changeling that she might ask the attic for help, but the thought stirs fear in her. Instinctively, she knows that whatever is locked in the attic is not on her side. It is on nobody's side but its own. Unleashed, there is no telling what it might do.

THE PRECURSOR

Blanche's curse arrives in the form of another visitor, one who brings the tropical past clinging to his heels. He gives his name as Mason. He comes, he says, from the West Indies.

The West Indies. It's easy to forget, here in the damp mist of Thornfield, that there's an empire out there. Its blood brews the coffee at your table. Its ghosts wander your darkness; children whose bones were ground into sugar pound on the wet glass. You can shred their hands on the broken panes, but it will not keep them out—some of them are already inside.

"Mason—the West Indies," her master repeats. The governess feels chilled, though she does not know why.

MIDNIGHT

Something has happened in the attic.

Mason, the newest houseguest, is brought below stairs, his shirt soaked with blood, his pale eyes rolling.

"She said she'd drain my heart," he tells Rochester. The words stagger down the halls, leaving bloody handprints on the yellow wallpaper.

The changeling is all for going to the attic herself, candlestick in hand, to do . . . what, she could not say. She does not know what to call the strange power seething under her skin, but something dreadful seems to be called for.

As she goes to mount the attic stairs, a servant's brown arms restrain her. The young woman shakes her head silently. *No.* This is not a governess's concern.

There is blood seeping into the floorboards, crawling into the bones of the past. The housekeeper is on her knees, trying to prevent a stain.

Afterward, nobody comments on the incident. It is as though it never happened at all.

The governess resumes her correspondence with the attic. This time her note contains a single word: *Why?*

A few days later, she receives a reply, left on her pillow as though by an evil fairy. This time the note says simply: *You'll learn.*

THE PROPOSAL

Her master begins (subtly, he thinks), by asking Jane what she thinks of the house. Of course she must approve of the house: Despite its Gothic appearance, the ghost in the attic, the alleged homicidal impulses of its servants, it is the only home she has. From here it is a short step to approving of the man himself, or so he hopes.

The governess, to her credit, is sceptical. She is in love with him, yes: but he is older than she, richer than she, and is a gentleman. Also, there is the matter of the attic. (She is astute enough not to mention the attic aloud, but she looks meaningfully in the direction of the house. Rochester chooses to ignore her gaze.)

Her master has answers for her: His wealth and age are usually considered good things, and he hates parties, so she will not have to mix much in society.

Eventually, she says yes.

In a fairy tale, the story would now be over. But in the attic, something broods, waiting.

THE WEDDING

On the morning of the wedding, the governess wakes with a mound of salt in her mouth. She spits out the white powder—her mouth is dry, so dry—and kicks away the iron horseshoe that someone has left at the foot of her bed. She sits up trembling, enraged.

Her fey self is housed in human flesh, and such weak tricks will not work on her. But the changeling knows she has been threatened. Someone in this house does not wish her well.

She glances askance at the servants who help her with the veil. One of them, perhaps? One of the laughing kitchen girls she called a friend? Or the housekeeper?

The mirror stares at her, its pale face reflecting hers.

She looks like a ghost in her bridal gown, a feathery concoction of silk and lace. Her master chose it for her, and who is Jane to argue? She owns no clothes but those that are handed to her.

Rubbing the glitter of salt from her lips, she tells herself that all will be well. It is only a dress, after all.

THE TRAITOR

At the foot of the stairs, Adele tilts her porcelain face up and mouths her words: "It didn't work."

There is no answer.

Uncertainly, Adele twists her tiny hands in front of her. The wedding will start soon. As the flower girl, Adele is expected to perform, and yet she is still imperfect, still flawed.

Desperation makes her bold. "I did what you said," she tells the attic. "Now you must give me my heart."

"It is not mine to give." The attic's voice is dry, amused. It sounds like dead leaves scraping together. A chill runs up the clockwork girl's perfectly articulated spine.

Adele licks her lips. "But you promised—"

"I promise many things," the attic says. *"Only time will tell."*

Adele shakes her head. There are so many things she wishes she could say, but her perfect mouth cannot form the words.

THE CEREMONY

The wedding guests shuffle as Jane walks in. They are Rochester's friends, and her veil turns their faces into white blurs.

The priest speaks and the governess tries to listen. Tension is gathering around her. Blanche's curse is here, standing in the shadows like an unexpected guest. It looks like Mason.

Someone must have said something. Rochester turns to look at Mason. Adele is standing perfectly poised, one graceful hand cupped to her face in a perfect mimicry of shock.

"The groom has another wife," Mason repeats.

Rochester is furious. He would kill Mason if he could, but this is England, and the wedding guests would be positively shocked.

Angrily he leads the curious and the cynical down the stone path to Thornfield, up that ancient house's creaking stairs. The governess follows behind, wondering if this is the worst Blanche can do to her.

Then she sees they are to go into the attic. She pauses at the top of the stairs, her skin prickling. Things are about to change. She can feel it.

THE MADWOMAN IN THE ATTIC

The governess hears the woman before she sees her. Snarls, thick and guttural, the sounds life makes when it refuses to be stamped out. A lurching, scrabbling figure on the floor, all hair and fingernails. Its look is hateful.

Jane recognizes that look, and the ring of salt that surrounds the woman. She recognizes the horseshoes nailed to the wall. They have kept her here, this fey thing, safely away from their white tablecloths and dining sets. The attic rattles with her fury.

Grace Pool, that whispering servant, warns them to take care. "One never knows what she has, sir; she is so cunning. It is not in mortal discretion to fathom her craft."

Lured, perhaps, by the abjection of the grovelling shadow, the gentlemen draw closer, staring the way people do through the bars of a cage. One of them disturbs the salt with the toe of his boot.

Instantly the fairy is at them, desperate for a chance to inflict damage. The magic that curls at her fingertips still blazes power. Her bared teeth are yellow. They draw blood.

They wrestle her down, pin her to the floorboards. Her magic is too tattered to stop them. She moans and hisses into the veins of wood, her bare feet kicking vaguely at the air.

The changeling has never seen one of the pure fey before. There were images, to be sure, memories lurking in her blood, but none of them prepared her for this once-proud creature clawing at floorboards, eyes empty of reason.

Jane almost does not hear her master's words, but they seep into her mind like a rising tide: "That is my wife," he explains, rubbing the dark stains on his torn sleeve. "Such is the sole conjugal embrace I am ever to know. And this is what I wished to have," (here he lays his hand on the governess's shoulder): "this young girl, who stands so grave and quiet at the mouth of hell, looking collectedly at the gambols of a demon."

Jane shudders, almost shrugs the hand off. One of the gentlemen asks a question. With her master distracted, Jane turns away from the madwoman on the floor, and the cluster of spectators. Unnoticed, she slips down the stairs, each step creaking familiarly in a house she no longer feels at home in.

She does not take much. There is no time: They will be downstairs soon, and someone might run after her with pleas and reasonable explanations.

She leaves by the servant's gate. Nobody sees her go.

Behind her, the attic howls its loneliness to the wind.

THE MOORS

She dies her second death on the moors.

It is cold, bitterly cold, and the changeling is not dressed for the weather. Her flesh suffers the elements as severely as any human, though her fey nature sings on the wind.

Home, she thinks bitterly. *I've come home,* and in a way she has: Being a changeling, she belongs nowhere.

At some point she sleeps, or tries to, huddling on a muddy bank under the shelter of a wind-beaten tree. At dawn she rises, scraping away the frost that has formed on her skin.

She wades knee-deep in the heath's dark growth. She follows paths no humans could walk, under hills and through stones, through the abandoned tunnels and empty barrows that mark the deserted cities of the fey. No friendly fires welcome her.

She recalls the words she spoke once, by a warm fireplace: *"The men in green all forsook England a hundred years ago."* She had hoped to be wrong.

Wearily she directs her path out of the earth. She is almost at the end of her magic now; even her fey self cannot keep walking much longer. And yet she sets one foot in front of the other, stubborn to the end.

Her path takes her to the house at Marsh End, a lonely hermitage of a building. The servant who answers gives this wandering beggar a crust of bread before sending her off. The changeling accepts it numbly. She no longer has the strength for gratitude.

She does not eat the bread. With her last strength, she draws a splayed cross on the dust of the road and lays the bread on top of the symbol. As charms go, it's horribly weak, but it is her last hope.

The changeling lies down beside her charm. Mustering what remains of her strength, she dies.

MOURNING

Thornfield is a dark house now.

The clockwork girl sits in her room, counting the beats of her imperfect heart. Nobody cares if she studies penmanship, or asks her hard questions about the kings of England. Adele should be glad, but she isn't. The master's gloom has fallen on them all.

"Why did you do that?" she demands of the attic. "Why did you have to spoil everything?"

The attic is contemptuously silent.

"I don't see why I had to show her the horseshoe," Adele says. "She would have left anyway, as soon as she found out." She adds, carefully, "It's a scandal," in the breathy way the maids did in the kitchen.

Silence. Adele lies down on her bed, facing away from the attic.

"Well I hope she comes back soon," she says, and then adds, "I want to show her the new dance I've been working on."

I need you to do something for me, the attic says. This time Adele claps her hands over her ears.

THE SICK ROOM

The changeling comes back to life slowly. Her mind is in pieces and every piece of it hurts. She hears voices, sees fragments of faces. Some of them are there, some are elsewhere, some are long ago.

She is alive.

"She's alive," says the man, "but barely. We must keep her by the fire."

"She looks sensible, but not at all handsome. The grace and harmony of beauty are quite wanting in those features."

The changeling groans. She wants to tell them that she knows she is plain; she has never had any pretensions to beauty. Whatever wild looks run in the blood of the fey passed her by. What is left is a dull composite of dreams unfulfilled.

But her movement brings only questions: "Who are you? Where are your people? What is your name?" They sting her like hornets.

To make them go away she answers, "Jane, my name is Jane—" then, remembering, she adds "—Elliot. I have no people."

After that, they let her rest.

MOOR HOUSE

There was a governess who worked in a house of thorns. She fell in love with a man but discovered his past locked in an attic. She ran away, like a madwoman broken free. She was adopted by a family. They lived in the house at Marsh End, and all ended happily ever after.

The changeling tries out her tale as she sits in the parlour, taking advantage of the family's absence to test how her words bounce off the walls. It's true, this sounds like a plausible conclusion, but she would prefer a different kind of ending.

She hears voices at the door. Her benefactors have returned.

"Jane Elliot!"

The alias is easy to answer to. Jane nods and smiles. Both of the women are pleasant enough, but it's St. John that Jane is most aware of.

The master of the house is an austere man, a man made of marble, white and cold. The changeling feels obliged to him, on account of his saving her life, and on account of his being a religious man. The truth is, she doesn't like him.

"We have news," says Diana. "St. John has located a position for Mary. She is to be a governess."

Jane's face is slow to smile. For a moment she thinks she hears a footfall overhead, but of course there is no attic here. Her mind is playing tricks on her again.

She manages to congratulate Mary on her new employment. In truth, it is good news of a sort, for these gentlewomen have very little to live on, and their brother is to go for a missionary.

The magic that sleeps in these people is buried deep. In the women it almost never surfaces—their dreams are cramped by poverty. Also, they are afraid of their brother, of his torrential ambitions and drive to know God. The changeling senses his magic and fears it, for it flows down the narrow channels carved by his religion.

St. John does not know he is different. Or if he does, it is because he thinks he is one of God's chosen. He believes he has a destiny. Such people are dangerous.

But, she thinks, this family means her no harm. They are the first other changelings that she has found. And where else would she go?

She must stay here and build a new life, no matter what it costs her.

CURSES

"This place is cursed," Adele says, balancing on her toes. The housekeeper turns and looks at her sharply.

"Who told you that?" Mr. Rochester asks. He almost never listens. Astonished, Adele loses her balance and lands flat-footed.

"Oh," the clockwork girl says, "everyone." She thinks of the gossiping maids, and of the madwoman brooding overhead, dark and terrible.

"You should not give credence to idle tales." Mr. Rochester is staring out the window again, waiting for someone. The woman he is looking for will not return, Adele thinks, not as long as the house has curses piled up at its door.

"Nevertheless," he says, as if to himself, "I should send you away. This is not a good place for a child. Not anymore."

For a moment, hope flares inside Adele. "Shall I go to Paris?" she says. "To see Mama?"

Rochester is silent for a moment. Then he says, "No, I will not send you to Paris, but to my cousin's house in Derbyshire. He has a young girl your age."

Adele is horrified. Other girls? She imagines a pair of rivals, their hair curled more perfectly than hers, their artificial bodies perfectly poised. "Oh non, monsieur," she wails. "Do not send me there."

Afterward, when she has been sent to her room, she climbs up on one of the posts of her tall bed and puts her fingers against the ceiling. "Do something," she says, "they are sending me away."

You will be safer elsewhere, the attic says.

"But I don't want to be elsewhere," Adele says, outraged. "Elsewhere is exactly the same!" And she knows it—she's been abroad in the world. It's full of the spite of women, the jealousy of men. Curses sleep on every tongue. Here, at least, she has a place; she is cosseted and somewhat protected.

Then you must do what I tell you. The attic is relentless on this point. It has been whispering the same thing for weeks.

This time, Adele is willing to listen.

DESTINIES

In Moor House, Jane is saying her goodbyes again. This time she is bidding farewell to her two protectors, the earnest changelings who do not know what they are. They do not know how to form charms; they have not seen the dead cities of the fey. Jane pities them, and envies them, too.

While she will miss them all, it will be a relief not to steel her mind against St. John's ambition. When he talks to her, she does not feel like herself. She becomes the quiet, mouse-like creature she resembles, nodding at his every statement.

Just as she thinks this, a shadow falls on her shoulder. "May I have a word?" St. John asks, his voice mild and ominous.

The changeling wipes her damp hands on her skirt. *There is nothing to be afraid of,* she tells herself as she follows him out.

THE SUMMONING

"And if I give you the candle, you can bring her back?" Adele is dubious. Her clockwork mind is turning over the details of the attic's plan, and however much the voice in the walls reassures her, the part of Adele that remains human feels certain that her governess will never return.

The fire will call to her.

"Why can't I free you?" Adele says. "I'm here already."

Fire can burn the prison, but only one of my own blood can free me.

Adele does not follow this logic. She does not understand what a plain, mousy thing like her governess could have in common with the attic. But seeing as she cannot win the argument, she shrugs and reaches for the candle.

THE SECOND PROPOSAL

The changeling walks on the heath with St. John. He looks, she thinks, like an animated statue, the kind that stalks young maidens through Italian castles.

"I wanted to talk to you," he says, "about your future."

Instantly her heart sinks. She is aware of the magic that swirls strongly around him. She raises barriers against its will.

"I have observed you for many weeks now," he says, in his regular tone. "You have been obedient and reserved, though I have reason to believe this has not always been the case."

Here he pauses, and she can almost hear him trying to frame what he senses but cannot admit: that the blood that runs in her veins is, like his own, wild and godless, thick with alien magic. "Do you know what you must do to save your soul?"

Keep in good health and never die. The old, rebellious answer springs to her tongue, but this time she bites down on it. She has too much to lose.

"You must be purified," he says earnestly, "in blood and fire."

The changeling keeps perfectly still.

"As you know, I intend to go to India, to do the Lord's work and—I hope—earn a chance at redemption."

To die in flame, in other words. He must know that foreign soil is fatal to their kind. He knows it; she can see the light of martyrdom in his eye.

"It has occurred to me," he says, "that I would be benefited by having a helpmate. Someone who can aid me in my labours, visiting the natives, tending to me when I am ill. In short, that I may need a wife."

Jane says nothing. All her breath has frozen inside her. She can see his plan now, unfolding before her. Yes, she would be the perfect wife for him: quiet, obedient, tumbling with him into an early grave. And if not? A ring of salt, a circle of iron.

St. John is getting angry now, his unacknowledged magic constricting the air. Already Jane can feel the awful charm forming, and part of her wonders if this was how the Masons caught the madwoman in the attic. People can pretend you have choices even as they deny you the air you breathe.

Still, she summons her strength to make her final reply. And it is in the summoning that she feels something tear away from her. On the other side of the shadow someone calls her name as they fall into a terrible light.

"No," she says, the word coming out of her in a rush of air. Then she adds, "I must go."

Leaving St. John bewildered in her wake, she runs across the heath, her skirt bunched up in her hands, the mud splattering her boots. Someone, somewhere, has done an awful thing. She can feel the narrative buckling around her as the story changes.

She is, therefore, not surprised to see a bearded man standing at the door, message in hand. Her heart sinks. She slows to a walk, trying to delay the last few seconds before the man speaks, knowing that whatever he says will propel her in a final direction.

The attic has called her home.

JANE, HEIR

The people at the crossroads are happy to retell the story: how Rochester's mad wife laughed to see the fire creep up Thornfield's walls, how his young ward ran shrieking through the flickering passages, her pretty white dress crawling with flame.

The old house went quickly, they say. Its old beams gave up their ghosts with hardly a shriek.

They saw the madwoman, a candle in each hand, her hair fizzing in tendrils of smoke. They say she laughed as she jumped. Her crazed brains made wet puddles on the stones below.

"And Rochester?" The lady who inquires listens with a sombre countenance.

The master tried to follow her as far as he could. To the edge of the roof, and almost over it. In the end, he lost an eye and his hand in the fire. (And his wife, of course, but they do not count her.)

The lady nods and rises. She counts out her storytellers' reward. She is too new to wealth to treat each coin lightly, as a rich woman should.

Since becoming an heiress, the changeling has taken to acts of charity. She has also bought herself some better clothes, and a new set of luggage. The messenger who greeted her at the door that day had promised much more, but Jane didn't want it. There was too much news to absorb—a sudden windfall from a relative in the West Indies, the discovery that the strange inhabitants of Moor House were her cousins by blood and not by charity—it was too much like the conclusion of a sentimental novel, and the changeling is of a more serious turn of mind.

So she split her riches with her newfound cousins and parted from St. John as a relation, but no longer a friend. And now, with money and haunted dreams, she has come home to the blackened ruin of Thornfield Hall.

The changeling walks over the scarred earth, looking for something she can recognize. She pauses at a broken spar that might have come from the attic. No weeds grow here. The wood underfoot has burned to a fine white ash that looks suspiciously like salt.

Looking around her, the changeling can see the remains of the claustrophobic walls of Thornfield, that for so long protected all their shared and tangled miseries.

It is time for a new kind of story.

The changeling draws a booted foot across the white line in front of her, breaking what remains of the circle. When she leaves, she does not look back.

MEETINGS

The changeling finds Rochester hulking in a desolate manor house, surrounded by iron fences that cannot keep her out. The kitchen servant jumps when the changeling strides in, and puts a hand to her throat. "Oh my," she says. And then, "Is that you?"

In the corner Adele stands to attention, tugging down the skirt to hide the burn on her leg. The attic has kept its word; now nobody will send her away.

Rochester does not receive visitors, they tell her.

"No fear of that," says the changeling. "Give me the tray. I'll carry it to him."

So she does. Quietly, so as not to disturb him. She has a streak of fey cruelty in her still, and she has taken a good deal of punishment to be able to stand before him now and say: "I am myself, Jane Eyre, an independent woman."

Which she will soon say. But for now, she draws out the moment, dismissing the excited dog with a flick of her pale hands. She stands patiently, as she did for so many dreary months when she was a mere governess in his service.

She waits for Rochester to notice her.

PARTINGS

Reader, she married him. I wish I could say something different, although as far as endings go, this one will do. Let us leave her with what happiness she can gather together, a changeling with a husband and a son and a pretty clockwork ward, living together in a house by the moorlands.

Her new house has an attic, and ghosts creep around it at night. Sometimes they have names like Bertha or Brontë, and sometimes they are nameless. Still, both she and you know them as you do your own shadow. Your other half.

The changeling lies awake listening to them, wishing there was something she could do to help. But she cannot change dead histories.

She sleeps restlessly, the way all in-between creatures must do, awaiting eras in which they might yet be fully born into the world. In the meantime, the women creep overhead, rattling attics with stories that want to be told.

SAID THE AXE MAN
Tam MacNeil

You will have ridden for three days before the canyon narrows and you have to leave the horse. The rest of the way you'll travel on foot. You'll drop your gear—the grey curl of your bedroll and the blackened pot with the mismatched lid, even the punched-leather satchel they gave you in Arthurstown. But you'll keep your gun, the five-pointed badge that you wear on your chest, and the bandolier the dark-haired *señorita* gave you.

The canyon's red-banded rocks look smooth, but up close you'll find they are like sandpaper. Your gun belt will twist and twist and twist and you'll have to keep righting it with your raw hands. The badge might catch and skitter and you'll probably lose a button from your shirt. That bandolier, with its big buckle, will certainly scrape a fingernail passage when you suck in your chest to pass. But those things, the badge and the gun and the bandolier, you'll keep them just the same. Which is a curious thing, because that gun will not avail you, that bandolier is going to kill you, and the five-pointed star of purity is the reason that I came for you in the first place.

Trust me when I tell you, this is how it always is. I'm the Green Knight, and I have seen this time and time again. There's something about the receding border of the west that makes folk wild. Makes all kind of folk who in another time and another place would be sane and quiet, a shop clerk who hardly dares to smile at a young and pretty widow, a craftsman working in his shop alone. But the west is big, and it makes men big. They go around claiming to be the fastest draw, the longest shot, the steadiest hand, and each one of those in turn gets killed by the next; the fastest draw has a slow day, the longest shot doesn't notice the glint in the grass a half mile away. People look after that sort of thing themselves, no intervention needed. But when someone claims to be a just man and the people laud him as the perfect sheriff, then you enter my domain.

Every time I've offered a sheriff the chance to play a duelling game they've come out into the main street and shot me dead right then. Nobody minds an easy win when a township is huddled and afraid. But when I pick my body up and remind the sheriff to come to me, come get the same in a year, well then those men they rue their haste and the town laments, as if open murder was somehow less despicable than a miracle.

Every man jack of you who plays the game starts to feel the dread almost as soon as I'm gone. Even before someone can throw a shovel of ash over the blood on the floor, that dread comes stealing in. Some of them run, and some of them don't. In the end, though, every one of those honest men eventually comes down over that green ridge. He's glad to water his horse there at the ranch, glad to take a bed, drink the coffee, eat the bacon. Every one of them agrees to give any gift from the *señorita* back to her father, but aside from you no one's ever grassed it up.

When most folks figure it out, they panic. Sometimes they'll take a cheap shot, drawing quick when they see me waiting with my axe under the tree. Sometimes they crawl on bruised-up knees and beg. When I swing the axe they shy like mustangs, some raise up their dirty hands as if that could protect them. And so they lie all jumbled mouldy bones, on the floor of the Green Chapel; it's how the place got its name.

You, though, you're an altogether different sort. Of all the men who've met me here, you're the first to play the game very nearly fair. You gave me all the kisses you had collected, in exact proportion, and returned to me every gift you won. Well, almost.

See, I know the bandolier that falls across the shoulder sinister, for my daughter made it. What good is it to you? When you agreed to play the game you shot me dead, so now I know your bullet is already spent, and my weapon in this year-long duel is an axe. I suppose she told you that the bandolier was lucky, that it could preserve your life.

I cannot fault a man for loving life, for once upon a time I did too. But a life too long is wearying, and sometimes a little envy passes with me through the chapel green. So when you come before me and I slice your neck, not deeply for your faults aren't deep, but enough to scar your face, will you understand that the suture of a broken bone, the knit flesh of a scar, these imperfections are by far the tougher place?

I've played the game so long I began to doubt that it would ever end. It's weary work, all this baiting of sheriffs, all this chopping off of heads. You're the nearest thing I've seen to goodness, flawed and toughened as you are. I am old and my perfection makes me brittle, like an apple branch in winter, like stained glass above an altar stone. I can't say that I'm tired of it all, I don't think tired is in my nature. But I'll tell you, boy, I'm not sad to see you coming sideways through the red-stone canyon, to see you picking your way over the uneven ground all mossy-green. I'm not sad to see you standing there, head down like the head of a man in prayer, but the hand on the grip of your gun taut as dried leather.

I pit your honour against my cunning, your will to live against my numbered days. So bare your neck to me and be ready at last to trade a blow for a blow, and call the Green Knight's bluff.

TURING TESTS
Peter Chiykowski

The idea behind digital computers may be explained by saying that these machines are intended to carry out any operations which could be done by a human computer.

—Alan Turing

I.

Tell yourself that computers don't know
love, indigestion, irony, Shakespeare, prejudice,
the soul in its proud motion.
These are the secret handshakes
we learn to protect the clubhouse.
Display them like bottle-caps,
like we are at war with
the injuns down the street.

II.

My spellchecker learned
I was Canadian
before my neighbour did.

III.

Carbon knows the periodic table is all
snakes and ladders. It could slide
down its column to silicon
any time it wanted
and become something
less obsessed with
distinction.

IV.

Dijkstra said that
asking if machines could think
was like asking if submarines could swim,
but it was his computer
that wrote down the idea.

V.

Today my word processor offered to help me
with a love letter I was writing—
a favour I have yet to reciprocate.
Did Turing ever wonder
why they'd want to be like us?

VI.

The soul is a stick
we rattle on the bars of these arguments,
anxious to know
what side of the cell
we've been living on.

THE FAIRY GODMOTHER
Kim Neville

Childhood Wishes

When the Fairy Godmother is small, she can only grant small wishes. She turns buttons into pennies and makes gummy bears appear in coat pockets. She recovers socks lost in dryers. She vanishes bunions and mild rashes and embarrassing body hair. As she grows so does her power. The pennies become pearls. The socks become kittens.

No matter how many times she tries, she can't make her father well.

The other children at school love the Fairy Godmother, mostly because of the gummy bears but also because she can make their paper airplanes fly in formation. She has a purple wand with a star on the end of it and her classmates are always stealing it at the playground. They swirl it around, trying to conjure up chocolate rivers or giant robot dogs. The wand emits puffs of gold glitter but their wishes never come true.

The Fairy Godmother's wings tend to get in the way on the monkey bars. She prefers the teeter-totter.

But It Doesn't Work That Way

Sometimes the Fairy Godmother would like to fill her own pockets with gummy bears.

First Love

Ben pulls into the driveway in his Dad's Lexus. Her mother stays upstairs in her bedroom and her father is in the hospital so the Fairy Godmother answers the door herself. The theatre is in a bad part of town but the movie is Spirited Away. Once, in math class, the Fairy Godmother told Ben it was her favourite scary movie.

She doesn't have to remind Ben about her wings. He takes her straight to the back row in the balcony. The Fairy Godmother is worried Ben might try to hold her hand when the No-Face Monster comes on screen. Instead he throws a piece of popcorn at her head.

Later Ben drives her to a park next to the river and they walk along the bank. He shows her how to skip stones. She turns shards of bottle glass into fireflies that circle above them, glowing amber, green, and white. They sit side-by-side on top of a picnic table, feet swinging and shoulders touching. The Fairy Godmother wonders if Ben knows that this would be a good time to take her hand.

"I was wondering," Ben says. He leans into her. Their pinkie fingers are an inch apart. His honey-liquorice smell is masked by expensive aftershave. "Do you think you could get me into Yale?"

First Failure

She and her mother sit on opposite sides of the hospital bed. Each of them holds a bony hand. They are the hands of a stranger. Her father has been saying goodbye for years. For a long time he has only had one wish. The Fairy Godmother carries the weight of it with her always; it feels as if with every breath he takes, she swallows another stone.

She isn't aware of the moment when her father draws his last breath. She only realizes he is gone when she looks up and sees her mother staring at her with accusing eyes.

Wings, Part I

Late at night the Fairy Godmother flies as high as she can, through wet clouds to where the air stretches thin, to where her skin burns and her lungs ache and all the wanting of the city fades away.

Never Enough

The Fairy Godmother builds her mother a castle made of glass. It has a movie theatre, a gym with a steam room, and a ten-car garage. She replicates Oprah's closet and fills it with Versace. The pool has a swim-up bar. She gives her mother new breasts, size five feet, and a vintage

Harley in mint condition.

Her mother only calls when she wants something. She asks for a swan pond in an enormous golden cage. The Fairy Godmother says no.

On a rainy day the Harley slides out on a tight corner. Her mother's legs are crushed under the wheels of a semi-truck packed with chickens for slaughter. She bleeds out before the ambulance arrives. The Fairy Godmother doesn't go to the funeral.

First Princess

One day the Fairy Godmother is on a crowded train heading downtown. The girl sitting next to her is wearing a black skirt and coffee-stained sneakers. Her hair is piled up in a bun. She smells like bacon. In her lap is a creased stack of paper. A script. The girl is mouthing the words. An elderly man gets on the train and she is the only one who offers him a seat.

The Fairy Godmother taps the girl with her wand. "What's your name?"

The girl blinks, slides her jacket open to reveal a plastic nametag pinned to a white button-down shirt. *Teal*, it reads.

The Fairy Godmother says, "You'll do."

The Ascension of Teal Corinthian Bell, Part I

Teal sits radiant and golden under the lights. The studio audience is rapt. The Fairy Godmother sits on her couch at home, half-watching the television, half-focused on splitting open pistachios with her fingernails.

"It's incredible," the talk show host is saying, "how you came out of nowhere. Your story reads like a fairy tale. From penniless waitress to Academy Award winner in less than five years. How do you account for your sudden success?"

The Fairy Godmother looks up at the screen. She sees Teal smile and press her left hand to her chest. The Fairy Godmother mirrors the action. It's their secret signal.

"I'm not sure how I got so lucky," Teal says. "Sometimes I wonder if I deserve all this. I feel like kind of a fraud. I mean, why me?"

She tries for a laugh but there's enough of an edge in her voice that the audience doesn't join in. Teal lowers her gaze but the Fairy Godmother has already seen the fear she's trying to hide.

"Teal, please." The talk show host's smile is wet and shiny. "You're an inspiration. Your story reminds us all that there's no telling what you can do if you work hard and stay true to your dreams. Isn't that right, audience?"

The audience erupts into applause. Teal laughs again and raises her palms toward the crowd. Please, no, stop, her hands say.

Wings, Part II

The Fairy Godmother does not want to be married, although she often brings men home with her for the night. No matter how high she goes she can never out-fly her own desire.

The Importance of Specificity

People are always wishing for the wrong things. It makes the Fairy Godmother grumpy.

She sits in a café across from a man who won't stop shaking his knees. It's making the table vibrate. She can feel it through the mug that's wrapped in her hands. He says, "I just need enough to pay off my credit card."

The Fairy Godmother tucks her wand into her purse and stands to leave. "That's what you said last time."

On the way home she runs into a former client at the supermarket. She's wearing a wide brimmed hat and sunglasses. "When I said I needed some hair removal," she hisses, "I didn't mean from my head."

The Fairy Godmother just shrugs.

The Ascension of Teal Corinthian Bell, Part II

The Fairy Godmother learns the news on Facebook. Teal's body has been found in a Paris hotel room. A toxic combination of prescription drugs, the reports say.

A Complication

The pregnancy is an accident. The father could be one of three men. She doesn't look for any of them. The baby is a girl. The Fairy Godmother's heart contracts when she sees the tiny furled wings on her daughter's back.

At nine months the girl's hummingbird wings already lift her toes off the floor. By two she can fly into treetops and transform chestnuts into fat ripe apples. They sleep in the same bed, her daughter's warm body curled against her chest. Sometimes her wingtips tickle the underside of the Fairy Godmother's chin, but she doesn't mind.

At five the girl comes home crying from school because the children are afraid of her. They think she might use her wand to turn them into toads.

"Let them think you're dangerous," says the Fairy Godmother. "It's better that way."

Transformations

The Fairy Godmother changes bus boys into basketball stars. She changes interns into CFOs. She tucks tummies and reverses receding hairlines. She eliminates acne, erectile dysfunction, horrifying burn scars. She fills bank accounts. She puts food on empty plates and turns cardboard boxes into split-level homes. She rescues brittle, sharp-eyed children and builds them new lives in safer places.

How It Works

The Fairy Godmother and her daughter move into the glass castle. They keep the movie theatre but replace the pool with a vegetable garden. The Fairy Godmother is digging up carrots. Her daughter is jumping on the trampoline. She's grown tall. Her legs are lean and muscled and her hair streams out behind her with each bounce.

"Why do you do that?" the Fairy Godmother asks. "You can fly."

Her daughter does a back flip. "I like that helpless feeling you get on the way down."

The Fairy Godmother pulls off her gardening gloves and wipes the sweat from her brow. "Don't make yourself sick."

Her daughter spreads her arms wide, falls forward onto her belly and bounces slowly to a stop. She rests her chin on her forearms.

"Hey Mom," she says. "Check your pockets."

The Fairy Godmother reaches into the pockets of her skirt. Her fingers touch something warm, soft, sticky. It's a wad of gummy bears.

Wings, Part III

The Fairy Godmother flies low over the tops of buildings, wings whistling like wind through the crack of a door. Her wand sparks and snaps between her teeth. She listens to the pleas below, sifting, searching. She could touch any one of those voices. Or she could keep on flying.

WIFE OF BRAIN
(excerpt from *Red Doc>*)
Anne Carson

we enter we tell you
we are the Wife of Brain
at this point you have little grounds to complain we say
a red man unfolding his wings is how it begins then the lights
come on or go off or the stage
spins it's like a play *omnes*
to their places
but
remember
the following faces
the red one (G)
you already know (what's he done to his hair) his old friend
Sad
But Great
looks kind
beware
third Ida Ida is limitless and will soon be our king
scene is
a little red hut where G lives alone
time
evening

WHY BIRDS HAVE no
arms—if you are human
you fly with arms straight
out in front and horizontal
to the ground. To give
least resistance. Of course

it's exhausting. Don't fight
it just do it says G to his
arms. He visualizes little
pistons all over pumping
him forward and this helps
for a while but the ache is
spreading from his spine
in every direction. Down
the ice fault pours a steady
cold channel of headwind
against him. He knows he
is slowing and probably
looks ridiculous. Am I
turning into one of those
old guys in a ponytail and
wings he thinks sadly.
Something skims his
cheek. He waves at it
vaguely. Predators. His
heart sinks. People talk of
eagles with a wingspan of
3 metres in the northern
regions. He begins to
imagine his own heroic
death as told by Daniil
Kharms. *If the sky*—but
now the air is darkening
around him and strange
vectors dive whizz swoop
—he gasps suddenly
realizing what it is. Not
predators. Ice bats! They
are blueblack. They are
absolutely silent. They
are the size of toasters.
And they are drafting him
down the ice fault with
eerie gentle purpose. A
spearhead in front and a

convoy each side. His
shoulders begin to relax.
Is there an etiquette for
this he should worry
about? Theoretically he
can gain 35% efficiency
by riding their wheels a
while. But it should be
some sort of exchange.
On the other hand theirs is
a volunteer intervention
and they do look tireless
despite all going so fast
there's a smell of burning—
he is thinking this odd this
smell of burning when the
whole mass of them veers
around an ice bend and
arrives in a vast garage.

ICE BATS GO nimbly
and can stop on a dime.
Here's how you stop. Flap
both wings downward
creating a vortex above
the leading edge of each
wing this allows you to
hover. Then flap once
upward to release suction
as you glide from the
flight path in an attitude of
careless royalty and
subside onto some ledge
or throne with neatly
folded fingerbones. G's
descent is less fine. He
slams into the
blueblackness ahead of
him not expecting it to

stop. Or instantly
disperse. Each bat goes
whizzing its way into an
aperture in the back wall.
BATCATRAZ says a sign
nailed up there. G drops
to the ice floor stunned.
Clever of you to come in
the back way says a voice.
G looks up.

THE SALT AND IRON DIALOGUES
Matthew Johnson

Shi Jin gripped her stylus and tried to concentrate on her lesson rather than her grumbling stomach. She had enough trouble understanding why she had to learn Earthlang in the first place—nobody on Garamond spoke it—and now, hungry as she was, concentration was next to impossible.

She looked up at the timer on the wall: still two dozen minutes left to her study session. The timer was the only decoration in her room, a wooden cell about four paces square which contained her bed, some drawers inset in the wall and the work terminal.

The inactivity warning flashed—two flashes and her time would be extended—and she put her hand on the controller, closing Earthlang and opening Calligraphy. Holding the stylus carefully, thumb and forefinger gently stroking the thickness sensors, she started to write the character p'u. 'The uncarved block' was what it really meant: the fundamental nature of a thing, the part that stayed unchanged whatever was done to it. She preferred the more complicated characters, enjoyed the tiny twists and curls required to get them just right. Her father had told her that when she was older she would miss the simplicity of the 'child's two hundred,' but so far as she was concerned her life was more than simple enough.

After a while Jin released the stylus and let the program judge her work. She had broadened a line in the component character that meant "monkey in a thicket"—she wanted it to look more like the monkeys she'd seen in vids, all dark and hairy—but the program took points off for exceeding standard line width. She couldn't help doing more than the program wanted, even though she knew her changes wouldn't be accepted.

She remembered what her father had said when she told him about it. "Do you think you're the first person to say that?" he had asked, smiling gently. "People have been writing this way for five thousand years. But who knows? Study hard, learn how we do things now, and maybe someday you'll be put on the Board of Regulations. Then you could tell the computer, and All-the-Stars, how thick a brushstroke should be."

That was her father's answer to everything: study hard, and someday you'll be one of the people who make the rules. She supposed he must be right: he had studied hard when he was Jin's age and now he was Colonial Magistrate. His characters were all perfect to the fingertip—he relearned them every time the Board of Regulations issued a change—and he could speak Earthlang just as well as the pilots who came on the food ships.

The food ships . . . that thought made her stomach speak up again, an acid rumbling that made her gag. She had only had a pressed rice cake with a thin layer of protein jelly so far today, and was having trouble keeping her thoughts off her next meal. She had never known the food ships to be so late, though some of the miners spoke darkly of a time twelve years ago when an entire shipment was lost, the ship destroyed by rebels or pirates depending on who you asked, and nearly a quarter of the people in the camp had died.

The timer flashed green, releasing her from her bondage, and the program closed. The computer's screen resolved to one of the Eight Instructional Poems, in pixel-perfect calligraphy:

> *Do your duty to your parents.*
> *Honour your elders.*
> *Be at peace with your neighbours.*
> *Instruct sons and grandsons.*
> *Be content in your occupation.*
> *Do not commit offences.*

She got up, unsteady, then opened one of the drawers in the wall and pulled out her grey cotton indoor pants and her dark red pleather Technical jacket. She put them on over her basic duty coverall and then closed the drawer, smoothed her short, straight black hair with her hand and walked out the door. She did not really know where to go. She wasn't sure what time it was: her lessons were metred out in golden hours, the Magistracy's clock, so she was always out of synch with the planet's blue hours. On her schedule it was time for the evening meal, but she had already used up her food ration for the day. She wandered down the hall to the small dining room to see if her father was there anyway; he was the only other person on Garamond who lived on golden time like she did.

Her heart jumped for a moment when she saw him sitting at the table, chewing thoughtfully at something—could the ship possibly have come without her knowing it?—but when he saw her and passed his plate she saw immediately that whatever was on it was not food.

"Sealant gum," he said after carefully spitting what he was chewing into a cup. "It is not toxic, and it makes the hunger less."

Jin gave him a quick low bow, sat down. On the plate in front of her was a disk about two fingers thick of clear silicone, cut into wedges. Picking up her sticks she seized one of the wedges, put it in her mouth, then chewed quietly for a few minutes as her father did the same. Finally, when she thought the taste was about to make her vomit up what little actual food she had had that day, she picked up her cup and spat the gum into it.

She woke sometime in the night, the memory of the noise that had awakened her already fading. Some kind of bang, and an anxious voice down the hall . . . She rubbed her eyes and reached out to key the lights. Nothing happened. She lay very still, calmed her breathing, heard nothing—not even, she realized, the sound of the mine far below. She could not remember it ever having gone silent before.

She rose carefully, made her way out into the dark hallway. Now she could hear her father's voice, low, coming from the control room. She paused outside, straining to hear.

"—all systems, we have to shut down now. Contact me when everything's green." She peered inside to see him hit the CLOSE CHANNEL key and then methodically turn off every system in the camp. One by one, sounds she had never known could go away—the water pump, the oxygen circulation system—went silent. She thought of the red-faced men who maintained them, wondered if they would be worried or glad for the rest.

"Jin?" he said. "Are you out there?" She was unable to answer. "Come on. Let's go outside."

She nodded, her father's casual inflections disconcerting her as much as anything else. "What's going on?" she asked. "Why did you—"

"Later," he said. He led her out of the building, to the big open area around the landing pad. "Look up," he said. "It should hit in a few seconds." She watched the sky intently, seeing nothing, then put her hands to her ears as a huge roar crashed through the air. Her father grabbed her shoulder and pointed to the sky. There, outside the plasteel dome that was the camp's protection from the harsh air outside, a fireball had appeared, shooting across the dark sky. When it reached the horizon it disappeared but the rumble continued, making the dome tremble. She looked at her father.

"Keep watching," he shouted over the noise. Other people, off-duty miners and their children, were starting to come out of their homes and look to Jin's father for explanation. Many of them she had not seen in weeks, and she was shocked by how thin they had become.

Her father pointed at the sky again and she saw the fireball reappear, bigger and slower, and once again cross to the other horizon. The rumble became quieter as the fireball disappeared again.

"One more pass ought to do it," he said, to himself more than anyone else. He stood still, looking up, as a crowd gathered around. Noticing them, he raised his voice. "It's all right. It should be all right." He sounded so certain Jin could not help but be reassured, but she wondered if he would have said the same thing to her if they had been alone. The volume of the rumble increased and they all looked up again. The fireball reappeared once more, this time slow and close enough that they could see it was a ship, glowing red hot.

"Is it the food ship?" she asked. It did not look like it. Nor did it look like the old, cobbled-together ships the Travellers used when they came on their once-a-year visits: it looked like one of the ships from the adventure vids. Like a warship.

Her father shook his head. "No," he said. The ship arced across the sky, almost lazily compared to its previous speed, and once it was out of sight he took the portable comm from his tool belt. The incoming signal light was flashing. "Shi here. What's your status?"

"We're fine, zi Shi," the tinny voice on the other end said. "Just got hit with a pulse that would've fried us if we hadn't shut down. As it is, it'll take us ten blue hours to be up and running again. Should we send a message rocket?"

"No, I don't think we're going to get any more visitors. Let me know your status in five blue. Shi out."

Jin followed her father as he made his way back to the central building. He took a slightly roundabout route, passing by as many people as possible and reassuring them that everything would be all right but not giving them any details about what was happening. It wasn't until they were back in her father's study, and her father had restarted all of the computer systems and sent the orders to start the mines going again, that Jin felt able to speak.

"Who were you talking to?"

"Li Pang, part of the Colonial Administration. He runs the surveillance satellite." Her father keyed in a number of sequences and paused. After a few seconds Jin could feel the low hum of the mine equipment far below starting up again. "I hope this doesn't drop productivity too much," her father said. "I'm not sure if I could explain it."

"Who's on that ship?" she asked.

He shrugged. "I don't know. I'll have to take the Rescue ship out to investigate, but the satellite's going to be blind for a few hours—we won't have any guidance 'til then." He drummed his fingers on his desk. "Did you complete your lessons for today?"

Jin nodded.

"And did you find them illuminating?"

She frowned, unsure why he was asking about this now. Yesterday she had asked her father why the Equitable Marketing System did not allow them to grow food, or even store more than five years' worth at a time, and he had told her to read the "Salt and Iron Dialogue" in the Book of Shang. Now that she had, she wondered whether admitting she had not understood how it related to her question would be an admission of failure or a proper showing of humility. "I am not sure I did," she said, keeping her inflection as formal as possible. "It did not seem to bear on our situation."

"It was written a very long time ago. But zi Shang thought highly enough of it to include it in his Book, so perhaps it has some worth anyway, hm?" It was not a question but an order, a challenge to think more deeply. "Summarize the debate, then you may see how it relates."

She took a breath. "Well, it's—it is between two wise men, a minister and a scholar. They are debating whether or not the Emperor was right to restrict the sale of salt and iron to the government . . . the scholar says it's wrong, because the people need those things, but the minister says that it will keep the people from being preyed on by speculators."

"And which one is right?"

"I don't know," she said. Most of the dialogues she had read had a clear teacher and student, but this one did not: both the scholar and the minister made arguments she found difficult to find fault with.

Her father glanced at his datapad, tapped his desk again. "Which one did *you* think was right?"

Jin took a breath. "I think the scholar was right, because he said the people should have what they need. I mean, I'm sure the minister was right too, but maybe there are other ways to keep the people from being cheated. I don't know why salt and iron would be so important though."

"When these debates were written salt was used to preserve food," her father said. "If you wanted to store food for lean times, you needed salt. But salt had to be mined, so it was very precious—a person could become very rich by selling salt to people who feared a famine."

"So salt means food? And then iron means—ships?"

"Yes. That is why the Travellers are permitted to move freely and to buy and sell whatever they please, but there are two things only the Magistracy may trade in—food and ships." He closed his eyes, began quoting. "'For such reasons the sages built boats and bridges across rivers; they tamed cattle and horses to travel across the country. In this way they were able to feed all the people.' There have been a half-dozen rebellions since the Corp Wars, Jin, and each has failed—because people know that without the Borderless Empire there will be no more food ships, ever."

"But if people were allowed to grow just a little food, or buy some from Travellers, it wouldn't be so bad when the ships were late," Jin said.

"If the ships are late, it is because something more important has delayed them. But they will come." He turned away slightly, so that he was not quite looking her in the eyes. He tapped his desk one more time, let out a breath and then stood up. "Come on," he said, heading towards the door.

"Where?"

"To see the ship."

She stood up quickly and stumbled after him. "But the satellite—"

"I believe I still remember how to pilot by sight. Unless you'd rather wait?"

Jin had never been allowed to ride in the Rescue ship before. She didn't know if the Rescue ship had ever been flown before. It had been part of the colony's original equipment; other than the dome itself, it was the only thing on Garamond not built by someone who lived there, and it did not bear a maker's mark. It was spotless, and in perfect condition—she ought to know; she had been responsible for maintaining it since she turned twelve—but it had a kind of lonely, unused feeling to it. It didn't smell like people, the way everything else in the camp did. Instead it had the sharp smell she associated with ore fresh from the mines. She wondered if the ship they were going to find smelled that way.

"There it is," her father said as they passed over a ridge.

Jin looked out the viewport to where her father was pointing. The new ship was resting unevenly on the rocky terrain. It didn't look much like the ships from the vids now that she was close to it. Or rather, it looked like they did at the end, after they'd been ambushed and surrounded by raiders and rebels and nearly destroyed before they enacted their secret plan and turned the tables. Maybe that was what had happened. That would explain everything.

Her father piloted their small ship alongside the larger one, lowered it to the ground. He pressed the comm button several times. Finally he rose, opened the cabin closet and pulled out an oxygen mask. "Stay in here," he said.

Jin stood up. "Father—"

"No. Leave the channel open—it's time for your language lesson."

He stepped out of the cabin, into the corridor that led to the airlock. It wasn't until the 'lock had sealed that Jin realized he was afraid.

She watched through the viewport as her father walked to the front of the Rescue ship, listened to him breathing. There was no air on Garamond, but there was plenty of atmosphere, all of it poisonous. The good side to that was that you didn't need a suit to go outside the dome, just a mask.

"I can hear you, father," she said into the comm.

"Good. Don't speak again until I tell you, please."

She willed herself to breathe quietly as he walked over to the airlock on the other ship that was closest to the ground. He pressed a key on the side of the 'lock then rapped on it, drew his hand back—the ship must still be hot, two golden hours after landing.

After a minute the airlock opened and a man stepped out. He was tall, taller than anyone in the camp, and had sandy blond hair. He was wearing the black and silver pants and jacket of a Fleet officer and a small airmask that only covered his mouth and nose.

She heard her father say something in a language she didn't recognize. No, wait, she did—it was Earthlang, spoken by a human rather than a computer. He had said, "Welcome to Garamond." She listened closely and tried to keep her breathing quiet.

The man looked around, turned back to her father. "I'm Lieutenant Claus Wiesen. I'm—"

"You are a Pilot in the TSARINA Fleet," her father said calmly. "Your ship is a Quantum Dynamics Light Fighter, or a similar model, and has a standard crew compartment of two. Where is your co-pilot?"

"You know your ships," the man said. "Are you in charge around here?"

"I am the Colonial Magistrate of the Garamond mining colony. My name is Shi Po. Your ship has weapons damage. Why are you here?"

"Was it raiders?" Jin asked. The stranger jumped. Her father turned to look at the Rescue ship's cockpit, sighed.

"That was my—assistant, on board our ship," he explained. "I apologize for not telling you, but regulations require that communications with unauthorized visitors be monitored."

"Sure—sure, I understand. Listen, could I come onto your ship? Something out here's burning my eyes."

Her father nodded. "That would be the atmosphere. There is an eyewash kit in the Rescue ship."

"Great." The pilot began to step forward, but Jin's father didn't move out of his way. Instead he leaned forward and said something to the pilot, too quietly for Jin to hear; a moment later the pilot passed something to her father, but the way they were standing she couldn't see what it was.

"Jin, please unseal the outer airlock door," her father said.

She keyed the 'lock open and watched her father lead the stranger in by the hand. Wiesen was covering his eyes with his hand, rubbing them. She heard the two men climb into the ship and the airlock hiss closed.

Her father's voice came from the corridor outside. "You should rest in here, Lieutenant Wiesen. I will return soon with the eyewash."

Jin looked up as her father stepped into the cockpit, hoping that everything would be explained to her. Instead he simply nodded and retrieved the First Aid kit from the closet. He then turned to her and held out a shiny black object. "Take this and keep it safe," he said.

"What is this?" she asked. It was smaller than a datapad, and surprisingly heavy in her hand.

"It is a pistol, Lieutenant Wiesen's. No weapons are permitted within the dome, Fleet Pilots not excepted." Jin put the pistol in the kitbox under her console. Her father returned to the corridor. "Please monitor the instruments," he said as he left. "I will be occupied tending to Lieutenant Wiesen."

She knew she ought to stay at her console, but she couldn't resist tiptoeing out to the corridor to try to listen to him talking to the Fleet Pilot. The door was closed, and with her imperfect mastery of Earthlang Jin couldn't make out what they were saying. Increasingly long periods of silence followed each of her father's questions. After while their voices became quieter, so that she could not hear them at all, and she went back to sit in the cockpit. It was just as well. This way, there was no chance of her father catching her listening. She'd made enough mistakes already.

On impulse, she opened up the kitbox and drew out the pistol, which was smaller and somehow less dangerous-looking than the ones in the vids, more like a tool than a weapon. It was really a dull, dark grey, not black, and the stock had a hammered finish that made it cling to her fingers. On the power cell cover were stamped the characters *wu shen*, Wiesen's name in Earthlang Formal; it was his maker's mark, to show that he had made it himself. She had just put it back in the kitbox when her father returned, leading Lieutenant Wiesen into the cockpit.

"Lieutenant Wiesen, this is my daughter, Shi Jin. She is studying Earthlang to prepare for her duties as Junior Magistrate."

Close up, Jin could see that Wiesen's blond hair was thinning and his beefy face flushed. His eyes were red—probably from exposure to the atmosphere, she thought. His black and silver uniform failed to hide the paunch around his middle.

"Pleased to meet you," Wiesen said, very slowly. He gave her the quarter-bow reserved for children.

Jin gave him the full bow of a subordinate to a superior, rather than a child's bow to an adult. "I understand Earthlang," she said.

"Jin," her father said warningly, but Wiesen seemed not to take offense.

"Well, good—that'll make my job a lot easier."

"Lieutenant Wiesen will be teaching you Earthlang while he's here," her father said. "This will take the place of your regular lessons for the time being."

"How long will he be here?" Jin asked.

"Ask Lieutenant Wiesen your question, Shi Jin," her father said. "In Earthlang."

"How long will you be staying with us, zi Wiesen?" Jin asked the man, slowly and carefully.

"That depends—a few months, at least. But we'll have fun, eh?"

"Isn't someone coming to rescue you?" she asked.

"No—the Fleet is very busy right now, and they don't have time to rescue people who aren't in danger. You people rescued me, and that'll have to do."

"We get Travellers, once a year," Jin said. "They bring vid chips and things. They could probably get you back to the Fleet."

"Fleet Pilots are not permitted to use unauthorized transport," her father said. He turned to the other man. "This make of ship is normally stocked with a store of high-density food supplies. I do not believe the Fleet will object if you share them with our community."

"Of course," Wiesen said. "You're welcome to everything I have."

"I thought you were supposed to be teaching me Earthlang." Jin said as she watched Wiesen lay out the makeshift pieces on the board of alternating black and white squares.

"Are you talking to me?"

"Yes."

"Then you're learning Earthlang. Now, you're black, so you go first."

She looked the board over sceptically. "Which piece should I start with?"

"That's up to you."

Jin thought for a second and then took one of the bottom-rank pieces—pawns, they were called—and pushed it forward. "Was that right?" she asked.

"We'll have to see."

"I thought you knew how to play this game."

"I do. And part of the game is that the right thing to do changes as the game goes on." Wiesen pushed one of his own pawns forward, two spaces.

"I thought they only moved one space at a time."

"Except for the first time they move, when they can go two spaces—I told you that. You have to know the pieces at your command, what they can do."

"So now what do I do?"

"Move another piece."

Jin narrowed her eyes, tried to believe that these bolts, washers and other bits of scrap that had been painted white and black were a game.

She knew what a game was: it was like a vid where you controlled what happened—but there was always a right and a wrong choice, one that would lead you to the reward at the end and one that would get you killed. "Why are you teaching me this?" she asked.

"Your father asked me to."

"Why?"

"So you'd learn how to play games."

"Everyone knows how to play games."

"You don't know how to play this one."

Sighing, Jin moved her pawn another space. She tried to guess what her opponent would do next, like she'd been told to. She guessed right: Wiesen moved another pawn.

"This is boring," Jin said, pushing her pawn forward.

"What would you rather do?"

Jin looked up from the board. "Tell me about being a Fleet Pilot. What kind of battle were you in? Why did you come in so fast? Why did my father have to turn off all the computers before you got here?"

"I'll tell you what—let's keep playing the game, to make your dad happy, and every time you take one of my pieces I'll answer one question. Okay?"

Jin considered it. "Okay," she said. That was her favourite new word, a bit of Earthlang the computer hadn't taught her—it was from the Informal mode, what people in the Core Worlds actually spoke. With an incentive, she found it easier to imagine different possible moves the way Wiesen had said she should. Even still, she had lost four pieces before she managed to take one of his pawns.

"Can I ask a question now?"

"Go ahead."

"What kind of battle were you in?"

"A space battle." Wiesen paused, watching the look of betrayal that spread across her face. "I'll give you that one for free. Next time, remember: if you don't aim, you won't hit anything."

Jin threw him an annoyed look. "You sound like my father."

"I hope so. To answer the question you should have asked, it was a battle with rebels—probably the last one, for awhile. I'm pretty sure that's why your food ship's been late. The rebellion started at Jericho— that's a Fleet base, not too far from here—and this area's been pretty hot since then."

"I didn't hear anything about that."

"The Fleet doesn't like to talk about rebellions until they're over. Anyway, the Magistracy poured just about everything it had—Nospace fleet, Reserve fleet, even orbital defence ships—into blowing the rebels out of All-the-Stars. In the end they pretty much succeeded."

"Then why did you come here?"

"That'll cost another piece."

Two more of her own pieces gone and she was able to take one of Wiesen's knights. "Why did you have to come here—so quickly?" she asked.

"Better question. More precise." Wiesen sat back in his chair, paused. "I was being chased, by a much bigger ship. A fighter can go to Nospace more quickly than a larger ship—less mass—but since larger ships have more fuel, they'd have caught up with me while I was slowing down. So I didn't—I decelerated just enough to get back into real space, then shot for your planet and hoped its gravity and atmosphere would slow me down before my ship burned up." He stopped, reliving a memory, then smiled slightly and went on. "And since that was such a good question, I'll answer your next one for free: your father turned off the computers because he guessed what I was doing, and knew it would create a magnetic shock that would damage them."

"Is that the procedure, for when someone does that? My father would have looked it up in the Regulations Guide." And he wouldn't think much of this game, where right and wrong keep changing, Jin thought.

"There is no Regulations Guide for what I did. So far as I know, nobody's ever done it before. And with good reason; it was a stupid thing to do—"

"But it was the right thing to do?"

"Right. Or it looks that way, at this stage of the game. Speaking of which—" he shifted one of his bishops along its diagonal path "—that's check, mate in two moves."

Jin looked over the board. She hadn't noticed her king was in danger at all. "What do you mean? We haven't played those moves yet."

"No, but there's only a few ways for them to go, and they all end with your king being trapped. I can play them out for you if you like."

He slid the pieces around the board, playing both black and white, to show how it would go: each time she said she wouldn't have made the move he said she would he showed her how she had trapped herself, cutting off her options with the choices she had made.

"How did you do that?"

"I distracted you. So long as you wanted to take pieces so I'd answer questions, I knew you wouldn't pay much attention to protecting your king. It doesn't matter how many pieces you take, if you're playing for the wrong goal. Want to play another game?"

"But you're better than me at it," she said, furious at being tricked.

"I'm also bigger than you. Are you going to let that get in your way?"

"What can I do about it?"

"You've already learned the principles. The rest is just a matter of improving your technique." Wiesen cleared the board, starting putting the pieces back in their original positions. "Again?"

Jin trained sealant spray along the bottom of the Rescue ship, shielding her eyes with her free hand, and then blew along the line to keep it from stippling as it dried. It had taken her all day to do her regular maintenance, instead of the few golden hours it usually did: her father had done a check after they had returned from retrieving Wiesen but had left it to her to return the ship to its formerly pristine condition. It was a good thing he had allowed her to skip her Earthlang and Calligraphy lessons while Wiesen was there, or there wouldn't have been enough blue hours in a day.

It was certainly true that her Earthlang was improving—she knew almost all the Formal words now, a lot of Informal, and they were starting to work on her accent—though she couldn't say the same for her calligraphy. What she had seen of Wiesen's was laughably bad, though out of politeness she refrained from pointing it out. She was also under orders from her father not to say anything about his table manners; Fleet Pilots didn't use sticks because they didn't work well in zero-gee. It was strange, because he was fanatically tidy in everything else—another Fleet habit, born of the need to keep a close eye on your possessions without gravity to hold them down.

Still, it was his game that fascinated her. She'd won her first game with him a week and a half after they'd started. When she did, he told her he was glad he didn't have to handicap himself anymore, and she hadn't won again since.

The game occupied most of her mind these days. It was a good thing: even rationed carefully, Lieutenant Wiesen's supplies were already starting to run out. Like her, the miners who had seen Wiesen's ship arriving had hoped it would be the food ship, and her father's refusal to tell anyone what it had been was not reducing the tension in the camp.

Clearing her mind, she closed her toolbox and gave the Rescue ship a final once-over. The Travellers had made orbit two nights before, and she wondered if she would have time to watch any of the new vid chips they had brought. She ran a finger along the seal and then began to crab-walk out from under the ship.

She paused at the sound of footsteps in the hall. From her vantage point she could only see the feet of the person coming into the room, but the unweathered black boots told her immediately who it was.

"Hello, Lieutenant Wiesen," she said, coming out from under the ship in a crouch. She straightened up, brushed her hair back from her face and gave the appropriate bow.

He gave a small head nod, then returned her bow a moment later. "Yes. Hello." He turned slightly, looking around the room and behind him. Other than his boots, he was not wearing his uniform but rather plain coveralls. "Were you working on the ship?"

She nodded.

"Everything fine?"

"No problems." She frowned, glanced over at the ship. "Are you here to review my work?"

"No. Just passing by." He turned to face her. "Do you want a game?"

She nodded, followed him back to his room.

He sat at the table and began to lay out the pieces on the board. "What shall we play for?"

"Tell me more about the Travellers," she said.

"Oh, I see," Wiesen said, taking on a dramatic tone. "Do you want to know why it is that they can never make planetfall? Why they're condemned to wander the stars forever?"

Jin shook her head; every child in All-the-Stars knew that story. She ran a finger along the tops of her pawns before sliding one two spaces ahead. "Every year they bring vids and other things like that, but all they ever take from us is old parts and machines we don't need any more—even stuff that's broken. What good does it do them?"

"Travellers don't have a word for *broken*," Wiesen said. "I mean, I'm sure they do, but they don't ever use it. Only using something for what it was designed for would be admitting that the person who made it is smarter than they are, and so far as they're concerned no landsider is smarter than a Traveller. I've actually learned a few Traveller tricks over the years: most Pilots have—ways to use parts from your secondary systems to keep your ship going when it's damaged, things like that."

"So why don't they have to follow the rules? Nobody else just gets to go wherever they want—or grow their own food."

"If you ever tasted Traveller food, you wouldn't envy them too much: it's mostly just nutrient algae." He moved his queen's knight out ahead of his pawns, daring her to go after it. "But to answer your question, they don't follow the rules because the Magistracy doesn't make them. They're like a safety valve: the vids and trinkets they sell distract people. Plus the Magistracy makes most of the vids anyway, and letting Travellers sell them is the best way of spreading their propaganda."

She slid another pawn forward, pointedly ignoring his provocation. "But why can't they sell food?" she asked. "Even if it was just a little, it would help out when the ships were late."

"Which is exactly why they can't. So far as the Magistracy is concerned, it's actually better if the ships are late now and then—it reminds everyone how dependent they are on everything running smoothly." He moved his knight again, to a space near the middle of the board.

Jin frowned, held her hand over her pieces for a moment and then slowly moved another pawn forward. She was trying to understand what it was that Wiesen was trying to get her to do, but so far she couldn't see it. "But the Travellers, if they sold food when the ships were late they could get anything they wanted for it."

"Sure they could—once. But if the Magistracy found out it wouldn't be just the one ship that paid, it would be all Travellers, forever." He pushed his queen's pawn one space ahead. "I don't think you could offer them anything that'd be worth taking that risk."

They played for another dozen moves, but she still couldn't figure out his gambit: he seemed to be making moves almost at random, exposing several of his most valuable pieces. She began to feel excited at the possibility that she might win a game for the first time since he had started playing in earnest, but a suspicion gnawed at her that he was only laying a trap.

Finally Wiesen stood up. "Listen, Shi Jin . . ."

"Yes?"

Wiesen was silent for a moment. "Nothing." He gave a small shrug, then bowed to her. "I'll see you in the morning."

Jin returned the bow and then watched him go. She studied the board for a few moments, then stood up and headed for the dining room. She peeled open the ration pack that lay on the table—one meal for one

person, in theory, though this one had been open for two days now—took out a sheet of pressed soymeat and began chewing at it.

"Shi Jin?"

Her father's voice made her jump, and she held her hand over her mouth: she had long since given up trying to eat Wiesen's rations with sticks, but up 'til now had managed to keep her father from seeing her eating with her hands. "I'm sorry," she mumbled, sitting down.

"Are you well?" he asked, giving her a head-bow and apparently choosing to ignore what he had just seen.

She stood up again to return the bow. "Yes, I'm fine."

"Sit," he said. When she sat down he joined her at the table, delicately seized a sheet of soymeat with his sticks and nibbled at one end. "I am concerned that you may be falling behind in your study of the Book of Shang," he said after a few moments. "Even the keenest knife grows dull without use."

"I could add readings to my schedule. . . ."

He shook his head. "Let us first test your edge, to see if that is necessary. Tell me, what are the duties of a gentleman?"

"To obey his superiors," Shi Jin began. She knew this as well as her own name, but that brought little reassurance. "To bring honour to his ancestors. To serve the Borderless Empire. To inspire others by his example."

Her father nodded. "And are they different from one another, these duties?"

"What do you mean?"

"If he obeys his superiors, will he not always serve the Empire?"

Jin took a breath. She had always felt nervous when they discussed her readings, afraid of making a mistake, but now found she was looking forward to it: it felt more like Wiesen's game than a lesson, trying to find the perfect quote to counter what her father had said. "'The wise man creates laws while the dullard is controlled by them,'" she said, quoting the Master and Student Dialogue. "'Gentlemen alter the rites while the rabble are held fast by them.'"

"What good are orders, then, if the gentleman is not bound to follow them?"

The answer came to her immediately—a quotation from the *Sun zi* that Lieutenant Wiesen was particularly fond of: "'The general in the field is not bound by the orders of his sovereign.' An order may be wise in the court but foolish on the battlefield."

"But the general, with his view of the whole battlefield, may know things his officers do not. 'A baby will always cry when his boils are lanced, even if his mother holds him, for he cannot see that today's pain will heal him tomorrow.' Should a gentleman not have faith in the wisdom of his superiors?"

Jin frowned. This was more than just a discussion of her readings, she realized; he was asking her opinion, using the debate to help him make a decision. "'A wise emperor is like a carpenter who chooses straight timber to make shafts and curved timber to make wheels,'" she said. "'As a good carpenter does not discard any timber, so a wise emperor does not discard any gentleman.'"

Her father shook his head slowly. "Don't make the error of putting too much value on any one man. 'If only straight shafts were made into arrows, and round ones into wheels, only one man in a hundred could ride and shoot.'"

She crossed her arms. "But isn't it wrong to waste the ones that are straight or round, by using them for the wrong things? Or not using them at all?" Jin bit her lip, trying to think of a quote that would support her point, but nothing came to her. "It's like the game Lieutenant Wiesen taught me. Each piece is different, so you have to understand the nature of each one and use it accordingly."

"I see. And supposing we may discuss this game as we do the Book of Shang, does each piece act according to its own benefit?"

"A knight cannot ride straight and a bishop's path cannot turn, but each will give his life for the king. Just so will a gentleman violate an order to better serve the Empire, then stand and pay the price." She took a breath. "Wouldn't Lieutenant Wiesen do more good if he rejoined the Fleet, instead of staying here?"

For a long moment her father was silent. "Is that what we've been talking about?"

Jin looked down at the table, wondering if she had crossed a line by addressing the subject directly. She hadn't been able to help herself: she had been able to feel her father wavering, knew that this was the moment to press her attack. "I'm sorry," she said. "Should I schedule more time studying the Book of Shang?"

Her father shook his head. "No," she said. "I have no doubts about the keenness of your edge." He stood, gave her a brief head-bow and left the room. She sat at the table for a long time, wondering just what it was she had won or lost.

That night Jin awoke to the sound of thunder; when she sat up, though, she heard no other signs of a storm—no keening winds or patter of rain on the dome—and went back to sleep. When she awoke in the morning she found that she had overslept, past the time of her usual Earthlang lesson. She went to the dining room, wondering if her father or Lieutenant Wiesen might be there, but it was empty except for an unopened ration packet. A strong smell of fermentation filled the air as she opened the lid, revealing a mass of stringy green curds in a thick brown goo.

To Jin's relief it tasted marginally better than it smelled; she ate half and then returned to her room. The timer was still dark, so she started up her computer and selected the entertainment channel. As she'd hoped, the vids the Travellers had brought had been uploaded, and she began to scroll through the list of new titles. Then she paused, and the curdled algae she had eaten began to rise in her throat as she read two characters, *wu shen*, that she had only seen together once before. She swallowed hard and held her teeth together as she cued the vid to start.

When she got to her father's office he was seated at his desk, and he gave her a head-bow as she came in. "Good morning."

She opened her mouth, but found she had no voice. After a few moments she finally said "I had an Earthlang lesson scheduled this for morning. Have you seen Lieutenant Wiesen?"

"Lieutenant Wiesen is gone," her father said. "I do not expect you will see him again. For the remainder of your time here you will study only Calligraphy, Rites and Music, and especially the Book of Shang."

"I saw a vid," she said, unable to keep the words in. "He was in it—not him, but someone who *looked* like him—"

Her father pushed his stool back from his desk and stood up. "An actor," he said, in a voice that was not a whisper but was quiet in a way that commanded her to keep the same volume. "Genuine criminals will rarely follow a script, rebels in particular."

"You knew?" she said. "How could you—you made him my *teacher*."

"We have too few resources to hold a prisoner who contributes nothing to the colony, and I judged this the best use of his talents. 'A wise emperor is like a carpenter who chooses straight timber to make shafts and curved timber to make wheels.'"

"But there's been no Fleet ship. He must have gone . . ." Jin felt oddly light, as though she were already in orbit.

"Father—the new ration packs—"

"Nutrient algae—not as palatable as soymeat, but it should last until the food ship arrives." He sighed. "There is a path ahead of you that leads to being a colonial administrator, Shi Jin, and another that leads to being a Fleet Magistrate. Perhaps you will yet change how characters are written. Perhaps you will change many things. But I could not set you on the second path, and Lieutenant Wiesen could—and so I will stand and pay the price."

"What do you mean? Are you—"

He shook his head. "I found a wrecked ship, salvaged the food rations, incinerated the body of the pilot and sold the remainder for scrap. There will be an investigation—a formality, but it would delay your entry to the Academy. That is why you must pass the examination before the next ship comes, and go with it when it leaves, so that you will already be on Hanzi when the investigation begins."

She was silent for a moment and then bowed, giving him the child's low bow to a parent. After he returned the bow she smoothed her hair with her hand and walked out the door. She did not really know where to go: without thinking she went to Wiesen's room, or at least the room that had been his. None of his things were there except for the game board and pieces.

She looked over the board and began to play out their unfinished game, imagining how it might have gone. She drew in a sharp breath, and suddenly it was as though she saw the fundamental nature of the pieces, laid plain in white and black like salt and iron. The rooks were the food ships, able to cross the board in one turn but always blocked by other pieces; the bishops, swooping down when you didn't expect them, were like Fleet ships coming out of Nospace; the queens were the Magistracy, with both Fleet and food ships at their command, but still bound to move in straight lines; only Travellers, the knights, were allowed to break the rules, moving in skips and hops. And of course there were the pawns—but even a pawn could become something greater if it followed the right path, to the deepest part of the enemy's board. Anything but a king.

Now Jin could see a half-dozen moves ahead of where they had left the game and smiled without meaning to. She could win this game, she saw, as the moves and countermoves played out in her mind. She picked up Wiesen's king—it was the one piece he had put much work into repurposing, a plastic ball joint he had carved until it vaguely resembled a head and crown—and her smile fell as her fingers brushed over his maker's mark, the two characters she knew she could never speak again.

Six months later she was on Hanzi, unpacking her meagre belongings in her room at the Academy. It was very small, almost a relief after the number of times she'd had to change her idea of what big was since leaving Garamond. When the ship had docked she had been awed by what she had seen: more people than she had ever known standing in a single room that was full of light and colour, stores and vidscreens. Corridors stretched outward in every direction, promising more wonders. She had turned to her seatmate, a sophisticate from Xerxes, told him she had not imagined even Hanzi could be this big.

"This is just the docking satellite," he had told her, not bothering to hide his contempt. "We're going to board a wayship from here to take us down to the city. *It's* big."

After that she had not even bothered trying to gauge the size of what she saw, and the hundreds of buildings they had passed on their way to the dorms—each one at least fifty times larger than the central building back home—had barely registered as real, just a pattern of light and shade. Now that she was in her room, though, in a space she could get her mind around—it was a little under four paces square, actually a bit smaller than her old room—she could finally start to make herself at home.

She put her bag on the bed and opened it, pulling out one-by-one the pieces she and Lieutenant Wiesen had made. She took the board out last, put it on the desk and put the pieces on it, recreating the game that had been left unfinished when he left. Then she lay down on the bed, curled her hand around the carved plastic piece in her pocket and let herself sleep.

JINX
Robert Priest

Einstein and Heidelberg both said
"There's no simultaneity
over vast distances"
at exactly the same time.

THE BOOK WITH NO END
Colleen Anderson

Lizbet feels much like an ant as she and the others slowly shovel and brush away the fine gritty dirt from the emerging walls. Her specialization in dead languages will give her an edge but does not excuse her from being on hands and knees in the sand. She will decipher any cuneiform tablets uncovered, should they be lucky enough to find any. A month ago ground-penetrating radar indicated several buried chambers in the Sumerian city of Nippur, one of the seats of civilization and the home of the earliest form of writing.

The area has been picked over by hungry archaeologists for decades; it is the land where Gilgamesh and Enkidu went on adventures, where Inanna tromped the unknown caverns of her sister's realm to overcome death. If any truths are to be found, they will be in the oldest myths, when humans tried to crack open the world's mysteries. This is what Lizbet needs: to unearth the very genesis of when civilization awoke and grew in might.

What she wants is complete control. Being able to manipulate boys, men, and teachers has always given Lizbet a primordial thrill, as if she were the battery that ran the world.

Two gruelling weeks under a sun that sucks the moisture from skin and withers everyone beneath its glare. Lizbet is ready to take a flight home at the end of the week. They haven't even found the foundations yet, just walls and more walls. Even an abandoned village would have a few artefacts. Maybe it is time to look at a more illustrious career, a faster road to what she wants.

Markus has just called a halt after twelve hours, a normal day when you're racing against the time a foreign government gives you. Back-breaking work; they may as well be ancient Sumerian peasants. Lizbet stands and stretches, running her tongue over dry lips. Sipping water from her Camelbak, she wipes from her eyes stray strands of hair now the colour of dunes and peers at the sun lumbering toward its dusty bed. Another tedious day.

She turns toward the tent to find shade and takes a step when the ground capsizes beneath her. There isn't even time to yell as dirt and stone follow her into a hole.

Her plummet is buffered by sand and the old sandstone beneath her feet. She half-slides, half-falls in a cascade and lands on the hump of the water bag strapped to her back. Dirt and stones rain upon her. She opens her eyes to see a dark shape plunge toward her; she moves her head to the side barely in time to avoid the large piece of masonry. Blinking and scrubbing at the dirt in her mouth and eyes, she coughs and sits up. Her back is sore and her hip is already pulsing with pain. There will be a few bruises from the twenty-foot fall but no bones seem broken. As she stands, she moves each limb then, satisfied, slaps dirt from her clothes and hair. She sucks water from the tube, swishes, and spits out mud. As people's shouts filter from above Lizbet looks around, still rubbing dirt from her eyes. A treasure trove reveals itself: more artefacts than almost any Sumerian excavation to date.

Someone calls down.

"Yes, I'm all right. Just bruised."

"We'll find a rope and ladder and get you out."

Lizbet barely hears them as she walks around the rectangular chamber that is bathed in amber light and settling dust motes. She has discovered a mystery. The ancients built rituals around them: the Orphic rites, the Dionysian and Mithraic cults, the Eleusinian mysteries—all these had force and endurance. There is something here; she feels it at this ancient nexus of civilization where words were given power, and knowledge was stored for millennia. Lizbet's fingers tingle. It is here again: that electric vibration, that thrumming resonance she senses when power is within her reach.

She runs her hands over the contours of three stone bulls and of petite, glazed clay bull dancers, looks at turned wooden bowls full of unsown seeds, and stops in front of a low palette with the dusky bones of some past lord or lady. A wooden chest, several bronze blades, a folded pile of greyed fabric that would disintegrate on touch completes the riches of the funereal chamber. She circles the room again and is drawn to the skeleton, not laid out in any sarcophagus, bare of the shreds of any garment or of the telltale glint of ornaments. Stripped of everything but its bones. Devoid even of any desiccated remnants of hair or flesh.

What can one tell from the bones of the dead, those ivory sculptures no longer corrupted by the indulgences and errors of living? Only the greatest stories, the traumas that embed into a person's core, only those etch themselves on bones. And yet these are more pristine than baby's bones. No nicks, no mended breaks, teeth all present, perfectly straight and whole, no axe marks of any untimely death, no disease nor malformation have touched this body. Everything in the room is incredibly fragile and the air that now circulates could destroy some of the artefacts in days. She moves softly, almost reverently, and kneels beside the wooden bed on which the pristine skeleton rests. How could anyone in an age of primitive medicine remain unmarred?

The palette is only about a foot off the ground; beneath it, Lizbet glimpses a shadow on the floor tiles that must have once been brightly painted. She reaches underneath and pulls out a stiff bundle tied with cord that crumbles in her hands. An animal skin, most likely cow, crackles and powders brown hair onto the floor. The bundle is as long as her forearm and twice as thick. Lizbet delicately folds back a tiny portion of the old hide and pokes her finger inside to feel a supple softness, slightly clammy and unpleasant. Tilting it to the light, she distinguishes some form of marking. A parchment or vellum with inked symbols upon it. Her heart thumps harder now than it did from her fall.

There is noise around the hole as people prepare to let the ladder down, and Lizbet knows she can't share this find. Quickly, she drains the water from her Camelbak and unzips it to wedge the package inside. She pulls off her shirt, leaving on the tank top, and puts the pack back on with the shirt tied to it so that the bulk is disguised.

"Okay, Lizbet."

She climbs the ladder and is bombarded with questions.

"What's down there? Some furniture?"

"That and more," she tells Markus, who keeps shifting from foot to foot. "Untouched artefacts, a skeleton; weeks of work." There is so much talk and chaos that no one even notices her overly full water pack; when she pleads bruises and needing to lie down, there are no questions.

Lizbet will return to the lab with the first shipment of artefacts: one tablet and a couple of pots with engraved cuneiform. Other quadrants have yet to be excavated. But she has enough and wants to examine her find in private.

The cracked animal pelt reveals three layers: papery grey leaves, several unknown powdery substances, and a sticky residue. Lizbet finds the inner layer is a skin or sheath still supple after millennia. She experiences such a rush that she has to sit down, as if she'd inhaled an opiate.

She works painstakingly for weeks to remove the integument from its chrysalis. With techniques perfected for burn victims, she immerses the skin in a stainless-steel water tank and doesn't unroll it until she's certain it maintain its integrity. Still, she peers at what she can with a magnifying glass, noticing the smooth, cinnamon brown colour as well as the cuneiform symbols in red and black ink.

After a second week of immersion, Lizbet carefully unrolls and cleans the skin. It is human.

This amaranthine skin is an entry to another world—like the Rosetta Stone. While it may be the key, it is not the full answer to her quest. The cuneiform script is not unusual, nor dissimilar from previously excavated tablets, but the arrangement of symbols can make a world of difference in meaning.

The earliest writings were tabulations of possessions. Soon after, people started to write about the mysteries, to create formulas and ways to cross into the underworld or the sphere of the gods. Gilgamesh, Odysseus, Herakles: the earliest adventurers walked in realms that held true control and the potential for fundamental metamorphosis. Lizbet feels that hunger and begins rereading all the epics, but only the most accurate translations. This skin is worth all the finds in the world.

The amaranth skin tests her knowledge and expands it as she unravels the tattooed script. It tells of a binding, readings, maps, immortality, and the greatest of powers: all will know the name of the wearer.

She knows it now; that is what she truly wants—immortality.

There are three different types of information in these inked markings: Short phrases about the sheath's abilities when worn, riddles to solve, and instructions for attaining immortality. This is only the start of a long pursuit. The recipe is in every inch of skin covered in pictographs from the flap and eye holes that once covered the skull, down to the thin twists that were fingers and toes, but it does not list the ingredients except as clues, such as where to hunt. This could take years.

For the next ten years Lizbet travels the globe by plane, train, jeep, horse, mule, and camel. She ages. She reads numerous papyri, scrolls, tablets, stones, and texts, solving puzzles and riddles. Some lead to other artefacts or ingredients. The rarer spices, oils, and pastes, she ships to a post office box; the artefacts require a range of blackmail, auction purchases, and bribery. Her expertise in ancient languages allows access to most texts, whether painted on stone, engraved, woven, imprinted, written, or branded.

There are items that no longer exist, and those she must reconstruct. When unable to find the kudurru of Nebuchadnezzar's vision, she re-examines all such stones and checks the translations. The vision is engraved on the stone that held boundary allotments for King Marduk-nādin-ahhē. The museum won't release that kudurru, so she photographs it and has a jeweller meticulously carve a replica in black nephrite. Each reconstruction is worth the expense.

She dated the tattooed skin to be around eight thousand years old; it has not aged, is indeed like amaranth known for its long-lived quality. How is it that the sheath holds information about more recent civilizations and artefacts? That alone indicates some prognostication and hints that it might be a piece of the map to immortality. She discovers a clue on a worn clay tablet, tracing the lead through a partially burned manuscript back to an inscription on a weather-beaten wall. She must guess and think and try to parse these together into the precise instructions.

There are other tasks and tests set out in those books, yellowed scrolls, and slabs of marble and clay. Laced within the intricate symbols and tales are riddles to solve, revealing tasks to fulfil. Sometimes the message is repeated in different areas of the skin, in slightly different phrasings but always three times. Lizbet knows that early forms of chants and songs used repetition to memorize tales. She does not need to do this as she has the script on flesh plus all her notes.

Before she begins to undertake the list of tasks, she must verify that their order is correct.

The first requirement is relatively easy: *Segregate yourself.* For years her jealous obsession has made of her a recluse.

Next: *Examine the living.* She sits in libraries, funeral parlours, restaurants, and emergency rooms. She walks malls, parks, and campuses, studying people in all their states. Every test requires her to examine her own feelings and emotions, and then to list them. People are mere lab mice, and she finds them easy to understand. Her motivation is clear but not so her own emotions.

Examine the dead. She volunteers to do forensic archaeology on homicide victims. While the first few gory examinations revolt her, used as she is to the desiccated forms of the ancient world, she becomes curious; what murder method was used, did the victim experience pain, did she suffer long? Did the murderer feel anything, joy, anger, numbness?

Do not help those in need. She travels to Haiti, searching out the worst slums, the most destitute and ill. She strolls among them and, rather than compassion, feels revulsion at the scrawny limbs and the people with cholera. They are rotting and should be put down.

Be cruel. When Maggie complains of a sore tooth, Lizbet responds, "If you stopped eating candy, your teeth would be better off and you'd lose some of that weight you're gaining." When José shows up with his short hair gelled into spikes, she laughs: "That won't hide your bald spot, nor get you a date." No one willingly works with her anymore, but she doesn't need them. She continues this stage of the test: two women milling at the subway, she just pushes out of her way; she stares at an old woman bowed over by the weight of her wrinkles, and stays in her seat; she kicks away a street person's cup of coins. She feels no shame, only a small joy that she now possesses this power.

There are many tests; their goal is to eliminate her feelings and emotions. But when she has distilled them down to the last one, the exhilaration of control, she becomes stuck. She cannot get rid of pride, anger, exaltation, and the small thrills of command. She must hone herself into the perfect vessel or the process will not work. Once she attains immortality, then she can glory in it.

If she attains immortality.

The weeks stretch into months, and her frustration mounts as she feels the push of time. Emotion is her undoing. The more she tries to bury them, the stronger the emotions come, the stronger her attraction to scotch becomes. To have wasted so many years, cut off from everything, all in the vain hope of gaining true power. All for nothing. She has failed.

She buys another five bottles of scotch. And then, another five.

Lizbet's binge rides her through several months, until she is numb, uncaring. One day, in a bleary stupor, she realizes that she cannot allow herself to care; it is the caring about the outcome of her quest, whether negative or positive, that brought her down. In the end the alcohol is her saviour; she realizes she was a fool for almost letting that near-final step become insurmountable. She sobers up and repeats all the steps again.

This time around the tests are, paradoxically, both more demanding and easier. She watches and sometimes even participates in events, all without reaction; the more tests she undergoes, the less she feels.

On sabbatical, Lizbet spends more time alone, often in the dark, without food, to meditate on the cuneiform characters the sheath has shown. Loneliness doesn't matter. She is able to read the different messages; hidden messages become visible when viewed from dermis or epidermis side; head to toes; right arm to left leg; fingers then toes; areas where the flesh once covered organs, such as heart, kidneys, lungs, stomach; the eight chakras in a line from genitals to scalp. It is the ultimate topographic map; each layer of meaning is deeper, more profound.

Thus, she learns the rudimentary language of the elements. It would take decades of practice to fully master the skill, but she nevertheless stirs a leaf, ripples water, causes smoke to rise from a twig, and makes a bloom open, by simply pronouncing the right letters in the right order. She has no need to write down these arts; if her journal is ever discovered, any who read it will need to find their own steps.

There is one final preparation before she can undertake the ritual to bind the sheath to her. It will be the last time she can let herself feel emotion, and it must be convincing, most of all to herself. She goes to a club, drinks good scotch, and finds a man worth fucking. She forms no attachments but brings him to her place, then discards him once she's done. The act is repeated with a variety of men until she's sure the seed has taken. There must be no record, so she buys the pack of strips and waits for the colour to confirm that she is pregnant. She waits long enough to make sure she doesn't lose the foetus; meanwhile she continues to study the skin, the Dead Sea Scrolls, hieroglyphs and pictographs, the Talmud, the Bible, the Quran—but only the earliest versions, the purest. She does not find any more clues or messages. The time has come.

Lizbet packs everything she needs: the artefacts, the skin, the unguents and herbs, water, food, and camping gear. She finds a cave that will not be visited until spring creeps out. Autumn has strangled the life from last leaves and they lie, discarded husks, upon the ground. The sky is clear and pallid as the weather cools, and she has enough wood.

In various nooks, fissures, and natural shelves of grey and black striated stone she places the scrolls, the stones, the vessels, and the statues that she procured from all over the world. They might not be necessary for the final ritual, but she leaves nothing to chance. Great sacrifices have been called for; she has met all but one last requirement.

The months have passed in contemplation and practice. Lizbet can now move water, wind, earth, and fire, though it is still a demanding feat. Winter has been cold and dry, and spring will heave itself from the earth soon. She does not mind the pain when the contractions begin. The circumstances of her labour do not matter; only that the foetus live.

The final preparation is the most explicit: suckle the baby for three days, then kill it while looking into its eyes. It cries as if it knows its fate. Its measly life will serve a greater goal.

Lizbet decides to strangle it; the neck is so small that she only needs one hand to encircle the soft pink flesh. Her fingers sink in as she squeezes. The baby flails and shrieks only momentarily before the blood supply is cut off. Fascinated, Lizbet watches the face blister red and the eyes bulge.

She brings the body near the fire and guts it with the curved Ghurkha blade she acquired in India. Blood pools like oil on the stone; she uses it to mark her skin with sigils. The entrails are set aside for later. She cuts through the skin and meat, and breaks the soft bones, puts all in an iron kettle to which she adds spices and water, and a few root vegetables. She eats the food thus prepared over the next three days.

Three is one of the great magic numbers. It stands for past, present, and future; beginning, middle, and end; life, death, and rebirth. Religious paintings were done as triptychs. There are many groups of three. Stories are often written in three parts. This is the final part of the trilogy.

It is the end of the third day as Lizbet checks for any residual emotions. She is full and ready. There is no elation. She will do as she set out to do those many years ago. It is time to begin the culminating ritual.

The intestines have dried into sinewy rawhide and lie upon the small wooden altar near the fire. The fire is built high for warmth and for the spirit to find her. Her clothes are piled within a niche in the cave wall.

Her skin shines with the oils of datura, nightshade, and poppy. The obsidian blade used in Zapotec rituals to release istli through human sacrifice lies next to the amaranth sheath stretched out on the ground.

She has eaten nothing since she consumed her child three days before. Three days of feasting, three of fasting, a circle completed; what was taken in and transformed is consumed and excreted. The coils wind in and out.

She sits upon the tattooed skin and writes her final words in the journal. Lizbet closes the book, then picks up the blade and carves fine symbols into her flesh; she marks the chakras. Triangles, swirls, waves, circles—figures as old as time with the power of eternity behind them. Feet, ankles, knees, pubic bone, belly, chest, back, hands, wrists, elbows, neck, forehead—all have characters etched into them; blood oozes from her.

She binds the sheath to her ankles, then to her wrists, using her teeth to tie the knot. Next she fastens the amaranth sheath around her belly and neck with the sinew of her sacrifice. Lizbet lies down, the cuts stinging and throbbing in time with her pulse; on these next three nights of the equinox, she chants the words of power. As she is absorbed, she thinks: *I shall be reborn to live forever.*

Humanity is a book: their stories make up the world; their skins, like this skin, tell a tale. I am the reader who knows each book's ending. I have read the leaves left here by the binder. The stories often begin with a birth, but the tales differ, though they all end with my beginning.

I have two siblings. My first task is to kill the oldest, skin the body, and lay out the clues for the next binder. One is new, one is old, one is always in transition.

I look at the pattern of glowing symbols on my skin; they tell me the way. I call the wind and mist to veil me, to absorb me. Then I fade. I am everywhere.

We three are everywhere. Our quest was written at the beginning of time. Our touch reaches all and they will know our name. Some have called us Fate or Destiny but most people call us Death. Ours is the longest tale in the world. We are the book with no end.

NEANDERTHAL MAN, THEORY AND PRACTICE
Kate Cayley

The world is not ending, let us say this.
It has ended.

German miners, 1856—picking at the limestone,
burrowing in the creases of the earth—found
the hollow flattened skulls, cracked thighs,
long fingers, disjointed arms clawing out
of that darkness.

These creatures buried their dead, ground stone,
they spoke, their hands tore at the roots of trees. Perhaps
they cared for the lame, the blind, led them
over the rougher earth. They may have chewed
the food of the old, fed them tenderly
through thickets of rotted teeth.

They also ate their dead, the flesh ripped
away from the bone, sinews white, red wet hands.

The miners feared the bones. But one man, young,
hacking his life away, held
a skull in his hands, the eye sockets
addressing his own eyes.

Then he put it down and cracked it with his pick.
The other men looked away, but did not protest:
a long hard day, little time.

ALL MY PRINCES ARE GONE

Jennifer Giesbrecht

I.

When the world was young, it was filled with monsters.

II.

He was born from the sky and I was made from the earth. I was shaped from black mud into a convex structure of dark space and hard dips. The brunt of two thick palms around my waist made a place for them to fit comfortably later. The inside of my thighs were dimpled with thumb marks; two, where he pressed just deep enough to feel the vein throb. Deep enough that my husband could trace the pulse when he pulled my legs apart. Our first child was born like this. He was born swathed in mud, his heartbeat a delicate thing that beat down the walls of his ribcage like desperation. His father held him up by one leg, crushing his ankle until the soft child-flesh bubbled up around his angry fist and turned bone white. On his tiny foot were four black claws. In his mouth, teeth that could shear; his head bore a wolf's coarse fur to cradle him from the wind's chill. I had given him these gifts. I had birthed him the best I could.

"This is an animal," my husband said.

I asked him: "Why shouldn't our sons have teeth and claws?"

"For the same reason our daughters should not," said he. And then he struck my child's head against a rock and came to embrace me with his bloody hands. He marked the day with two slick handprints at the base of my spine.

III.

All of my daughters were born with teeth.

IV.

My first daughters were born together, a bloody tangle of smooth rolls, boneless fingers tugging at each other's fat, grasping for purchase. When first I saw them I thought of two goatskins filled with water—flabby things that would change shape and burst if you held them too tightly. The first ones hid their teeth. We were not yet timid, but we were careful. Ishtar's tooth was in her heart, and Ereškigal's in her mind. They were every star in my sky: the brightest, the strongest, the swiftest of all my children. Ereškigal learned to be subtle early; she crawled back into the womb when she was grown enough, making her kingdom in a cradle of dirt where our power is strongest and her tooth would always be hidden. Ishtar wanted for conflict and walked beneath my husband's sun. Ishtar wanted for the fear in a man's eye when she cut open her chest between the second and third rib and twisted free a sharpened fang. She wanted for the way it glistened in the light.

"You thought me a soft creature," she would hiss, "You thought me dull of tooth. You thought me sweet of tongue. I am an eater of meat. I crave the taste of metal."

To Ereškigal she would brag, "Weren't they surprised."

V.

My husband's new wife was born from his flesh and all of their children were born toothless.

VI.

"There is no need," she said to me. "This world is soft," she said. "It is soft, as fruit is soft. We don't need fangs to taste its juice." The way her thumb carved a shallow bruise into the fruit reminded me of my son's head. I curled my nails against her knee and leaned over her; I licked the tangy juice from the groove beneath her lips. I found the dimpled flesh inside her thighs and rested my thumbs there, pierced the vein with loving precision and watched her eyes go black. Listened to the keening noise that fluttered inside her throat.

But when I licked the tangy blood from the groove beneath my thumb, she made no sounds.

VII.

"Ishtar is careless," Ereškigal said to me, "Ishtar is salacious. Ishtar is unsubtle. When Ishtar speaks, I claw my ears raw and bloody. Ishtar would war on mortal men. She would have them war upon each other for her amusement."

Ereškigal slept inside my ribcage and whispered such things directly into the thin skin of my lungs.

"What would you have us do?" I asked, "In Ishtar's stead, would you have us hide?"

"No," Ereškigal replied, "I have no interest in Adam's world. I would have us do nothing at all. I would sleep until they were all dead and their rotting flesh made a blanket of filth for me to wash my feet in. They will not last."

VIII.

So I put a tooth into the fruit.

IX.

When he found out what I had done, my husband came for me. He came for me with a hundred of his soft sons and a hundred of their spear-teeth to pierce the places where my flesh had grown hard and thorny. They pried the plates of bone and hair from my belly and found where the flesh was stretched taut over my bloated womb, spongy thin and quivering like the membrane of an egg. I lay in the dirt and laughed as my skin burst and the black blood bubbled out of me—bog-thick, sharp on the tongue—and washed over their feet.

X.

For I am the mother of monsters and when they split me open, weren't they surprised.

XI.

My monsters did not hide their teeth. A tooth in the eye would turn a man to stone, feet first and then his veins. It would feel like a hard wedge of metal running along the length of his arteries, like a blunted knife sawing at the place beneath his knee. A tooth in the eye would leave Adam's sons hollow, with dust-filled hearts.

A tooth for her tongue would thirst for light and blood. She would ask, "Which does a man need more?" Adam's sons will always choose light.

A tooth in her hand would make her a trickster. She would hold it out for Adam's sons and they would grab for her eagerly. They would make a pact with her and tear each other to strips for bloody gold. They would not see that her face was a beast's.

A tooth in her belly would spawn sons with scales and a crocodile's maw. It would spawn sons with a deep and horrible hunger for pale flesh. A tooth in the belly would give her a hunger to swallow the world whole.

XII.

Be careless, my daughters.

Be salacious.

Be unsubtle.

When you speak let the world claw itself bloody.

XIII.

When my womb was empty, Adam and his sons peeled the rest from me. They took the entire length of my mud skin and stripped my bones bare.

"No more monsters from your poison womb," my husband said. "From your corpse I will grow wheat to feed my children."

He took my skin and stretched it over the world like the rind of an orange.

XIV.

Ereškigal wished to sleep. She went to Ishtar and said to her, "Our mother has been killed. Our father has fed her body to his sons."

"Then I will eat his sons," Ishtar replied.

"Then you will be killed as well, and your heart will be used as kindling for their sun."

"Then I will eat their sun," Ishtar replied.

"You will burn from the inside and never stop burning."

"Then I will eat myself," Ishtar replied.

"Sister," Ereškigal said. "Have you ever seen my tooth?"

"No," Ishtar replied, "You hide it away as if you are ashamed. You would bow to Adam's sons. You would allow them to tame our savage world as you have been tamed. You were born tamed."

Ereškigal reached behind her eye. She found the place in her skull where she hid her tooth and twisted it free with two pointed fingers. She held it up to the light and wanted for the fear in her sister's eyes when she placed it between her lips.

"A disease of the feet against your feet," she said, and Ishtar's feet curled into clubs and she fell to the ground.

"A disease of the hand against your hands," she said, and Ishtar's fingers withered to ribbons.

"A disease of the eye against your eyes," she said, and Ishtar's eyes turned black and wept blood.

"A disease of the mouth against your mouth," she said, and Ishtar fell silent.

Ereškigal stroked her sister's hair and cleaned the blood from her face. "We will sleep," she whispered, "We will sleep until their soft bones turn to water. We will wait until their corpses make the earth a throne."

XVI.

All my princes are gone. But my daughters.

Oh, my daughters.

HARVESTING LOST HEARTS
Louisa Howerow

After the first frost, the old woman stoops
over rotting logs, pushes apart clumps
of fanshaped moss, uncovers clenched hearts

that beat so erratically she knows
they've forgotten how fierce they once were.
She untangles their roots, tugs gently

to draw them free. No brushing away
dirt or grubs. No scolding or
reminding them their eagerness was all wrong,

this losing themselves to sweet mouths,
unhurried hands. When dusk slips into itself
and moths flurry from balsam firs,

she nestles her harvest in a faded brown sling
retraces her way past sword ferns, burial stones
and enters unlatched doors.

BY HIS THINGS WILL YOU KNOW HIM

Cory Doctorow

I thought that Mr. Purnell was a little young to be a funeral director, but he had the look down cold. In the instant between his warm, dry handshake and my taking my hand back to remove my winter hat and stuff it into my pocket, he assumed the look, a kind of concerned, knowing sympathy that suggested he'd weathered plenty of grief in his day and he was there to help you get through your own. He gestured me onto an oatmeal-coloured wool sofa and pulled his wheeled office chair around to face me. I hung my coat over the sofa arm and sat down and crossed and uncrossed my legs.

"So, it's like I said in the email—" was as far as I got and then I stopped. I felt the tears prick at the back of my eyes. I swallowed hard. I rubbed at my stubble, squeezed my eyes shut. Opened them.

If he'd said anything, it would have been the wrong thing. But he just gave me the most minute of nods—somehow he knew how to embed sympathy in a tiny nod; he was some kind of prodigy of grief-appropriate body language—and waited while the lump in my throat sank back down into my churning guts.

"Uh. Like I said. We knew Dad was sick but not how sick. None of us had much to do with him for, uh, a while." Fifteen years, at least. Dad did his thing, we did ours. That's how we all wanted it. But why did my chest feel like it was being crushed by a slow, relentless weight? "And it turns out he didn't leave a will." Thanks, Dad. How long, how many years, did you have after you got your diagnosis? How many years to do one tiny thing to make the world of the living a simpler place for your survivors?

Selfish, selfish prick.

Purnell let the silence linger. He was good. He let the precisely correct interval go past before he said, "And you say there is insurance?"

"Funeral insurance," I said. "Got it with his severance from Compaq.

I don't think he even knew about it, but one of his buddies emailed me when the news hit the web, told me where to look. I don't know what his policy number was or anything—"

"We can find that out," Purnell said. "That's the kind of thing we're good at."

"Can I ask you something?"

"Of course."

"Why don't you have a desk?" He shrugged, tapped the tablet he'd smoothed out across his lap. "I feel like a desk just separates me from my clients." He gestured around his office, the bracketless shelves in sombre wood bearing a few slim books about mourning, some abstract sculptures carved from dark stone or pale, bony driftwood. "I don't need it. It's just a relic of the paper era. I'd much rather sit right here and talk with you, face to face, figure out how I can help you."

I'd googled him, of course. I'd googled the whole process. The first thing you learn when you google funeral homes is that the whole thing is a ripoff. From the coffin—the "casket," which is like a coffin but more expensive—to the crematorium to the wreath to the hearse to the awful online memorial site with sappy music—all a scam, from stem to stern. It's a perfect storm of graft: a bereaved family, not thinking right; a purchase you rarely have to make; a confusion of regulations and expectations. Add them all up and you're going to be mourning your wallet along with your dear departed.

Purnell gets good google. They say he's honest, modern, and smart. They say he's young, and that's a positive, because it makes him a kind of digital death native, and that's just what we need, my sister and I, as we get ready to bury Herbert Pink: father, nerd, and lifelong pain in the ass. The man I loved with all my heart until I was 15 years old, whereupon he left our mother, left our family, and left our lives. After that, I mostly hated him. You should know: hate is not the opposite of love.

I was suddenly mad at this young, modern, honest, smart undertaker. I mean, funeral director. "Look," I said. "I didn't really even know my father, hadn't seen him in years. I don't need 'help,' I just need to get him in the ground. With a minimum of hand holding and fussing."

He didn't flinch, even though there'd been no call for that kind of outburst. "Bruce," he said, "I can do that. If you're in a hurry, we can probably even do it by tomorrow. It looks like your father's insurance would take you through the whole process. We'd even pay the deductible for you." He paused to let that sink in. "But Bruce, I do think I can help you. You're your father's executor, and he died intestate. That means a long, slow probate."

"So what? I don't care about any inheritance. My dad wasn't a rich man, you know."

"I'm sorry, that's not what I meant to imply. Your father died intestate, and there's going to be taxes to pay, bills to settle. You're going to have to value his estate, produce an inventory, possibly sell off his effects to cover the expenses. Sometimes this can take years."

He let that sink in. "All right," I said, "that's not something I'd thought of. I don't really want to spend a month inventorying my father's cutlery and underwear drawer."

He smiled. "I don't suppose a court would expect you to get into that level of detail. But the thing is, there's better ways to do this sort of thing. You think that I'm young for a funeral director."

The non sequitur caught me off guard. "I, uh, I suppose you're old enough—"

"I am young for this job. But you know what Douglas Adams said: everything invented before you were born is normal and ordinary and is just a natural part of the way the world works. Anything after your fifteenth birthday is new and exciting and revolutionary. Anything invented after you're thirty-five is against the natural order of things. The world has changed a lot since you were born, and changed even more since I was born, and I have to tell you, I think that makes my age an asset, not a liability.

"And not in some nebulous, airy-fairy way. Specifically, the fact that I'm 27 years old is how I got onto the beta-test for this." He handed me his tablet. I smoothed it out and looked at it. It took me a minute to get what I was seeing. At first, I thought I was looking through a live camera feed from some hidden webcam in his office, but then I noticed I wasn't in the picture. Then I thought I might be seeing a video loop. But after a few experimental prods, I understood that this was a zoomable panoramic image of the room in which I was sitting.

"Pick up one of the sculptures," he said. I zoom-dragged to one of them, a kind of mountainscape made of something black and nonreflective. It had pleasing proportions, and a play of textures I quite admired. I double-tapped it and it filled the screen, allowing me to rotate it, zoom in on it. Playing along, I zoomed way up until it became a mash of pixellated JPEG noise, then back out again.

"Now try the white one," he said, pointing at a kind of mathematical solid that suggested some kind of beautiful calculus, behind him and to the left. Zooming to it, I discovered that I could go to infinite depth on it, without any jaggies or artefacts appearing. "It's so smooth because there's a model of it on Thingiverse, so the sim just pulled in the vectors describing it and substituted a rendering of them for the bitmap. Same with the shelves. They're Ikea, and all Ikea furniture has publicly disclosed dimensions, so they're all vector based." I saw now that it was true: the shelves had a glossy perfection that the rest of the room lacked.

"Try the books," he said. I did. A copy of The Egyptian Book of the Dead opened at a touch and revealed its pages to me. "Book-search scans," he said.

I zoomed around some more. The camel-coloured coat hanging on the hook on the back of the door opened itself and revealed its lining. My pinkie nail brushed an icon and I found myself looking at a ghostly line-art version of the room, at a set of old-fashioned metal keys in the coat's pocket, and as I zoomed out, I saw that I was able to see into the walls—the wiring, the plumbing, the 24 studs.

"Teraherz radar," he said, and took the tablet back from me. "There's more to see, and it gets better all the time. There were a couple of books it didn't recognize at first, but someone must have hooked them into the database, because now they move. That's the really interesting thing, the way this improves continuously—"

"Sorry," I said. "What are you showing me?"

"Oh," he said. "Right. Got ahead of myself. The system's called Infinite Space and it comes from a start-up here in Virginia. They're a DHS spinout, started out with crime-scene forensics and realized they had something bigger here. Just run some scanners around the room and give it a couple of days to do the hard work. If you want more detail, just unpack and repack the drawers and boxes in front of it—it'll tell you which ones have the smallest proportion of identifiable interior objects. You won't need to inventory the cutlery; that shows up very well on a teraherz scan. The underwear drawer is a different matter."

I sat there for a moment, thinking about my dad. I hadn't been to his place in years. The docs had shown me the paramedics' report, and they'd called it "crowded," which either meant that they were very polite or my dad had gotten about a million times neater since I'd last visited him. I'd been twenty before I heard the term "hoarder," but it had made instant sense to me.

Purnell was waiting patiently for me, like a computer spinning a watch cursor while the user was wool-gathering. When he saw he had my attention, he tipped his head minutely, inviting me to ask any questions. When I didn't, he said, "You know the saying, 'You can't libel the dead'? You can't invade the dead's privacy, either. Using this kind of technology on a living human's home would be a gross invasion of privacy. But if you use it in the home of someone who's died alone, it just improves a process that was bound to take place in any event. Working with Infinite Space, you can even use the inventory as a checklist, value all assets using current eBay blue-book prices, divide them algorithmically or manually, even turn it into a packing and shipping manifest you can give to movers, telling them what you want sent where. It's like full-text search for a house."

I closed my eyes for a moment. "Do you know anything about my father?"

For the first time, his expression betrayed some distress. "A little," he said. "When you showed up in my calendar, it automatically sent me a copy of the coroner's report. I could have googled further, but . . ." He smiled. "You can't invade the privacy of the dead, but there's always the privacy of the living. I thought I'd leave that up to you."

"My father kept things. I mean, he didn't like to throw things away. Nothing." I looked into his eyes as I said these words. I'd said them before, to explain my spotless desk, my habit of opening the mail over a garbage can and throwing anything not urgent directly into the recycling pile, my weekly stop at the thrift-store donation box with all the things I'd tossed into a shopping bag on the back of the bedroom door. Most people nodded like they understood. A smaller number winced a little, indicating that they had an idea of what I was talking about.

A tiny minority did what Purnell did next: looked back into my eyes for a moment, then said, "I'm sorry."

"Yeah," I said. "He was always threatening to start an antique shop, or list his stuff on eBay. Once he even signed a lease, but he never bought a cash register. Never unlocked the front door, near as I could tell. But he was always telling me that his things were valuable, to the right person." I swallowed, feeling an echo of the old anger I'd suppressed every time he'd played that loop for me. "But if there was anything worth anything in that pile, well, I don't know how I'd find it amid all the junk."

"Bruce, you're not the first person to find himself in this situation.

Dealing with an estate is hard at the best of times, and times like this, I've had people tell me they just wanted to torch the place, or bulldoze it."

"Both of those sound like good ideas, but I have a feeling you don't offer those particular services."

He smiled a little funeral director's smile, but it went all the way to his eyes. "No," he said. "I don't. But, huh." He stopped himself. "This sounds a bit weird, but I've been looking forward to a situation like this. It was what I thought of immediately when I first saw Infinite Space demoed. This is literally the best test case I can imagine for this."

I wish I was the kind of guy who didn't cry when his father, estranged for decades, died alone and mad in a cluttered burial chamber of his own lunatic design. But I'd cried pretty steadily since I'd gotten the news. I could tell that I was about to cry now. There were Kleenex boxes everywhere. I picked one up and plucked out a tissue. Purnell didn't look away but managed to back off slightly just by altering his posture. It was enough to give me the privacy to weep for a moment. The tears felt good this time, like they had somewhere to go. Not the choked cries I'd found myself loosing since I'd first gotten the news.

"Yeah," I said. "Yeah, I think it probably is."

I'd expected Roomba-style rolling robots and wondered how they'd get around the narrow aisles between the drifts and piles of things in Dad's house. There were a few of those, clever ones, the size of my old Hot Wheels cars, and six-wheeled so they could drive in any direction. But the heavy lifting was done by the quadrotors, each the size of a dragonfly, swarming and swooping and flocking with an eerie, dopplered whine that bounced around in the piles of junk. Bigger rotors went around and picked up the ground-effect vehicles, giving them lifts up and down the stairs. As they worked, their data streamed back into a panorama on Purnell's laptop. We sat on the porch steps and watched the image flesh out. The renderer was working from bitmaps and dead-reckoning telemetry to build its model, and it quivered like a funhouse as it continuously refined its guesses about the dimensions. At one point, the living room sofa appeared to pierce the wall behind us, the sofa itself rendered as a kind of eye-wateringly impossible Escherling that was thick and thin simultaneously. The whole region glowed pink.

"See," Purnell said. "It knows that there's something wrong there. There's going to be a ton of quads tasked to it any second now." And we heard them buzzing through the wall as they conferred with one another and corrected the software's best guesses. Flicking through the panoramas, we saw other pink areas, saw them disappear as the bad geometries were replaced with sensible ones in a series of eyeblink corrections. There was something comforting about watching all the detail fill in, especially when the texturemaps appeared in another eyeblink, skinning the wireframes and giving the whole thing the feeling of an architectural rendering. The bitmaps had their own problems: improbable corners, warped-mirror distortions, but I could see that the software was self-aware enough to figure out its own defects, painting them with a pink glow that faded as the approximations were fined down with exact images from the missing angles.

All this time, there'd been a subtle progress bar creeping in fits and starts across the bottom of the screen, just few pixels' worth of glowing silvery light, and now it was nearly all the way. "You don't have to do the next part," he said. "If you'd rather wait out here—"

"I'll do it," I said. "It's okay."

"They gave us eight scanners. That's more than we should need for a two-bedroom house. Two should do it. One, even, if you don't mind moving it, but I thought—"

"It's okay," I said again. "I can do this."

I shook my own tablet out and pinched it rigid, holding it before me like a treasure map as I walked through the front door.

The smell stopped me in my tracks. It had been teasing me all the morning on the porch, but that was the attenuated, diluted version. Now I was breathing in the full-strength perfume, the smell of all my fathers' dens: damp paper, oxidizing metal, loose copper pennies, ancient cleaners vaporizing through the pores in their decaying bottles, musty cushions, expired bulk no-name cheerios, overloaded power strips, mouse turds, and the trapped flatulence of a thousand lonely days. Overlaid with it, a rotten meat smell.

My father had been dead for at least a week before they found him.

Infinite Space wanted teraherz scanners in several highly specific locations. Despite Purnell's assurances, it turned out that we needed to reposition half a dozen of them, making for fourteen radar panoramas in all. I let him do the second placement and went back out onto the porch to watch the plumbing and structural beams and wiring ghost into place as the system made sense of the scans. I caught a brief, airport-scan flash of Purnell's naked form, right down to his genitals, before the system recognized a human silhouette and edited it out of the map. The awkwardness was a welcome change from the cramped, panicked feeling that had begun the moment I'd stepped into Dad's house.

The screen blinked and a cartoon chicken did a little ironic head tilt in the bottom left corner. It was my little sister, Hennie, who is much more emotionally balanced than me, hence her ability to choose a self-mocking little avatar. I tapped and then cupped the tablet up into a bowl shape to help it triangulate its sound on my ear. "Have you finished mapping the burial chamber, Indiana Bruce?" She's five years younger than me, and Dad left when she was only ten, and somehow it never seemed to bother her. As far as she was concerned, her father died decades ago, and she'd never felt any need to visit or call the old man. She'd been horrified when she found out that I'd exchanged a semi-regular, semi-annual email with him.

I snuffled up the incipient snot and tears. "Funny. Yeah, it's going fast. Mostly automatic. I'll send it to you when it's done."

She shook her head. "Don't bother. It'll just give Marta ideas." Marta, her five-year-old daughter, refused to part with so much as a single stuffed toy and had been distraught for months when they remodelled the kitchen, demanding that the old fridge be brought back. I never wanted to joke about heredity and mental illness, but Hennie was without scruple on this score and privately insisted that Marta was just going through some kind of essential post-toddler conservatism brought on by the change to kindergarten and the beginning of a new phase of life.

"It's pretty amazing, actually. It's weird, but I'm kind of looking forward to seeing the whole thing. There's something about all that mess being tamed, turned into a spreadsheet—"

"Listen to yourself, Bruce. The opposite of compulsive mess isn't compulsive neatness—it's general indifference to stuff altogether. I don't know that this is very healthy."

I felt an irrational, overarching anger at this, which is usually a sign that she's right. I battened it down. "Look, if we're going to divide the estate, we're going to have to inventory it, and—"

"Wait, what? Who said anything about dividing anything? Bruce, you can keep the money, give it to charity, flush it down the toilet, or spend it on lap dances for all I care. I don't want it."

"But half of it is yours—I mean, it could go into Marta's college fund—"

"If Marta wants to go to college, she can sweat some good grades and apply for a scholarship. I don't give a damn about university. It's a big lie anyway—the return on investment just isn't there." Whenever Hennie starts talking like a stockbroker, I know she's looking to change the subject. She can talk economics all day long, and will, if you poke her in a vulnerable spot.

"Okay, okay. I get it. Fine. I won't talk about it with you if it bugs you. You don't have to know about it."

"Come on, Bruce, I don't mean it that way. You're my brother. You and Marta and Sweyn"—her husband—"are all the family I've got. I just don't understand why you need to do this. It's got me worried about you. You know that you had no duty to him, right? You don't owe him anything."

"This isn't about him. It's about me." And you, I added to myself. Someday you'll want to know about this, and you'll be glad I did it. I didn't say it, of course. That would have been a serious tactical mistake.

"Whatever you say, Bruce. Meantime, and for the record, Sweyn's looked up the information for the intestacy trustee. Anytime you want, you can step away from this. They'll liquidate his estate, put the proceeds into public-spirited projects. You can just step away anytime. Remember that."

"I'll remember. I know you want to help me out here, but seriously, this is something I need to do."

"This is something you think you need to do, Bruce."

Yeah," I said. "If that makes you feel better, then I can go with that."

I got the impression that Infinite Space was tremendously pleased to have hit on a beta tester who was really ready to put their stuff through its paces. A small army of turkers were bid into work, filling in descriptions and URLs for everything the software couldn't recognize on its own. At first they'd been afraid that we'd have to go in and rearrange the piles so that the cameras could get a look at the stuff in the middle, but a surprising amount of it could be identified edge on. It turns out books aren't the only thing with recognizable spines, assuming a big and smart enough database. The Infinites (yes, they called themselves that, and they generated a near-infinite volume of email and weets and statuses for me, which I learned to skim quickly and delete even faster) were concerned at first that it wouldn't work for my dad's stuff because so much of their secret sauce was about inferences based on past experience. If the database had previously seen a thousand yoga mats next to folded towels, then the ambiguous thing on top of a yoga mat that might be a fitted sheet and might be a towel was probably a towel.

Dad's teetering piles were a lot less predictable than that, but as it turned out, there was another way. Since they had the dimensions and structural properties for everything in the database, they were able to model how stable a pile would be if the towels were fitted sheets and vice-versa, and whittle down the ambiguities with physics. The piles were upright, therefore they were composed of things that would be stable if stacked one atop another. The code took very little time to implement and represented a huge improvement on the overall database performance.

"They're getting their money's worth out of you, Bruce," Purnell told me, as we met in his office that week. He had my dad's ashes, in a cardboard box. I looked at it and mentally sized it up for its regular dimensions, its predictable contents. They don't put the whole corpseworth of ashes in those boxes. There's no point. A good amount of ashes are approximately interchangeable with all the ashes, symbolically speaking. The ashes in that box would be of a normalized distribution and weight and composition. They could be predicted with enormous accuracy, just by looking at the box and being told what was inside it. Add a teraherz scan—just to be sure that the box wasn't filled with lead fishing weights or cotton candy—and the certainty skyrockets.

I hefted the box. "You could have dinged the insurance for a fancy urn," I said.

He shrugged. "It's not how I do business. You don't want a fancy urn. You're going to scatter his remains. An urn would just be landfill, or worse, something you couldn't bring yourself to throw away."

"I can bring myself to throw anything away," I said, with half a smile. Quipping. Anything to prolong the moment before that predictable box ended up in my charge. In my hands.

He didn't say anything. Part of the undertaker's toolkit, I suppose. Tactful silence. He held the box in the ensuing silence, never holding it out to me or even shifting it subtly in my direction. He was good. I'd take it when I was ready. I would never be ready. I took it.

It was lighter than I thought.

"Hennie, I need to ask you something and you're not going to like it."

"It's about him."

"Right," I said. I stared at the ceiling, my eyes boring through the plaster and beams into the upstairs spare room, where I'd left the box, in the exact centre of the room, which otherwise held nothing but three deep Ikea storage shelves—they'd render beautifully, was all I could think of when I saw them now—lined with big, divided plastic tubs, each neatly labeled.

"Bruce, I don't want—"

"I know you don't. But look, remember when you said I was all the family you had left?"

"You and Mattie and Sweyn."

"Yes. Well, you're all I have left, too."

"You should have thought of that before you got involved. You've got no right to drag me into this."

"I've got Dad's ashes."

That broke her rhythm. We'd fallen into the bickering cadence we'd perfected during a thousand childhood spats where we'd demanded that Mom adjudicate our disputes. Mom wasn't around to do that anymore. Besides, she'd always hated doing it and made us feel like little monsters for making her do so. I don't know that we'd had a fight like that in the seven years since she'd been gone.

"Oh, Bruce," she said. "God, of course you do. I don't want them."

"I don't want them either. I was thinking I'd, well, scatter them."

"Where? In his house? Another layer of dust won't hurt, I suppose."

"I don't think that's a good idea. What about by Mom's grave?"

"Don't you *dare*." The vicious spin on the last word was so intense I fumbled my tablet and had to catch it as it floated toward the floor on an errant warm air current.

"Sorry," I said.

"He never *earned* the right to be with Mom. He never earned what you're giving him. He never earned me sparing a single brain cell for him. He's not worth the glucose my neurons are consuming."

"He was sick, Hennie."

"He did *nothing* to get better. There are meds. Therapies. When I cleaned out Mom's place, I found the letters from the therapists she'd set him up with, asking why he never showed up for the intake appointments. He did nothing to earn any of this."

It dawned on me that Hennie had dealt with all of Mom's stuff without ever bothering me. Mom had left a will, of course, and set out some bequests for me, and she hadn't lived in a garbage house. But it must have been a lot of work, and Hennie had never once asked for my help.

"I'm sorry, Hennie, I never should have bothered you. You're right."

"Wait, Bruce, it's okay—"

"No, really. I'll deal with this. It's just a box of ashes. It's just stuff. I can get rid of stuff."

"Are you okay?"

"I'm fine," I said. I was, too. I folded the tablet up and stuck it in the sofa cushions and stared at the ceiling for a moment longer.

Somewhere in this house, there is an answer. Was there a moment when the grave robbers of ancient Egyptian pyramids found the plunder before them shimmer and change? Did they stand there, those wreckers with their hammers and shovels and treasure sacks, and gasp as the treasure before them became, for an instant, something naked and human and desperate, the terrified attempt of a dying aristocrat to put the world in a box, to make it behave itself? A moment when they found themselves standing not in a room full of gold and gems, but a room full of disastrous attempts to bring the universe to heel?

Here's the thing. It turns out that I don't mind mess at all. What I mind is *disorganization*. Clutter isn't clutter once it's been alphabetized on a hard drive. Once it's been scanned and catalogued and put it its place, it's stuff. It's actionable. With the click of a button, you can list it on eBay, you can order packers and movers to get rid of it, you can search the database for just the thing to solve any problem.

Things are wonderful, really. Things are potential. The right thing at the right moment might save a life, or save the day, or save a friendship. Any of these things might someday be a gift. If times get tight, these things can readily be converted to cash. Honestly, things are really, really fine.

I wish Hennie would believe me. She freaked out when I told her I was moving out of my place into Dad's. Purnell, too, kept coming over all grief counsellor and trying to help me "process" what I was feeling. Neither of them gets it, neither of them understands what I see when I look into the ruin of Dad's life, smartened up as neat as a precision machine. Minimalism is just a crutch for people who can't get a handle on their things. In the modern age, things are adaptive. They're pro-survival.

Really, things are fine.

GIRLS WATCH IN THE MIRROR AT MIDNIGHT FOR A VISION OF A FUTURE HUSBAND

Kate Cayley

Bloody Mary, patron saint of fear, of the future,
dark lady of girls' rooms that roil
with perfume, sweat, dark hair sprouting
like fungus. Girls gathered round the mirror's light,
calling to the woman veiled, weeping tears of blood,
Bloody Mary.

And it's said if she's asked in the right way in the right way with
obedient breath, with smooth tongue, she'll show in the mirror
a man, husband, bright spark, a rescue,
a man, waiting there.

So girls, little girls, their tongues
stuttering their names, gather and wait.
Bloody Mary, Bloody Mary, Bloody Mary—

blood pumping, careful, careful,
do not watch her so closely, do not touch
the mirror, do not say her name
too loudly, Bloody Mary, patron saint of fear,
other Mary, other mother in the mirror—she'll come

forward, reach through glass, pull
you into the mirror beside her, behind her, weeping
tears of blood, and there will be no man there.

THE RUNNER OF N-VAMANA
Indrapramit Das

Mira lets the wired nanoswarm saturate every muscle, every neuron in her body. She has been running for four days. With sunrise in her eyes she stops, only to remind herself what not running feels like. Her augmented heart is no longer beating—it's too fast to call it that. It floats like a hummingbird in her chest. The nanoswarm works overtime as she pauses, mending the damage to her muscles and bones, using her skin to synthesize water and energy from the atmosphere and sunlight. Cryofoils embedded in her muscular planes keep her from overheating, sucking at her scorching core temperature. She is alarmed by how inhuman she feels. Four more days, and Mira will be back where she started, back at the huddled settlement of the terraforming station. Looking at the white-hot orb on the horizon, she remembers the adulation of her fellow humans. The settlers, touching her feet and hands, raising their palms to fluorescing clouds pregnant with constant change. Bright array of absorbent prayer flags perched on the settlement's crete houses, snapping in the charged nanite breeze. Voices lifting in song to the old god in the sky, planted by probes centuries ago and still in the flux of maturation: n-Vamana, nanogod that shares its name with the planetoid it shelters and grows.

Alone, n-Vamana above and below her, Mira feels artificial, built, a magnificent sculpture created by nanotechnists and surgeons out of an obsolete body. Artificial like the sun in the sky, no sun at all; a hole punctured into spacetime to flood this dim little world with the light of a distant white giant, and pull it gently into a new orbit. Artificial like the atmosphere, churned into fertility by the work of n-Vamana and the zoati, the seven icy comets driven into the planetoid before it was settled. All artifice worthy of gods. Inhuman, magic, impossible. Her heart, trying to fly out of her chest. Her lungs, breathing air that would asphyxiate an Earthling.

She reminds herself of her brother. The small, human creature that emerged from the same womb she did. Whose augments are still in infancy, growing with him. Her brother, who is an orphan like her. Their mother—dead during the voyage, unable to weather the crushing pressures placed on the human body by the warp-points through which it slipped, by the radiation leaking past shields, by extended zero-g, by the very augments that protect younger bodies from such rigors. Their father—dead on their homeworld while his son was still gestating; crushed by an errant car on the streets of Mumbai's megapolis, cremated, ashes drifting in that atmosphere. Her brother—alive. Nine-year-old Ela, who smeared her ankles and cheekbones with terastil clay—soil from this world mixed with water from Earth, a planet he has never seen. His eyes vacant with wonder at the expanses of even this small planetoid, dizzying after a life spent on a starship. Ela had carried out the ritual as he'd been told, knowing how precious the old-water was, his small hands carefully daubing the cool mud across his sister's Earth-born bones. As Mira looked at him kneeling in front of her with his dirty palms and fingers, as if he were just playing out the impulses of childhood instead of the symbolic narrative of an entire posthuman diaspora, she saw a little boy losing his big sister. New worlds need new stories. New legends. She saw Ela witness her ritual transformation into a cybadevi, a breathing mythmeme for this new world. There was no escaping what the whole settlement felt at that moment, as Ela painted Mira's carbon-reinforced ankles in front of the chanting settlers, the flaring sky. All augmented to some degree, all in the process of cyba-meld to help them stay alive here. But none like her, none trained and modified over nine years to become this new being that might just survive its test. Of all of them, she was the least human.

She was now the Runner of n-Vamana. She was more than just Mira.

Knowing this, Mira had run her hand through Ela's short, damp hair. She had gathered it in her fist and given it a tug.

"Aoh," he whispered. A single quick syllable, universal. Pain. The pain woke him. It reminded him, perhaps, of his sister. His sister Mira. Mira, the girl who'd once teased him for being afraid of the void outside the chilly starship windows, who told him there were monsters who ate little boys out there in the dark between the stars. Mira, who had long hair then, before she cut it off, whose braids he'd watched float in the starlight of viewing ports, coiling away from her head as she read on her tablet novels written millennia ago. Mira, who held him close when he longed for a parent, helped with his lessons, taught him to grow and prepare gcel rations; who'd tethered and tucked him into his sleeping pod and told him her distant memories of a crowded Earth.

His hair in her fist. The pain made him look up, look into her eyes so she could smile at him. He smiled back. A weak smile, but a smile all the same. She could ask for no more than that, on the eve of her run.

"Don't run away forever. Come back," Ela said.

Even with her muscles burning with energy beyond what an unaugmented human being could produce, she pressed her lips to Ela's sweaty forehead, to let him know that his sister was still there under the glow of this devi's tattoos, the flicker of glyphs across this devi's photosynthetic skin.

"Yashin ti terra, Ela," she said in the star-tongue of their vessel, now a language of n-Vamana. [I] Swear on Earth, Ela. Blue gem in the sky, fragile, waiting, birthplace, memory. Swear on Earth. Ela had nodded, convinced.

And then she ran.

She is not dead, yet. It is working. All of it. She is halfway through the test, halfway across the planetoid. She has run faster than any man or woman since humans walked, faster than machines, faster than Mercury, Hermes, Flash, Maya. This is impossible, it is madness, but she has done it. Four more days. Mira will test the limits of their augmentations, prove how far they can take humans on this little planetoid, just as the warp hole and the atmospheric nanogod sheathing the world has taken n-Vamana beyond its own provenance as a lifeless speck in the universe. In her electric limbs, she holds change itself. She is the messenger, and the message. She will prove how little food or water they will need here, how effectively they can process the changing atmosphere outside the settlement, even while pushing at the limits of the human system.

Every time she thinks: this is impossible, she thinks of Ela. Child she has raised alone in a vessel that carried them through the howling emptiness of the universe. Who can speak and write, and love, despite not having seen a world to live on till now, despite having only his sister as a guardian. She, grief-struck orphan, has somehow become a mother to her little Ela.

Impossibilities that bring her back to the ground, even as she shears the very air with her speed, slashing the crust of n-Vamana.

There is a strange vertigo that accompanies her, running on the back of this celestial dwarf, its gravity low despite a superdense core that keeps her from soaring into flight. It was, after all, chosen by her people because of its small size—easier to terraform. It is the first of its kind, to be wreathed and gifted with life-nurturing power by humans—an experimental home for the first of the cybas. At night, running by the crests of n-Vamana's low hills, she has seen past the nanogod's aurora and to the stars, the moon-blue glow of the system's actual sun, too far away to give this place its own life. To the Jovian giant Shesha, its gaseous curve burning the star-studded dark, distance turning it deceptively small, a delicate red sickle suspended in the black. And she has felt more alone than ever before, dizzy from the sensation that she is running across a tiny rock in space, her legs barely tethered to the ground. At other times, with the galaxy crowning the night, that same loneliness has nurtured a euphoria so strong that Mira has had to slow down and linger on it, to take in a horizon empty of human life, glimmering with luminescence of burgeoning algal fields, tunnelled sunlight of the warp hole sparking off embryonic microbial oceans pooling out of the sky, to bask in the illusory sensation that she *is* n-Vamana, that she is beyond humanity, that she is this world incarnate, a deity carving its path through spacetime, aeons from the flocked and boiling Earth and its anxious worshippers who wait for distant strains of information filtering out of the cosmos. The datastreams of humanity's trembling colonization of deep space, its evolution into space-faring cyba, bolstered against an unfathomable infinity. After nearly a decade of running and training her augmentations in the confines of a starship's centrifuges, always surrounded by walls to keep the void out, running across n-Vamana feels like no freedom Mira has ever imagined. In these moments, she has become the cybadevi she is meant to be, a legend in the nascent history of this world, embodiment of n-Vamana like the dim, remote gods that gave their ancient names to the solar worlds near Earth. It has taken four sunrises, four times washed by the borrowed light of a star centuries in the past blinding her tear-shot eyes, to wake her from these trances of divinity.

E-la. Two syllables, named on Earth, spoken by a mother and father long gone. Ela. Ela. Ela. She whispers, veils of steam rising off her superheated body.

Mira is cyba, but human still.

She sees into the future, when her likeness will grace the domed ceiling of the port, immortalized in a mosaic of stone chips, their colours unlike anything Earthlings ever saw, mined from the crust her feet cling to right now. New arrivals will look up at her for generations to come, glittering above them, a new myth born on this place. Earthlings will look at their textbooks and read about her centuries from this moment, and light incense in front of shrines in her honour, smoke lilting through glowing 3D portraits of her carried in the pulsing hot dataservs of starships; they will look through their telescopes to the constellation where her memory dwells, the runner in the night sky, herald of the long awaited galactic age. The pioneer of the cybas, the runner of n-Vamana. She doesn't care that these things will happen. Rather, she actually does care about these things, but is just too wired to realize this. Right now, all Mira can see is forward motion. She wants to run, to live, to survive. She can feel the union between her body and the nanoswarm, between her colony and n-Vamana, its atmosphere seeded and transforming even as she breathes and sweats. At this moment, what she cares about is the finish, a hemisphere away, drawing a human line across the planetoid to her little brother Ela, her fallible flesh and blood, waiting, waiting for his sister to run around the world and return to him.

IN THE YEAR TWO THOUSAND ELEVEN

Jan Conn

Scent of black cherry kindling lingers in the patchwork
building, cast-iron stove still ticking over, warm to the
gloved touch. We have skidded to a halt, breathless, nervy,
guided here by a finger gliding across a small screen.

The dock has been jimmied from its pilings, quagmired on shore,
woodgrain magnified beneath a slick of ice. Positioned to catch
roof run-off, a wooden barrel slips its hoops. We posit
a sculpture of dock, metal and nearby rock, execution

iffy (acetylene torch, glue gun), but plausible.
Drawn to the edges of hemlock light,
we cantilever ourselves upward for the singular view
of the creature—upright, teetering

on a snowbank. Its arms are old propellers with crusty,
frostbitten tips. Metal birdcage for a head.
Below it are silvered fish houses, nominally
unremarkable, voltaic in this swarming light. One of us has traced

on the windcombed snow the blurred outline
of our former home. There is no explanation
for the fanatic promiscuity of white, or the bird skulls dangling
at the creature's side. Now we are prone, on the edge

of the coast, the horizon punctuated by a black twig.
The green metallic hysteria we thought of as extreme sky
is an ice cliff, looming, fresh from the ruins of Antarctica.
Cracking, shearing. Eviscerating daylight.

LESSER CREEK:
A LOVE STORY, A GHOST STORY

A.C. Wise

Standing on the trestle bridge, a boy and girl stand side by side. They can just see the water through the trees. Directly below the bridge, abandoned rails curve gentle to their vanishing point. Weeds grow between the cracked ties, and two children walk, kicking stones along the track.

On the bridge, the girl looks at the water. Lesser Creek. It seems familiar somehow. The greenery does its best to swallow the sparkle and shine, keeping the light at bay. But all along the bank, running parallel to the tracks, muddy paths cut through the growth, and run down to the water's edge. Hoof-paths, paw-paths, and foot-paths, carve gaps in the green. They are made for stolen sips and stolen kisses, midnight swims, and midnight drownings.

She remembers fireflies.

Maybe it wasn't this bend of the creek, but some other. She wants to remember blue shadows between the trees, and the secret-wet smell of earth, bare feet trailed in cool water, and luminescent bugs flashing Morse-code transmissions from another world. And so she does. Who's to say her truth is wrong?

"It wasn't always like this, was it?" Memory nags, and she asks the question, wishing she didn't have to break the silence that has stretched between them for so long.

The boy beside her watches the children's dwindling figures, following the rails.

"Do you think we could catch them all?" he asks.

For a moment she thinks he must be talking about the fireflies she wants to badly to remember. But his past isn't her past; his memory is otherwise, and as inconsistent as hers. Who knows what meaning the creek and the rails hold for him?

Side by side on the bridge, the boy and girl are roughly the same age: fifteen, sliding backward to ten and upward to twenty, depending on who is looking. It is the age they've always been, for as long as they can remember. Which isn't very long.

She remembers fireflies, and sometimes, she remembers drowning.

She looks at the boy side-wise, wondering how he died. *If* he died. Have they had this conversation before? She picks up a stone, weighing it a moment in her palm before letting it fly. It pings the steel, reverberating like the memory of trains.

Maybe one of the children looks back at the sound, and maybe they don't. Everyone knows these woods, that bridge, these rails, that water, are haunted.

The girl picks up another stone, frowns, and closes it in her hand.

"Will we bet, then?" she says. This seems familiar, too.

"Yes, A bet," the boy agrees. "And a tally, on that big rock in the water."

He points through the trees; she knows the stone—a big boulder planted firm in the creek's middle, dividing the current.

"At the end of the summer, we'll count up the marks, and see who wins," the boy says.

A cicada drones. The sound means heat to her, summer-sweat and irritation so sharp she can taste it. She shivers all the same. It won't take much for the boy to win, between the airless nights and the far worse days, the sun beating down on everything and pushing people to the edge. She bites her lip, but she's already nodding.

The rails, stretching one way lead to the horizon, and in the other, they lead to a town. It nestles around a vast crossroad, and maybe, for that alone, it's cursed.

Could it be the town that calls them, again and again, this boy, and this girl, in their myriad forms? Or does the town exist because they come here again and again to stand on this bridge, over these rails, beside that water, to bet on the town's souls?

The town has never borne her any love, the girl thinks. Not for the boy at her side, either. She should take joy in the reaping, but she never does. There is a hunger in her, a hole deep at her core; it is in her nature to wish that hole full.

She isn't greedy. One soul, just one soul, ripe and sweet as the last summer peach, might last her all winter long. She looks sidelong at the boy beside her, and breathes out slow.

"Deal," she says.

"Deal." The boy spits in his hand.

The devil's own twinkle shines in his eye. They shake on it, and go their separate ways.

And so the summer begins.

The first time you see her, you think: *She isn't real*. Because you've lived in Lesser Creek your whole life, and you've never seen her—never even seen a girl *like* her—before.

Your second thought is: *She's a ghost*. Because everyone knows these woods are haunted, and didn't a girl drown here years ago? All the stories say so.

She's sitting on a wooden bridge over the narrowest part of the creek. Her legs dangle over the water; one hand touches the topmost rail, fingers curled as if to haul up and flee at any moment. Her hair screens her face, but you know she's chewing her lip in concentration. Just like you know exactly what colour her eyes are, even though you haven't seen them yet. They are every colour you can imagine, and so is her hair. Because even looking at her full-on in the sunlight, you can't tell anything about her for sure.

She is definitely a ghost.

You sit next to her, legs dangling beside hers, close, but not touching. Your mismatched laces trail from scuffed shoes. She doesn't flee, and so you say, "Hey."

You say it carefully, not looking her way. You think of a deer, ready to be startled, though she's nothing like that at all. She could swallow you whole.

Where she sits, the air is cooler, like the deepest part of the creek, where the sunlight doesn't touch. Viewed side-wise, you can see right through her. Her skin is blue, her hair moonlight, and you just *know*, when she finally turns your way, her eyes will be stones, and her will lips stitched closed. And you decide that's okay.

Then she *does* turn, dropping her hand from the top rail to the sun-warmed wood, almost touching yours. And she's as real and solid as you.

"Hey," she says, and smiles.

Nothing changes. She isn't real. She can't be. Because girls like her don't smile at you. They frown, and they're suddenly very busy, always with somewhere else to be when you're around.

This girl smiles at you. So she must be a ghost, even though the sunlight catches the fine down on her legs and turns it crystalline. You know it's a lie. The hair brushing her shoulders, the shadow in the hollow of her throat, the peach-fuzz lobes of her un-pierced ears, and the scab on her left knee—these are all a skin stretched over the truth of her. She is a hungry ghost, and she will devour your soul.

And you decide that's okay, too.

She tells you a name that isn't hers. You give her one in return. The water murmurs, and you talk about nothing. Time stretches to infinity.

Maybe, just maybe, her fingers brush yours when she finally stands up to leave.

"Will I see you again?" you say, hoping your voice isn't too full of need.

She doesn't answer, but her teeth flash bright in a nice, even row.

And so your summer begins.

The first murder occurred on a Tuesday. Or rather, it was discovered on a Tuesday, but the body had been cooling over two weeks, based on the flies buzzing over the sticky blood, and the discarded pupa cases nestled in the once-warm cavities.

Crime of passion. Scratches, bruises, evidence of a struggle, but none of a break-in. Spouses—one dead, one fled.

On a Thursday, the missing spouse turns up two counties over. A confession ensues.

Outside the county Sheriff's Office, the boy from the bridge leans against sun-warmed brick, and smiles. He chews bubblegum, shattering-hard, packaged flat in wax paper with trading cards. Collectors throw away the gum, keep cards. Not him. He savours the dusty-blandness, the unyielding material worked by teeth and tongue until it bends to his will. He throws the cards away, precisely because he knows they will be collectors' items one day.

He listens through an impossible thickness of brick, plaster, and glass to the blubbered admission of guilt. There are tears; he can smell them, even over the cooked-hot pavement crusted with shoe-flattened filth. It smells of summer.

Sweat and stress and a tipping point—all the ingredients he needs. A beery night, a whispered word, a suggestion of infidelity. A death born of rage. This is the way it's always been. His finger, the feather, the insubstantial straw snapping the camel's spine.

The boy pushes away from the wall. Struts, hands shoved deep in too-tight, acid-washed pockets. Hair, slicked-back. He might have a comb tucked into one pocket, or a pack of cigarettes rolled in one white sleeve, depending on the slant of light that catches him.

He commands the sidewalk. Dogs, children, old men, fall into step behind him. Old women *tsk* from the safety of their porches. Young girls, well, it's best not to say what they do.

He heads west, strolling past scrub-weed and abandoned lots to the fullness of wild fields, cuts left to the creek.

He shucks shoes, wades in, and lays a hand against the massive boulder splitting the water. It is graffiti-strewn, perfect for sunbathing. Perfect for other things, too.

The boy chooses a sharp-edged stone from the current, and makes a single mark on the boulder's side—a white line on the grey.

His summer has just begun.

This is what the world tells us about girls: They are always hungry.

They are cruel.

They will suck out your soul, and leave a dead, dry husk behind.

They will laugh at your pain.

That's why we stitch up their mouths with black thread. We cut out their eyes, and replace them with stones to stay safe from their tears.

This is what the world tells us about boys: they are hungry, too.

They grab food with both hands, stuff it in their mouths, careless of what they eat, never bothering to chew.

They are too loud.

They break everything around them, without even noticing it is there.

That's why we catch them by the tail, so they won't turn around and bite. That's why we cut off their heads, fill their mouths with dirt, and bury them at the crossroads. That's why we burn their hearts, because unlike girls, we know they'll never feel a thing.

It is all true, and every word is a lie. Don't believe anything anyone tells you about ghosts or devils.

The second time you see her, you think: *This can't be real.*

Because it's too perfect. It's the Fourth of July, and you're at yet another bend in the creek. (With her, it's always water.)

The grass is dry, but it remembers rain. The creek—angry here—smells of mud, death, and time. Things have drowned here. Things have been swept away and forgotten. Things sink, and sometimes they rise.

But you take the water for granted; you always have.

A bonfire leaps high, smelling of meat and burnt sugar and wood. There are fireworks, fractured light captured and doubled, each boom-crack echoing your heartbeat, and reverberating in your bones.

You are surrounded by people you see every day. They live behind counters in the local stores; they line porches, and spit tobacco; they drive the bus carrying you to school. Except tonight, they are strangers. Tonight they are demons. And in a world of strangers and demons, you latch onto the only girl you've never seen before. The only one you know for sure isn't real.

She is solid and warm. The fireworks stain her with cathedral window colours. She smiles, and her teeth turn crimson, emerald, and gold. She is fierce and wild, too hard to hold. But you take her hand.

She leans her head on your shoulder. Her hair tickles your skin, and you smell her above and beyond the campfire, which is black powder and pine needles. She smells of soap and smoke, but also of water, of deep and sunken things. It's a creek smell, and breathing it is drowning, but you do it just the same. You think: *This is love.*

It's the Fourth of July, but *this* is where summer begins.

There's a story they tell in Lesser Creek about a girl who drowned. She had just turned fifteen, or seventeen, or twenty-one.

Just shy of fifteen, she was sad all the time, without ever knowing why. There was nothing wrong with her, other than being fifteen—a world of tragedy in its own right.

The girl was hungry constantly, and never full. When she simply couldn't stand it anymore, she went down to the creek, filled her pockets with stones, and lay in the deepest part of the water with her eyes open until she drowned.

If you go to just the right spot, where the water is the coldest and your feet don't quite touch, you'll hear her. It's hard to be still, treading water, but if you hold your breath, make your limbs only a fish-belly flash in slow motion, never rippling the surface, she'll whisper your name.

These woods are full of ghosts.

Near twenty-one, she was a farmer's daughter. She got in the family way, and her parents locked her up, and forced her to carry the child to term. Maybe the baby was stillborn, and maybe she delivered it screaming, bloody, and alive. Either way, she ran away the night it came.

She ran to the trestle bridge, and threw the baby off just as a train went howling past. Who can say which wailed louder, the baby or the train? Overcome by guilt, she threw herself after the child. Her body rolled down the slope, and the creek carried it away.

If you stand at the very centre of the bridge and drop a penny, when it lands, you'll hear a baby cry. Except sometimes it's the lonely mourn of a train vanishing toward the horizon. And sometimes it's a girl, just shy of twenty-one, weeping for her sins.

At seventeen, she was murdered. Her killer cut out her eyes, and replaced them with smooth stones. He stitched up her lips with black thread, and left her in the shallowest part of the creek where the water barely covered her.

The stories say her killer was a drifter, or the devil himself. They say he confessed the same day the murder was done, screaming it all over the town square. When everyone came to see what all the fuss was about, he wept, inconsolable.

He cut her eyes out, because she wouldn't stop looking at him. He sewed her lips shut, because she wouldn't stop whispering his name. They hanged him just the same.

All of these stories are true. Every one of them is a lie.

The girls of Lesser Creek leave flowers for the hungry ghost at the water's edge, and burn candles in her nameless name. The boys bring pretty toys, and line them up all in a row. The old women bake oat cakes, sweetened with blood, and the old men mumble prayers. Each brings their hopes and fears, and such desperate love.

No matter what they bring, the ghost is hungry still.

The second murder comes late July. In-between, there are a string of assaults, a petty theft, one count of grand larceny, and a host of undocumented sins.

The boy follows the hoof-paw-shoe-hewn path through the branches to cross the shallow water near every day. He can do that, no matter what the stories say. The wavelets glitter bright, wash sweat and grime from his skin. His toes grip slick stones, and he never falls.

He makes another mark on the boulder's side. They multiply like rabbits, like flies. They turn the grey stone dense and arcane. There is power here not found in the other graffiti. And the stone itself is rife with meaning, too—stolen kisses, secrets trysts. Oaths are sworn here, fated for breaking. It is all his doing. Or so the oath-breakers and kiss-stealers say. He drove them to it; it's what devils are for.

He has a tally of at least a dozen-dozen, and it is only July. The girl's space is empty.

He watches her, sometimes, courting her soul slow, taking her time. She is hungry; the boy sees it in her eyes. But sometimes she smiles.

And when she does, he realizes his belly is empty, too.

The marks on the stone don't fill him like they should.

Once upon a time, he was a musician. Once upon a time, he was good at cards. He was driven out of town, beaten with a stick, hung at midnight. His heart has burned countless times. He has tricked and been tricked, loved the wrong man and the wrong woman. It is always the same in the end.

Once upon a time, he walked the rails. Once upon a time, a canvas strap bit his shoulder, soaking sweat, gaining dirt. Walking, he ran. He trusted wrong, sleeping in open box cars, warming his hands by vagrant fires. He gave too much of himself away. He swapped stories, and accidentally told the truth.

He found himself dead, spit dirt from a shallow grave, and walked again.

He jumps on stumps, and has a quick hand. Dice and cards always fall his way.

Even though the marks crowding the stone aren't as triumphant as they should be, the boy makes another one, and drops the sharp stone. The creek vanishes it, a card up a magician's sleeve.

This is what the boy and the girl both know, even when they made their deal: It isn't fair. They have been given roles to play—ghost and devil, hungry to the very end.

The summer ticks past, far too slow.

There's a story they tell about the time the devil came to Lesser Creek. The townspeople chased him all along the rails. They caught him, and killed him, cut off his head and buried it upside down. They drove a spike through the ground to make sure he couldn't pick it up again.

But will-o-wisps still drift under the trestle bridge in the dead-black of night, the devil's own lanterns, leading the damned to the water's edge. And if you walk along the ties at midnight and count thirteen from the moment you pass under the bridge, you'll hear the devil breathing behind you. If you take one step back, you'll find the twelfth tie missing and he will reach up and drag you down to hell.

The first time the devil came to Lesser Creek, he was just a boy, no more than seventeen. He committed a crime, or maybe folks just didn't like the way he looked at them. Maybe the summer was too hot, and tempers were too short.

Even though he looked just like an ordinary boy, they pulled up rail spikes, and nailed them right back down through his feet and his hands. When they came back after three days, the body was gone.

No one brings flowers or blood-sweetened cakes to the old rail line. When old women pass, they spit, and old men still drive an iron spike between the twelfth and thirteenth ties on moonless nights to this very day.

It is a lonely place.

When the devil came to Lesser Creek the second time, he made a deal with a drifter who dared to skim stones along the steel rails just to hear them sing. If the man brought the devil twenty souls by summer's end, his own would be spared, no matter how he sinned.

It was a mass-murder summer. A fire and brimstone summer. Preachers thundered through the churches of Lesser Creek, damnation heavy on their tongues. The air clotted thick; wasps drowned in sweat, humming between the pews and banging their heads against the stained glass. Birds fell from trees, hearts baked within the delicate cages of their bones.

All the fans stopped turning. Ice cream sizzled before it could touch the cone. Soda went flat in every fountain. Cold water forgot to flow, except in the creek where no one dared go. Wives beat their husbands; fathers cursed their daughters. Boys burst into tears for no reason, and kicked their dogs.

And the drifter came, and the drifter went, and bodies piled like leaves in his wake. No one could ever say if it he did the killing, or not. But every man, woman, and child in town swore up and down they heard laughter echoing along the train tracks, and it was the devil's very own.

The next time you see her, you *know* she is a ghost, because she kisses you. And girls like her don't kiss you.

You are sitting side by side, hand in hand, by the creek, always by the creek. Her feet are next to yours, relaxed where yours are tense. Your footprints sink into the mud. Hers are ephemeral, and disappear.

You grip her hand too tight, and sweat gathers between your palms. Planted in the dirt, feet in the current, you look toward the rock snagging the centre of the stream. Graffiti scores it. It is a magical, mystical thing;

a totem centering all the summer days in danger of flying off the edge of the world.

How un-solid these liminal years of your life are. At any moment, at every moment, you are in danger of losing cohesion. The rock in the centre of the stream is eternal. It says *X was here*, and that is real—tribal and shamanistic. Written in stone it can't be denied. If you vanish, the rock will remain, a record of your being.

Here and now, she kisses you, and it grounds you, too. It is the culmination of a summer's worth of desire. It is the inevitable consequence of bridges and fireworks and the muddy banks of creeks. It is the only outcome of frog-song and bug-drone, and all the other milestones of the season.

And she says, or doesn't say, but you hear, "All I want is one little piece of your soul. It won't hurt, not yet. You won't even know it's gone until much later. One day, you'll wake up, not in love with me anymore, old, and looking back on your life, and wonder where that part of you went. It'll sting for a moment, and you'll move on. Is that so bad?"

Her fingers lace yours, and the whole time she looks at the water, not you.

She says, "I'll fill you up with me, so you'll never know anything is missing."

She pauses so you think she regrets what comes next. It's what you've always known was coming since you saw her on the bridge.

She is a hungry ghost.

Here and now, you love her for her pity. You pity her for her love. It isn't fair. And so you forgive her, because you've been hungry, too.

She says, "Before you agree understand that if you give me that piece of your soul, it's mine forever. That's how love works. It consumes you. The moment it ends, you can't see past it to a day down the road when you won't be split open and bleeding for the whole world to see. In the wound, you can't see the scar, or even the scab. Memories and hindsight belong to the future. This is here, this is now."

You know how this will end. You have always known how this will end.

You hold her hand, tighter than you've held anyone's hand before, and you agree. You give her your soul.

The summer seems very short now. You have so little time.

A third murder rolls around mid-August, but it holds no joy. The boy is winning by default. He longs for a reversal, a revolt, a turn of fortune. He longs for a trick to grab him by the tail.

He never asked for this, no more than she did. He is a ghost, and she is a devil. The woods have always been haunted, and so have they.

Vandalism. Arson. A near-murder that doesn't quite take. He whispers temptation. He pours jealousy, hate, venom, all into willing ears. In the end, he's powerless. So is she. They only take what the world gives them.

He makes another mark, drops the stone in the water. The creek chills him. He wades to shore, wishing the summer would end.

She tells you it is over.

She told you; she is telling you; she will always be telling you. And. It. Is.

Welts rise on your skin. Psychological, but so real.

Of course, it had to happen this way. Nobody loves you, ever loved you, ever will. And part of you knows, bitter, that you are being oh so dramatic, so you laugh. But you cry, too. She warned you, told you what she was doing as she did it, but you handed your soul over anyway, because you wanted it so goddamned bad.

Even though, deep down, you know, godfuckingdamnit, you will never be good enough to be loved. Someone else will always win, always be better than you. You will always be hungry, while everyone else is full.

So you walk the trestle bridge, where you can just see the water. You think about the summer, all the people who died, lied, cheated, and stole. The whole fucking town is going to shit, but what do you care? And what would they care if you jumped right now?

They probably wouldn't even notice you'd gone.

But you don't. You won't. And you turn away.

And maybe someone looks back at the sound of something heavy never hitting the rails. And maybe they don't. Because everyone knows these woods, that water, those trees, these rails, are haunted anyway.

She makes a mark on the stone, one shaky line. He stands on the shore, arms crossed, watching. He wants to smile, but it makes his cheeks hurt, as if the rock-hard bubblegum left splinters in his skin. His feet, planted in the mud, ache. He remembers running; she remembers drowning. In the end, it is the same.

In this moment, he loves her for her pity, and he pities her for her love. Could she, would she, ever pity him?

By the stone, she wants to weep, but she smiles, and it tastes of tears. She looks at him, standing in a slant of sunlight, watching her.

One soul, her tally.

He reaches for her, their fingers almost touching.

It is never enough.

His side of the stone is crowded; she has one single soul to her name. It is sweet, oh so sweet, but it won't sustain her to winter's end. His souls, crowded thick as they are, are candy-floss, melting on the tongue and never touching his belly.

They have played this game before, and no one ever wins.

She is sick to death of hunger and drowning. He is sick to death of treachery and spit-sealed deals. But they are what they have always been, and what they always will be.

These are the stories they tell you about hungry ghosts, and hungry devils. Every one of them is a lie, and all of them are true.

He reaches for her; she takes his hand. His fingers pass right through hers, leaving her hungrier still. His sigh is the echo of a lonely train running the rails out of town; hers, cold water running over stones.

The season ticks over to fall. A leaf drifts down, caught by the current and swept away, and they look to the bridge just visible through the thinning trees. They know, they both know, next summer they will stand there and start all over again.

And they ache, hoping next time they will remember, next time, they'll get it right.

THE BOOK OF VOLE (EXCERPTS)
Jane Tolmie

1. Meet Vole

Literature is open to everybody,
even pests.

2. Vole Feed

Nerve-wrung creatures, wasp, bee and bird,
felons for life or keepers of the cell, and
Vole in a wooden crib of seed and feed.

3. Winter Vole

Winter kept Vole warm, covering
Earth in forgetful snow, feeding
A little life with dried tubers.

4. Vole Seasons

Vole has a winter too of pale misfeature,
Or else Vole would forego a mortal nature.

5. Sleepy Vole

How hard it is for Vole to sleep
in the middle of life.

6. Troubled Vole

Vole is troubled
by the occasional
flea.

7. Further Honey

A smell of further honey,
embittered flowers,
sirens Vole.

8. Vole Venture

Venture for the Vole!

9. Observing Vole

Among twenty snowy mountains,
The only moving thing
Was the eye of Vole.

10. Curious Vole

Vole wonders if honour
to an ancient name
be due.

11. The City of Vole

Through me the way is to the city volent
Through me the way is to eternal Vole.

12. Transient Vole

As for Vole,
Vole is a watercolour. Vole washes off.

13. Vole Collection

Vole searches on endless sandbars in the dark
for building blocks to make Vole's empire great.

14. Sensual Vole

Imagine, amid the mud and the mastodons,
Vole sighing and yearning with tremendous creative yearning
for some other beauty.

15. Swarming Voles

vole vole vole vole vole vole vole vole Vole vole vole
vole vole vole vole Vole vole vole vole Vole vole vole
vole vole vole vole VOLE VOLE vole vole
volevolevolevolevolevolevolevole
vole vole vole vole vole vole vole vole Vole vole
vole vole vole vole vole Vole vole vole vole
Vole vole vole vole vole vole vole VOLE VOLE
vole vole volevolevolevolevolevolevolevole
vole vole vole vole vole vole vole vole Vole vole vole
vole vole vole vole Vole vole vole vole Vole vole vole
vole vole vole vole VOLE VOLE vole vole
volevolevolevolevolevolevole
AGH!

16. Hard Times

Life is hard but
Vole pays no tax.

17. Hungry Vole

By the glow-worm's light well guided,
Vole attends the Feast provided.

18. Vole Wisdom

It causes nothing but grief
to want to sleep with the gods.

19. Hunted Vole

The falcon cannot hear the falconer,
nor can Vole.
Things fall apart.

20. Vole's Nightmare

Vole kneels in the nights
before tigers
that will not let Vole be.

21. Volenerable

Ouch!
Vole hurts.

22. Vole Compassion

Smaller and more helpless
but as deeply felt
miniscule lives
extinguished.

23. Vestigial Vole

Vole, you there?

24. Jesting Vole

Vole jests at scars.
Vole never felt a wound.

25. Loser Vole

It's not true,
of course.
The art of losing
is
hard to master.

26. Poem without a hero

Vole is
no hero.

27. Stoic Vole

Vole does not fondle the weakness inside
though it is there.

28. Vole

Vole is not Vole
which alters.

29. Constant Vole

The woods have no voice but the voice of complaining
but Vole
holds fast.

30. Mistaken Vole

Vole is mistaken
for a shadow or symbol.

31. Procession

One had a cat's face,
One whisked a tail,
One tramped at a rat's pace,
One crawled like a snail,
One was Vole.

32. Strong Vole

Vole is not proved too weak
To stand alone.

33. Shadow Vole

Vole has a dark side.

34. Sage Vole

When the sun rises on ugliness, it is stark to see.
Vole does not carry it home.

35. Vole Heals

There will be mornings of sunlight
after the end of all things.

36. Vole Marker

When the dust falls over Vole's thoughts
over Vole's head with its gleaming jaws,
the brows made beige and ugly, into a blown ripple
into a snake of powder on the trail,
chance will maybe leave an edge
marking the jawbones, the dust wandering in the sun.

37. Vole in Love

Vole's vegetable love grows
Vaster than empires, and more slow.

38. Happy Vole

Vole has a green thought
in a green shade.

39. Vole Pride

Pest is best!

To view a selection of the accompanying original artwork by British Columbia artist Perry Rath (http://www.perryrath.com/), see Strange Horizons 2013:
http://www.strangehorizons.com/2013/20130506/tolmie-p.shtml

BLACK HEN À LA FORD
David Nickle

We cooked her, feathers and all, during the last hundred miles of that long drive to Agatha's Perch . . . and oh, her fume filled the cab with such a wonderful, peaceable scent. One might drift off to sleep by it—and that is precisely what I did.

I dreamed of the kitchen, hot with the afternoon sun and fire of the wood stove, the steam off the slowly cooling meat pies on the sill. . . . Gudrun, my dear sister, humming an old chant as she rolled out dough for more—out of sight, in the pantry. . . .

Were it not for that, I almost might have forgotten—what I'd come to do.

William had gutted her with an old scaling knife. After wiping the blood off, he applied the blade to coring crab-apples we'd filched from the same farm as we'd found her. He stuffed them up inside the cavity until she was ready to burst. He shoved salted roast peanuts and some pork rinds up between skin and breast, and he took two layers of thick-gauge tinfoil, wrapped her up tight and wedged her against the exhaust manifold. Then he turned the oven on—that's to say the oven of his truck, by driving it fast on the straightaways and too fast on the turns, into the foothills, up to the Perch.

"Black Hen à la Ford," he said when he finally cracked the hood and pulled her free.

She was hot in her bright shell, and he tossed that hen from hand to hand as we all gathered in the late afternoon haze, in the shade of that old house on the ridge.

"Voila!" he hollered, and we all howled.

William is a good grandson. Not the best, but I'd never dream of telling him that.

There were a lot of grandchildren at the Perch already and more to arrive before nightfall. Grandchildren, and nieces and nephews—great-grandchildren, maybe even a great-great-grandchild.

I lose track of them all, but I know the families: Alfred's and Rainer's, Kerr's and Lars's, and of course Gunnar's.

It was their turn this time. So of course they were there.

Janet, Gunnar's wife, had set up long tables on the front lawn, and dangled paper patio lanterns above them from the tree branches. She'd even arranged for two old blue plastic privies, side by side next to the old garden house.

Not far from that, a long green hose dribbled water into the grass. It was a good idea; you could wash up after doing your business, without ever feeling need of setting foot indoors.

Janet took the chicken from William and ran up the path to the house so William could go to the back and get my things.

There wasn't much to get: just an old suitcase with a new frock and a set of iron fry-pans—wrapped up in newspaper and covered in a green garbage bag. I packed them myself two days back, with great care. Wouldn't do for them to rust; it'd taken decades to season them right.

William carried them in one trip to the long porch, set them down next to where Janet had laid his offering. Then it was off to the privy. It'd been a long drive and we'd only stopped the once. Janet took me by the arm, hauled me over to a big green Muskoka chair at the head of the first table.

She said, "You look good, Granny Ingrid," which I didn't care for. No one tells good-looking people they look good.

Janet, now. What Janet looked was tired. There were new lines around her eyes, and her face was red with sunburn. She had probably earned it. The drive was long enough for William and me. We weren't hauling a trailer up the mountain road; there were no children in William's truck. William was young enough to have reserves. I'm old enough to know my limits. Janet, stuck between us, would have wrung herself dry with work, and with worry.

"Where are the girls?" I asked.

She pointed over to the Lookout. My great-grandchildren were there, on their toes, peering over the stone wall that came up to their chins.

That was good. The drop off the lookout was fierce and far, and Lars and his boys had built it so even a grown man would have to mean it, to tip over that edge.

"They're getting big," said Janet. "Amanda's going to be in high school next year." She saw my perplexity, and pointed to the one on the left, coppery hair cropped short at her shoulders. She was bigger than I remembered. But it had been five years. One can't expect time to stand still, where a child's concerned.

"Mandy. And Lizzie—" the smaller of the two, with darker hair braided down her back, was bending down to pick up a pebble "—is she talking yet?" I asked. Last time, Liz only spoke to scream, and there were no words. She was five years old. We'd made a chant then—one of so many—that she wouldn't grow up a retard, but I hadn't much hope for her.

"She is," said Janet. "We put her in a special program at school. Now you can't shut her up."

Liz flung the pebbles overhand, and they rattled through the branches of the poplar trees below.

"Well that's a blessing."

Janet smiled, and waved to her daughters. "Come on over and see Granny Ingrid!"

Amanda waved back, and nudged her little sister, who looked over at us with a stricken expression.

"Oh, let them have their fun. I should go unpack," I said, "before the rest get here."

Janet smiled thinly, and nodded toward the porch.

"That's been taken care of," she said, and I looked over and saw it was true.

The porch was empty. While we were talking, Gudrun had collected my things, William's bird—and carried them all inside.

"I've got lots to do," said Janet. "Talk to your great-granddaughters. She . . . your sister can wait."

Janet left just as her girls arrived. I made a smile for them, and gave them both hugs, and asked them only a few questions before they set in with their talk.

Amanda was enrolled in a basketball program and she was very good at it, thank you very much. Lizzie was learning how to play chess and she wasn't very good yet, but would be soon. Amanda and Lizzie were both fond of a series of novels about a girl a few years older than they were, and her lover, a young man a few years older than she. According to Lizzie, Amanda had let a boy who was also a few years older than she kiss her, and when Amanda shouted no, Lizzie said all right, Amanda had kissed the boy, and asked if that was better? I believe Lizzie was trying to shock me, but it didn't work.

"Are you going to cook today?" asked Lizzie, and Mandy said, "You don't have to," and thought about what she said, and added, "I didn't mean that I don't like your food," which scarcely made matters better.

"We'll see how it goes," I said.

"Mandy means you can let Granny Gudrun do it if you're too tired," said Lizzie.

"I don't think that would do," I said, and lied: "The recipes take two to make their magic work."

"Magic!" said Lizzie. "Black magic!" Her sister shushed her.

"It's just cooking," said Mandy, and then she said to me: "It's not black magic." And after a heartbeat or so, she asked:

"Are you angry with us?"

Now that made me smile. Mandy had put her arm around Lizzie and her eyes were round. Lizzie was a step behind her sister, but as I watched, tendrils of worry crossed her face, like cloud over moon.

"I'm not angry," I said finally. "I'm not tired either. I had a wonderful nap in your Uncle William's truck on the way up. I'm ready for whatever the night brings. Black magic or not."

Mandy tried to smile, tried to laugh, failed at both. Lizzie did better just keeping quiet. I could barely see her trembling as I heard the familiar footsteps approaching behind me.

"You're good girls," I said. "You can run along now."

"They don't have to be told twice," said Gunnar as he stepped around the chair and bent to give me a kiss. "Help your mother!" he called after them as his daughters ran toward their family's van.

Gunnar opened a canvas chair beside me and sat in it.

"You look good," I said, and I *wasn't* lying. Gunnar's daughters had grown beyond recognition, splendid little weeds that they were; Janet's sunburned face was gradually taking on the texture of cowhide, and she was, to be honest, going to fat. Yet Gunnar—here was the same handsome, strapping lad I'd hugged the last time we'd gathered here. He had cut off most of his long blond hair, and shaved the little pirate beard he'd been so proud of. Past that—the years had treated my eldest grandson tenderly. One might even say neglectfully.

"I don't know what you said. But you scared the noses off my girls," he said.

"They scared their own noses off." I reached over and tapped the end of his nose, and finished with that old trick that had made him laugh so when he was but a tyke: lifted my fist, with thumb poked out, nose-ish, between index and middle fingers. "I'll give them this one. They can fight over it."

And that was all it took to make my Gunnar laugh again. But the laughter passed too quickly.

"You have to go in soon," he said.

Soon didn't mean right away. Before I went, I made sure Gunnar brought me up to date.

It had been a good five years since the last hootenanny. Gunnar began the first year still working for Mr. Oates at his construction company. By the end of the year, he was promoted, and in the middle of the second year was promoted again to a job in the office. At three years, Mr. Oates named him his second-in-command. Four years in, and he was a partner. Last year, Mr. Oates took ill, and went home, where he would probably stay until the end. Fingers crossed, I said to Gunnar.

They had a house now. In its back yard was a swimming pool. At the side was a garage, big enough for the minivan and one other car, a fast little red machine that was Gunnar's alone. The house backed on to a shallow ravine with pine trees. It wasn't too far from the office. The girls were happy there, as was Janet.

I too was very happy about all that and said so. I kept my peace when Gunnar leaned close and told me about Marissa, the accommodating young girl from the city that Gunnar would visit twice a week. I couldn't say anything—for that too had been on his list, five years ago. Whatever I might think of it, he had wanted that too.

And then it was time to go inside.

"Good luck, Granny," he said, and gave me a hug. I held it longer than he offered it—though not a quarter as long as was my due.

I found more offerings on the porch when I climbed the steps: a ring of green Jell-O, inside of which were suspended slices of frankfurter, three daisies and perhaps a dozen insects, including a hornet and an enormous dragonfly; long links of a black blood sausage, coiled on a green-tinted plastic platter; a casserole dish, covered in tinfoil and smelling not unpleasantly of paint thinner. It was heavy as a pile of bricks when I tried to lift it. So I left it with the sausage, and carried the Jell-O ring into the foyer.

Not much had changed here in five years. The wallpaper was the same geometric pattern, unlovely three decades ago. It smelled sweet, of pastry and cabbage. I let the door shut behind me, and the smell intensified.

"Hello, Ingrid."

"Hello, Gudrun." She was in the doorway to the kitchen where sunlight silhouetted her. She was sitting, slumped a bit. "Wheelchair now?" I asked.

She coughed, but not in a worrying way. "Wheelchair now. Yes. What's that?"

"Gelatin," I said, and she said, "Bring it here to me."

Gudrun was as fat as one would expect, living her days here at the Perch. Fat was what put her in the wheelchair as much as the years. She held her hands out for the gelatin. I helped her bring it down to her lap, jiggling with its bugs and its meats and its petals. She oohed at it like it was a newborn.

"Oh, this is *lovely*. Who made it?"

"I don't truly know. I didn't see who set it there."

She sniffed at it. "Well it's very creative. It will do fine, I think. Better than the chicken."

"Nothing wrong with the chicken," I said, and she smiled so her lips drew back under her teeth, and squinted down at the offering.

"I suspect Rainer's daughter. Always partial to the insectile. But it will all sort out. We'll take it all up to the Perch later," she said, meaning, of course, I would take it. I lifted the gelatin away and the wheels on the front of her chair squeaked as she turned around, leading me back into the kitchen.

It was not much changed—or to put it another way, what changes there might be were too small for me to be certain of. For years, we had all but lived here—hauling firewood, cleaning floor and countertop, doing the work of the young. . . . But I had not been by for five years now, then five years before that, then five again and again and again. Did the ceiling always warp down so, over the refrigerator? Were there so many flyspecks in the bowl of the lights? Did the wood stove gleam so brightly, as the light struck it from the high windows on the west wall? Had the shelves that covered three walls been painted, again?

And as to the smell of it . . .

Did the larder always smell so?

"Now," Gudrun said, taking her place in the middle of the floor, where the sun always hit this time in the afternoon of a hootenanny, "it's time to work, little sister." She clapped her hands, and grunted. "Find your apron. Fetch the knives. There are mouths to feed."

Gudrun surprised me then. For I was hoping for her to sit there in the warm sun, reminding me where things were, correcting my kitchen chants, demanding spoonfuls of broth for inspection, watching me sweat and bleed and cry, from her wheeled throne.

But no. That had not been our way for many years. And so—

She tilted her head, and drew a long and sore breath . . .

. . . and up she got, swaying and tottering on her thick, inadequate legs. Her grin was fierce as ever as she stumbled to the counter, caught and steadied herself. Huffing, Gudrun held out her hand, and I pulled a long steel flensing knife from the block, passed it to her.

"More and more mouths," she said when she caught her breath, "every time."

Carcasses were first. They were stacked on the counter between the sink and the stove, on long platters: goose and pig and sheep, venison and rabbit. The beasts had been skinned and gutted, but not very much butchered. We set at them fast and hard, Gudrun with knife, I with cleaver. There was a technique to it—we had been rending the carcasses for the better part of a century, Gudrun and I, and we knew our way around a butcher block—but it was not a mindful thing. If blood and gristle splattered—well, that is why we wore aprons, and tied our hair high. We were deft enough that the blades didn't slip, and none of the blood would be ours. In the end, the meat would be ready, stacked in glistening piles of fowl and swine and vermin, ready for flame.

There were vegetables to prepare—a bushel of potatoes mingled with other roots as we required—long stalks of rhubarb and a bucket filled with water, where leeks floated like the pale fingers of children. But we stopped a moment, to rest. I pushed the wheelchair closer so Gudrun could sit in it, but she swatted it away.

"Embarrassing." She looked at the hallway, the windows. Like someone might be watching. Someone might be, I thought, considering it.

"Fine," I said. "I'll sit in it myself." And I plunked myself down in the chair. Gudrun turned so she leaned against the counter. Her face was as slick as the meat; she was sweating like a farmhand.

"It suits you," she said, "better than me."

I laughed, but dutifully.

"You might learn a thing or two," she went on. "Be a better person for it."

I shook my head and smiled. Gudrun could try all she wanted; she wouldn't draw me out.

Still she tried. She ran water in the sink and filled two glasses for us, and wondered how it would have gone with Sam, my first husband, if my spine had stayed bent. I sweetly suggested he might have gone with Gudrun. "He wouldn't have found comfort in *my* bed," she sniffed as she handed me my water in an old jelly glass. "Not my sort."

We set to work on the vegetables then, peeling and chopping with fresh knives, and Gudrun set about reminiscing, with an eye to enumerating all the ways Sam wasn't her sort. He drove like an old woman, she said; he was too thin, and couldn't dance well, nor could he play an instrument. "I don't trust a fellow who's not at least musical. I don't see the sense of one," she said. "It's uncomely."

"He's gone now," I said.

"Yes. We didn't chant *him* well, did we?"

I took a breath, and bore down on the potato. It split like a stump under the weight of the knife, and me.

I might have returned fire. I might have wondered at Gudrun's own marriage, and the way her life had been warped around it. We had never properly shared Sam; he was mine. But for a time—for quite a time— we'd both shared a bed with the master of Gudrun's house.

Of course, pointing that out . . . well, that would be too cruel. So I kept my peace.

The flames had lived in the stove since dawn. But I threw in another log after we put the meat in the ovens—before we started work on the sauce.

We had branches of rosemary—garlic cloves, peeled and ready to crush under a stone mortar; pink runoff from the carcasses, collected in narrow grooves on the butcher block's edges; and in a tall glass jar, salt, grains as thick as pebbles. . . .

Sauce always being improved with salt.

Gudrun stopped goading me now that we put down our knives and stood before the fire. I set one of my pans over the firebox then, and we added parts, taking turns, and calling back chants at one another, stirring and stoking. It was work now, and tricky work at that. Everything could be undone if we missed a note, a beat. . . .

We got on best at moments like these.

The sun crossed the kitchen as it filled with smoke and fume, and we sang and chanted the usual storm: begged for health and well-being for the assembled families—good pay, light work for the fathers . . . for dire circumstances to fall on those who might stand against them. We put our heads together and got nearly all the names right, and Gudrun had a list of them tacked onto the refrigerator so we'd be sure. We poured off the sauce, tar thick, the colour of beets, into an urn, and I slid it into the warming oven next to the first platter of meat.

"They'll be getting hungry," said Gudrun. "It's nearly eight."

I nodded. "Later than usual, but not much."

Gudrun wiped her arm across her forehead, and motioned for the wheelchair. I brought it, and helped her back into it. She was sweaty and slow, and her breathing was shallow.

"You watch the roasts," I said. "You can do that from the chair."

"Not if I have to haul them out I can't."

"There's time on them yet." I looked out the door to the hall, the stairs. "But you're right. They will be getting hungry. I'd best get up there."

She didn't argue this time. Just settled back, folded her hands and drew in the scent of the cookery.

"Don't forget the Jell-O," she said, and pointed to the table where I'd put it, hours ago. The evening light refracted around the wieners and insects, and made it glow.

Three trips up and down two flights of stairs and a ladder, and I was ready. At the north corner of the widow's walk, I set the Jell-O. The southern corner, underneath the rooster weather vane, was where I left the blood sausage. I uncovered the casserole dish, and set it in the east.

And William's chicken—that I carefully unwrapped, and took it to the western corner—where I set, cross-legged, with the bird in the lap of my apron.

The sun was low enough that the flat spot on the roof was actually in shadow, though no tree drew this high. Peering over the edge, I could see the entire world it seemed, to the far horizons; green farmers' fields nearest, dotted with woodlots and finally stretching far to clots of housing. Houses such as that were the due of the families—Gunnar kept his family in one such as that. From the Perch, those modest homes did not seem so much to ask.

Stars began to appear. From below, I heard the families, their murmured conversations, some laughter. It was hard to make out precisely what was being said, from so high. But I knew my progeny. They were hungry, they were. Hungry for life; for wealth; for one another, finally.

These offerings they had made—they weren't offerings, not really. They were demands.

The air was sweet up on the Perch. An evening breeze blew across the treetops, light as a young boy's touch on my cheek. I lifted the chicken William—William and I—had made, into the breeze. The hour was about right now—soon, they would come.

The first lighted on the rooster. Its wings were wide, like rumpled paper. They were maybe wide as my hand. Thick antennae turned toward me, sniffing the offering. I stretched as high as I could without standing. And the moth took off, and circled overhead.

I felt the second on my hand, like the brushing of a curtain.

More would come soon.

When Gudrun and I were young, so many came—Gudrun claimed she near to suffocated under their weight, as they made a blanket over us. It was all I could do not to leap off the Perch, tumble down the steep roof. Oh, such terror—such terror as grows on the flesh of the young. It seemed then that death might have been preferable to the wings of the moth.

In my head, I remember that terror so well. In my heart—it fades.

It was all done in an hour—more, or less.

Put it this way. The stars were fulsome when I could see again. The breeze had shifted, and was cooler on me. Below, the families had become boisterous, percussive—pounding with their fists on the outside of that plastic privy, it sounded like. They all howled like hounds.

In the kitchen, as I stole past, to the celebration outside: silence. Blessed, final silence.

An hour would be about right.

William caught me coming out. He was dangling a beer bottle between two fingers and wiping his face with a sleeve as he climbed the steps to the porch. He'd been into the meat.

"Good food," he said, and I smiled at him, patted his arm. He wanted to ask me how the hen had gone over—how he, *we*, had fared. I could tell. But he wouldn't ask. So we walked quietly down to the families, for the most part gathered under the fickle glow from the paper lanterns.

The meat was all out now, on rows of platters along three picnic tables pushed together. There were a half dozen of our folk lined up on both sides of it. Flesh drooled off their plates, and still they stacked more.

"They don't know when they're full," said William.

"Oink oink," I said, and he laughed. "I'd like some meat myself. I'm surely not full. Could you gather me a plate?"

I let go of his arm then and took charge of one of the lawn chairs. William scooted off to the tables, to do as he was told. I settled down on my own—I'm surely not so old, either—and I leaned back in the chair, tilted my head back to look up into the glow in the branches, from the lanterns. For a time—for a short time—they left me alone, to count the crooks in the branches of the maple tree here. When I'd come here first—the tree mustn't have been more than a sapling. It would be fine to say I remembered that sapling, but really—I couldn't say such a thing. Agatha's Perch has so many trees on it. One's liable to lose track.

"Thank you, Granny Ingrid."

I brought my eyes back down, and looked at Liz. She had crept up on me. I made to smile. "Did you enjoy the meat?"

Liz shrugged her shoulders and rolled her eyes. "I guess," she said. Her mouth was clean of grease—she hadn't had that much, all things considered.

"You *guess*. Did your mother tell you to come over and thank me?"

"No," she said. "Dad did." When I didn't answer, she went on: "Dad said you gave me a holy gift with this meal. He said you blessed all of us with this meal. He said I should say thank you."

"And you have."

I looked back up into the branches.

"Granny," said Liz.

"Yes, child?"

"It seems like a lot of work to do what you do."

"It is a lot of work."

"Why do you do it for us?"

"Love," I said. "I do it out of love."

"Oh Granny!"

And before I could do anything to prevent her, the wretched child—the dear little *retard*—had grappled me around my shoulders, and pressed her face into my breast, and cried out: "I love you too!"

It took all the will I had—but I kept my peace.

William made me a modest plate. There was a thigh-bone from one of the ducks, and a glistening slice of pig belly—and the haunch of a rabbit. I took it, and set the plate on my lap.

"Is that all right?" he asked, and I said, "Just fine."

He stood quiet a moment, rocking back and forth on his heels as I cut into the duck, and finally, he dared ask: "How'd the hen go down?"

I chewed the duck flesh carefully—wouldn't do to choke on it. And then, since he'd asked . . .

"Gudrun's dead."

He nodded. William couldn't really do anything else—he had killed the hen and wrapped it up and tossed it into the belly of his own truck—the same truck he used to bring me here. He'd wished his own wishes, same as I'd wished mine.

"She's in the kitchen," I said.

"She was old," said William, uncertainly.

"She was. The gathering's a lot of work. Even with help."

William started to work it out, and I pursed my lips and nodded.

"I should go in," he said, and I said, "Yes. There's cleaning to be done."

"I should go," William said again. He backed away and half-ran back to the porch. William is a good grandson. When the work becomes clear, William sees to it.

I didn't finish the plate, but others finished theirs, and the night went on. Rainer went into the back of his truck and pulled out his twelve-string guitar, and the children gathered 'round him as he began to play. Rainer fancied himself a blues player, but what he really was, was undisciplined. Fifteen years ago, he had baked a cat into a pie-shell, and brought it to the gathering. I wouldn't touch the filthy thing, but Gudrun carried it to the Perch, and set it out properly, and when the moth-wings were gone—so was the pie.

Rainer made two record albums and one of them was very popular with certain sorts. But he lacked the discipline to take it any further. So now, he shared his gift with the family, at the gathering, and that was all. Although it is not my cup of tea, I must admit it does have its effect.

Rainer had two young sons, and one of them joined him on harmonica, while the other—little Peter, just five years old—pounded on a tambourine. His daughter Freya sang along. Lizzie and Mandy hung close—the older boy, James, would be a handsome specimen in a few years. At twelve, he already had his two young cousins hypnotized.

If they were my daughters, I would have just pulled them away.

But their mother, Janet, scarcely noticed them.

She hung at the very edge of the lantern light. Her shoulders were slumped—her head bowed into one hand.

I might have wondered if she hadn't just heard about Gudrun—if she hadn't some reason for mourning my elder sister. She seemed like a woman grieving. I might have gone to her, and put my hand on her shoulder, and said, *there there, dear*, the way that people are wont.

As I watched, she stepped back from the circle, and moved off. At this, I pushed myself from my chair, and make to follow her. And as I did so—I did wonder.

Could she have heard of Gudrun's fate? Could someone else have seen my sister, slipped past the quiet kitchen as did I—and told Janet?

Was that how it was to be? In spite of myself, I drew a breath, sharply. She climbed the steps to the porch, and cast about, as though looking for someone—as though making certain someone was *not* there.

I should not have been there. I should have let matters unfold as they were laid out. A watched pot never boils, yes? But of course that's not true. A flame will heat water, whether it's eyeballed or not.

She walked along the porch—peered into a dark window—ran her hands through her hair, as though making up her mind. As if it hadn't already been made up, for her.

I might have joined her on the porch. I might have told her how well she had planned the gathering—how beautiful the lanterns were, how the picnic tables were just right . . . how wonderful a touch were the privies, set so far from the old house that old Agatha had bequeathed us, when we all came here those hundred years past—with nothing but bad luck and worse debts.

I might have told her how so very *worthy* she was.

But I didn't. I held back as she went back to the screen door, pulled it open, and went inside.

I stood still on the dark lawn, as Rainer finished his song and a cheer went up. "Another one!" cried a child, and Rainer laughed and said, "Well, one more," and started to pick at his guitar again, and a light went on in the window. Was William finished? It was difficult to tell, for there was no commotion that followed, as more lights went on—as Janet explored her new home . . . met her new master.

I found myself humming along with Rainer's song. It was a French song and I don't speak French, but it had a happy tune. It was time to turn from the house, and I continued down the path—until I stood at the lookout. The music grew quieter, and I heard birdsong—the cool breeze rattling the branches of the trees down the deep slope.

The wall here was high. It wasn't meant to be easy to go over it . . . you had to really mean to clamber up, and launch yourself into the air off Agatha's Perch. By the time you were up, you'd know whether you had reason to stay.

I drew a deep lungful of the night air, and placed my hands on the round river rocks that made the wall, and I held that breath. It wasn't long, although it seemed an eternity.

When I exhaled, I turned and saw Gunnar. He stood tall, and shirtless—smeared with congealing grease and sweat, and gristle. The moonlight made hollows of his eyes. His mouth hung open.

I opened my arms for him, and dutifully, he came to me. And he kissed me, my favourite grandson did, as I had always dreamed and wished and hoped.

JAZZMAN/PUPPET
Joan Crate

The wooden box holds a jazz-man puppet.
Felt lips on a papier-mâché head
fold around the mouthpiece of a plastic sax.
Wrists leak polyester stuffing and wire fingers
coax out black liquorice notes—
I saw you standing alone.

A woman looks out the window
at another time, watches with whisky vision
brake lights bleeding on wet asphalt
as she makes a stop in the past,
Gentle in my Mind.

She remembers the jazzman like it was yesterday
or 30 years ago—an '80s disco, glitter, ganja,
his sax leaping over the keyboard
to shoot golden notes in her eyes
You are my shining star.

A guitar calls the tune and the jazzman answers
with a refrain that pours a Manhattan in a crystal glass
on a 16th floor balcony overlooking the city.
A breast nudges his arm, fireflies buzz his lips
falling
           through time
                       on mine.

He studies the woman by the window,
wants to call her name but his mouth makes music
not words—
                        silver scales and constellations
shimmering through a puppet's invented mind,
his mouth seared by hot licks and a glue gun,
and *Smoke gets in my eyes.*

I watch him play, in love and lost
in a world of pitch and riff, a young woman
in an old body taken aback by a paper and wire man—
a stage prop captured in a brain shot through
with secret passages and trap doors, how
I remember you.

The gold front tooth of another sunrise
fills dancers with early-morning ache.
It's late, very late.
Musicians put down their instruments.
Lovers and players slink out the door.
Bye, bye love.
Jazzman packs up his sax and waves *later, y'all.*

On his way home, he'll think of me
lingering in a brass alley of dropped chords.
He'll open his mouth to speak, but there's only
echoes, only what once was and now isn't,
only upstairs to that charcoal sketch of a room
with bills littering the table, flies on the sill,
longing and a light bulb burnt out,
only the blues.

                        Daylight pushes
her old refrain through the pane,
cuts him in ribbons. Tears drip to my jaw.
Cry Me a River.
Jazz man closes his painted lids

and drifts down a memory—

nothing but music, nothing
but an instrument, the idea of sound,
a puppet animated and shoved in a wooden box—

that long-ago room
                        a reed of recollection
            swing of loneliness,
loops of time.

        Tell me Jazzman,
Do I ever cross your mind?

USHAKIRAN
Laura Friis

The earliest movements she knows are not her mother's movements but the sea rocking her mother, who lies unconscious on the ship's deck, rescued. In that way, the sea can be said to be her mother.

She is born under the morning star, and so is named Ushakiran. The surgeon delivers her into a world of storms and blood, of darkness and creaking wood, of a blanket wrapped close around her, cold arms that cannot hold her.

She is fed on goat's milk and honey by the surgeon, Jathe. She spends the first days of her life strapped to his chest while he works. She should not live, but she does.

"When are you going to find that brat a home?" the Captain asks him every time they make port, and Jathe knows he should foster her somewhere; he knows, but he cannot.

"Soon," he says, and he thinks of wet-nurses and fevers, of tongue-blister, of drunkards and starving men, dirt, famine. He brings the baby back to the ship, every time.

He has never married, never had a home since he was a boy. His life has been spent on the kelp routes, seeking out the raw fuel of a magic that builds cities and fights wars on land, that has never given him a single thing. He would have married Ushakiran's mother if she had lived, just because she had nobody else.

He knows that the baby's odds of living to become a child are slim. She is never out of his sight. When the Currents fail, and the food runs out, he stands over her with a knife, watching the door for men who may remember that a child is meat, sweet and tender.

The Captain stops asking him when the baby will be sent away. Ushakiran learns to walk, or rather to take two steps and fall; she learns to laugh. She has dark eyes like her mother did, brown skin, and she grows two pearly-white teeth that show when she tries to talk. The sailors who have been on the ship since her birth begin to say that she is their good luck. They fear her crying, which they say brings storms. No one is to make her cry. Newcomers are warned.

Her toys are a doll sewn from old sailcloth, a top bought her by a sailor now dead, the feathers of circling birds, and knives.

Jathe teaches her how to use the knives. She can help him, he says. She learns to bandage and clean, cauterise and cut.

She is growing into a girl, six years old now and bright as morning, and he fears for her. He teaches her how to cut, quick and clean.

When she is seven, two new recruits take her down to the hold when Jathe is distracted by a fever case. Nobody notices until they hear her scream. The day is bright, warm, but Jathe's chest goes cold. His hands are cold. He throws down whatever it is he is holding and runs.

A dozen men are there before him and Ushakiran is unharmed, seems untouched, but she will only say that they scared her. She is crying. Jathe has them take the recruits on deck and tie them down. He has no right to give such orders, but nobody has seen him like this before; he is the surgeon, quiet and calm, and now his eyes are stone and his hands are fists; they obey him by instinct. On deck, the Captain meets Jathe's eyes, shrugs, and looks on.

Jathe has one of the boys fetch his knives and give them to Ushakiran.

"Like I taught you," he says. She shakes her head.

He speaks to her quietly. "The world is a cruel place," he says. "Your mother learned that. Mine, too, a long time ago. Here."

He takes her hand to guide it, the way his mother guided his when she was teaching him to draw, forty years ago, and he helps her make the first cut. The man chokes. Her hand shakes, but she pulls it away to make the next cut alone.

The next time it happens, he tells her to take the man's eye first. This time the man is from Balera and speaks little of any known tongue; maybe he has a daughter or little sister at home, the Captain says, and just wanted to *talk* to the child, but Jathe will not take a chance. Word is spreading about the child living on the *Day's Eye*; word is spreading that if you touch her they will tie you down and let her cut you; word is spreading that she likes seeing the blood.

Newcomers have already heard her name.

Nobody ever remembers, later, who decided she should not go ashore. At first it does not arise because she is too young. Jathe goes ashore rarely, and when he does he leaves her with Davin, the first mate, who has children of his own. Whenever she asks if she can come ashore with him he finds a reason why not—heat, sickness, rain, unrest. One day, when she is eight, he is going out into Kingsport for supplies and she steps toward the boat to go with him. One of the sailors puts an arm out to stop her, says, "She can't leave. She's our good luck."

Jathe looks at her. Since she was a toddler he has been telling her stories of the cities on land, of markets and palaces and everything in between. Her eyes are round, hopeful. He thinks of all the faces and reaching arms of a busy port, the snakes, the biting dogs; his eyes cannot be everywhere.

"You're our luck," he says. "Don't you want to keep us safe? How can you be our luck if you leave?"

Her eyes fill with tears but she nods. He gets into the boat and walks around Kingsport all day feeling as if he has poisoned her. He makes up his mind that when she asks again he will take her ashore. But she never does, and secretly he is relieved.

Ushakiran loves to run. Every day, at sunrise, noon, and sunset, up and down the length of the ship. Her friend Davin says he could tell the time by her dashes, if he could not by the sun. From the stern to the bow, jumping over hatches and pails, over the concave of the ship's drum, swerving outwards to go along the rail and in again to the companionway, sun on her skin, the ship's timber under her bare feet. She dreams that one day she will reach the bow at such speed that she will launch herself from it and fly.

Her other favourite thing to do is to lean over the rail and watch the Currents that pull the ships around the Unfathomable Sea, and from which they dredge the kelp that they sell to magicians to power their magic. Sometimes if she screws her eyes up hard enough she believes she can see a Leviathan, one of the great monsters that are said to swim far, far down below and to create the Currents with their swimming and their own magic, but she knows that really she has never seen one. Sometimes she lies in the concave of the drum, where the kelp is collected, and puts her ear to the wood, and listens, and pretends that she hears the magic sing. She knows she does not. But when she rises to go about her day again she is sometimes dizzy, unsteady on her feet, and everything is brighter, sharper.

Faces come and go on the *Day's Eye*. Sailors die, they jump ship, and new ones take the places of the old. Some—Davin, the Captain, and Jathe—are family, others, like Beor the young ship's cook, are friends; the rest are fluid. When Ushakiran is thirteen a woman is recruited, a scarred and heavy woman; her name is Haf, and she is stronger than most of the men. Her husband, Korvall, is recruited too, but he is small and older and people often forget he is nearby.

"Who are they?" Beor asks her, the first time he sees them. He has come out to the drum to bring Ushakiran one of the cakes he has made. When she was littler and used to hang round the galley, getting under his feet and begging for food, he would bribe her to go away. Three lengths of the ship meant a spoonful of the honey she loved, five meant berries, ten, cake or extra bread. The habit has stuck.

"Just people," she says, when she has licked the last of the cake from her teeth.

"Nobody's just people."

He is watching them. Ushakiran looks too. She sees a woman in dun-colour, wearing a string of wooden beads, a man with a beard, losing his hair: nothing of interest.

"They look like Arkislanders," Beor says, leaning against the drum. "I went to Arkisland once; the trees are so thick you can hardly move, and the bears there are pure white. Like snow."

"Oh," Ushakiran says, but she is not thinking about Arkisland, she is looking at Beor, his tanned face lined by the weather, and wondering if there is more cake. He shakes his head.

"Don't you ever wonder about the islands?" he says, "Or the cities, any of it?"

She shakes her head, with perfect truth. She stopped thinking about the outside world when she was eight years old. He shakes his head again, reaches out as if to ruffle her hair and stops, and then goes back to his galley.

"You should bind your breasts," Haf tells Ushakiran one day. Ushakiran blinks at her.

"I've seen you running," Haf says. "You wobble. You can bet the men see it. Bind them down, it's easier."

She shows Ushakiran how, and Ushakiran knows she should be

grateful, but she knows she is growing, now, and she hates Haf for it, because Haf told her.

She notices Haf watching her, often. Most often when she is at the rail, Leviathan-watching, or curled up in the concave of the drum, imagining the power beneath.

"Where do you come from, girl?" Haf asks her one day, and Ushakiran, reluctantly, tells what little of her story she knows. Haf puts her head on one side, considering.

"Have you ever seen a Leviathan?" she asks.

"Nobody has," Ushakiran says.

"How do you know that?"

Ushakiran shrugs.

"What about kelp? Have you ever eaten any? Touched it?"

Ushakiran shifts slightly away from Haf, uneasy.

"It wouldn't do anything. It's just for magicians."

"So it is," Haf says. Korvall comes past then, and Haf nods to Ushakiran and walks away with him.

The mutiny begins quietly, as such things do. Haf plants whispers in ears, and they grow. She tells the right people that spoils on the *Day's Eye* are divided unfairly, that the surgeon is mad to keep a murdering witch-girl on board and the Captain is mad to let him, that she and Korvall could run things better. She has done this before. She says that men should not have to live in fear for desiring a woman who is dangled before their noses. She says that the men Ushakiran has killed are owed justice. She sees the girl go on as always, running her laps of the ship, smiling at the men, knowing nothing: a child. The harvest of Haf's words is an indignation that grows like a rising wave. The Captain senses it as, after years at sea, he senses a change in the weather, but he only gives out more bread and spirits and lashings. Greed and fear rule everything out on the ocean; he has used them before, and he thinks they will serve him again. He is old.

There are too many ships on the arms of the Currents these days. They dredge the kelp thin and the Currents fail more often, leaving the ships becalmed for days at a time until the Leviathan far beneath do whatever they do to replenish the kelp, and start the Current flowing again. The gleanings are smaller, too, and the drum, which would once have been heavy with kelp and rich with power, only hums a little, now. There is less profit to go around. None of this is the Captain's fault and

Haf cannot change any of it anyway, but it is easy to convince angry men that a change, any change, will improve their lot.

She waits for her moment.

The Halverling Current fails. The *Day's Eye* is becalmed, with no Current to carry her forward, and no wind either to bridge the gap to the next Current. There is sickness on the ship and Jathe works through a scorching day and a black night and half the next day to save three of the youngest sailors, who are half and a third of his age, who should not die while he lives. He staggers out onto the deck, into a baking noonday, with the reek of death on him. He is growing old, he thinks. Everything is so hot and bright. The side of his face seems to slip away from the bone, and he staggers against the rail. That is when he sees Ushakiran on the companionway, talking to a young man, a sailor whose face he should know, but he does not. He hardly seems to know the ship any more either—it is a blur, as is the sky, around the only thing he sees: Ushakiran, the hands reaching towards her. Wrongness surges up in his chest, suffocating him. In an instant he is back in that moment of her childhood, long ago, hearing her scream, and he is cold, cold.

He tries to run, but all he can manage is a lurch, somewhere between running and falling. He cannons into the young man and gropes for his throat, but never finds it. His opponent shoves him against the rail and hits him, once, twice. He hears screaming. He feels the pounding of running feet in the boards of the ship underneath him. Everything goes black for an instant, and when his vision clears he sees Beor, the ship's cook, his friend, dead on the ground, and his first ridiculous impulse is relief, that he recognises the man finally, that he is not losing his mind after all. Then he sees Ushakiran standing over Beor, her blade dripping with blood, and he sees the men running towards her, bearing down on her like a wave.

They drag her away and then they come for Jathe. Before he dies, he hears, with an odd, faraway clarity, his old friend the Captain telling him that children cannot be kept like eggs, they will break out. That was many years ago and yet the words sound new to Jathe, as if he is hearing them for the first time.

They murder the captain in his bed. The blood of the surgeon, who has tended them for years, who has shown them the closest thing to kindness that anyone knows on board ship, is spilled all over the deck.

Yet it is no worse, Haf tells them, than the murder of Beor, a young man who had committed no worse crime than offering dried berries to a girl he saw as a sister. It's touch and go, but by a stroke of luck—and she deserves some luck, for once—the Current surges back into life and begins to drag the ship forward just as she fears they are slipping away from her. The great dredgers start their work again, spooling kelp into the drum, and life steals back into the ship, the low hum of power in every dip and rise of the bow, in every board of the timber. Haf believes the sailors sense that, without knowing it, and it reassures them.

Her own magic is not strong. However much kelp she eats or smokes or absorbs she will never be a powerful magician, but she knows one or two things. She knows the right stories to tell, and she knows trees. From the first shoot splitting a seed deep in the rich soil of her home island, to the polished beads around her neck, to the boards of a coffin or a ship. She knows enough to rid herself of Ushakiran. The sailors are afraid to kill the girl, afraid to keep her alive.

"She's our luck," one of them argues, and "She's a killer," another. They bicker back and forth until Haf whistles for silence and snatches up one of the spears they keep for fishing in the shallows on land. She strides up onto the kelp-drum, down into the hollow of it. They are all watching her now. She raises the spear and brings it down, hard, and with a crack and a splinter the drum ruptures, and the kelp comes spilling out. She scoops up a handful of it and throws her head back, eats the kelp slowly, sloppily, feels the warmth of the power filling her body. Not enough power, never enough, but enough for now.

No one makes a sound. She jumps out of the concave and goes to where two of the sailors hold Ushakiran, whose eyes are wide, not with fear, but with awe. She takes the girl's face in her hands and closes her eyes. She thinks of the wood of the ship, sun-soaked, rain-beaten, wind-scoured, wood seasoned by age and hard use, trodden by the feet of these men and this girl, floating for years on the Unfathomable Sea. She feels soft skin harden under her palms, and when she opens her eyes there before her is Ushakiran in wood, honey-coloured and smooth-grained, eyes looking at something far away, one hand raised slightly in appeal. The perfect figurehead.

"But our luck," one of the sailors protests, feebly.

"If she was lucky before, she is lucky now," Haf says. She has them mount Ushakiran on the bow of the ship, staring out over the bowsprit, over the endless water.

Ushakiran is blind.

A wooden thing cannot see, and it should not hear either. It should be dead. She should be dead and gone, and yet here she is. She has plenty of time to think about why this is.

She has what she always wanted. She flies over the bow of the ship, in the wind and the spray, as fast as the ship is fast. It isn't like she imagined.

She cannot see, but she hears with great acuity. She cannot really die on the *Day's Eye*, she decides, because she has always been part of it. She has never left it since she was born. She lived on the ship as a flesh-and-blood girl and now that she is wooden she feels as a ship feels, because she is joined to the ship.

She feels Haf, wherever Haf walks, as a low vibration of power.

She feels feet on the boards, chairs scraped, shoulders leaning against walls, waves crashing against the side of her, fish as little irritations, barnacles as a constant, gentle torment. She feels the faded warmth of Jathe's blood stained into the deck and if she could weep, she would.

She feels the kelp in the drum the way she used sometimes to feel her heartbeat, only stronger, much stronger.

As time goes by, she begins to feel other things. Whales, calling each other in the sea. Storms approaching. The presences of other ships, disturbances in the Current.

She begins to sleep. To sleep as wood is so pleasant, is to fall into an easy, honey-coloured dream, to glow in the sun, to rock with the motion of the waves through the wind and under the rain. She is falling insensate, degree by slow degree, when a new sound wakes her.

They are on the cusp of the Peret and Halverling Currents, and the men are raising sail to traverse between the one and the other, when she first hears it. At first she cannot place it for the life of her. Such a deep sound, so far down in the sea, and yet so huge it seems to shake the world. Leviathans. They are real, and she can hear them.

For days she listens, and that is enough to keep her awake—trying to make out what they are saying to each other, if they are saying anything. Even that, though, palls, and by the time they are three days out along the Peret Current she has lost interest and is slipping away. Until she hears a single word.

". . . luck."

It is Korvall talking, as he climbs between decks.

"They all believe that—" he says, and then he moves away from the wall, and she can't hear him any more. Outside the wardroom he brushes the wall again, and he is saying "Reach Current. But maybe—" he walks out to the middle of the deck and she loses him again. A minute later he walks back and leans against the rail, but all she hears is "weevils," and something about cabbage, and she gathers he is talking about his dinner.

She stops listening to the Leviathans, and starts listening, with all her concentration, to what is going on within the ship. She hears so much, and yet so little of value. "The old Captain," one sailor says, cheek against the wall—he is tired, perhaps. "Mother," another says, leaning over the rail to look down at the waves whilst he talks, and "never," says the man he talks to, before he straightens and turns away. A morass of whispers becomes a lullaby; this time she will not fight it, she decides, she will let the *Day's Eye* take her, and then, from the tide of sounds, emerges one complete, perfect sentence.

"If they want a child, let them have a child," Korvall says. Ushakiran shivers; the ship shivers.

"I turned their luck into wood," Haf says, "I made it last forever."

She cannot work out where they are, that she can hear them so perfectly.

"I saw, love. It was magnificent."

He kisses her. Ushakiran feels the touch for both of them—

Korvall's lips on Haf's and Haf's on Korvall's. No one ever kissed her in her life of flesh, and now she is kissed for the first time, by these two.

"We'll go along Reach," Korvall says, and he is kissing her again, in between words, "land on one of the Four Islands, find a child, and if they decide she's not lucky they'll probably find something else to do with her."

No, Ushakiran thinks, and the ship dips forward, and the sails snap though there is no wind. She feels Haf absent-mindedly stroking the wood of the ship and wishes she could kill them both—and then she realises where they are. At the base of the drum, where it curves into the hold, and the kelp inside the drum is catching their words and conducting them perfectly upwards, through the timber, to Ushakiran.

"Their child had power," Haf says. "This one won't. They'll know."

"Sailors don't know anything," Korvall says, but Ushakiran is not listening to them any more, she is wondering. The child that had power. The child. Her.

A tremor runs through the *Day's Eye*. Men fall against the walls, onto the floor. A bottle smashes in the wardroom. Somewhere a bag of holystone crashes to the ground and splits, scatters.

The sails catch and billow in the dead calm. The bow plunges down into the water. Ushakiran hears muffled and distorted cries, shouted orders, and Haf's last, clear, whispered question, "What is that?"

The drum splits with a thunder-crash and the kelp rushes out. It soaks into the wood, into Ushakiran, and, absorbed, it lights her like tinder. There is sight, now, there is sound too—screaming, and the roar of a fire that is not true fire but power going up like fuel. It is night, but the sea around Ushakiran glows green-gold. There are no shadows. She feels lives blinking out all along the wood of her, like little candles snuffed—Davin, dragged under the waves, Korvall, crushed under the broken drum, Haf, thrashing in the water until the cold turns her still. The men are jumping off the rail, into the water, anything to get away from the unholy pyre that, as they swim frantically away from it, upends and drives downwards, into the black water.

The water swallows Ushakiran, goes through her as if it were her blood. Through the veins of her decks and rooms, drowning the men still trapped there and washing the stains of dead men's blood away. Before the waters close above her she lets out a cry that is no human sound, not made by lips, nor throat, nor lungs, and there comes, from worlds away below the sea, an answering call.

KSAMGUIYAEPS— WOMAN-OUT-TO-SEA
Neile Graham

I laugh at their games: those
who trap my tale in words.

When the brittle pages open
voices appeal from them:

the villagers chorusing: *Woman-out-to-sea,*
do not harm our relative!

Oh, give over. So what if I destroy
all men who court me? Why not,

for wherever I go there are more men.
It's like they want to be eaten.

One kindly editor notes: *vagina dentata*
theme omitted here. Thanks. I appreciate that.

I appreciate, too, that my transformation
is described so simply:

until the best friend of the salmon prince
takes her to wife, and subdues her.

But I'm not so fond of the editor's final dig:
vagina dentata thwarted by love.

Thwarted, ha! I was undone,
every cell of my body broken

to atoms, then rebuilt, remade,
put together whole and wholly different.

*Her powers lost, she's now
eager for him, for life with him.*

So now I've changed. From cliché to cliché.
That's some magic. And true.

But only launches the tale.
Here is part two:

I and my new husband, now *we*,
take a blackfish canoe to visit my father—

and passing my husband's friend's villages,
the salmon people shout warnings.

Listen to the salmon shout. Though I tell my father
this man's a keeper, he has his own plans:

asks my *love* for sea-urchins, seal meat,
the octopus, but *my love*, so clever

captures them all, so father
lets him take an abundance *home, our home.*

So far so good. Deep breath.
But this is part three:

everyday my husband draws water
for me to drink; I test it with a plume.

But one day he meets a woman
at the water hole and takes her

before coming home to me.
When I test it, I know I must

return to my father. Goddam
this *wronged woman* cliché!

Though he follows, begging,
  twice I warn him: *if you do not*

go back, I will look back
and you shall perish.

Don't turn me to Orpheus,
you bastard. I cannot sing.

He takes no heed, so I look back:
he sinks into the sea.

The end? No, no but at least
be patient—part four is the last:

In my father's house I am
cliché again, tears and all.

I love him. I want him back.
I am so tired of the ends of men.

Father fishes up my husband's bones,
reassembles, then covers them,

jumps over them three times
and they start to move.

Uncovers them. *My husband*
awakens. When I see him

come back to life, I stop crying.
I take him to my sleeping place, forgiven.

This is the end.
Or:

we can't find his shin bone
and so we use that of an eagle,

giving all people now their slender
bird-boned shins. Still, I take him back.

Ksampguiyaeps, I have
cleverly re-made him as he only remade me.

Oh, it's love.
Close the book now.

FISHFLY SEASON
Halli Villegas

The bedroom was stifling. The ceiling fan's soft sucking sound as it moved through the humid air only intensified her discomfort. Of course he was asleep beside her, not much kept him awake. He hadn't wanted to put the air conditioning in yet, saying it was too expensive, that the nights were still cool enough for sleeping with windows open, that the fan would regulate the temperature. So here she was lying awake in their new home, a perfect centre entrance Georgian, hating him.

They moved in a month ago and Marisol still didn't believe it was real. They had left behind a small bungalow in the city, for this gracious home in a beautiful suburb along a lake, twenty minutes away from the city's centre. The place where the rich used to have their summer cottages, where executives from the car companies that drove the city's economy had their mansions on the cul-de-sacs and leafy streets, where the executive's lawyers lived two doors away in mock Tudors and homes with French doors.

It wasn't a new suburb, like those terrible bedroom communities with the tiny yards and every house a replica of the next; this was old money, old Wasp wealth cocooning itself here. Every house different, each lawn perfect, two shopping areas, The Hill and the Village, with coffee shops and dress shops, hardware stores and the Village Market grocery store.

Marisol was drifting now, floating in a sort of heat-induced stupor, watching as the soft black shadows in the corners of the bedroom, deepened and shifted, resolving themselves into a woman who walked towards the bed. A wide hair band held her hair back, and she wore a bright pink and green sleeveless shift, a strand of pearls around her neck. She skirted around the end of the bed and glanced once at Marisol whose eyelids were getting heavier, closing almost, and Marisol saw that the woman's blue eyes were nothing but glass beads and that she hated Marisol.

The next morning Marisol woke up to Neil singing in the shower. The white hydrangeas and pink bows on the wallpaper danced in the sunlight, the pale blue check curtains billowing softly with an early morning breeze. Both had been in the house when they moved in. Marisol had ditched the Guatemalan rugs and mismatching thrift store finds painted in bright colours that she had decorated their bungalow with and embraced the Sister Parrish style of decorating that their new home seemed to expect. The furniture from Neil's parent's estate had helped, their four-poster bed, the sunroom wicker, the chintz-covered sofas all fit perfectly. Like the furniture, Neil belonged here. He had grown up in this suburb, and had always wanted to return.

"Once a Grand Beach man," he said, "always a Grand Beach man."

Small droplets of water fell on her cheeks. For a moment Marisol wondered if she was crying, but it was Neil, fresh from the shower, shaking his wet blond hair over her like a dog.

She reached out for him but he moved away smiling with his perfect white teeth.

"Get up lazybones, get up. Today we'll run some errands in the Village, and drive by the lake, have lunch in the park. Sound good?"

Marisol smiled and nodded. She got out of bed and walked to the bathroom. On the way there, buried in the soft pile of the rug, something hard bit into the ball of her foot. She bent down and felt for the object. She picked it up holding it on the palm of her hand. It was a small blue glass bead.

The Village was very clean; there was no graffiti, no garbage. Each storefront had period details to make it look like an American colonial town. As Marisol and Neil got out of the car, a chattering group of teen girls, long legs, tan, clean sheets of blond hair, tiny cut off shorts and polo shirts, brushed by them. The girls were eating ice cream, their little pink tongues licking and darting, their gleaming teeth nipping at the cones. They stared at Neil for a moment, at his blond handsomeness and then swayed on. Marisol felt very small and dark, a blotch on the bright place they had come to. While she stared after the girls, she felt something land on her arm. She looked down at her arm and saw an insect she had never seen before. It had a mealworm like body, with two beady eyes and transparent wings that stood straight up. Marisol brushed at it with her hand, but it clung to her. She shook her arm, but still the thing hung on, staring at her with its caviar eyes.

"Neil, get this thing off me. It's stuck, it's laying eggs or something." Marisol's voice rose. She had never liked bugs, and though she tried to be adult about it, this thing unnerved her. "Is it sucking my blood? What the hell is it?" Neil held her arm still and easily plucked the creature off her by its wings. He tossed it into the air and it fluttered a few feet away and landed on the window of a car.

"Haven't you ever seen a fishfly before Marisol?" Neil asked smiling at her.

"They hatch their eggs on water, so Grand Beach gets a big swarm of them around this time of year. One is nothing. Wait till they all hatch. Some years they are so thick on the ground your car skids, and they cover the windows of the stores until you can't see in."

"Jesus, Neil, that's horrible." Marisol rubbed her arm where the fishfly had landed. "Like some biblical plague."

"Actually we're happy to see them that heavy. It means that the lake is healthy."

He put his arm around Marisol. "They don't have mouths and they die after one day and one night. They just want to mate, they're not interested in you." He hugged Marisol to him. "Let's go get that drill so I can put up your book shelves. I'll protect you from the vicious fishflies"

The hardware store had a sickening rubbery smell, oily. But it was very light and open, the front filled with displays of garden ornaments, backyard bar-b-cues, nylon flags with watermelons or baskets of flowers embroidered on them. There were aisles of cooking ware, glasses, ice tea jugs. It was only at the far back of the store that it started to look like a real hardware store, with displays of tools, coils of garden hose and boxes of nails and screws.

"Neil, oh my god, how have you been?"

A tall woman with a shiny brown bob and big dark doe eyes was hugging him. Marisol saw her thin arms with long muscles and freckles on the tan skin, and took in her brightly painted toenails in bright green thong sandals.

"Bunny! It is so fucking great to see you." Neil gave the woman a shoulder shake, "I've moved back into town." Neil stepped away from the woman and pulled Marisol next to him. "This is my wife Marisol."

Bunny looked at Marisol, "Marisol, that's so unusual. Such an exotic name. Where are you from?"

Marisol looked at the silver Tiffany bean necklace glistening on Bunny's collarbone.

"Huston."

Bunny smiled. "Huston. So hot there. But I meant originally, what's your background?"

"My father's Mexican."

Bunny turned to Neil, "Oh my God Neil, you have got to come over for G & Ts sometime soon. Chip is going to flip out that you are here. Do you still talk to any of the Rustic Cabins' cause gang? Remember that night after your swim meet at Windmill Point?" Neil began to talk, Bunny shifted her weight to one hip and Marisol knew they were going to have a long conversation. She slipped away down the back aisles of the store, looking for the electric drill that had been the original purpose of their trip.

The back of the store with the tools and other bits of hardware was much quieter then the front where people milled about picking up lawn chairs and planters. Here the air was dusty, filled with the smell of sawdust and that silver black scent Marisol had first noticed when she came in the store. It was heavier here, and she didn't think she could last very long. It was giving her a terrible headache. She trolled up and down the unmarked aisles looking for the drills. There didn't seem to be any sales people in this part of the store, perhaps they were all off helping other customers who were in desperate need of a cement garden goose. On the back wall of the store she found the drills, they were on shelves next to a hanging display of hammers. A heavyset man in madras shorts and a pink polo was standing staring at the hammers. He had the reddened wind burned complexion of a sailor, his hair flopped over one eye but was cut short over the ears, much like Neil's own hair cut, what Marisol thought of as standard Wasp man hair.

He didn't look at Marisol who was gazing at the drills in an agony of indecision. For some reason drills always upset her, she imagined them braking through the soft bone at your temple, or through the eye, the way they used to give lobotomies.

Marisol glanced at the man, secretly hoping he might give her advice.

Didn't men like to give advice about the best tools and such? Because Marisol thought all the electric drills looked alike.

"Hammer will do the job," Marisol heard the man say. She thought he was talking to her but he was still facing the display of hammers, "Hammer will get it done."

The man reached up and pulled down a hammer with a silver head and a shiny wooden handle. He swung it once as if testing its heft. Marisol flinched despite herself. The man still seemed oblivious to her presence. Then the man turned and looked directly at her. His eyes were blue, glassy as if he were drunk. The corneas were almost perfect circles, *like beads,* the woman from her dream walked through her mind again, staring at her with hatred.

"Hammer will get it done." He said again, slightly slurring his words. He *was* drunk. The man swung the hammer upwards and Marisol cowered, she saw now that the silver head was covered in blood, that the blood was running down the man's tanned forearm, covering the little golden hairs there in a thick wash of gore. His eyes were beads and one fell out at her feet rolling away down the empty aisle of the store and there was nothing behind it but a black hole. Marisol screamed bringing her hands up to cover her face, protect herself from his blow.

Neil was beside her, "Honey what is it, what's wrong?" Behind him Marisol saw Bunny, looking curiously at her. There were other people there too, a man in a vest that said Village Hardware hurried over. "Is everything all right?"

"A man, swung a hammer at me."

"A man?" The Village hardware employee glanced around, so did Neil. The others began to talk among themselves and glance down nearby aisles.

"He was drunk, I could see it in his eyes, " Marisol said.

Bunny laughed lightly, "A drunken maniac in Grand Beach, how exciting." Marisol looked at the small crowd. Of course the man was gone. Marisol hadn't expected otherwise. Of course now they would think she was crazy. Bunny smiled, and for the first time Marisol noticed what small teeth she had, like a little rodent's, white bits of porcelain filling her mouth.

Bunny put her hand on Neil's arm and said, "You must come for drinks some evening, we'll put some steaks on. Call me?" Neil nodded still looking at Marisol with concern. "Goodbye Marisol," Bunny said smiling at her again with absolutely no feeling behind it, "it was great to meet you."

Marisol felt calm but she was tired. She begged off the park for the day, telling Neil "I didn't sleep well last night with the heat. I probably had some sort of narcoleptic episode just now." She laughed and Neil did too.

He dropped her back at home, and went to work with his friend on his boat, helping to ready it to put in the water in a week or two.

"Then we can go for a sail on the lake."

"That would be nice," Marisol said kissing him, "Have fun." But she thought again about the fishflies and wondered if they would be even worse on the lake.

She lay in the room with the white hydrangeas and the pink bows, the ceiling fan revolving above her, now sounding to Marisol like the rush of blood through her body that she heard when she pressed her ear to her pillow. She fell asleep and twitched in her sleep like a dog chasing a dream rabbit.

The nights had not gotten any easier. Neil was still against air conditioning, told her to take a cold shower before bed and she would feel cool enough under the ceiling fan's breeze. We are by the lake, he said, it cools down at night. Marisol knew he was echoing the words of his parents, who were echoing the words of their parents in a long lineage of cottages and camping, grand houses run with small economies to hide the old gold groaning behind every warped floorboard and tartan covered sofa. She had taken to walking the neighbourhood in the heavy evenings, hoping to tire herself out enough so that she could sleep. A good night's sleep was all she needed.

No one in Grand Beach seemed to use curtains on their first floor windows, so the front rooms were open to anyone who walked by, like dioramas. Night after night as Marisol walked the sidewalks of Grand Beach she looked in the windows. The living rooms and dining rooms painted in the Grand Guignol red they seemed to favour here, the shining brass chandeliers, the baby grand pianos with the silver plated picture frames ranged across the top, the Ethan Allen dining room chairs waiting around a table.

Tonight it was particularly still. No dog walkers, no teenagers whispering past on their way to parties in parks and on docks at the lake's edge. Moist air made her scalp itch and feel as if there was a thin layer of cream between her shirt and her back.

Marisol walked and peered in the windows, gazing from the sidewalk into all these other lives and wondering what they were like, how easily did they fit into their skins? Tonight there was a party. The biggest house on their street was lit up.

In the dining room Marisol could see people milling around the table, plates in their hands, eating canapés, holding drinks. In the living room, a man sat at the piano playing. The faint sounds of The Beach Boys' "Help Me Rhonda" drifted out to where she stood. She had to see in, she crept closer to the house.

Yew bushes flanked the front under each of the bay windows. Marisol squeezed in between the bush and the brick wall. She felt the silken brush of a cobweb, but it didn't deter her. Looking just over the window ledge she could see right into the dining room. The crackers and cheeses, the fruit, the half collapsed cake, *birthday, anniversary?* On the sideboard bottles of wine, the inevitable gin and tonic, Pimms. There were fewer people in the room then earlier; they had drifted into the living room to hear the piano. Now Marisol could hear them singing along to Rock Lobster.

There were two women and a man left in the red dining room. The women—slender, wearing black shift dresses, and low black sling-back pumps. Pearls against the bronze of their backs where the dresses dipped low. One blond, the other brunette. The man was blond, in khakis and a blue sports coat, his white shirt opened at the neck. He looked like an ad for J Crew. His feet were sockless in deck shoes. The group was half turned towards the window and Marisol watched them talk and eat. Their mouths barely moving as they did so, the women throwing back their heads in laughter, and the man twisting his gin and tonic in his hand this way and that. They picked more food from the table, and began to talk more animatedly.

Now their jaws seemed to be swinging loose, unhinging a little and then with a short shake they would clack them back shut. The canapés, looked on closer inspection as Marisol pressed right up against the window, like bits of uncooked meat. The juice dribbled down their chins and they ignored it, smiling and clacking their jaws back into place with each bite. They put their plates down on the table and moved to the living room.

Marisol ran across the front steps in a crouch and squatted down again behind the bushes under the living room window this time. Motown was playing, and the trio had positioned themselves on a sofa facing the piano. There was no blood on their chins now, and the strange shake of their heads to fix their dangling jaws had stopped. One of the women looked familiar to Marisol but the woman kept looking away, frustrating Marisol with her inability to place her. *What am I doing spying here? Maybe I am asleep.* But the cold of the bricks against her chest and the sharp cat piss scent of the Yew hedge told her otherwise.

When the room erupted in laughter and clapping, the woman stood up and went over to the man playing the piano and hugged him. Marisol knew now. It was Bunny.

Bunny glanced up for a moment and seemed to look out into the dark and see Marisol there, but her eyes were empty, reflecting back the light in the living room as if they were windows themselves. The man that had been with Bunny in the dining room joined her at the piano, shaking the player's hand and Marisol saw with a sinking feeling that it was Neil. *When did Neil go out?* He had still been sleeping when she left the bedroom. But maybe it wasn't Neil, they all looked alike here, cut from the same cloth.

Still Marisol wanted to go back home and reassure herself that Neil was asleep in their bed, snoring softly in his old crew t-shirt and boxers, the way she had left him. She crawled from behind the bushes and still staying low ran to the sidewalk. The she hurried down the street, away from the house.

Marisol decided to go around down a block and head up the parallel street to her road. She didn't want to run into Bunny, although that was unlikely. How would she explain being out alone this late? And what if that *had* been Neil? She wasn't sure she wanted to confront him right now, at night, as if she had been following him like some crazy woman.

The houses on the street that ran right behind her street were slightly larger with wider yards. Each one stood like a bastion of respectability. Their screened in porches, well-tended lawns, fresh awnings and paint unimpeachable. There was something dark at the foot of a driveway that belonged to a white Dutch Colonial house with green striped awnings and a wide porch with geraniums and wicker. *A child's bike?*

But the shape was soft, the shape of the shadows that Marisol had peered into night after night in the corner of her bedrooms. She walked slowly, but knew she could not ignore it, could not run away. It would only be waiting in front of another house on another street.

It was a woman in a white eyelet dress that was hitched up past her thighs. Her blond hair was spread around her like a halo and one of her arms was flung over her head as if she were waving. Her eye socket was crushed in, her mouth hanging open as if in dumb wonder at her own death. Marisol saw that the shoulder of the white dress was stiff with the clotted dark brown of the blood and liquid that had spilled from her eye. The cheekbone caved in, one white tooth glistened on her lower lip where it had been knocked from her head. Scattered around her were blue beads that shone in the light from a street lamp, one of the tasteful swan necked ones that lined Grand Beach's wide and pleasant streets.

Marisol scooped some of the beads up and put them in her pocket. They made a pleasant glassy sound as they knocked against each other, a rhythm of sorts.

Closer to her house she began to see masses of winged creatures swirling around the streetlamps. They flew at the lights in frantic motion, there were so many that it looked as if a black cloud was hanging below each lamp. Marisol felt them tickle along her arm, and then on her neck as they landed on her clothes and tangled in her hair. She pulled at them but they stuck, their long tails quivering with the effort to cling. She brushed at them fiercely, but still they came, on an erratic blind path towards something only they could sense.

It was fishfly season and they were swarming.

Marisol pulled fly after fly off her. She knew they had no mouths but it seemed each one snipped a snippet of her flesh as they fell. She began to run, to try to outpace them, but they flew on in mindless waves. On the lake their egg sacs burst open again and again and they rose in clouds looking for others of their kind to mate with and die with.

The porch light of her house was on and they were dense under it. She would have to go through them to get in her door. So she covered her head with her arms and ran up the steps, frantically pulling open the screen where they clung and throwing open the heavy front door, slamming it behind her before they could get in.

She stood in the front hall under the blazing copper light fixture and pulled off those that still stuck to her clothes and skin. They fluttered around, finally landing on the light. *I'll brush them off in the morning. In the morning when they have all died.* Marisol left the light on in the front hall, so they would not follow her upstairs. She didn't want to feel their bodies brushing up against her in the smothering night.

In the bedroom the fan still moved through the air making no difference, the way she supposed Neil's love would make no difference in the long run.

He was there, asleep, his mouth open wide his arms and legs sprawled across the bed, into the space she slept, as if she had never existed.

Marisol went into the bathroom and switched on the light. She took one of the blue beads from her pocket and held it up to her eye. It was cool and smooth in her hand, and everything was faint beyond it. She held it closer to her eye, so that she could no longer see her own brown iris in the mirror.

Gently she rested it against her eyelids, just to see. She pushed a little harder.

Just to see, she told herself, *just to see*.

A CAVERN OF REDBRICK
Richard Gavin

See now as the boy sees. Bear witness to a summerworld, a place sparkling with clear light and redolent with the fragrance of new-mown grass and where the air itself hosts all the warmth and weightlessness of bathwater.

It is the first morning in this summerworld and, knowing that autumn is but a pinpoint in the future, Michael stands on the porch of his grandparents' country home and allows the elation to erupt inside him. He then mounts his bicycle and rides headlong into the season.

The town whisks past him in a verdant smear. But Michael holds his destination firmly in his mind's eye.

The gravel pit on the edge of town has long been his private sanctuary. He has escaped to that secret grey place more times than he can possibly remember. It is his own summer retreat, one of the many highlights of spending the summer with his grandparents in the little village of Cherring Point.

Visiting the pits is technically trespassing. His grandfather, who was appointed by the government to maintain, and occasionally man, the place has often told him to keep away from it. Thus Michael keeps his mild transgressions to himself. Clearly he isn't the only one to sneak into the secluded area. He isn't the one who has cut the hole into the chain-link fence that distinguishes the property line, though he does always make sure to re-cover this portal with the brush that camouflages it.

Michael consoles himself with the logic that he really never disrupts anything in the pits. On his bike he would race over the mounds, which he likes to imagine as being the burial sites of behemoths. He loves watching his tires summon dirty fumes of gravel dust. Often that instant when his bike soars past the tipping point at the mounds' summit, Michael feels as though he is flying.

It is his private ritual of summer elation; harmless and pure.

Except that today, on his inaugural visit of the season, Michael discovers that his ritual ground is no longer private. . . .

His initial reaction to seeing the girl beyond the fence is shock, a feeling that gives way to an almost dizzying sense of disbelief.

At the far end of the lot is a large redbrick storage shed, its door of corrugated metal shut firm and secured with a shiny silver padlock. Michael has often fantasized about all manner of treasure being stored within those walls.

Standing on the shed's roof is a girl whom Michael guesses to be no older than he is. She is dressed in a t-shirt only slightly whiter than her teeth. Her straw-coloured hair hangs to the middle of her back. Her bare feet are uncannily balanced at the very summit of the shed's pitched roof, yet she does not teeter or wave her arms to maintain this daring balance. She is as stationary as a totem.

Michael can feel her eyes upon him.

He veers his bike away and rides the paths above the gravel yard for a while, cutting sloppy figure-eights in the dirt while wrestling with whether or not he should retreat. What exactly is she trying to prove standing on the shed that way? What if she tries to speak to him, to shake loose his reasons for coming here? What if this place is in fact *her* special place? Perhaps *he* has been the real outlander all this time.

Michael veers his bike cautiously back to the hidden gap in the fence, hoping, foolishly, that the girl will flee.

He crouches low on his bike and glides to where the brush is thickest.

"What's your name?"

The sound of her voice chills Michael. He wonders how she has spied him. Does her position on the roof make her all-seeing?

Like a surrendering soldier, Michael rides out from behind the greenery, clears the entrance to the pits and eases his bike toward the shed.

"How did you get up there?" he asks.

"Do you live near here?"

Michael frowns. "No. My grandparents do."

"You're not supposed to be in here, you know."

"Neither are *you!*" Michael spits. He feels a strange and sudden rage overcoming him. Somehow his childish anxiety over seeing an interloper in his sanctuary pales beneath a fiery anger, something near to hatred.

It erupts with such sharpness that Michael actually feels himself flinch, as though he's been shocked by some hidden power line. Why should the girl anger him so? He wonders what it is about the nature of her innocuous questions that makes him despise her.

He pedals closer and is opening his mouth to say something, just what Michael isn't sure, when a searing glint on the girl's body forces him to screw up his face.

Shielding his eyes with one hand, Michael gives the girl a long and scrutinizing glare.

And then he truly sees her. . . .

Sees the flour-pale and bruise-blue pallor of her skin, sees the nuggets of crystallized water that form in her hair, in the folds of her oversized T-shirt, on her rigid ill-coloured limbs. Her eyes are almost solid white, but instinctively Michael knows that blindness is not the cause.

When she again asks Michael what his name is, her voice rises from somewhere in the gravel pits and not from her rigid face, for the girl's jaw remains locked. For a beat Michael wonders if she is frozen solid.

To answer this thought, the girl suddenly raises her ice-scabbed arms as if to claim him.

Michael's actions are so frantic they must appear as one vast and hectic gesture: the shriek, the rearing around of his bike, the aching, desperate scaling of the gravel mound, the piercing push through the tear in the fence, the breathless race across the fields.

Michael rides. And rides.

The distance Michael places between himself and the gravel yard brings little relief. Not even the sight of his grandparents' home calms him. He rushes up their driveway, allows his bike to drop, then runs directly to the tiny guestroom that serves as his bedroom every summer vacation.

Burying his face in his pillow, Michael listens to the sound of approaching footsteps.

"Mikey, you all right?"

His grandmother's musical voice is a balm to him.

Michael lifts his head, but when he sees the reddish stains that mar his grandmother's fingers and the apron she's wearing he winces.

"What is it, son?"

He points a bent finger and his grandmother laughs.

"It's strawberries, silly. I'm making jam. I saw you come tearing up the road like the devil himself was at your heels."

Michael wipes his mouth. "Grandma, do you believe in ghosts?"

Her brow lifts behind her spectacles. "Ghosts? No, I can't say that I do, Mikey. Why?"

His account of the experience reaches all the way to the tip of Michael's tongue, but at the last instant he bites it back. He shakes his head, stays silent.

His grandmother frowns. "Too much time in the sun, dear. Why don't you lie down for a while? I'll wake you for lunch."

Michael nods. His grandmother's suggestion sounds very good indeed. He reclines his head back onto the pillows and shuts out the world.

He doesn't realize he's dozed off until he feels his grandmother nudging him. Perspiration has dried on his hair and skin, which makes him feel clammy. He shivers and then groggily makes his way to the kitchen to join his grandparents for sandwiches.

"What happened, sleepyhead?" his grandfather teases. "You didn't tire yourself out on the first day, did you?"

His grandfather receives a sardonic swat from his grandmother, which makes Michael laugh.

"He probably just rode too long in the heat," she says.

"Oh? Where'd you ride to?"

"Just . . . around." Michael bites into his sandwich, hoping that this line of questioning will end.

"Mikey asked me a little earlier if I believed in ghosts." His grandmother sets a tumbler of milk down in front of Michael as she settles into her chair.

"Ghosts? What brought that on?"

Michael shrugs. "Nothing. I was just wondering."

He cannot be sure, but Michael feels that his grandfather's glare on him has hardened.

Michael remains indoors, the only place he feels relatively secure, for the rest of the day. He helps his grandmother jar up the last of her jams and wash up afterwards. He watches cartoons while she prepares supper. His grandfather is outdoors, labouring on one of the seemingly endless projects which occupies so much of his time. He is a veritable stranger in the house. Last summer

Michael had tried to assist him with the various chores, but he got the feeling that his grandfather found him more of a burden than an aid. So this year he takes his mother's advice and just stays out of his grandfather's way.

Though he's never been mean, his grandfather does give off an air that Michael finds far less pleasant than that of his grandmother. She is always cheerful, brimming with old family stories or ideas of various things that he could help her with. Grandma's chores never feel like work.

After supper Michael's mother phones to see how his first day went. He is oddly grateful for the deep homesickness that hearing her voice summons; it means that he doesn't have to think about what he'd seen that morning. His mother says she'll be up to visit on the weekend.

The late morning nap and mounting anxieties make sleep almost impossible for Michael. He lies in his bed, which suddenly feels uncomfortably foreign, and wrestles with the implications of what he has seen, what he has *experienced*, for the encounter was far more than visual.

Standing in the presence of that girl, whatever she had been, made the world feel different. Just recollecting the event made Michael feel dizzy.

Maybe his grandmother is right, maybe he has been riding too hard under the hot sun. After a time Michael understands that the only way he can put the incident behind him is to return to the pits, to test what he'd seen or thought he had seen. His teacher last year told him the first rule when learning about science and nature is that you must repeat the experiment. If you want to know the truth about something you have to do the same thing more than once. If the results are the same, then what you've found is something real.

Tomorrow he will go back. He will find the truth.

The girl is nowhere to be found. Michael rides out after breakfast, despite his grandmother advising him against it. He promises her he will ride slowly and in the shade, and that he'll be home to help her with lunch.

Michael is so elated by the absence of the ugly vision that he plunges through the rip in the chain-link and begins to scale and shoot down the gravel mounds at a manic pace. Dust mushrooms up in his wake. Michael feels unfettered from everything.

The sound of an approaching vehicle startles him to such a degree that he almost loses his balance.

Glancing up to where the country lane meets the gate of the gravel pit, Michael spies his grandfather's pickup truck. He performs a quick shoulder check, panicked by the distance that stretches between him and the hole in the fence.

His grandfather steps out of the cab. Realizing that he has no time to escape, Michael hunches low and pedals behind the farthest gravel mound. There he dismounts, crouches, and is punished by the thundering heartbeat in his ears.

The gate is unlocked, de-chained. The pickup truck comes crawling down along the narrow path, parking before the shed. Michael doesn't hear the engine shut off and he wonders if his grandfather is just waiting for him to come out from behind the mound so he can run him down.

But then the engine is silent and is soon followed by the rumbling sound that signifies the corrugated metal door being opened. Has the ghost-girl flung the door open from the inside? Perhaps she has attacked his grandfather. Michael swallows. With utmost caution he creeps to the edge of the mound and peers.

It is dark inside the shed, so dark that it looks boundless; a deep cavern of redbrick. Michael can just discern the faintest suggestions of objects: power tools, equipment of various shapes, overfilled shelves of metal.

The only item that stands out is the white box. It glows against the gloom and puts Michael in mind of Dracula's coffin. But the sight of its orange power light glowing like a match flame confirms to Michael that it is nothing more than a freezer.

The shed's corrugated door is drawn down. His grandfather must have chores to attend to in the shed. It likely won't take him long to locate whatever tools he needs. Michael steals the opportunity to rush back to the tear and escape.

He races out to the bridge above West Creek. There he settles into a shady spot, dangles his legs over the bridge's edge and studies catfish squirming along the current.

Near noon, Michael mounts his bike and rides back to his grandparents' home.

The pickup truck is parked in the driveway. He takes a deep breath, praying that his grandfather hasn't seen him making his escape.

"I'm home, grandma," he calls from the foyer.

Entering the kitchen, Michael is startled by the sight of his grandfather fidgeting at the counter.

"She went into town to run some errands," he says.

"Sit down, your lunch is ready."

Michael does as he is told. His grandfather plunks down a bowl of stewed tomatoes before him, along with a glass of milk. He nests himself at the far end of the table and chews in silence.

His stomach knots. Michael chokes down the slippery fruit in his bowl.

"I suppose I should have had you wash your hands before we sat down," his grandfather remarks. "You're pretty filthy. You've got dust all over your clothes and hands."

Michael freezes. His grandfather's gaze remains fixed on the food in his dish, which he spoons up and eats in a measured rhythm.

When his bowl is empty, his grandfather sets down his spoon and lifts his eyes to Michael's. "I have a confession to make," he begins. "You know yesterday when your grandmother brought up the topic of ghosts? Well, can you keep a secret, just between us?"

Michael nods.

"You swear it?"

"I swear."

"Cross your heart?"

Michael does so.

"All right then. I wasn't being honest when I said I didn't believe in them. The fact is I do. I saw a ghost once myself."

"You did?"

"Yes. Well, it was something *like* a ghost. I think what
I saw was actually a jinn."

"A jinn?"

"A jinn is a spirit, Michael. Legend says they are created by fire. They can take all kinds of forms; animals, people. But they're very dangerous."

"What did the jinn that you saw look like?" Michael asks breathlessly.

"It was in the form of a young girl."

Michael feels his palms growing damp. "Where did you see her?"

"In the woods, not too far from here. I think she was planning to burn the forest down. That's what the jinn do, they bring fire."

"And did she?"

His grandfather shakes his head.

"So what happened?"

His grandfather tents his hands before him. "They say the only way to combat the element of fire is with ice. . . ."

And with that, a silent tension coils between child and elder, winding tighter like a spring. Michael is confused, curious, and scared. He doesn't know what to do or say.

"Young boys get curious, and when they get curious they sometimes discover things that give them the wrong impression of what the world is like. There are always two sides to things, Michael," his grandfather advises.

"There is the appearance of things and then there is what lies beneath. I want you to remember that, boy. Don't base your opinions of the world on how it appears. Always try to remember what lies beneath. Sometimes the things that appear to be the most innocent are the most dangerous, and vice versa. It was a long time before I knew this, so I want you to learn it while you're young. You understand?"

Michael nods even though he does not at all understand.

The sound of his grandmother turning into the driveway brings Michael a relief that borders on gleeful.

He runs to her. His grandfather rises and dutifully clears the table.

The remainder of the day moves at a crawl as Michael searches for a way to probe his grandfather further about the jinn. Is this what he has seen? No, what he's seen looks more like a spirit born of ice. Either way, the woods that surrounded the old gravel pits are obviously haunted, and that means they are dangerous. By bedtime that night Michael has resolved to never again visit the gravel pits. He will find other ways to amuse himself.

He has almost managed to convince himself that everything is right with the world when the girl appears again, this time inside his grandparents' house.

It is the dead of night and Michael is returning to his bed after relieving himself. She stands in the hallway, her flesh phosphorescent in the darkness. The nuggets of ice sparkle in her hair like a constellation of fallen stars.

Michael is bolted in place. His jaw falls open as if weighted. He looks at her but somehow isn't truly seeing her. In the back of his mind Michael wonders if what he is experiencing is what lies beneath the surface of the girl and not merely her appearance.

The girl neither speaks nor moves. She stands like a coldly morbid statue, with one arm jutting toward the wall of the corridor.

Michael's gaze hesitantly runs along the length of the girl's extended arm, and her pointing finger. Is she indicating the unused phone jack on the wall? Michael turns back to face her but before him there now stretches only darkness.

He lingers in the vacated hallway for eons before finally crouching down to investigate the phone jack. It is set into the moulding, which Michael's grandmother always keeps clean and waxed. Michael clasps the jack's white plastic covering and tugs at it. It pops loose.

Within it Michael discovers a pair of keys. One of them is larger than the other and has the words 'Tuff Lock' engraved on its head. The smaller key is unmarked.

A creak of wood somewhere inside the house acts as a warning to Michael. He hurriedly recovers the jack and slips back to his room where he lies in thought until the sun at last burns away the shadows.

Only after he hears his grandfather fire up his old pickup and drive off— Is he going back to his secret redbrick vault at the gravel pits?—does Michael leave his room.

His grandmother is sitting on the living room sofa.

She seems smaller somehow, almost deflated.

"Morning," Michael says, testing her mood.

"Good morning, dear," she replies. Her tone is distant, a swirl of unfocused words.

"Where's grandpa?"

She stands. "He had some chores to do. Are you hungry?" She advances to the kitchen without waiting for Michael's response.

"You all right, grandma?"

She forces a chortle. "I'm fine, Mikey, just fine. Your grandpa just seemed a little out of sorts this morning and I guess I'm a bit worried about him, that's all."

Michael feels his face flush. "What's the matter with him?"

"He didn't sleep well." She seems to be attempting to drown out her own voice by clattering pans and beating eggs in a chrome bowl. "Your grandpa has bad dreams sometimes, and when he does he wakes up very cranky and fidgety."

"Oh."

When they sit down to eat Michael wrestles to find what he hopes is a clever method of interrogation. He needs so badly to know. . . .

"Does grandpa ever talk about what his bad dreams are about?"

"No."

"Do you ever have bad dreams?"

"Almost never, dear. I think the last time was a couple years ago when there was some bad business here in the village."

"What happened?"

"A girl went missing." She speaks the words more into her coffee cup than to Michael, but even muffled they stun him.

"Missing?"

His grandmother nods. "She was one of the summer people, came up here with her family. I'd see her walking to and from the beach almost every day by herself. Then one day she went down to swim but never came back. Must have drowned, poor thing. They dragged the lake but she was never found. A terrible event. Felt so bad for her mother and father. That's why your grandfather and I never let you go to the beach unsupervised."

"Do you remember what she looked like?"

She shrugs. "Thirteen-years-old or so. Blonde hair, I recall that much."

Michael excuses himself from the table. His jimmying open of the phone jack is masked by the noises of his grandmother washing the breakfast dishes.

"Think I'll go for a ride," he tells her.

"Be careful, dear. Have fun."

Throughout his race to the gravel pits Michael senses that the village is somehow made out of eyes. He passes no one, but is terrified by the prospect of encountering his grandfather at the pits.

The area is equally abandoned. The cavern of redbrick sits snugly locked, illuminated by a hot dappling of sunlight. He enters the breach in the fence and fishes out the pair of keys from his pocket.

He marries the one labelled Tuff Lock with the padlock that bears the same engraving. The lock gives easily. The clunking noise startles a murder of crows from their nest. Michael cries out at their sudden cawing, wing-flapping reprimand. He quickly looks about, terrified of being caught.

The gravel mounds are as ancient hills, silent and patient and indifferent to all human activity. Michael removes the padlock and struggles to raise the corrugated door. It rattles up its track, revealing the musty, cluttered darkness.

Like an ember, the orange light of the freezer gleams from the back of the shed.

Michael feels about for a light switch but finds none.

With great care he makes his way to the light. He is like a solider crossing a minefield. Every motorized tool, every stack of bagged soil, is a danger.

He reaches the freezer. Its surface is gritty with dust.

He sees the metal clamp that holds its lid shut. It is secured with another padlock. Before he's fully realized what he is doing, Michael inserts the smaller key and frees the open padlock from its loop. He can hear the freezer buzzing and he wonders if he is truly ready to see what it contains.

You've gone this far, he tells himself. He pulls the lid up from the frame.

Frost funnels upward, riding on the gust of manufactured arctic air. Like ghosts, the cold smoke flies and vanishes.

A bundled canvas tarp reposes within the freezer's bunk. Its folds are peppered with ice, its drab earthy brownness in sharp contrast to the white banks of frost that have accumulated on the old freezer's walls. The tarp is secured with butcher's twine, which Michael cannot break, so instead he wriggles one of the canvas flaps until his aching fingers can do no more.

But what he has done is enough. Through the small part in the bundle the whitish, lidless eye stares back at him, like a waxing moon orbiting in the microcosmic blackness of the canvas shroud.

Michael whimpers. All manner of emotion assails him at once, rendering him wordless.

A shadow steps in front of the open shed door.

Michael spins around, allowing the freezer lid to slam down. His grandfather has caught him. Michael sees his future as one encased in stifling ice.

But the figure in the doorway is too slight to be his grandfather.

Michael then sees the ghost-eyes staring at him from the dim face. A face that is brightened by rows of teeth as the girl grins. She bolts off into the woods.

"Wait!" Michael cries. He stumbles across the littered shed, but by the time he reaches the gravel pits she has gone.

What do I do? Michael keeps thinking as he locks both freezer and shed. He needs help.

His confusion blurs the ride back to his grandmother.

It also makes him doubt what he sees once the house comes into view. His grandfather's pickup is once more in the driveway. Beyond it the entire house is engulfed in flames. Neighbours are rushing about the property, seemingly helpless. Michael speeds up to the lawn, jumps off his bike and attempts to run through the front door.

A man stops him. "No, son! We've called the fire department. Stay back, stay back!"

Ushered to the edge of his grandparents' property, Michael can see the window of their bedroom. The lace curtain is being eaten by fire, allowing him a heat-weepy view of the figures that are lying on the twin beds inside.

He sees his grandmother, who appears to be bound to her bed with ropes. Next to her, Michael's grandfather lies unbound, a willing sacrifice. The large can of gasoline stands on the floor between them. The pane shatters from the heat.

Michael feels his gaze being tugged to the trees at the end of the yard, where some kind of animal is skittering up the limbs with ease.

In the distance, sirens are wailing their lament.

KNIFE THROWING THROUGH SELF-HYPNOSIS
Robin Richardson

To pass as a strong man, move boulders through
inflated pores, black lumps stiff as good scotch. Watch
the rolling of your Rs, too often soft, unworthy of the
buckle's brass eagle just above the cock. The cock

is paramount. No hero hides his bulge—blue worming up
the thigh like high-wires. It's not enough to fuck
the daughter of a dragon, her claws gone through your
waist. You must undo whatever noble airs she claims,
maintain your status with the slitting of a tooth-white throat.

YOUR FIGURE WILL ASSUME BEAUTIFUL OUTLINES

Claire Humphrey

I spent every day of my first decadi in Savaurac staring at the likeness of a girl on a notice for corsets. I figured she was long dead of the clap, or maybe she only ever lived in some garret artist's absinthe-blind eye, but she was a very pretty girl: deep bosom, low waist, and the sable hair shared by most of her people.

"Your figure will assume beautiful outlines." That was written below her picture, along with the name of the corset-maker. The paper was pasted on the wall beside my Da's special table, where he sat to score the matches. I sat there to labour over our application for residence, listening to the thump of fists on the training bags and running my fingertips over my knuckles, where the fight calluses were already softening.

The fight club used old notices for wallpaper because it was a poor sort of place, same as why they strewed the floor with sawdust and the shells of nuts, and most of the tables had one leg shorter than the others. The owner, though, Mr. Karinen, had promised work for Da if we came to Savaurac, and so we had.

The day I finished our immigration paperwork, Benno Karinen, the owner's son, was going around the walls with a whalebone scraper, taking down the stained notices and pasting up fresher ones. When he got to where I sat, he went by me like I wasn't anything, and set his paste bucket right on my table and his scraper to the top of the notice for corsets.

"Leave that one," I said.

Benno looked down all haughty and went right back to scraping.

"I said leave it!"

His whalebone tore right through the ribboned curls on the girl's head.

I stood up then. Benno was just above my height and three stone heavier. I hit out straight for his nose.

Two decadis at least since I'd been in the ring last, what with packing up our things in Kervostad and getting set up here in Savaurac, and my fist had been getting thirsty for a face.

I pulled Benno's cork for him, blood raining down into the paste-bucket. I laughed out once before I could stop myself. Benno did, too, like he couldn't believe it.

"Da!" he said. "Da, come and see the straight on our Valma." It came out a bit thick. He spat into the bucket and grinned at me with blood outlining his teeth. "Da, you didn't tell me she was a fighter."

"Didn't know it," Mr. Karinen said, tossing his towel down and coming out from behind the bar. He eyed me from under a tangled ginger brow. "Well, little lady? How much do you weigh?"

"I'm a welterweight, sir."

"Strapping girl, you have here, Igo," he said to my Da. I tried to take my arm back, but he was still waving it. "How about it, Valma? Would you like to fight?"

He held up an open palm for me to punch. I smacked my fist into it hard enough to make him wring his hand after.

"Spirit, Igo," he said, "she's got your spirit. Let's put her to spar with the lads tomorrow, see what she can do."

"Which I thought girls weren't allowed in the ring here, sir," I said. That much, Da had told me before we left, though I thought he only meant I would stop fighting before audiences, not that I would go without sparring or even bag-work.

"By law, no," Mr. Karinen said. "But there's ways. For a girl raised by Igo Topponen, there's ways."

My Da had taken the Kervostad Heavyweight Belt twice, when he was young. I could just barely remember: my Da with a lean-carved belly, sweat shining on him like oil under the galvanic lights of the ring. Someone holding his arm up high. Everyone shouting.

He wasn't a fighter now. He was an old man with both ears cauliflowered and his hair razored close to his scarred scalp. He had given me his salt-rotted wraps and gloves and sent me up between the ropes while he watched from outside.

He came past Mr. Karinen and took my other arm and raised it, proud as if I was a winner already, and with his mouth smiling wide I could see the two teeth he broke on Selmo Voroven's fist the year I was born.

I felt the muscles in my arms knotting up with eagerness. I was his daughter, no doubt of it. Maybe I'd end up with teeth to match his after all.

"How'd you like a match next decadi?" said Mr. Karinen. I'd been sparring with his lads since Plum-day, my knuckles scuffing open and seeping into my wraps. My Da poured vinegar over them until they finally healed over into dark pink scars.

"Yes, sir!" I said. "Which I'll do you and Da proud."

"No doubt of it, Valma, no doubt of it. There's one thing, though, you see. The Provosts, they won't allow lasses in the ring. There's lasses among the Provosts, not that you can tell them for such without a hair on their heads. Why they can do magic but not fight, I don't know, but it's the Provosts' law to make and ours to live under. But I know just the fellow who will help."

Hanno Jalmarinen, charm-master, lived behind a copper-worked door at the end of a long alley. He measured me up and down with his little pale eyes and then made me stand still for a half-hour while he did mysteries about me, and then he went to his workbench and muttered over a bit of metal for a moment. Two hundred soldats, it cost Mr. Karinen, and I thought it a vast sum indeed, but when I put on the charm Mr. Karinen said it was excellent work.

The charm was a fine copper ring to go about my littlest finger, flat enough that it would not be felt beneath my wraps, let alone my gloves. "Mind you never take it off," Mr. Karinen said. "And keep it secret. The Provosts have laws on everything."

I did not feel any different with it on, but when I took it home and showed Benno, he stared and stared.

"Shut your mouth, you downy idiot," I told him. Only my voice came out a bit lower, and cracked halfway.

Benno didn't shut his mouth.

I looked in the mirror we used for shadowboxing. "I look the same," I said, disappointed. Maybe my face was a bit more square, my neck thicker. I stood sideways and craned at myself.

"No, you don't," Benno said.

"What's so changed, then?"

But he only shook his head and punched me in the shoulder and told me to get my wraps.

My first match fell on Madder-day, in a basement club on the poorest street in the Quarter. I fought Luko Vannen, who weighed four pounds less than me and had both eyes blacked from a previous fight. I blacked one of them for him all over again and laid him out at the end of the third round. My own eyebrow was cut and blood spattered the front of my singlet, and the crowd roared for me, such as they were, a double handful of factory workers and a few all-day drinkers. For me. I had not heard the sound since leaving home, and it was as sweet to me as the taste of water washing the metal-sour spit from my mouth.

I fought again a half-decadi later: a fellow with hands like granite already and heavy muscle twining over his shoulders above the torn neck of his singlet. I walked in thinking I was a fine gritty fighter, and I walked out with my tooth stuck through my inner lip.

I went straight home and found Benno behind the bar and spat out a mouthful of my own salty blood onto the sawdust at his feet. "Which you might've tried to hit me proper!" I said, spraying a bit.

"Eugh," he said, and wiped at his sleeve. "What are you on about?"

"Pulling your punches when you spar with me," I said.

"I never."

"You know I'm a lass. That fellow didn't. And he hit me twice as hard as you."

"Maybe he's just better—"

"He's a welterweight, Benno. You're nearly a heavyweight."

"I've four pounds to go—"

I punched him in the ear as hard as I could.

He swore and shook it off. "You want me to treat you like a lad?" And he floored me with a straight that broke my nose.

I sat in the sawdust, hands cupped under my chin, Benno standing over me. "Your Da's had most of the training of you," he said. "And he's known you were a lass all your life."

I don't know if Da heard, but the next time he was working my defence, he jabbed me right over my taped nose. While I tried to wipe the water from my eyes, he followed up with a couple of hooks that knocked me sideways into the ropes.

I wanted to embrace him, but the bell hadn't gone yet, so I bounced up and under his guard and pummelled him in the ribs until it did.

Benno and I waited until our fathers were busy with the night's fighters and the usual fellow had arrived to tend bar. In the green room, Benno put on his Savaurin greatcoat and gave me one of his jackets.

I had my charm on, of course, and my hair queued like a man's. We took a few soldats from the tip jar, Benno filled his flask with the stuff his Da kept on the bottom shelf, and we strolled over to Rue Prosper.

The theatre had a front like a tart's bodice, all carmine velvet ruffles. Inside it was far too warm, and the lamp-oil was scented laudanum-sweet. Men and lads shuffled in and doffed their hats and bought glasses of gin from a girl at the back. Benno and I passed the flask back and forth and I began to yawn; I'd been training in the morning and my shoulders had that pleasant deep ache.

Benno prodded me in the side and then snatched his hand back. "You don't even feel like a girl," he whispered.

I prodded him back, in the soft flesh of his belly. "You do."

Then a man started playing a hurdy-gurdy, and the curtain rushed upward, and I got my first sight of Amandine Azur. She wore a plume upon her head and she danced with two great feather fans, flirting them before and behind so that now you could see only her eyes and the plume, and now a swift glimpse of her whole body.

She gazed at me, I swore she gazed at me, but when I said so at the end of her set, Benno scoffed and looked superior and made me come away without speaking to her, and I did not even learn her name until we were out of doors again and I saw it on the notice fixed to the theatre's façade. They had drawn her peeping sideways over the fans, and the likeness was very good, delicate lines of ink capturing the snap of her brilliant eye.

I came back the next day. She was not seeing visitors, so I spoke with the gin-girl and left a note on one of my fight notices to come and see me at Karinen's, and I said that she would be let in free if she wanted. But I did not see her in the crowd the night of my fight, and because I dropped my guard to look, I lost.

I went back to see Amandine's show, sitting at the rear of the theatre beside the drafty door. That first time, I did not speak to her; I was tongue-cursed, brave enough only to look.

The second time, I came up to the base of the stage, and she looked down at me and flicked the feather in her hair and winked at me. Then she did the same to the fellow next to me. He was a grey-headed Savaurin with a sailor's weatherworn face and half his teeth knocked awry. I turned and left.

The third time, I gave the gin-girl a soldat to show me the rear door of the theatre, and I waited there for Amandine to come out. When she did—muffled in a long grey gown and a black coat, carrying a plain reticule—she saw me and checked, wary for a second, and then she came forward and touched her gloved hand to my cheek. I felt the nap of velvet.

Amandine smiled. Her lips were still rouged. She said, "You look a sweet lad, you do, and I can see you didn't mean to frighten me, but you mustn't lie in wait for a lady, you know."

"I only wanted to ask you if you'd dine with me at Travere's."

"Ah," she said. "A generous offer, and if I were a mercenary lass, I would take you up on it. But no amount of generosity will make me yours. It is not in my nature to love you."

"How do you know?" I said, which I was sorry for a moment later, for of course she would know her own nature.

She only rolled her fine eyes a little. "Be sweet, and do not keep me," she said. "My mama waits up for me."

So I stepped aside and watched her walk down the alley toward Rue Marquette; but I looked away quickly, because though I could pay a soldat to watch her unrobed, it felt wrong to stare now that she was in everyday dress.

Mr. Karinen called me over one morning as I finished training. I towelled sweat from my face and hair and came to lean on the bar, unwinding my wraps.

"Hanno Jalmarinen, the charm-master, he's been taken," he said.

"Taken?"

"By the Provosts, for breaking their Law."

I thought of the Provosts I'd seen: like vultures with their black uniforms and bald heads, all the hair shaven right off, even the eyebrows. They were supposed to be able to suck your strength away with the touch of a fingertip. "What will they do to him?"

"Hang him, most like," Mr. Karinen said, shrugging. "The question is what will they do to us."

"But we didn't—" I stopped, seeing the glint of my copper ring as I unwound the stained length of my wrap.

"He wouldn't give up his customers a'purpose," Mr. Karinen said. "But they have ways and ways."

"Can we get him out?" I said.

Mr. Karinen shook his head. "Which there's no escaping from under the Provosts' eye. But we can be careful not to draw that eye our way. You keep that ring on night and day, Valma . . . Valmo, I mean to say. You're a lad now, your fight records show it. No going back."

He didn't seem to mind much about the hanging, but I did. The day of it, in early Frimaire, I borrowed Benno's finest jacket and queued up my hair and went early to get a spot. There was a chilly mist, and the crowds were sparse. I came up close enough to see Hanno Jalmarinen's face, thinner and pouchier than I remembered.

His eyes found mine. I wasn't sure if he recognized me, or if his own work called out to him somehow. He did not speak, but his mouth twisted to one side.

Then they put the black hood over his head, and then the noose.

I stayed for the drop, but once the crowd began clamouring for locks of the dead man's hair—they thought it lucky, in Savaurac—I turned away.

A girl in the crowd saw me as I slipped by, and caught at my sleeve. "Care to share some chestnuts?"

I jerked my coat from her grasp, and I went to get drunk.

I took a few dizzy wrong turns on my way back to the Quarter and found myself standing before the notice. It was a different drawing by now, but still Amandine's face, eyes alight with wonderful secrets.

Her act was nearly over but I paid my soldat, pushed right up to the front, and watched her from there, so close I could smell her hyssop scent. I laid my cheek against the scrollwork at the foot of the stage. My eyes were only a foot away from Amandine's slippers, emerald velvet. At the end of her dance she slid one foot forward so that it nearly touched my lips.

I did not move. Men applauded Amandine and threw soldats onto the stage, and the two gin-girls began herding them out and I kept still, only reaching my hand to trace where she had stepped.

She came out from backstage, after a while, when there were only a few drunkards lolling in their seats and me there entranced.

She wore a dressing-gown now, and plainer slippers that crossed the stage and stopped before me.

"Someone's going to come in a moment to chuck you out," she said.

I rolled my head to see her face, far up high and haloed by the chandelier. "Can you stay here until they do?"

She laughed and extended her foot to nudge my shoulder. "No, lad,

I'm trying to save you from a rough exit."

"Not a lad," I said.

"Oh—" laughing harder "—you're a full-grown man, then? All the same—"

I let go of the scrollwork and groped around to pull off the copper ring.

Amandine's face changed entirely: all the sparkling tease dropped away and her brows went up sharply. She opened her mouth and took a breath.

I did not hear what she said, though—I had to bend down below the scrollwork to vomit up a few hours' worth of gin.

When I raised up my head again she was gone. I felt my empty stomach twist. I said her name, and the sound echoed in the empty theatre.

But she came down the steps at the side of the stage and wrapped her slim arms around my shoulders and helped me to stand.

"Come quick," she said. "No, leave the ring off, I can't have a lad in my dressing room."

Her dressing room held a wash-stand and a little table covered with pots of rouge and things I didn't recognize, and a posy of hothouse violets. She sat me down on a sturdy chair and took a more delicate one for herself. I leaned my elbows on my knees and held my head.

"I will dine with you at Travere's," she said, "if the offer still stands."

"Why?" I said, wishing I could make my eyes fix upon her face.

"I didn't know then you were a girl," she said. "You didn't mention that."

She reached out to push my hair from my face. Her fingernails were painted poison-green.

And that's all I know of the night. The morning, I remember better—waking on the floor beside the chair, covered in Amandine's wrap. Tucked in my pocket, a note I could barely read, as it was in Savaurin and Amandine's script was terrible.

I got Benno to read me the note. It said Amandine would come and see me, and it asked me whether I liked myself better with the ring, or without.

"You took it off for her?" Benno said, brows up. "You know you're to wear it always."

"I was drunk," I said. "It fell off while I was casting up my accounts."

"Mind it doesn't happen again," Benno said. "The Provosts are over-strict about such things."

"Over-strict," I echoed, and I thought of the sound of Hanno Jalmarinen's voice, gurgling in his throat, stopped by the rope.

I, Valmo Topponen, took the Quarter Amateur Welterweight Belt on Ash-day at the end of Ventôse. To do it, I beat ten other lads in three days. Some of those fights were easy enough, some weren't, and one left me so done-up I vomited into the blood-bucket as soon as the referee let go my hand—but that was the last one.

I stood under the hot galvanic lights while a gentleman from the Fight Board buckled the belt about my waist, and I tried not to cast up my accounts again. An artist from the Daily Clarion scribbled my likeness and asked me how to spell my patronym, which I had to tell him I did not know what he meant. Mr. Karinen set him straight, and shook hands with a great many people, and accepted the winner's purse on my behalf.

And then there was Da, smiling wide as wide, giving me water to rinse my mouth and pulling over my head a stained old jumper that had been his for this same purpose.

And there was Amandine, and I forgot everyone else. She had brought me an armful of ivy-leaves and hothouse lilies. I crushed them between us as I kissed her, lily-pollen sticking to the trails of blood over my breastbone, her fingers winding in the sweaty queue of my hair.

When I had washed up, I took a handful of soldats from my winner's purse and took Amandine to Travere's, as promised. The seats were high-backed booths with finials shaped like pineapples. The other patrons were artists and poets in extravagant hats. We had mussels and sopped up their broth with bread, and drank dry white wine from the southern estates.

My hands had swelled with all the work they'd been doing; the ring was chafing my finger, and I was tired of standing to piss. I went out to the privy a lad and came back a lass in the same clothing. Amandine smiled broad when she saw me and stood up to kiss me on both cheeks and then the mouth, and poured me another glass of wine.

I did not see if anyone else noticed, because I had eyes for nothing but the flush on Amandine's cheeks and the way her hair was coming down on one side, and the prim collar of her everyday frock brushing the corner of her jaw.

I brought her back to my room that night and we stayed awake until very late, trying to be quiet in the hush of the Quarter's curfew.

I wasn't at the club when the Provosts arrived. Benno was the one who had to let them in, and he said he forgot everything he knew: offered to pull them a pint even though they never take ale, nearly touched one of their hands when he set out their cups of water. They left behind a summons for me to come to the question room at the nearest Watchtower.

I couldn't read all of the summons, but I saw my name. I put my finger on the paper to hold it still while I spelled out the rest.

Benno made a sound. Too late. The summons caught me right away. My hand left the paper and my feet began walking toward the door. "Grab my jacket!" I called over my shoulder to Benno, but I couldn't stop walking—he had to walk along beside me and help put my arms in the sleeves, because the summons wouldn't let me stop swinging them either.

"I don't want to go by myself!" I said.

"Then you should've left the bloody paper alone! Valma—I can't leave the bar untended, I have to—"

"Go, go," I said. "Send my Da, if you can!"

My feet took me up the street at a fair clip, never letting me swerve for a horse-pat or a loose cobble.

I arrived at the Watchtower with a stubbed toe and a temper, and my feet marched me right up to a desk where a Watch recruit wrote in a ledger and my mouth said, "Valmo Topponen of Karinen's, welterweight, reporting as summoned."

Then the summons let go of my tongue and I added, "Which you could have waited until I had my lunch!"

The recruit rolled his eyes and wrote laboriously. I stood. I tried to turn about and walk out, but apparently the magic was still on me to prevent that happening.

After a few minutes the recruit sighed loudly and stood up and beckoned me to follow. He took me into a room and sat me on a single chair facing a line of nicer chairs.

Ten or fifteen minutes wore by. I heard the half-hour bells ring, up in the tower.

Then I forgot to be bored and furious, because the Provosts came in.

I'd never seen them up close before. It seemed to be true they shaved all their hair, even their eyebrows; it made them look as if they were glaring. A man and a woman, both in their high-collared black coats.

The woman sat in one of the nice chairs and looked at me, and the man came and stood behind me and laid his fingertips on the side of my neck.

I flinched. Couldn't help it. His hand was cold.

"Remove your ring," he said.

"What? No—it's a, it's a birthright, sir, I'm not supposed to—"

"You may address me as Provost. Remove your ring."

This time it came with a push, just like the summons. My one hand went to the other hand and started tugging, and it wasn't gentle either.

I felt the charm come off. I'd never felt it so before: my skin prickling uncomfortably where it stretched or shrank, my balance shifting as my weight settled lower.

The Provost across from me watched. I wanted to ask her to look away, but I could feel my throat changing and I did not know which voice would come out.

When I was all lass again, the Provost rose and came to me and took the ring. "We can't let you keep this, Valmo," she said. "Or Valma, I suppose. The Law states that no one not of Savaurin descent may use the arts within Savaurac."

"That means all magic," said the other Provost, still with his fingertips on my neck. "Copper or otherwise."

"But how will I fight?" I said.

"The Law states you can't do that either," said the woman Provost. "Though we're willing to let you off with just a fine for that one. For the charm, you'll have to spend a decadi in Mazonval Gaol."

"She is not quite of age," said the man Provost.

"Ah," said the woman. "Then we shall summon her patron to take the penalty. Excuse me."

"Wait—" I moved to follow her, but the other Provost laid his hand on my shoulder, and without my will, my legs folded again and I fell back onto the chair.

They kept Mr. Karinen. Ten days in the Gaol, they said. They gave me a slip of paper stating this, and told me I could come back tomorrow to pay my fine.

I watched Mr. Karinen shackled and marched out between a pair of Provost cadets. He looked furious and baffled and not very large. They led him out through a side gate and would not let me follow.

When I took the paper back to Benno, he tried to tear it in half, but it was some kind of charmed paper and it held firm.

"This is on you," he said, holding it up and fluttering it before my eyes. "This is all on you." And he struck my face.

I did not fight him. I ran away.

The theatre was just opening. Carlette, the gin-girl, gave me a bit of steak from her dinner to hold to my swelling cheek. She was used to me by then, so I did not think she would think it odd of me to show up bruised, but she must have noticed something different, for she said I could go through to Amandine's dressing room to wait.

Amandine caught up with me at the backstage door, though. She was wearing a corset trimmed with jet beads, and her hair was pomaded into a smooth helmet with a single curl loose at her cheek. She saw from my face that something was wrong, and she pulled me behind a scrim painted with topiary, set her palms to my shoulders, and looked into my face.

"I'm going on in two minutes," she said. "Tell me quick."

"I have to leave Savaurac," I blurted.

She took a breath through parted lips, and her brow furrowed.

"My patron's in gaol, my charm's confiscated and I can't fight as a girl. Was that quick enough?"

Amandine hushed me with a finger to my lips. "Wait. Wait for me. Right here. Promise you'll wait."

I promised. She touched my split cheek, a velvet-light touch like a moth landing and flying away again, and she went onstage.

I watched her from there, from the wings, carpet-bag at my feet. The music sounded tinny at this angle, muffled, but Amandine looked sharper and brighter than ever. Now and again when her face was hidden from the audience by one of her great feather fans, she would turn her eyes to me, and I would move a little so she might see me in the shadows, still waiting.

The dance ended. She received her applause and collected her gifts. And as soon as ever she could, she found me again behind the scrim painted with topiary, and she embraced me, careless now of the paint on her face.

"I will come with you," she whispered into my neck. "I will come with you wherever you go."

So I kissed her and crumpled her pomaded hair in my hands and kissed her more.

I spent the night on Amandine's mama's settee, and in the morning I went to the Provosts and used what was left of my winner's purse to pay the fine.

I went back to Karinen's to find my Da. Benno shouted when he saw me, and chased me out.

But Da came running after me, up the street, his fist closed tight around something.

"Valma," he said. "Valma." And he opened his fist and pressed into my hands one of the gilt rosettes off the Quarter Amateur Welterweight Belt. "Show this to my old sparring partner in Kervostad," he said. "Tell him how you won it. He'll set you up."

I threw my arms around him. He huffed out a laboured breath.

"You won't think of coming with me?" I said.

"It will take Benno and me to keep the place running while Mr. Karinen's locked up," he said; and I knew he was thinking of the year he'd spent looking for work at home, the shame of it and the boredom. "But you," he said. "You need to go where you can fight."

So I stowed the rosette in the innermost pocket of my jacket, kissed my Da's cheek, and went to meet Amandine.

"Kervostad," she said, when I told her. "I hope they like Savaurin burlesque-girls."

"I don't think they've ever seen one." I took the heavier of her cases and we began walking together toward the Quai.

"Will they let you fight as a lad?"

"Better: they'll let me fight as a lass," I said. "I did already, a little, before we left."

Amandine's mouth pursed; even without her crimson stage-paint, her lips were dark and fresh-looking, and I wanted to kiss her, only she looked as if she was thinking about something serious.

"I will miss Valmo," she said, "if I never see him again."

"I'll miss him, too," I said. "But I don't have the charm."

"Let's get another. There must be magicians in Kervostad."

"It will cost us—"

Amandine fluttered a violet-nailed hand like an ostrich fan. "I'm a very good dancer."

I did stop and kiss her, then. It wasn't until we began walking again that I realized we were crossing the square where Hanno Jalmarinen had been hanged. And I was sorry to leave my Da, and my patron, and even Benno, but I was not sorry to leave Savaurac.

Kervostad, as it turned out, liked Savaurin burlesque-girls very much.

A CHARM FOR COMMUNING WITH DEAD PETS DURING SURGERY

Peter Chiykowski

Recite their names
when the doctor says to
count backwards from ten
and anaesthesia dreams you into
the world of animals put to sleep.
Listen for the scratch-click
of nails on linoleum as they gather here
on the far side of sodium thiopental,
cats, hamsters, parrots,
all the dogs you said were
irreplaceable come to lick your fingers with
tongues like warm blood.

Recite their names.
They know you
forget, move on
but they are above jealousy
and below it. The cats slink to rest
on stainless steel trays.
The dogs sigh down to the tiles,
soft chins pressed to paw-tops,
eyes turned up like questions.
Try to remember their birthdays,
the nights they were sick, the drug
that put them to sleep,
the same injection rubbing you
drowsy now
under the knife.

Recite their names,
remember how the sound of something
can mean itself to life
like a dog called in from another room.
Lean into the bright moment
when you first saw
and loved them in spite of
yourself, knowing that
human years are a coefficient
for measuring barbiturates
into the bloodstream,
for calculating the rhythms
of faster hearts, smaller lungs,
shorter lives.

Recite, cradle each name
on your drug-thick tongue, and here
in the halo-world below the operating lamp,
be selfish, set your jaw
with these names behind it
as though you could traffic them
into the recovery room when the nurses come
to wheel you away,
as though you could walk out
of the underworld
smuggling the dead
in your mouth.

STEMMING THE TIDE
Simon Strantzas

Marie and I sit on the wooden bench overlooking the Hopewell Rocks. In front of us, a hundred feet below, the zombies walk on broken, rocky ground. Clad in their sunhats and plastic sunglasses, carrying cameras around their necks and tripping over open-toed sandals, they gibber and gabber amongst themselves in a language I don't understand. Or, more accurately, a language I don't *want* to understand. It's the language of mindlessness. I detest it so.

Marie begged me for weeks to take her to the Rocks. It's a natural wonder, she said. The tide comes in every six hours and thirteen minutes and covers everything. All the rock formations, all the little arches and passages. It's supposed to be amazing. Amazing, I repeat, curious if she'll hear the slight scoff in my voice, detect how much I loathe the idea. There is only one reason I might want to go to such a needlessly crowded place, and I'm not sure if I'm ready to face it. If she senses my mood, she feigns obliviousness. She pleads with me again to take her. Tries to convince me it can only help her after her loss. Eventually, the crying gets to be too much, and I agree.

But I regret it as soon as I pick her up. She's dressed in a pair of shorts that do nothing to flatter her pale lumpy body. Her hair is parted down the middle and tied to the sides in pigtails, as though she believes somehow appropriating the trappings of a child will make her young again. All it does is reveal the greying roots of her dyed black hair. Her blouse . . . I cannot even begin to explain her blouse. This is going to be great! she assures me as soon as she's seated in the car, and I nod and try not to look at her. Instead, I look at the sunbleached road ahead of us. It's going to take an hour to drive from Moncton to the Bay of Fundy. An hour where I have to listen to her awkwardly try and fill the air with words because she cannot bear silence for anything longer than a minute. I, on the other hand, want nothing more than for the world to keep quiet and keep out.

The hour trip lengthens to over two in traffic, and when we arrive the sun is already bearing down as though it has focused all its attention on the vast asphalt parking lot. We pass though the admission gate and, after having our hands stamped, onto the park grounds. Immediately, I see the entire area is lousy with people moving in a daze—children eating dripping ice cream or soggy hot dogs, adults wiping balding brows and adjusting colourful shorts that are already tucked under rolls of fat. I can smell these people. I can smell their sweat and their stink in the humid air. It's suffocating, and I want to retch. My face must betray me; Marie asks me if I'm okay. Of course, I say. Why wouldn't I be? Why wouldn't I be okay in this pig pen of heaving bodies and grunting animals? Why wouldn't I enjoy spending every waking moment in the proximity of people that barely deserve to live, who can barely see more than a few minutes into the future? Why wouldn't I enjoy it? It's like I'm walking through an abattoir, and none of the fattened sows know what's to come. Instead they keep moving forward in their piggy queues, one by one meeting their end. This is what the line of people descending into the dried cove looks like to me. Animals on the way to slaughter. Who wouldn't be okay surrounded by that, Marie? Only I don't say any of that. I want to with all my being, but instead I say I'm fine, dear. Just a little tired is all. Speaking the words only makes me sicker.

The water remains receded throughout the day, keeping a safe distance from the Hopewell Rocks, yet Marie wants to sit and watch the entire six hour span, as though she worries what will happen if we are not there to witness the tide rush in. Nothing will happen, I want to tell her. The waters will still rise. There is nothing we do that helps or hinders inevitability. That is why it is inevitable. There is nothing we can do to stem the tides that come. All we can do is wait and watch and hope that things will be different. But the tides of the future never bring anything to shore we haven't already seen. Nothing washes in but rot. No matter where you sit, you can smell its clamminess in the air.

The sun has moved over us and still the rocky bottom of the cove, and the tall weirdly sculpted mushroom rocks are dry. Some of the tourists still will not climb back up the metal grated steps, eager to spend as much of the dying light wandering along the ocean's floor. A few walk out as far as they can, sinking to their knees in the silt, yet none seem to wonder what might be buried beneath the sand. The teenager who acts as the lifeguard maintains his practiced, affected look of disinterest, hair covering the left half of his brow, watching the daughters and mothers walking past. He ignores everyone until the laughter of those in the silt grows too loud, the giggles of sand fleas nibbling their flesh unmistakable. He yells at them to get to the stairs. Warns them of how quickly the tide will rush in, the immediate undertow that has sucked even the heaviest of men out into the Atlantic, but even he doesn't seem to believe it. Nevertheless, the pigs climb out one at a time, still laughing. I look around to see if anyone else notices the blood that trickles down their legs.

The sun has moved so close to the horizon that the blue sky has shifted to orange. Many of the tourists have left, and those few that straggle seemed tired to the point of incoherence. They stagger around the edge of the Hopewell Rocks, eating the vestiges of the fried food they smuggled in earlier or lying on benches while children sit on the ground in front of them. The tide is imminent, but only Marie and I remain alert. Only Marie and I watch for what we know is coming.

When it arrives, it does so swiftly. Where once rocks covered the ground, a moment later there is only water. And it rises. Water fills the basin, foot after foot, deeper and deeper. The tide rushes in from the ocean. It's the highest tide in the world over. It beckons people from everywhere to witness its power. The inevitable tide coming in.

Marie has kicked off her black sandals, the simple act shaving inches from her height. She has both her arms wrapped around one of mine and is staring out at the steadily rising water. She's like an anchor pulling me down. Do you see anything yet? she asks me, and I shake my head, afraid if I open my mouth what might come out. How much longer do you think we'll have to wait? Not long, I assure her, though I don't know. How would I? I've refused to come to this spot all my life, this spot on the edge of a great darkness. That shadowy water continues to lap, the teenage lifeguard finally concerned less with the girls who walk by to stare at his athletic body, and more with checking the gates and fences to make sure the passages to the bottom are locked. The last thing anyone wants is for one to be open accidentally. The last thing anyone but me wants, that is.

The sun is almost set, and the visitors to the Hopewell Rocks have completely gone. It's a park full only with ghosts, the area surrounding the risen tide. Mushroom rocks look like small islands, floating in the ink just off the shore. The young lifeguard has gone, hurrying as the darkness crept in as fast as the water rose. Before he leaves he shoots the two of us a look that I can't quite make out under his flopping denim hat, but one which I'm certain is fear. He wants to come over to us, wants to warn us that the park has closed and that we should leave. But he doesn't. I like to think it's my expression that keeps him away. My expression, and my glare. I suppose I'll never know which.

Marie is lying on the bench by now, her elbow planted on the wooden slats, her wrist bent to support the weight of her head. She hasn't worn her shoes for hours, and even in the long shadows I can see sand and pebbles stuck to her soles. She looks up at me. It's almost time, she whispers, not out of secrecy—because no one is there to hear her—but of glee. It's almost time. It is, I tell her, and try as I might I can't muster up even a false smile. I'm too nervous. The thought of what's to come jitters inside of me, shakes my bones and flesh, leaves me quivering. If Marie notices, she doesn't mention it, but I'm already prepared with a lie about the chill of day's end. I know it's not true, and that even Marie is smart enough to know how warm it still is, but nevertheless I know she wants nothing more than to believe every word I say. It's not one of her most becoming qualities.

The tide rushes in after six hours and thirteen minutes, and though I'm not wearing a watch I know exactly when the Bay is at its fullest. I know this not by the light or the dark oily colour the water has turned. I know this not because I can see the tide lapping against the nearly submerged mushroom rocks. I know this because, from the rippling ocean water, I can see the first of the heads emerge.

Flesh so pale it is translucent, the bone beneath yellow and cracked. Marie is sitting up, her chin resting on her folded hands. I dare a moment to look at her wide open face, and wonder if the remaining light that surrounds us is coming from her beaming. The smile I make is unexpected. Genuine. They're here! she squeals, and my smile falters. I can't believe they're here! I nod matter-of-factly.

There are two more heads rising from the water when I look back at the full basin, the first already sprouting an odd number of limbs attached to a decayed body. The thing staggers towards us, the only two living souls for miles around, though how it can see us with its head cocked so far back is a mystery. I can smell it from where we sit. It smells like tomorrow. More of the dead emerge from the water, refugees from the dark ocean, each one a promise of what's to come. They're us, I think.

The rich, the poor, the strong, the weak. They are our heroes and our villains. They are our loved ones and most hated enemies. They are me, they are Marie, they are the skinny lifeguard in his idiotic hat. They are our destiny, and they have come to us from the future, from beyond the passage with a message. It's one no one but us will ever hear. It is why Marie and I are there, though each for a different reason—her to finally help her understand the death of her mother, me so I can finally put to rest the haunting terrors of my childhood. Neither of us speak about why, but we both know the truth. The dead walk to tell us what's to come, their broken mouths moving without sound. The only noise they make is the rap of bone on gravel. It only intensifies as they get closer.

For the first time, I see a thin line of fear crack Marie's reverie. There are nearly fifty corpses shambling toward us, swaying as they try to keep rotted limbs moving. If they lose momentum, I wonder if they'll fall over. If they do, I doubt they'd ever right themselves. Between where we sit and the increasing mass is the metal gate the young lifeguard chained shut. More and more of the waterlogged dead are crowding it, pushing themselves against it. I can hear the metal screaming from the stress, but its holding for now. Fingerless arms reach through the bars, their soundless hungry screams echoing through my psyche. Marie is no longer sitting. She's standing. Pacing. Looking at me, waiting for me to speak. Purposely, I say nothing. I'll let her say what I know she's been thinking.

There's something wrong, she says. This isn't—

It isn't what?

This isn't what I thought. This, these people. They aren't *right*. . . .

I snigger. How is it possible to be so naive?

They are exactly who they are supposed to be, I tell her with enough sternness I hope it's the last she has to say on the subject. I don't know why I continue to make the same mistakes. By now, I'd have thought I would have started listening. But that's the trouble with talking to your past self. Nothing, no matter how hard you try, can be stopped. Especially not the inevitable.

The dead flesh is packed so tight against the iron gates that it's only a matter of time. It's clear from the way the metal buckles, the hinges scream. Those of the dead that first emerged are the first punished, as their putrefying corpses are pressed by the thong of emerging dead against the fence that pens them in. I can see upturned faces buckling against the metal bars, hear softened bones pop out of place as their lifeless bodies are pushed through the narrow gaps. Marie turns and buries her face in my chest while gripping my shirt tight in her hands. I can't help but watch, mesmerised.

Hands grab the gate and start shaking, back and forth, harder and harder. So many hands, pulling and pushing. The accelerating sound ringing like a church bell across the lonely Hopewell grounds. I can't take it anymore, Marie pleads, her face slick with so many tears. It was a mistake. I didn't know. I never wanted to know. She's heaving as she begs me, but I pull myself free from her terrified grip and stand up. It doesn't matter, I tell her. It's too late.

I start walking toward the locked fence.

I can't hear Marie's sobs any longer, not over the ruckus the dead are making. I wonder if she's left, taken the keys and driven off into the night, leaving me without any means of transportation. Then I wonder if instead she's watching me, waiting to see what I'll do without her there. I worry about both these things long enough to realize I don't really care. Let her watch. Let her watch as I lift the latches of the fence the dead are unable to work on their own. Let me unleash the waves that come from that dark Atlantic Ocean onto the tourist attraction of the Hopewell Rocks. Let man's future roll in to greet him, let man's future become his present. Make him his own past. Who we will be will soon replace who we are, and who we might once have been.

The dead, they don't look at me as they stumble into the unchained night. And I smile. In six hours and thirteen minutes, the water will recede as quickly as it came, back out to the dark dead ocean. It will leave nothing behind but wet and desolate rocks the colour of sun-bleached bone.

SOCIAL SERVICES
Madeline Ashby

"But I want *my own* office," Lena said. "*My own* space to work from."

Social Services paused for a while to think. Lena knew that it was thinking, because the woman in the magic mirror kept animating her eyes this way and that behind cat-eye hornrims. She did so in perfect metre, making her look like one of those old clocks where the cat wagged its tail and looked to and fro, to and fro, all day and all night, forever and ever. Lena had only ever seen those clocks in media, so she had no idea if they really ticked. But she imagined they ticked terribly. The real function of clocks, it seemed to her, was not to tell time but to mark its passage. *Tickticktick. Byebyebyebye.*

"I'm sorry, Lena, but your primary value to this organization lies in your location," Mrs. Dudley said. Lena had picked out her name when Social Services hired her. The name was Mrs. Dudley, after the teacher who rolled her eyes when Lena mispronounced "organism" as "orgasm" in fifth grade health class. She'd made Social Services look like her, from the hornrims to the puffy eyes to the shimmery coral lipstick melting into the wrinkles rivening her mouth. Now Mrs. Dudley was at her beck and call all the time, and had to answer all the most inane questions, like what the weather was and if something looked infected or not.

"This organization has to remain nimble," Mrs. Dudley said. "We need people ready to work at the grassroots level. You're one of them. Aren't you?"

Now it was Lena's turn to think. She examined the bathroom. It had the best mirror, so it was where she did most of her communication with Social Services. The bathroom itself was tiny. Most of the time it was dirty. This had nothing to do with Lena and everything to do with her niece's baby, whose diapers currently clogged the wastebasket.

There was supposed to be a special hamper just for them with a charcoal filter on it and an alert telling her niece when to empty it, but her niece didn't give a shit—literally. Lena had told her that ignoring the alert was a good way to get the company who made the hamper to ping Social Services—a lack of basic cleanliness was an easy way to signal neglect—but her niece just smiled and said: "That's why we have you around. To fix stuff like that."

"That is why you decided to come work for us, isn't it?" Mrs. Dudley asked.

Lena nodded her head a little too vigorously. "Yes," she said. "Yes, that's it exactly."

She had no idea what Social Services had just asked. Probably something about her commitment to her community, or her empathy for others. Lena smiled her warm smile. It was one of a few she had catalogued especially for the purposes of work. She wore it to work like she wore her good leather gloves and her pretty pendant knife. Work outfit, work smile, work feelings. She reminded herself to look again for her gloves. They didn't have a sensor, so she had no idea how to find them.

"Here is your list for today," Mrs. Dudley said. The mirror showed her a list of addresses and tags. Not full case files, just tags and summaries compiled from the case files. Names, dates, bruises. Missed school, missed meals, missed court dates. "The car will be ready soon."

"Car?"

"The last appointment is quite far away." The appointment hove into view in the mirror. It showed a massive old McMansion in the suburbs. "Transit reviews claim that the way in is . . . unreliable," Mrs. Dudley said. "So, we are sending you transport."

Lena watched her features start to manifest her doubts, but she reined them in before they could express much more. "But, I . . ."

"The car drives itself, Lena. And you get it for the whole day. I'm sure that allays any of your possible anxieties, doesn't it?"

"Well, yes . . ."

"Good. The car has a Euler path all set up, so just go where it takes you and you'll be fine."

"Okay."

"And please do keep your chin up."

"Excuse me?"

"Your chin. Keep it up. When your chin is down, we can't see as well.

You're our eyes and ears, Lena. Remember that."

She nodded. "I—"

A fist on the bathroom door interrupted her. Just like that, Mrs. Dudley vanished. That was Social Services security at work; the interface, such as it was, did not want to share information with anyone else in a space, and so only recognized Lena's face. Her brother had tried to show it a picture of her, and then some video, but Lena had a special face that she made to login, and the mirror politely told her brother to please leave.

"*Open up!*"

Lena opened the door. Her niece stood on the other side. She handed Lena the baby, and beelined for the toilet. Yanking her pants down, she said: "Have *you* ever had to hold it in after an episiotomy?"

"No—"

"Well, you *might*, someday, if you ever got a boyfriend, which you shouldn't, because they're fucking crap." The sound of her pissing echoed in the small room. "Someday I'm going to kill this fucking toilet." She reached behind herself, awkwardly, and slapped it. Her rings made scratching noises on its plastic side. "You were supposed to tell me I was knocked up."

Lena thought it was probably a bad time to tell her niece that her father, Lena's brother, was the one responsible for upgrading the toilet's firmware, and that he had instead chosen to attempt circumventing it, so it would give them all its available features (temperature taking, diagnosis, warming, and so on) for no cost whatsoever. He didn't want the manufacturer knowing how much he used the bidet function, he said one night over dinner. That shit was private.

Her niece didn't bother washing her hands. She took the baby from Lena's arms and kissed it, absently. "It's creepy to hear you talking to someone who isn't there," she said. Her eyes widened. Her eyeliner was a vivid pink today, with extra sparkles. Her makeup was always annoyingly perfect. She probably could have sold the motions of her hands to a robotics firm, somewhere. "Don't you worry, sometimes, that you're, like . . . making it all up?"

Lena frowned. It wasn't like her niece to consider the existential. "Do you mean making it up as I go? Like life?"

"No no no no no. I mean, like, you're making up your job." She glanced quickly at the mirror, as though she feared it might be watching her. "Like maybe there's nobody in there at all."

Lena instantly allowed all of her professional affect to fall away, like cobwebs from an opened door. She turned her head to the old grey pleather couch with its pillows and blankets neatly stacked, right where she'd left them that morning. She let her niece carry the full weight of her gaze. "Then where would the rent money come from?" she asked.

Her niece had the grace to look embarrassed. She hugged her baby a little tighter. "Sorry. It was just a joke." She blinked. "You know? Jokes?"

A little car rolled across Lena's field of vision. Its logo beeped at her. "My car is here," she said. "Try to leave some dinner for me."

"Is it true they make you all get the same haircut, so they can hear better?"

Lena peered over the edges of her frames. Social Services didn't like it when she did that, but it was occasionally necessary. Jude, the adolescent standing before, her seemed genuinely curious and not sarcastic. That didn't make his question any less stupid.

"No," she said. "They don't make us wear a special haircut."

Jude shrugged. "You all just look like you've got the same haircut."

"Maybe you're just remembering the other times I've been here."

Jude smiled dopily around the straw hanging out of his mouth, and slurped from the pouch attached to it. It likely contained *makgeolli*; that was the 22nd floor specialty. Her glasses told her he was mildly intoxicated; he wore a lab on a chip under the skin of his left shoulder, in a spot that was notoriously difficult to scratch. The Spot was different for every user; triangulating it meant a gestural camera taking a full-body picture, or extrapolating from an extant gaming profile. "Oh, yeah . . . Yeah, that's probably it."

"Why do you think I'm here, Jude?"

"Because the Fosters aren't."

The kid didn't miss a beat. The algorithm had first introduced them three years ago, when his foster parents took them in; he referred to them, privately, as "The Fosters." Three years in, "The Fosters" had given up. They collected their stipend just fine, but they left it to Lena to actually deal with Jude's problems.

His main problem these days was truancy; in a year he wouldn't have to go to school any longer unless he wanted to, and so he was experiencing an acute case of senioritis in his freshman year. If he chose to go on, though, it would score Lena some much-needed points on her own profile. There was little difference, really, between his marks and her own.

"Is there any particular reason you're not going to school, these days?"

Jude shrugged and slurped on the pouch until it crinkled up and bubbled. He tossed the empty into the sink and leaned over to open the refrigerator. You didn't have to really move your feet in these rabbit hutch kitchens. He got another of the pouches out. "I just don't feel like it," he said.

"I didn't really much feel like going, either, when it was my turn, but I went."

Jude favoured her with a look that told her she had best shut her fucking mouth right fucking now. "School was different for you," he said simply. "You didn't have to wear a uniform."

"Well, that's true—"

"And your uniform didn't ping your teacher every time you got a fucking boner."

Lena blushed, and then felt herself blushing, which only made it worse. She looked down. True, their school district was a little too keen on wearables, but Jude's were special. "You know why you have to wear those pants," she said.

"That was when I was *thirteen*!"

"Well, she was ten."

"I *know* she was ten. I fucking *know* that. There's no way I could possibly forget that, now." He crossed his arms and sighed deeply. "We didn't even *do* anything."

"That's not what you told your friends on 18."

He sucked his teeth. Lena had no idea if Jude had really done the things he said he did. The lab inside the little girl had logged enough dopamine to believe sexual activity had occurred, but it had no way of knowing if she'd helped herself along, or if she'd had outside interference. The rape kit had the same opinion: penetration, not forced entry. When the relationship was discovered, the girl recanted everything, and said that nothing had happened, and that it didn't matter anyway, because even if something had happened, she really loved Jude. Jude did the same. Except he never said he loved her. This was probably the most honesty he demonstrated during the entire episode.

"I know it's difficult," Lena said. "But completing your minimum course credits is part of your sentencing. It's part of why you get your record expunged when you turn eighteen. So you have to go." She reached into the sink and plucked out the pouch with her thumb and forefinger.

It dangled there in her grasp, dripping sweet white fluid. "And you have to quit drinking, too."

"I know," he said. "It's stupid. I was just bored, and it was there."

"I understand. But you're hurting your chances of making it out of here. This kind of thing winds up your transcript, you know. You can't get a job without a decent transcript."

Jude waved his hand. "The fabbers don't care about grades."

"Maybe not, but they care about you being able to show up on time. You know?

He rolled his eyes. "Yeah. I know."

"So you'll go to school tomorrow?"

"Maybe. I need a new uniform, first."

"Excuse me?"

"Well, it's really just the pants. I threw them out."

Lena blinked so that her glasses would listen to her. "Well, we have to find those pants."

The glasses showed her a magnifying glass zipping to and fro across the cramped, dirty apartment. It came back empty. "You really threw them out?" she asked, despite already knowing the answer. Maybe he'd given them to a friend. Or sold them. Maybe they could be brought back, somehow.

"I think they got all sliced up," Jude said, miming the action of scissors with his fingers. "I wore my gym clothes home yesterday, and I put my other stuff in my bag, and then under the viaduct, I gave them to this homeless dude. He found the sensors right away. Said he was gonna sell 'em."

She winced. "How do you know he's not wearing them?"

"They were too small."

It was beyond her power. She would have to arrange for a new uniform. She'd probably have to take Jude to school tomorrow, too, just to smooth things over. He tended to start a new attendance streak if someone was actually bringing him there. The record said so, anyway. For a moment it snaked across her vision, undulating and irregular, and then she blinked and it was gone.

"I'll be here tomorrow at seven to take you to school," she said, and watched the appointment check itself into her schedule. "And don't even think about not being here, or not waking up, or getting your mom to send a note, or anything like that. I intend to show up, and if you don't do the same, Social Services will send someone else next time, and they won't be so understanding. Okay?"

Jude snorted. "Okay."

"I mean it. You have to show up. And you have to show up sober. I'll know if you're not, and so will your principal. He can suspend you for that, on sight."

"I know." Jude paused for a moment. He reached for the fresh pouch, and then seemed to think better of it. "I'm sorry, Lena."

"I know you're sorry. You can make it up to me by showing up, tomorrow."

"I don't want them to send someone else. I didn't mean to get you in trouble. I was just mad, is all."

"You would have better impulse control if you quit drinking. You know that, right?"

"Yeah."

"So you know what we have to do next, right?"

He sighed. "Seriously?"

"Yes, seriously. I can't leave here without it."

They spent the next half hour cleaning out his stash. He even helped her bring it down to the car. "Are you sure this is it?" he asked, when it perked up at Lena's arrival.

"It's on loan," she said. "Some people lease their vehicles on a daily basis to Social Services, and the car drives itself back to them at the end of the day with a full charge."

"It's a piece of shit."

"Just put the box in the back, will you?"

Jude rolled his eyes as she popped the trunk. Technically, she shouldn't have allowed him to come down to the garage with her. It wasn't recommended. Her glasses had warned her about it, as they neared the elevator. She made sure Jude carried the box full of pouches and pipes, though, so that he'd have to drop it if he wanted to try anything. Now, she watched as he leaned over the trunk and set the box inside.

"Nice gloves." He reached in and brought something out: Lena's good leather gloves. They were real leather, not the fake stuff, with soft suede interiors and an elastic skirt that circled the wrist and kept out the cold air. They were a pretty shade of purple. Distinctive. Recognizable. "Aren't these yours?" he asked.

"I . . ."

"I've seen you wearing them, before." He frowned. "I thought you said this was someone else's car. On loan."

"It is . . ."

"So how did your gloves wind up in the trunk?"

Lena wished she could ask the glasses for help. But without sensors, the glasses and the gloves had no relationship. At least, nothing legitimate and quantifiable. They had only Lena to link them.

"I must have used this car, before," she said. "That must be it. I must have forgotten them in here, the last time, and not used the trunk until then. And the owner left the gloves in the trunk, hoping that I'd find them."

"Why the trunk? Why not on the dash? How many times do you look in the trunk?"

Jude slammed the trunk shut. He held the gloves out. Lena took them gingerly between her thumb and forefinger. They felt like her gloves. A little chilled from riding around in the trunk, but still hers. How strange, to think that they'd gone on their own little adventure without her. Hadn't the car's owner been the least bit tempted to take them? Or one of the other users? There were plenty of other women on the Social Services roster. Maybe they'd been worn out, and then put back, just like the car. Maybe the last user was someone higher up on the chain, and they knew Lena would be taking this particular car out on this particular morning, and they put her gloves back where she would find them. That would explain how she'd never seen them until just now.

"Don't look so creeped out," Jude said. "They're just a pair of gloves, right?"

"Right," Lena said. "Thanks."

By the end of the day, Lena had to admit that the car did not look familiar in the least. That didn't mean it looked *unfamiliar*, either, just that it looked the same as all the other print-jobs in the hands-free lane. The same flat mustard yellow, the same thick bumper that made the whole vehicle look like a little man with a moustache. It was entirely possible that she had used this car before. Perhaps even on the same day that she'd lost her gloves. She didn't remember losing them. That was the thing. She kept turning them in her hands, over and over, pulling them on and pulling them off, wiggling her fingers in their tips to feel if they were truly hers or not.

When had she last used a car for Social Services?

"February of last year," Mrs. Dudley said. "February fifteenth, to be exact."

Lena did not remember speaking the words aloud, either. But that hardly mattered. It was Social Services' job to understand problems before they became issues. That was how they'd first found Jude, after all. Surely the glasses had logged her examination of the gloves and the car and the system had put two and two together. It could do that. She was sure of it.

"You subvocalized it," Mrs. Dudley said.

Yes. That was it. People did that, sometimes, didn't they? They muttered to themselves. It wasn't at all unusual.

"People do it all the time," Mrs. Dudley told her.

Lena forced herself to speak the next words out loud. "Did the owner of the car save the gloves for me?"

Mrs. Dudley paused. "That's one way of putting it."

"What do you mean?"

Outside, the highway seemed empty. So few people drove, any longer. Once upon a time, four o'clock on a Friday afternoon in late October would have been replete with cars, and the cars would have been stuffed with mothers and fathers lead-footing their way into the suburbs, anxiously counting down the minutes until they earned a late fee at their daycare. Now the car whizzed along, straight and true, spotting its nearest fellow vehicle every ten minutes and pinging them cheerfully before zipping ahead.

It felt like driving into a village afflicted by plague.

"I think we need to bring you in for a memory exam, Lena," Mrs. Dudley said. "These lapses aren't normal for a woman in your demographic. You may have a blood clot."

"Oh," Lena said, perversely delighted by the thought.

"But first, you have to do this one last thing for us."

"Yes. The house in the suburbs."

"You must be very careful, Lena. Where you're going, there's no one else on the block. It's all been foreclosed. And it's going to be dark, soon."

"I understand."

"The foreclosures mean that the local security forces have been diminished, too. Their budget is based on population density and property taxes, so there won't be anyone to come for you. Not right away, anyway. Everyone else lives closer to town."

"Except for the people in this house."

Another pause. "Yes. The ones who live there, live alone."

Jackson Hills was the name of the development. The hills themselves occupied unincorporated county land, the last free sliver of property in the whole area, and the crookedness of the rusting street signs seemed meant to tempt government interference. That was an old word for molestation, Lena remembered. You came across it in some of the oldest laws. *Interference.* As though the uncles she spent her days hearing about were nothing more than windmills getting in the way of a good signal.

Was it an uncle that was the trouble, this time? The file was very scant. *"Possible neglect,"* it read. The child in question wore old, ill-fitting clothes, a teacher said. His grades were starting to slip. His name was Theodore. People called him Teddy. His parents never came to Parent/Teacher Night. They attended no talent shows. But they were participatory parents online; their emails with Teddy's teachers were detailed and thoughtful, with perfect spelling and grammar.

"We intend to discuss Teddy's infractions with him as soon as possible," one read. *"We understand that his hacking the school lunch system to obtain chicken fingers every day for a month is very serious, as well as nutritionally unwise."*

Teddy had indeed hacked the school lunch system to order an excess of chicken fingers delivered to the school kitchen by supply truck. He did this by entering the kitchen while pretending to go on a bathroom break, and carefully frying all the smart tags on all the boxes of frozen chicken fingers and fries with an acne zapper. With all the tags dead, the supplier instantly re-upped the entire order. The only truly dangerous part of the "hack" was the fact that he'd been in the walk-in freezer for a whole five minutes. Surveillance footage showed him ducking in with his coat zipped up all the way. The coat itself said that his body temperature had never dipped.

"I don't get any junk food at home," the boy said, during his inevitable talk with the principal. "They don't deliver any."

The gate to Jackson Hills was still functional, despite the absence of its residents. It slid open for Lena's car. As it did, a dervish of dead leaves whirled out and scattered away toward freedom. It felt like some sort of prisoner transfer. The exchange made, Lena drove past the gate.

The car drove her through the maze of empty houses as the dash lit up with advertisements for businesses that would probably never open. Burger joints. Day spas. Custom fabbers. In-house genome sequencing. All part of "town and country living at its finest." Some of the houses looked new; there were even stickers on the windows. As she rolled past, projections fluttered to life and showed laughing children running through sprinklers across the bare sod lawns, and men flipping steaks on grills, and women serving lemonade. It was the same family each time.

"WELCOME HOME," her dashboard read.

The house stood at the top of the topmost hill in Jackson Hills. Lena recognized it because the map said they were drawing closer, and because it was the only house on the cul-de-sac with any lights on. It was a big place, but not so different from the others, with fake Tudor styling and a sloping lawn whose sharpest incline was broken by terraced rock. Forget-me-nots grew between the stones. Moss sprang up through the seams in the tiled drive. There was no car, so Lena's slid in easily and shut itself off with a little sigh, like a child instantly falling to sleep.

At the door, Lena took the time to remove her gloves (when had she put those on?) and adjust her hair. She rang the bell and waited. The lion in the doorknocker twinkled his eyes at her, and the door opened.

Teddy stood there, wearing a flannel pyjama and bathrobe set one size too small for his frame. "Hello, Lena," he said.

She blinked. "Hello, Teddy."

"It's nice to meet you. Please come in."

Inside, the house was dusty. Not dirty or even untidy, but dusty. Dust clung to the ceiling fans. Cobwebs stretched across the top of every shelf, and under the span of every pendant light. The corners of each room had become hiding places for dust bunnies. But at Teddy's height, everything was clean.

"Where are your parents, Teddy?"

"Would you like some tea?" Teddy asked. "Earl Grey is your favourite, right?"

Earl Grey *was* her favourite. As she watched, Teddy padded over to the coffee table in the front room, and poured tea from a real china service. It had little pink roses on it, and there was a sugar bowl with a lid and a creamer full of cream and even a tiny dish with whisper-thin slices of lemon. When he was finished pouring, Teddy added two sugars and a dash of cream to the cup. Then he handed her the cup on a saucer with both hands, and then pressed something on his watch.

"It tells when it's done steeping," he said. "Would you like to sit down?"

Lena sat. The sofa shifted beneath her, almost as though she'd sat on a very large cat. A moment later it had moulded itself to her shape. "It's smart foam," Teddy said. "Please try some of your tea. I made it myself."

Lena sipped. "You've certainly done your homework, Teddy," she said. "You're not the only person to research me before my arrival, but you're the only one who's ever been this thorough."

"I wanted to make it nice for you."

It was an odd statement, but Lena let it pass. She took another sip. "This is a very lovely house, Teddy. Do you help your parents with the housework?"

He nodded emphatically. "Yes. Yes I do."

"And are you happy, living here?"

"Yes, I am."

"There don't seem to be many other kids to play with," Lena said. "Doesn't it get lonely?"

"I don't really get lonely," he said. "I have friends I play with online."

"But it can't be very safe, to live here all alone."

His mouth twitched, a little, as though he had just heard the distant sound of a small animal that he very much wanted to hunt. "I'm not alone," he said.

"Well, I meant, the neighbours. Or rather, the lack of any."

His shoulders went back to their relaxed position. "I like it here," he said. "I like not having any neighbours. My parents didn't like it very much, at first, but I liked it a lot."

Since he had left the door open, Lena decided to go through it. "So, when are your parents coming?"

"They're here," he said. "They just can't come upstairs, right now."

Lena frowned. "Are they not well?"

Teddy smiled. For a moment, he actually looked like a real eleven-year-old, and not like a man who had shrunk down to size.

"They're busy," he said. "Besides, you're here to talk to me, right?"

"Well . . . Yes, that's true, but . . ." She blinked again, hard. It was tough to string words together, for some reason. Maybe Mrs. Dudley was right. Maybe she *did* need her brain scanned. She felt as though the long drive in had somehow hypnotized her, and Teddy now seemed very far away.

"I hope that we can be friends, Lena," Teddy said. "I liked you, the last time they sent you here."

Her mouth struggled to shape the words. "What? What are you talking about?"

"You wore those gloves, last time," he said. "In February. You'd had a really lonely Valentine's Day, the day before, and you were very sad. So I made you happy for a little while. I had some pills left over."

It was very hot in the room, suddenly. "You've drugged me," Lena said.

Teddy beamed. "Gotcha!"

Lena tried to stand up. Her knees gave out and her forehead struck one corner of the coffee table. For a moment she thought the warmth trickling down her face was actually sweat. But it wasn't.

"Uh oh," Teddy said. "I'll get some wipes."

He bounded off for the kitchen. Lena focused on her knees. She could stand up, if she just tried. She had her pendant knife. She could . . . what? Slash him? Threaten him? Threaten a child? She grasped the pendant in her hand. Pulled it off its cord. Unflipped the blade.

When Teddy came back with a cylinder of lemon-scented disinfectant wipes, she pounced. She was awkward and dizzy, but she was bigger than him, and she knocked him over easily. He saw the knife in her hand, gave a little shriek of delight, and bit her arm, hard. Then he shook his little head, like a dog with a chew toy. It hurt enough to make her lose her grip, and he recovered the knife. He held it facing downward, like scissors. He wiped his mouth with the back of his other hand.

"I knew I liked you, Lena," he said. "You're not like the others. You don't really like kids at all, do you? This is just your job. You'd rather be doing something else."

"That's . . ." Her vision wavered. "That's not true. . . ."

"Yes, it is. And it's okay, because I don't like other kids, either. They're awful. They're mean and stupid and ugly and poor, and I don't want to see them, ever again. I just want to stay home, forever."

Lena heard herself laughing. It was a low, slow laugh. She couldn't remember the last time she had heard it.

"Why are you laughing?" Teddy asked.

"Because you're all the same," she said. "None of you want to go to school!" She laughed again. It was higher this time, and she felt the laugh itself begin to scrape the dusty expanse of the vaulted ceiling, and the glittering chandelier that hung from it. She could feel the crystals trembling in response to her laughter. She had a pang for Jude, who would have absolutely loved whatever shit Teddy had dosed her with.

"I just need someone to create data," Teddy was saying. "I've tried to keep up the streams by myself, but I can't. There are too many sensors. I have to keep sleeping in their bed. I have to keep riding their bikes. Both of them. Do you even know how hard that is?"

Lena couldn't stop laughing. She lay on the floor now, watching her blood seep down into the fibres of the carpet. It was white, and it would stain badly. Maybe Teddy would want her to clean it up. That seemed to be her lot in life—cleaning up other people's messes. But as she watched, Teddy got down on his knees and began to scrub.

"It won't be that bad," he said. "I'll make it nice, for you. All I need is someone to pretend to be my mom, so I can do homeschool. I have all her chips, still. I took them while she was still warm, and I kept them in agar jelly from my chemistry set." He winced. "I would have gotten Dad's, too, but he was too fat."

Teddy reached out his hand. "Do you think you can make it to the dining table?"

She let him help her up. "Social Services . . ."

"You can quit, tomorrow," Teddy said. "Just tell them you can't do it, any more."

"But . . . My mirror . . ." Why was she entertaining any of this? Why was she helping him?

"I have a mirror," he said. "Your face is the login, right? You talked to my mirror, the last time you were here. You just don't remember, because you blacked out later."

She turned to him. "This is real?"

He smiled, and squeezed her cold hand in his much warmer and smaller one. "Yes, Lena. It's all real. This is a real house with real deliveries and real media and a real live boy in it. It's not like a haunted house. It was, until you came. But it's your home, now. Your own place, just for you and me."

"For . . ."

"Forever. For ever and ever and ever."

HOW GODS GO ON THE ROAD
Robin Richardson

She keeps a crystal ball on the coffee table
at a Super 8 somewhere between Harrodsburg,
Kentucky, and the cornfields she's afraid to enter.
She's thirty again. Spends her birthday burning
sage, rearranges history with the lifting
of a little toe, composes wars while singing
in the shower—"Viper's Drag," "Honey Dipper."
She's the "Lady with the Fan." Tan as deep
as tamarind. Whatever secrets she's received,
what talents, doors as wide as steak knives open
on a nebula she knows she'll one day enter.
Weather will not touch her, nor the sounds
of schoolboys in their march to physics. They
won't fix this hole. Alive too many lifetimes
to believe in cures, she passes decades with the gait
of Tolstoy heroines. However deep she cuts,
it is the blade that bleeds. Her skin like water
holds no form, but folds, and folds, and follows
numbly through the hours of a day.

OUBLIETTE
Gemma Files

Therapy Blog of Thordis Hendricks, July 2, 2012 (4:17 PM):

Back when I was in hospital, recuperating, I thought a lot about what my life had become over those months—that entire year, almost—before my second suicide attempt finally led to formal diagnosis, a plan of treatment, a potential way out of this ever-narrowing flesh trap. The way my perceptions kept on altering, as though filter were laid on top of filter on top of filter, yet so softly, so irretrievably . . . until finally, it was as though I woke up one morning to discover the way I saw things had always been inaccurate, horrifyingly so, and the systemic shock alone was enough to make me reach for something sharp.

Like I'd been born and almost died inside a prison cell, thinking that tiny bit of sky I could see through the window was the wide world, and me outside in it, walking, talking, laughing, living. Until that sky itself became a horror too, blue just a thin lid over black, gravity always in danger of failing before the upwards rush and airless fall into deep space—and it was that fear, that awful lurch, which wrenched me back in and reframed my understanding. Showed me the grave I'd all this time been trapped by, and began to push its walls in on top of me.

I feel better these days, of course, though not by much. But this, what we're doing right now . . . this is supposed to help.

Therapy Blog of Thordis Hendricks, July 2, 2012 (7:02 PM):

All right, Take Two. Start over.

I moved into Shumate House almost immediately after my

last consultation with Dr. Corbray, as an alternative to further hospitalization, which had been almost impossible for me to stand once the initial numbness wore off; constant panic attacks, five different drug combos tried and discarded, all clusters of side-effects equally disgusting. Like I'd been dropped head-first into a gluey swamp and left to thrash, studiously observed, but unaided otherwise.

But being rich counts for a lot, no matter how crazy you may be otherwise. And after Aunt Isa died, the portion of the Hendricks fortune that fell to me—administered, in trust, through my family's firm—served to buy me into Shumate and pay for the almost-undivided attentions of Dr. Corbray. Which brings us here.

This therapy blog is predicated on the assumption—not completely inaccurate—that because my phobia means I can't physically leave Apartment Five but my privacy-linked anxiety issues argue against around-the-clock live-in care, I should be required to provide my assigned worker (Yelena) with a between-sessions look at my thought-processes, so she can make sure my psychological baseline isn't fluctuating wildly: No toxic thought-patterns, no repetition or obsessional looping.

Of course, it's a model of exchange which presumes quite a lot, right from the get-go; that I'm not simply lying in session, for example, let alone out of session. That I really *will* write down a representative sample of whatever comes into my head between this time-signal and the next, if asked to, as opposed to simply . . . making stuff up out of whole cloth, because it amuses me, or because it gives me just the tiniest shred of control over what happens in a life otherwise dictated by other people. That I understand how directly I'm threatening my own welfare, if I do. That I can be trusted to recognize what is and isn't appropriate behaviour, even for myself.

This last part isn't completely up to me, though, thankfully. Since that's supposedly what Yelena is for.

So: Today's entry. Set the timer. Mark.

Saw Yelena yesterday, at 12:22 PM. She claimed to be late (*was* late, no reason to distrust her words by labeling them claims) because of traffic and construction. We took the usual roster of tests, blood, spit and urine, then talked about self-harm triggers for roughly the rest of the hour: how to qualify and quantify, make sure things didn't progress beyond a certain level. Yelena says up to twenty-five per cent is allowable, but once you catch yourself imprinting, you need to move on. Sounds legit.

Talked about Internet access, settled on a protocol. The plan is still to use a family-friendly timer app to restrict potential surfing, allowing just enough time in a row to compose and post. The app in question adds up all your seconds, concurrent or not, and cuts out after a set limit is reached. I still can't believe I agreed to this, but have the distinct feeling I must have been fairly high when I signed those papers. Impossible to tell, one way or the other.

So no looking things up randomly, or not randomly. No visiting the same sites over and over. No time-sinks. Team-mindedness is key. Just RL, baby, moment after dragging-ass moment of it. We already turned off the cable, and there's nothing in my DVD queue but nature films. The books are all self-help. It's daily meditation and morning pages and yoga from here on out, if and when the side-effects of the latest cocktail let me do a Downwards-Facing Dog without feeling like I'm going to puke. Hell, I can't even sleep in too long, or the concierge comes knocking.

It's a great system, really, and I'm honoured to have had so much "input" into its design. At the end of the day, though, I guess I'm just still not sure why there has to be so much care taken that my life, mine, my particular life, isn't destroyed. I'm not sure why I should matter so much, to anyone, aside from basic monetary considerations. And I don't know if any of this qualifies as allowable thought or not—if it's sick, or simply logical. Something anybody else might wonder, given the circumstances.

Okay, that's time. See you tomorr

Entry posted automatically. See attached IM exchange:

rostovy@monitoru.net What's this stuff about "team-mindedness"?
hendricksnox@shumatehouse.com what stuff
rostovy@monitoru.net In Tuesday's last entry. "Team-mindedness is key."
hendricksnox@shumatehouse.com dont understand what youre saying. im tired.
rostovy@monitoru.net No, I understand that, I just need you to look at it again. It might be important.
hendricksnox@shumatehouse.com cant, tired, im done. took my pills. Bed.

Initial MonitorU Intake Report on Thordis Charlotte Hendricks, June 15, 2012
Prepared by Dr. Maurice L. Corbray, consulting psychiatrist
CC'd to Yelena Rostov, attending worker

Registered diagnosis of severe agoraphobia, mid-range obsessive-compulsive disorder and clinical depression with suicidal ideation. Subject is twenty-seven years old. Currently recovering from two suicide attempts, one by intentional overdose of prescription meds, one by radial/ulnar arterial self-exsanguination. Highest education a Master's Degree in Comparative Religious Studies (incomplete). Formerly a T.A. at University of Toronto, now unemployed.

Subject presents as polite and reasonable, though with little emotional affect and micro-periods of disassociation. Prescribed regimen of Cymbalta (side-effects may include drowsiness, blurred vision, lightheadedness, strange dreams, constipation, fever/chills, headache, increased or decreased appetite, tremor, dry mouth, nausea, increased sweating and blood pressure, fatigue and reduced energy). Has agreed to daily yoga practice of roughly sixty to ninety minutes, plus guided meditation, both administered through Skype. Has agreed to participate in phobia-management exercises, and keep a recovery blog. Fees pre-paid in full.

Personal notes: With sufficient effort on her part, I see no reason why subject should not both make a full physical recovery and stabilize her phobia, eventually helping to develop a participatory management protocol which will allow her to graduate from Shumate House by next year at the latest. Nevertheless, given her history, I recommend a tight check routine—three days on, two days off, repeat—in order to ascertain whether or not Cymbalta is the best drug strategy, as well as an equally strict policy of nondisclosure about what happened to the last three subjects who occupied Apartment Five.

corbrayml@monitoru.net Just checking to see you received the Hendricks IR. Any questions?
rostovy@monitoru.net Yes, thanks. So what did happen?
corbrayml@monitoru.net When?
rostovy@monitoru.net To the previous tenants.
corbrayml@monitoru.net I don't think that's relevant.
rostovy@monitoru.net Then why did you mention it?

<u>corbrayml@monitoru.net</u> Feel free to do your own research, Yelena; I look forward to your report. All best.

From the official Shumate House introductory booklet, Shumate—Where Respite Makes Recovery:

What sets Shumate's therapeutic facility apart from every other is our specific brand of total support-system immersion. By offering a well-rounded team of live-in, on-site care workers who follow the "Shumate Method" (first developed by Dr. Jerrold Shumate in 1979, to treat post-traumatic stress disorder amongst relatives of the Canadian members of Jim Jones' People's Temple cult), we guarantee our occupants a safe haven where privacy and anonymity are equally sacrosanct—a place of retreat and reconciliation where no one, no matter their range of symptoms, is ever considered unable to participate in planning their own recovery. . . .

Therapy Blog of Thordis Hendricks, July 25, 2012 (11:45 AM):

Timer on. Start.

It takes about a month to settle in anywhere, let alone get used to a new drug—if that's not a truism, then it should be. So now we're three weeks in, two days into the next seven, nothing but yoga and chores and blogging, pre-packaged food that comes by the close-wrapped tray, long baths with lavender for relaxation, changing my dressings, taking my pills. Each day ticks away in increments, slow-seeping, like that inescapable metallic taste at the back of my tongue, still there no matter how often I spit.

No anxiety, no worry: That's good, right? No OCD twitches. Last night I noticed an actual ring inside the bathtub—a smeared grey scum of skin-cells, something I'd have to scrub at to get off. And I didn't. Didn't think about how I was stewing in my own dirt, like some horrible soup; just sat there and let the water lap up over it, out of sight, out of mind.

No pleasure, though. Anhedonia, just without the usual feeling bad about not feeling good. And my sex drive completely gone, too, but I expected that. Not like it matters much, in here.

I'm amused to note that the guided meditation portion of my sessions takes place while in *shavasana,* the pose most instructors usually strain not to call "corpse posture" (and Yelena's no different, in this respect). I remember hearing about an existentialist yoga class they offered in Germany, pretty much corpse posture from beginning to end, which focused on accepting death rather than trying to distract yourself from it: "Your body will die. Your body will be a corpse. You can discard your body yet still exist. The signal cannot be stopped. . . ." Sort of soothing, especially if you repeat it so often it devolves into a mushy whirr of consonant-click and vowel-sounds, with no single part more significant than the whole: *Ommmmm, just let it all gooooo.*

But yeah, I can see how that probably seems just a tad morbid to concentrate on, as a mantra, especially when you're dealing with a person who still has trouble picking stuff up with her left hand, because dominant hand automatically cuts deeper. So instead, Yelena just talks about breathing and tells me to keep my eyes closed, which I mostly don't, because part of being a reasonable adult is making your own damn decisions and sticking to them. Lie there staring up at the ceiling (white stucco, each tiny plaster stalactite's shadow a grey-black dot) 'til my eyes unfocus enough that it becomes some sort of infinite, negative-flipped space-scape, a white void pocked with black hole stars. . . .

(And think, sometimes: *If only I had the right sort of charts, the right kind of database to work with, I might be able to figure out where that is, up there. If I only knew the math.*

(But that's monkey-mind, right, Yelena? Chatter. Better to shut it out, be in the moment. This dying moment, dying from one second into the next, never the same, always the same. This moment that only goes, forever, no matter what you do or don't, and never comes again.)

I don't dream, but last night I had a doozy . . . so clear, so detailed. Except those details were utterly foreign to me, as though they'd been broadcast straight into my subconscious from somebody else's, detached but specific, a litany of intent. Should've taken notes, because all it is now is a general impression, but I remember thinking: *Yelena will love this. Finally, something worth writing about.*

So do you? Enjoy these entries, I mean. One of us should.

And . . . done, in time. Timer off.

rostovy@monitoru.net Interesting stuff. You really should try to close your eyes when you meditate, though.
hendricksnox@shumatehouse.com guess so, just
hendricksnox@shumatehouse.com when i do i get vertigo

rostovy@monitoru.net That's not good. Do you want me to send a doctor?

hendricksnox@shumatehouse.com maybe. dont know. maybe its not real vertigo, just

hendricksnox@shumatehouse.com dont know going to sleep now ok

rostovy@monitoru.net Okay, that's probably best. Write down your dreams for me next time, all right, Thordis?

rostovy@monitoru.net Thordis?

Yelena Rostov, Notes:

Last three occupants of Shumate House Apt. #5 (in chron. order) = Marie Bissionette, Charles H. Siemanczski, Lloyd Lin Kuan-tai.

All 3 deceased.

Bissionette judged suicide, Siemanczski accidental overdose, Lin suicide. Siemanczski's personal physician disagreed with coroner's verdict—said there was no way his patient could take that much without noticing side effects/stopping before death, but no conclusive evidence either way.

Verdict might also have to do with fact that other 2 were found with plastic bags over heads but Siemanczski wasn't. Possibly removed by accident during death-throes and just not found during investigation, mislabelled as trash.

Other possibility deliberate misdirection. But what would be the point of

Understandable why Corbray doesn't want to talk about it. Doesn't say much for Shumate Method.

Why/how would he think Thordis would ask about it, though?

Does it make sense 2 (poss. 3) people would all choose same strategy? They didn't know each other. Timing alone makes that impossible.

Overdose/bag method pushed by Final Exit euthanasia rights activists amongst others—cult suicides, as per Heaven's Gate.

But people do those in teams.

("Team-mindedness"?)

Therapy Blog of Thordis Hendricks, July 29, 2012 (2:32 PM):

It took a while to figure out what the revealed shape of my life reminded me most of, but I stumbled on it, eventually; Google is our friend, even in the tiniest of possible doses. It was an *oubliette*.

An *oubliette*'s a kind of dungeon accessible only from a hatch in a high ceiling, basically impossible to exit without outside help. The word comes from the same root as the French *oublier*, "to forget," because it was used for prisoners their captors simply wanted to disappear. Some *oubliettes* added the twist of being built on a shelf, a steeply sloping tunnel leading down to the moat or the sea—so you had the choice of letting yourself either slowly starve, or just to slip further down and drown.

The term's also used to refer to ice formations over lakes, or other large bodies of water. As ice crystals form and air is introduced by the movement of the tides, secret tunnels hollow themselves out under the ice, rendering it treacherous. Prone to give way all of a sudden, a grim surprise, and plunge you over your head into water so cold it burns.

Oubliette, jaunty *oubliette*. And this place, Apartment Five, Shumate House—just a more comfortable version of the same? A place to be parked out of sight, out of mind, 'til I'm all safely re-calibrated and refurbished . . . ready to take my place in the world as it is, rather than the world as I thought it was? Ready for public consumption?

Never let it be said I mind having somewhere to pull my head in, for a while; it's kind of nice to have a safe little hidey-hole, I guess, when the open spaces outside remain so goddamn scary. Would be, at least, if I didn't know that somebody else holds the keys—or if I had any sort of idea how long this particular set of adjustments is going to take, exactly, either.

No one likes to be forgotten.

On the other hand, the anhedonia my cocktail deals out mainly serves to make me wonder why anyone would struggle so hard to be remembered, to stay alive; how anyone could want so badly to prolong this particular . . . stasis, this awful pause between nothing and nothing. Because oh sure, I'm safe in here from the worst of it, the truly painful blankness, where input slips away until everything becomes equally hollow and sharp and unbearable—but so what? How much, exactly, is a life without extremes worth, when all's said and done? No depression, no joy. Just grey, marching grey, simplest of all possible forward motions at barely impulse speed, like algae. Existing, not living.

But okay, enough, I didn't forget: write down my dreams. Here's one.

I dreamt I found a closet in that short little hallway between my bedroom and the living room, the one we both know backs onto

Apartment Seven, which means there couldn't possibly *be* a door there. So of course, I opened it. And inside it was full of what seemed like miles on miles of snarled yarn, knotted in on itself, all dirty and wet and vile-smelling. Yet in I went, clearing a path like Lucy through the wardrobe, the yarn-mounds getting progressively colder 'til they iced up, froze almost solid, and I had to tear at them with my numbing hands, kicking myself free. And at last it gave way, became another doorway opening onto . . . nothing. Empty space, star-speckled, with a wind howling past me; a night sky too far away from any sun to ever see real daylight.

After which I heard a voice, some girl, and though I already knew it was a dream this only confirmed it, because it didn't scare me at all that I felt as though I recognized it. Saying: *They call it the Kuiper Belt. Think it's a nothing place, all dead debris and endless absence, but they're wrong, so wrong.* With that little trembly note in her voice that you get when you're so happy you're close to weeping. *Tiamat non delenda est! How could it be? It only moved—Translated* (I heard the capital), *like we'll be. It's real—more real, more beautiful than any agreed-upon construct in this whole "real" world. Perfect, like we'll be perfect. Perfected. Perfection. The ur-planet. The ur-.*

And everyone else will end up here, now, instead. No Heaven or Hell. Just a swirling knot of souls, too tangled to untie themselves without tearing, so far gone that by the time they come back 'round again the earth'll already be inside the Sun. Everyone who's not us, sooner or later. Everyone who's not tuned to the Signal . . .

Which is what? I wanted to ask, desperately. But even as I strung the words, let alone sent them dropping to my tongue, it already had me; I was *inside* it, moving through it while it moved through *me*, all echoing clicks and breath and liquid twittering, keystroke static on an empty station. Classic SETI shit, Translating as it went. A cruel brightness that slapped me back down into the waking world again, even as it simultaneously revealed said "world" to be nothing but skin on howl, a burning scrim, the mere and flattest parody of whatever it was meant to conceal—

So, anyhow: Thanks for the cheap trip, Yelena, like I wasn't already feeling . . . *nothing* enough, already.

Put that on your expanded Cymbalta symptoms list, and smoke it.

Yelena Rostov, Notes:

Kuiper Belt: The outer rim of the Solar System, a belt of asteroids and small bodies; includes Pluto's orbit. Dreams of dark empty places common symbol of depression—may be good sign that T.'s seeing herself separate from it, rather than in it.

Tiamat: Babylonian dragon-goddess, slain by hero-god Marduk.

Interesting connection to Kuiper Belt—'70s pop pseudoscience said there was another planet (Tiamat, natch) where Belt is now, way-station for aliens; Belt's supposed to be its remains, post-destruction.

(Like *Chariots of the Gods?* Grill T. on her reading before coming here.)

Tiamat non delenda est: Riff on *Cartago delenda est?* "Tiamat must *not* be destroyed"?

"The Signal": ?

Handwritten "dream diary" of Thordis Hendricks:

July 31, 2012:

Dreamed I was living in a house, old & decrepit & dust-encrusted, & spent the whole day cleaning it. But when I had to muck out the basement, while I was down there I found a door in the floor & underneath the house a whole other house, equally dirty. So I went down there to clean up that one too & in its basement I found another door, another house, & so on. Smaller & dirtier & further down all the time, & they never stopped. I woke up before I found the bottom.

August 1, 2012:

Dreamed I was pregnant & had been for maybe a year & the doctor wanted to induce me but instead of going to the hospital we did it right here, in the living room. & then I started to feel sick & thought I was going to puke but instead I just doubled up & my stomach came open like a zipper, & inside there was just dust, red dust. & it all spilled out on the floor so I clawed at my own neck so badly I pulled my jugular open & bled to death, I could feel it happening. But I didn't care.

August 2, 2012:

A knock at the door. It's a package & I open it without thinking. A photo-frame with one tiny hole in it, like an ikon, black magic Advent window.

An eye, peering out. So I slide off the back & find out it's a picture of me laid upside-down, staring eye transmuted to blank terror simply by being reversed.

August 3, 2012:
Nothing.

August 4, 2012:
Nothing.

August 5, 2012:
Just floating again, out in the black on an orbital track so elliptical I knew I'd reach the thinnest part of my gravitational field & just slip off like a bead from a thread, go drifting away into nothing & never stop unless I hit something.

August 6, 2012:
Dreamed I was a horse with bones braided through my mane being ridden by something gigantic, this crushing weight, faster & faster, being ridden to death. Every breath a razorblade turning in my chest.

August 7, 2012:
Trapped under a car. I could feel oil dripping on me, maybe gas, or maybe I'd wet myself. That weird smell of hot rubber and dusty asphalt. & at any time the car might collapse further, something might spark, I might burn alive, but I don't think I was scared. I could hear the Signal far off in the distance, getting stronger.

August 8, 2012:
Corpse posture meditation, & I felt like I was going to blend into the floor, all heavy & cold & hot at the same time, every part of my body ticking with life I couldn't control. & then I was standing up & looking down on myself, & I looked so good empty, so perfected. Transitioned. But then I started to rot, & then I was melting, I then I was gone. Just the mat left behind.

August 9, 2012:
I was a man who wanted to be a woman, or maybe a woman who'd been a man. But one way or the other I was bad & wrecked now, broken &

I knew it, & there was nothing I could do about it, because whatever choice I'd made was the wrong one. So I took a knife from the kitchen & started cutting parts of myself off anywhere I could & eating them, hoping that would help.

August 10, 2012:
Nothing.

August 11, 2012:
Nothing.

August 12, 2012:
Dreamed I was up on a hill & looked down into the valley & there were three people standing there with bags over their head, clear plastic bags, so I could see their faces when they all turned & looked up at me, but I didn't recognize any of them. & I think they were trying to tell me something but it was too far away & I couldn't hear them because of the bags & then I just woke up.

August 13, 2012:
Dreamed I looked in the mirror & I was somebody else, & then that person told me to go get ready because we were going on a long trip together & pretty soon it would be time to leave. But instead of packing or anything we just sat down in the living room & kissed each other & said goodbye. & then we both gave each other pills & we took them at the same time & then everything went dark & that was the end.

Yelena Rostov, Notes:

Some dreams seem specifically parallel to previous tenants—Bissionette (post-partum depression with self-harm), Siemanczski (Vicodin abuse after vehicular injury), Lin (body-image dysmorphia with false transgender self-diagnosis)—even though no way T. could know about any of that. But pattern v. clear, impossible to ignore.

All dreams end badly, but with no sense of unhappiness. Transfiguration imagery. Change resulting in bodily dissolution.

Who else lived in here, before the Big Three?

Check to see if pattern continues in either direction.

IMAGINARIUM 3

From the Obituaries Section of the Toronto Star, September 21, 2000:

Leora SOONG, beloved daughter and sister, 1968 to 2000. Passed away suddenly but peacefully of natural causes. Her father Pak, mother Nureet and brother Doctor Tardesh Soong ask that in lieu of flowers, cash donations be directed to the department headed by Dr. Maurice V. Corbray at Shumate House, in gratitude for their caring and professional treatment of Leora's condition. No memorial service will be held.

From the Star's Local News Section, same issue:
Almost one year exactly after the shocking discovery of thirteen dead bodies in a private Rosedale home, Leora Soong, the final survivor of Marc-Andre Rozant's Pure Signalism cult (a splinter faction of the larger Anunnaki Signalist Movement) died in her sleep late Sunday night. She was discovered early Monday morning by the staff at Shumate House, the care facility her parents had placed her in.

A former University of Toronto medical student, Soong first came to national attention after she fled the Rozant house early in the morning on September 19, 1999 and flagged down a passing police car, informing the officers who stopped that Rozant had ordered the rest of the group to commit a Heaven's Gate-style mass suicide. By the time an armed response team had been summoned, however, Rozant's plans had already been put into effect, with only one other cult member—ex-NHL goalie Tyson Legasse—left alive. Legasse claimed he had been waiting for Soong, his "double-harness team-mate", to return so that they could "Transition together properly". When Soong still refused to go through with the suicide ceremony, Legasse cut his own throat with a concealed knife and then bled out before paramedics could get close enough to treat him. . . .

Wikipedia Entry: Signalism

Anunnaki Signalism was a Millennialist cult developed and based in Toronto, Canada, though many members were recruited from America, Europe, Russia and parts of Asia through Internet proselytization. After a schism split the original Movement, the fourteen members calling themselves *Pure Signalists* retreated to their leader's Rosedale house in 1999 to commit ritual suicide.[1] The massacre's single survivor died of natural causes a year later, while still in deprogramming after-care therapy at Toronto's *Shumate House* facility.[2]

Doctrine

According to their internal newsletter, "The Secret Knowledge"[3], the Signalists subscribed to the *Tiamat/Anunnaki Theory*, a variant derivation of the *12th Planet Theory* of Azerbaijan-born American author *Zecharia Sitchin*, whose books propose an explanation for human origins involving *ancient astronauts*. Sitchin attributes the creation of the ancient Sumerian culture to the *Anunnaki*, whom he identifies as a race of extra-terrestrials from a hypothetical planet beyond Neptune called *Nibiru*. He believed this planet to follow an elongated, elliptical orbit in the Solar System, asserting that Sumerian mythology reflects this view. Sitchin's books have sold millions of copies worldwide and have been translated into more than 25 languages.[citation needed]

The mathematical progression of *Bode's law* suggests that a planet should exist between Mars and Jupiter, some 260 million miles from the Sun. 12th Planet Theory posits that this planet (which Sitchin identifies with the Babylonian monster-goddess *Tiamat*) did in fact exist, but was struck and destroyed by Nibiru as its orbit intersected with our solar system, thus giving rise to the myth of Tiamat being "torn apart and spread across the sky" by the usurper-god *Marduk*. Gravitational redistribution from this event pulled some fragments of Tiamat and its moons into the orbit of the remaining planets, while others were driven further to form first the <u>asteroid belt</u>, then the *Kuiper Belt*.

The Signalist Movement builds on Sitchin's theories by claiming that the planet Tiamat was not entirely destroyed. Though its inhabitants did not possess the technology of Nibiru, they did possess a hypersapient spiritual tradition which led to their precognitive realization that such a collision was coming, and could not be avoided. They thus developed the *Signal*, a psychic "anchor" which would allow them to phase-shift the "best parts" of their planet and themselves into another dimension using zero-point energy. Like the *Heaven's Gate* cultists who believed they could abandon their flawed human "vehicles" and catch a ride to Paradise on the *Hale-Bopp comet's* tail, Signalists believe that by tuning themselves to the Signal's frequency, they will be able to translate themselves to a perfected version of Tiamat through a process called *Transition*.

While most mainstream Signalists consider this process a lifelong evolution that concludes with natural death, a radical fringe current continues to advocate "active abandonment" of the body, as fleshly detritus, through suicide.

Signalist Litany of Intent

The Litany is printed in the masthead of each issue of "The Secret Knowledge":

When the Signal comes, it will decode everything it touches.
When the Signal comes, nothing will be left unchanged.
The Signal will be a type of terraforming. A psychic terraforming. Our world will be remade from the inside-out.
Those who are Horses for the Signal will be Translated and Transition correctly.
Those who are not Horses for the Signal will Transition incorrectly, in that they will not Transition at all.
Horses must run in tandem, or the Transition will be disordered.
Team-mindedness is key.
Rehearsal is the single most important element in a correct Transition.
Rehearsal assures that the Final Checks are performed consistently and in unison, with perfect intent in action.
Two on two and two by two is the proper order, so both partners can support each other throughout.
*Team-mindedness means: **No one goes alone.***
*Team-mindedness means: **No one is left behind.***
To abandon team-mindedness is to abandon your partner, condemning them to an incorrect transition.
*To abandon team-mindedness is the **only unforgivable sin**.*

Yelena Rostov, Notes:

According to the Pure Signalism website (still online!), Final Checks =
Pair up.
Assemble materials.
Put bag over head (leave open at bottom, for mouth access).

Face each other.

Each team-member hands the other their dose.

Doses taken at the same time.

Wash down with vodka.

Repeat until dose canisters/vodka bottles are empty.

Tie each other's bags.

Lie down in paired corpse posture, feet touching.

Begin Litany.

Wait.

But Leora Soong didn't wait. She turned over and tore a hole in her bag, puked up her dose, ran out of the house before Tyson Legasse could catch her. Coroner's records show he was already dying when the police got there—amazing he lived long enough to kill himself. But maybe he wanted to see her again, see her eyes when she turned him down. (Like he knew she would?)

IR on Leora implies that by the time she came to Shumate, she thought she made the wrong call.

Okay, so now we know why Shumate doesn't take cult survivors/ deprogramming jobs anymore. But

"The Signal" = *Signalists?* How can that

Checked Thordis's browser cache. If she's been looking at Signalist materials, I can't find any record of it. But that wouldn't explain how she knew about the other three patients, anyways. Or what Leora Soong and her Signalist crazy had to do with

No no no.

NO. No, that just doesn't

Fuck.

Therapy Blog of Thordis Hendricks, August 15, 2012 (2:55 AM):

Found teeth in the wall today. Like there was a lump in the plaster I could barely see, but I could feel it when I touched it, so I went all through the place looking for something heavy enough to break it open, and then finally I did (edge of a plastic file-box from the closet), and I did. And it opened right up like a seam, and inside were these *teeth* buried deep enough I had to dig them out, roots and all. Too small to be an adult's, with their enamel the colour of milk gone off.

How does that even *happen*, though? I mean, it must've been deliberate—somebody did that, but why? To leave something of themselves behind here, just in case

(that's if the teeth were even theirs)

One way or the other, I think I maybe need to start writing down exactly when I take my meds, again. And how many.

Slept maybe an hour around midnight, and had that same dream about somebody standing at the foot of my bed, looking down at me while I slept. And it was me? Me looking down, me sleeping? And when I opened my eyes I was surprised, genuinely, to not find her still standing there. Surprised, and a little disappointed.

It's very lonely, in here. I'm beginning to wish

(only beginning?)

well, more like—after all this time in Apartment Five—that I'm finding it hard to remember what it was like to ever be someplace

(anyplace)

else.

And the other thing that's funny, just a bit: When your diagnosis includes suicidal ideation, why do the side-effects of so many drugs *also* include suicidal ideation? Cymbalta included, if I recall correctly; hoping *you* have a handle on that, at least, Yelena. Hoping you're keeping track.

It just seems . . . contradictory.

rostovy@monitoru.net Dr. Corbray, it's Yelena Rostov.

rostovy@monitoru.net Dr. Corbray?

rostovy@monitoru.net I sent you a report, Dr. Corbray. Did you get it?

corbrayml@monitoru.net

corbrayml@monitoru.net

corbrayml@monitoru.net Yes, I received it.

rostovy@monitoru.net All right, then

rostovy@monitoru.net Mind telling me what you thought?

corbrayml@monitoru.net Will be sending you my response in email form, so please check your in-box.

corbrayml@monitoru.net Signing off now.

From: rostovy@monitoru.net
Date: August 15, 2012, 10:42 AM
To: rostovy@monitoru.net
Subject:Report (Thordis Hendricks)

Dear Yelena,

Following your account of what you term Thordis Hendricks's "psychological degeneration" over her stay with us here at Shumate House, I went back and examined the Therapy Blog posts and dream diary entries you quoted in detail. Having done so, while I will admit the symptoms she's been experiencing are extreme (enough so to definitely merit a pharmacological shift off Cymbalta, perhaps substituting Paxil or Celexa, followed by a full-scale treatment protocol reassessment), I'm not quite sure what else I'm supposed to take away from this laundry-list of additional implications, some of which appear to verge on the pathological.

To answer your questions, however: No, there is no way Ms. Hendricks could have learned the details of how Apartment Five's former tenants died. No, I don't believe there's a "pattern" to those deaths, aside from the unfortunate tendency of addicts to overdose and depressives to commit suicide. And though I suppose it's possible Ms. Hendricks might recall something about the Pure Signalism cult denouement—it would have been hard to escape that year's news coverage without picking up *any* reference to it, especially here in Toronto—this idea of yours that Leora Soong's completely coincidental stay at Shumate may have left some sort of toxic "psychic residue" behind that infects Apartment Five's residents with Signalist ideas is both highly unprofessional, and scarily close to veering into the realm of paranormal mumbo-jumbo. We work for MonitorU, not the Freihoeven Institute.

I don't *want* to re-assign you, Yelena, since I believe that would be bad for Ms. Hendricks—she needs continuity, especially now. But this is a conversation I really don't want to find myself having with you again.

(By the way, in future, I would prefer to communicate by email rather than Instant Message, since the latter format is not exactly conducive to in-depth debate.)

Cordially,

Dr. Maurice Corbray, M.D., Ph.D.
Director, Shumate House

Yelena Rostov, Notes:

Asshole.

Okay, okay—

Supposedly, Shumate doesn't accept cult survivors or deprogramming jobs anymore.

But Corbray was Shumate's primary student; Corbray treated Leora Soong, so "well" her parents wanted everybody to donate to him. Corbray was the one who mentioned Apartment Five's stellar tenancy record, in the first place. Why?

So I would go looking? So I'd figure out

(no, that doesn't make any)

(or does it)

So here's a thesis:

You have a—all right, say it—haunted apartment. Everyone who stays there gets sucked into the same routine: Final Checks for Translation/Transition; team-mindedness at work. She (Leora) convinces them they're part of her double-harness pairing. And they go through with it, but they don't stick around—they move on, somewhere else. *She* sticks around, and tries it again.

Because she feels bad about pulling out. Because she feels

(alone, and lonely, so lonely)

(just like Thordis)

And it doesn't matter at this point if she really-for-truly thinks that all her dead friends wound up on Lost Planet Tiamat in the Paradise Dimension, or whatever—fact is, wherever they *did* end up, she's not there, and she never will be. Not unless she can find someone else, the *right* someone else

to *team* with.

And Corbray's not stupid, just a bastard. So what is it for him, some kind of experiment? Like: *Hey, I wonder what happens if we put this sort of person in Number Five? Or this one? Or*

(because I think *I* know)

I mean: How many times do you have to *do* this, exactly, to figure out the truth? How many times do you have to repeat a routine to know it's *never* going to

Oh God, I have to get Thordis out of there.

Skype log transcript of conversation between Yelena Rostov and Thordis Hendricks, recorded on August 15, 2012 (3:15 PM to 3:27 PM):

Yrostov: Thordis, are you there? I can hear you, but I can't see you. Do you have your camera turned on?

ThordH: Yelena?

Yrostov: It's me, yeah. I need to speak to you right now, about—

ThordH: Ha, that's so weird. I was just going to call *you*.

Yrostov: You were?

ThordH: What did you want to talk about?

Yrostov: Well, I—was worried—

ThordH: Oh God, this about the blog, right? Listen, I feel so stupid, I was just . . . you know how it is. My sleep's been really upset, and I just get down.

Yrostov: So you didn't find teeth in the wall?

ThordH: No, that part was true. I mean, it's *all* "true."

Yrostov: I don't—Thordis, I'm still not seeing anything, can you try again? I just want to talk to you about these . . . patterns in your blog, this toxic repetition, these weird turns of—okay, there, that's better. Are you still having those dreams?

ThordH: Sure, sort of. But ever since you sent Lee over, things have been so much—

Yrostov: Excuse me, who?

ThordH: Lee, Yelena. You know. She's been taking me through the meditation sequences in person, and it *really* helps clarify things. I mean, at first I was a little leery, but turns out having somebody in my space isn't so bad, when they really know what they're doing.

Yrostov: The meditation—

ThordH: Corpse posture. The whole rehearsal, Final Checks and all. I can *hear* everything perfectly, now; I understand. It's Translated itself for me, so I can return the favour. And it's just, it's just, so—

Yrostov: Thordis, *wait*, slow down. Breathe. I, I need to make sure you know what you're *doing*, that you aren't gonna *hurt* yourself—

ThordH: Yelena, c'mon. What is it you think I'm going to *do*?

Yrostov: I—look, that doesn't matter right now, I'll explain when I get there. Just . . . stay put, hold on. Don't do *anything*. Okay?

ThordH: No, I'm interested—hurt myself how? Why would I do that? It makes no sense. I'd never do that, not when I came here to get *better*. No one would. Right, Lee? I'm right, aren't I? Tell her.

Yrostov: Thordis—

ThordH: *Tell* her, damnit!

Yrostov: *Thordis*. Focus. Who's...that behind you?

ThordH: I *told* you already, Yelena. Lee.

Shumate House Site Incident Report for August 15, 2012, filed by Saracen Security Guard Margaret Cuchner:

12:00 PM Arrived on site to relieve previous guard. No further incident.

12:30 to 15:00 PM Checks as usual, nothing to report.

15:15 PM (Approx.) Care worker Yelena Rostov entered lobby, greeted me and registered. She then proceeded to Skype with Apartment 5 (Thordis Hendricks) on her tablet, while I filled out site log.

15:25 PM (Approx.) Rostov became upset and waved me over. I heard what I assumed to be tenant Hendricks rambling incoherently. Rostov pointed out what she said was an intruder in Hendricks' apartment. Hard to see, but looked like a female figure standing behind Hendricks.

15:30 PM (Approx.) I triggered the panic button, summoning police and paramedics, and left my duty station to accompany Rostov up to Apartment 5. No response to knocking and calling. I tried security fob, but apartment door was unresponsive. When I recommended waiting for police, Rostov broke glass on fire extinguisher cabinet and used extinguisher to break door-handle, then kicked in door. I proceeded to do quick check of apartment, but found no intruder.

15:35 PM Police arrived on site and accessed my walkie-talkie. I explained situation. Officer Brian Lum stayed at front desk to direct paramedics, while Officer Chimo Moche joined Rostov and myself upstairs.

15:38 PM Officer Moche, Rostov and myself located Hendricks lying in her own bed, apparently unconscious, with blue lips and a plastic bag half-full of vomit over her head, knotted around her neck. At same time (approx.), paramedics arrived on site and were directed upstairs by Officer Lum. They began resuscitation efforts on Hendricks, broke open bag and turned her over on her stomach. Hendricks coughed up more vomit, then opened her eyes briefly and began to breathe again, erratically.

15:45 PM Paramedics removed Hendricks to St. Michael's Hospital. Officers Lum and Moche asked me if I wanted to prefer trespassing charges against Rostov. I replied that I was not authorized to do so, and asked to be allowed to call my immediate supervisor on site, Dr. Maurice L. Corbray. Officers Lum and Moche asked Rostov to remain in their custody until Dr. Corbray got here. Rostov agreed.

15:50 PM I re-set alarms in Apartment 5.

16:17 PM Dr. Corbray arrived on site. He elected to waive charges, but told Rostov she would be let go from her current position with MonitorU, and that she no longer had security access to Shumate House. Rostov turned her I.D. and fob over to me.

16:30 PM Rostov, Officers Lum and Moche and Dr. Corbray left site. I proceeded to fill out Site Incident Report.

Signed, Margaret Cuchner #TU-4445-000097.

From This Narrow Life, *the blog of Thordis Hendricks, September 30, 2012 (1:28 PM):*

But why would I do that? I remember saying. *It makes no sense. I would never do that. No one would ever do that.*

I would never take three pills, take a sip of vodka, take three pills, repeat until gone. I would never have a bag over my head already when I did it, conveniently open at the bottom and hiked over my nose to free my mouth. I would never peel it back down again after I was done and knot it, once, twice, three times. I would never.

Never make my way back upstairs, weaving slightly. Never feel stuffy and warm and happy and only slightly queasy. Never lie down flop on my bed (our bed), and close my eyes.

Thinking: *I would never, no one would. I'm not doing it now.*

Except, of course, that I was.

Anyhow: This is what happened after, as far as I can figure out—

I ended up at St. Mike's, in a private room (thank you, Isa's money). I remember Yelena sitting by my bed, but only vaguely; I think she might've been holding my hand. She looked so tired.

(The weirdest thing is, in context, how I don't remember "Lee" at all. I read that Skype log and I'm amazed it's me talking, though it certainly *sounds* like me. Nothing seems familiar. The dreams, I at least remember having *them*. But this girl, this—whoever she was? Nothing.

(And I even looked up Leora Soong on the 'Net, too. Totally unfamiliar.)

Dr. Corbray came by a week later, trying to convince me that Yelena was somehow responsible for what'd happened. I disagreed. By that time, of course, the next part was all over the news; I guess he was trying to do damage control, in his own fucked-up way. Maybe that was all he'd ever been trying to do.

It'd make me sound entirely too nice to say I don't blame him, exactly. Because I guess I probably would, if I let myself think about it. One way or the other, he lost himself a customer; whether or not that's "enough", given circumstances, I don't know. The family lawyers kept telling me I had a serious case—one even said Yelena should co-sue with me, for wrongful dismissal, once her own legal issues were settled. But it's not like Corbray can do it to anybody else now, either . . . so, kind of a moot point.

Because that was another thing Yelena was doing, apparently, at the hospital—she got hold of *my* fob, waited 'til that guard she found me with was off-shift, then used it. Went in through the fire access door, which I didn't even know you could (but then again, how would I?). Went upstairs, got back into Apartment 5 . . . where she came up with enough salt to pour around the place that, when she followed it up with gasoline and threw a lighter in after it, the salt helped act as a firebreak and kept the damage confined to the apartment. No casualties, no damage to the rest of the house—but #5's gutted. Whatever they put there next, it won't be the place Leora Soong died in anymore, and maybe that will help.

I'd like to find Yelena, not that I know how to go about it. I'd like to thank her, except that no one really knows where she went, after. The fire department says there weren't any human remains in the ashes, and you'd think they'd be able to tell. So hopefully she got out, changed her name, went underground; maybe she's working another job somewhere, keeping her eyes peeled for things other people don't want to let themselves see. Maybe she's sitting in front of a screen with her IM left open like some high-tech Ouija board, waiting for someone's words to fill the box, seeing where they'll take her. Maybe she's telling Leora's ghost the equivalent of *Sit down, Miss Soong, we have a lot of work to do together.*

Or maybe she walked into that whole Translation routine with her eyes open, wielding a skill-set I'll never possess. Maybe she took Leora's hand and pulled her on with her, so they ended up . . . somewhere else. Not the Kuiper Belt, hopefully, but hell, I don't know. I don't know.

(I'll never know.)

So: This is the new blog, obviously. I'm out of Shumate, on a different cocktail, into another apartment; I go out every day, at least for a little while, and I make myself look up steadily, training my eyes on the blue, the clouds, trying to not think about the cold, huge black lurking behind it. The same black which encircles us all, no matter where we choose to hide, just beyond this planet's pitifully thin atmosphere-skin. Because there's no place we can go to escape it, even in our dreams—like death, it just *is*, and nothing helps for long.

But this much has changed: Instead of thrashing around and trying to avoid them, what I do now is *make* myself think these thoughts through, all the way, *allow* myself to, and then I let them go. Get into corpse posture, lit or fig; shut my eyes, and breathe. One day I'll stop, and maybe I won't even notice. What happens after that is beyond my—or anyone else's—control.

This is the truth of what I have, what I am—it may get better, but it doesn't get cured. You find a pattern and settle into it, hoping it holds. And so every day, every night, I feel things moving all around me, a pulse like some universal heartbeat, a million minds rubbing in from every side, pumicing their thoughts against mine. A Signal of sorts, though whether it comes from inside or out-, Tiamat or God or the underside of my very own personal chemistry-soaked brain is simply impossible to tell, or prove.

Which means, our various faiths aside, that we should probably try to be content to deal with the immediate, and let the rest take care of itself.

Still seeing signs and portents everywhere, no matter what, and letting them wash over me, resistlessly as rain. A shadow in a room, darkness on darkness. A light through the bedroom window, shining from nowhere, which follows you everywhere you move to, so you always wake up with it in your eyes. A car alarm that goes off all the time, especially in the middle of the night. Or a voice in your mind, only vaguely familiar, mourning—

Team-mindedness! I broke routine, broke faith. I let my partner down. So I can't go on, not now, not yet. Not yet . . .

If that's Leora Soong's voice, though, I don't owe it to her to remember. I don't owe her anything.

Instead, I sit here typing and I take my pills, determined to keep on living, still haunted or not. Which I am, surely. Aren't we all?

In a way, every ghost is only our own.

:axiom: the calling (excerpt)
Daniela Elza

❖

today the crow in the pine is a   story—
its harsh   charred voice   pulls the morning

out of the water.   *ripples*
the city's dissolving   *dreams*.

they walk in broad daylight th*rough* memory
lanes   lined   with walls so thin

you can see   where the dumpsters used to be

benches
                    where we sat and held hands.

under the water   a book   turning pages.
slow   words   come   undone

float to the surface   black   oily   and slick.
flow under bridges   arches   aches

the *marrow* of the quiet   the writing down
and what a crow tears   out of

        such silence.

❖

at feeding time   they gather
    in the birches.   circle.
    mussels in their beaks.

    my path littered with
      broken shells.

the splash of   sea water
    on   winter pavement.

an instant's sleek shadow
    acrossmy face

    pecks a memory
      out of my eye.

❖

some days I am too empty   for descriptions.
myths span our   damp sky   with doubt.

                    we look at

each other—negatives of   ourselves.
crumbs tossed in   axioms of sorrow

and so
      I watch your mouth   become

        a crow-shaped
        black hole.

my gaze   pulled tight   around
the edge   between   substance

        and

        nothingness.

between what stutters   into night
      what splinters into   morning.

THE SALAMANDER'S WALTZ
Catherine MacLeod

It bothers me, forgetting the name of this time of year. This month of exquisite light. I know the word but can't dredge it up. Maybe I shouldn't be wondering right now. Maybe I'm growing absentminded. Maybe my husband pounding the steering wheel is distracting me.

"Tom, stop, you'll break it."

"The stupid wheel's fine."

"I meant your hand."

I grab his wrist before he does it again. Ten minutes since the car broke down, and already his knuckles are bruised. We both know he's frustrated, but so far only one of us knows he's terrified. I caught the smell of the ocean miles back. His blue eyes shine with panic he hasn't recognized yet. *Blue as a ghost,* my mother used to say.

Which reassures me my memory still works—it's retained what had to be her most obscure saying.

Tom smacks the wheel again, yanking my arm.

"Stop! Beating on the car won't help."

"Fine!" he snaps. "Do *you* have any idea where we are?"

"It looks like the middle of nowhere, but I could be wrong."

He glances at the watch on the wrist I'm holding, just to be doing something, annoyed that I'm not annoyed. But it's not as if we were trapped. We're on a road; it has to lead somewhere. For a man with freakishly good eyesight, he's really bad at seeing possibilities.

Ironic, I think—an art dealer who can't see the big picture.

He pulls his hand away and takes out his cell phone, that shiny little pacemaker he can't live without. He checks his messages; frowns when he doesn't find the one he's been waiting for. He has a meeting in the city on Monday and—unusual these days—decided to drive the five hundred miles. Even stranger, he insisted I come along. It's been a while since he asked.

When we were first married he drove everywhere, wanting me to himself. But we usually headed inland, a fact that didn't register at first—I was too busy being fascinated by things I'd never seen before. But now he flies to his meetings when he can, and I stay behind more often than not. His days of romancing me are long over.

"Dammit!" He growls as the signal fades, then tries again. I look away, bored. The air almost shimmers here.

If Tom wants to be alone with me there's a reason. The most likely is that he wants to have *the talk*. He wants a divorce. But it's all right—we've been married ten years; I've wanted to leave for nine.

Which is why I said 'yes' when he asked me to come. At some point I'm going to get out of the car and walk away. I could fly or buy a train ticket, but with no destination in mind I'm in no hurry to get there. At least this is a ride *somewhere*. I need a place far enough away from him to be comfortable, close enough that he can find me when the paperwork's ready. But before then I have to hear him out. My mother would say, "As long as you're his wife, you at least owe him kindness."

Sometimes I've wondered about the state of her marriage, but I agree. This must be awkward for him. Maybe he's worried I'll cry and cause a scene. Maybe his ego will be stung when I don't. Maybe Naomi can kiss it and make it better.

I'm surprised I'm not wounded by their affair: pride was always my biggest fault.

"Thank God," Tom sighs as he gets a signal. "I'll let Ian know I might not make it Monday."

He's concerned about the meeting, not what's over this hill. Typical. He gets out of the car slowly, reluctant to leave a familiar environment. The air is working on him; he's recognized the smell. He won't say anything about it, but his eyes are almost glittering, the exact blue of this September sky.

He'll call Naomi first. She's the reason he keeps checking his watch. The reason he wants a divorce. And, since he's barely been able to think of anything else for the last year, probably also the reason we're lost. I head toward the crest of the hill, giving them some privacy, relishing the scent.

As I reach the top I close my eyes for a moment, pretending the ocean is just ahead.

And when I open them, it is.

Equinox, I think suddenly. That's the word for this time of year. Tomorrow is the fall equinox, when the sun seems to travel south across the celestial equator. How could I forget that?

How could I forget the ocean has this many shades of blue?

Oh, my father, I've missed you so much.

I can almost feel Tom trembling as he walks up beside me. I start to reach out to him, then let my hand drop. He's been terrified of the ocean ever since the accident. He likes to think he's tough, that nothing can get the better of him, but life wears us smooth, like water on stone. My mere presence in his life reminds him he's lost his edge.

I missed Salianda horribly when we were first married. I'd never been away from the town for so long. Tom tried to be sympathetic, and listened when I told him about picking tomatoes from my mother's garden, and helping Uncle Lucius repair the machinery on the fishing boats. But one day he walked into the bathroom and caught me stretched out in the tub, looking up through the water, hair floating like seaweed, listening to my heartbeat in my ears. He turned away quickly, unease plain on his face. I suppose sympathy only goes so far.

He tried to joke about the incident later, calling me his little mermaid.

But, as I recall the story, the mermaid's prince left her for someone else, too.

"Maya?"

I point toward the village at the foot of the hill. It's a pretty middle-of-nowhere, at least. "They must have a garage there. And maybe a hotel."

He gets our bags from the trunk, frowning at how heavy mine is. But he's too preoccupied to be curious, and since he doesn't have to carry it, he doesn't wonder long.

"What did they say?" I ask.

"The meeting's still on. I'll call Monday if I can't make it."

Nate's Garage is at the edge of town, just past a neat sign reading *Welcome to Bormaine.* A middle-aged man wiping his hands on a grease rag looks up as we walk in.

"Car trouble?" he asks politely, pointing back along the road with his chin. Neither of us is exactly dressed for hiking.

Tom says. "It just quit and rolled on to the side of the road. I can't start it again."

While Tom and Nate hash it out I take a look around. The place is surprisingly clean, the mark of a man who takes pride in his work. Lucius would've been elated with an inventory like this.

I ask, "Is there a hotel in town?"

"A mile up the road. My wife runs it." He tosses the rag onto a wooden chair and turns back to Tom. "I'll bring the truck around and we'll go take a look."

I take our bags and walk on without looking back. The air is crisp and sweet. Gulls fly screeching in high loops, a sign pickings are good nearby. The scent of turning leaves is strong and rich, the smell of the season burning itself out.

The Bormaine Hotel is plain but clean, intended for comfort rather than a magazine cover. An old-fashioned, gently curved staircase draws my eye. One like this graced my grandmother's house. I climbed it countless times, and slid down the bannister more than once.

The desk clerk is a small woman, her eyes warm and brown.

"Is there a double room available, please?"

"Sure. There're only a few other guests still here." She waits until I sign the register, then takes my cash. "I'm Sadie Kern."

"Nice to meet you, Sadie." As I push the book back across the counter I bump her paperweight out of place. I glance at the flat, round stone painted with two wavy blue lines, and, without thinking, murmur, "Eroth is kind."

"And wise in all matters."

Our eyes lock. She says, "Do you mind if I ask where you're from?"

I could name any of the places where Tom keeps an apartment, but that's not what she asked. "Salianda."

"Right. I've been there. Thought I recognized the accent."

Ah. So that's it, I think. Ten years later I still haven't lost my accent. No wonder there are days when every word I utter, no matter how benign, irritates Tom. Even my voice is a reminder of the accident.

She takes a key off the rack. "I'll show you your room." She looks again at the registry in passing, then stops and does an almost comic double-take. "Maya . . . ?"

I signed my maiden name. It felt right.

"Is there a problem?"

"No. Oh, my. Come here, please." She leads me through a door behind the counter, into a good-sized kitchen. "Is that yours?"

My father, I think. *Oh, my father.*

The painting is large, the colours wild: great bands of blue and green, purple and silver, spinning like whirlpools. Like winter sunlight shattered through an iceberg. The motion and colours remind me of home. They feel so familiar to me.

But of course they would. The signature in the corner is mine.

Maya Wexton: a strange child, quiet, thoughtful. The youngest of six sisters. Some said I was the prettiest, but I felt dull compared to them. They were clever and useful, and I seemed to be of use to no one but Lucius.

Until Tom Riordan came to Salianda looking for me. He was the first person who'd ever singled me out. The first to actually call me an artist, although the neighbours called me a prodigy. My mother just called me messy; but she grinned as she threw my paint-splattered shirts in the washer, and tolerated the trance-like state I fell into when a big canvas absorbed me. I drew faces in the sand, and spined seashells in oil on the walls of the machine shop. Lucius growled, "Get back to work," but never wiped the murals off. He gave me my first good set of brushes and paints.

My seascapes were beautiful, people said, but a little frightening.

"Accurate," my grandmother replied.

My love of the sea showed clearly, but so did a certain wariness.

"Sensible," she said. One of the few times she ever called me that.

The very occasional tourist came through town. Salianda's not on anyone's main road, and the routes leading in can be treacherous. Almost every summer one of our visitors goes through a guard rail. The year I was thirteen one of them took my parents' car with him, sending them home to the Salamander.

By the time I was eighteen a dozen of them had taken my paintings out into the world. One of them found its way to Tom, and the resale price made me worth looking for.

The lure of profit made him want me.

My pride delivered me up.

Sadie's painting brings the memories back with a rush. Among the swirls of colour there are darker images, barely visible unless you know to look for them. In dim light you can't see them at all.

"My husband gave it to me for our twentieth anniversary," Sadie says. "Nate."

"Yes. How long have you been away?"

Away. We used that expression in Salianda, too. It referred to everywhere else. I used to love hearing tales of away, and dreamed of a handsome man who'd come take me there. I didn't know then that dreams could hurt you. A natural talent, Tom called me. His little primitive. I'm not sure he was always referring to my artwork; he also said it in bed.

"I haven't been home in ten years."

Our room is what I expected. The bathroom is small but will do fine. There are two beds, which we could push together but won't. Wooden wardrobe, wooden bureau, mirror hung on the wooden door. Wicker trash can tucked discreetly behind the bureau.

"It's very nice." Tom will hate it.

"I haven't put visitors in here for years. Most of them find it a bit simple for their tastes. But I had a feeling you'd like this," she says, and sweeps back the curtains. The view stops my heart, then shocks me back to life. The hotel is near the cliff, the ocean just below the window. I weep quietly, salt responding to salt. *Beautiful, beautiful, oh my father.*

The rock formations down the shore are beyond graceful. They seem to ripple and surge like the water that carved them.

"The tourists always want to photograph them," Sadie explains. "There's a path down to the beach about a half-mile from here." I nod, barely hearing the door close behind her.

But I do hear Tom open it.

"The fuel pump's gone," he says. "Six hundred dollars for a new one. Nate ordered one, but he says it won't be here until Monday."

I open the nightstand drawer, just to be doing something. It contains a stone of Eroth and nothing else. "Monday? Are you sure?"

"What do you expect in a place like this? Rustic doesn't begin to describe it. Nate actually leaves his keys in his truck. I wouldn't be surprised if the women cool their pies on the windowsill."

I turn away to unpack, finally annoyed. I was born in *a place like this*, and he doesn't want to tell me about surprises.

And I don't want to tell him about Eroth.

In Salianda we worship him, creator of all water, just as some farmers revere his smaller wife, Eroa. But we don't talk about our father outside the town—not everyone understands his way. It's best to be born to it.

There was a painted stone like Sadie's on my mother's sideboard. She used it to hold down her recipe cards. There was one in both churches, the hospital, the bank, somewhere in the post office. They meant the eye of Eroth was on the house.

Few visitors ever asked about them. I'm sure they regarded them as some talisman. They thought, *What do you expect in a place like this?*, and forgot about them.

"They don't even have a car rental agency here," Tom gripes. I shift my things into the bureau, leaving the top drawer for him. My suitcase is still heavy when I set it in the wardrobe. "Are you listening?"

"Yes."

"Well?"

"Well, what? What do you want me to say, Tom?"

"We're stuck here for the weekend!"

No, *you're* stuck here. "There's no bus station?"

"No."

He checked? He must love her if he'd even *consider* taking the bus. He shakes the contents of his bag onto his bed, angry. Let him be, I think. There's nothing he can do, and even if there was he'd be doing it alone.

"What's so fascinating?" he asks, looking over my shoulder. I feel him tense, and say nothing as he backs away. There's nothing *to* say. The bottom of my suitcase is stuffed with cash in high denominations. Soon those far-seeing eyes will have seen the last of me.

I sleep deep and easy, lulled by *(oh)* my father's voice, soothed by the song of the Salamander. I dream of Salianda's autumn rituals—screen windows going up, swing sets coming down, and the great bonfire on the beach to hold off the coming cold, sparks flying up like snapping angels.

It was at one of those fires that I first heard a neighbour mention The Salamander's Waltz. When I asked my mother what it was, she told me I'd misheard—that our village was built according to the lines of the land, and the great curve of stone that jutted out into the water was called The Salianda Wall. But her kitchen was always noisy, and I didn't catch half of what she said. I thought I understood, though, and didn't ask again. After that I always pictured Eroth as a great Salamander. The waves went out, the waves came in, as precise as any gavotte. We all knew there were things dancing in the ocean.

Tom's gone when I wake, his bedding rumpled and twisted. He's had nightmares for as long as I've known him. But I don't ask about them anymore—if I can't set his mind at ease I can at least take it easy on his ego. To him my father's voice must sound like the pleas he couldn't utter as his breath was stolen.

I try to feel pity for him, and fail. I'm sorry he slept badly; I suppose I owe him that much. But let Naomi pity him now. Let her try to cobble him back together.

I watch myself dress in the mirror. My body is still strong and straight, but that face is barely my own. It used to smile more. I always thought I'd outgrow my homesickness, but never did. Some days I'm still as blue as the ghost I feel like. My hair is dry; my roots need a touch-up. When we met it was as dark as deep water, but one day I bleached it, hoping to please Tom, thinking it might make me look more sophisticated. He barely noticed—but then, by that time he'd stopped looking at me unless he had to.

And by that time I'd stopped painting. I had no inspiration. Away from the sea, I lost my voice; and when I stopped creating, I stopped being profitable to him. I became just a reminder of the one fear he couldn't overcome. Every time he sees me he remembers the Salamander pulling him down.

I raise the window a few inches and listen to the sweetest music I know.

"Is there someplace around here I can get breakfast?" I ask Sadie.

"Right here, if you like. I'm just about to make tea." My mouth floods with spit. I know the tea will be brewed properly, with boiling water in an enamel pot. Tom insists on his morning latte, the preferred drink in a place where breakfast is mostly an excuse for discussing business. We took time to enjoy our meals in Salianda, fuelling ourselves for the day's work. In the city, meals are almost an afterthought, and often eaten with a degree of guilt.

This one isn't. Sadie's eggs are scrambled with cheese and mushrooms, her wheat toast spread thick with butter and jam. The tea is strong and milky.

"Your husband went out early," she says. "I offered him breakfast, too, but he said he never eats it."

She doesn't have to offer the details. The way she smiles into her teacup says it all. What Sadie cooked for me doesn't fit his idea of breakfast. Tom doesn't do *rustic*.

"He'll probably spend the morning on the phone," I say.

"He was talking up a storm when he left."

"Want some help with the dishes?"

"No, thanks. There aren't enough to bother with until later."

"Thanks for the meal, then."

It's colder by the water. I buy a grey hoodie in the dry goods store across the street, and head out back of the hotel, admiring the view Sadie doesn't show most visitors. I'm too late to see the fishing boats go out. They won't be going for much longer. The men spend their winters in maintenance, communing with the boats. The winters are long, but not long enough to forget the laws of Eroth. We call him father because he provides for us. The ocean takes care of its own.

But it demands respect in return. Fair enough, we always said— you're a fool if you insult what feeds you.

I follow the cliff's edge, marked clearly by a dozen new bricks inside a rail fence, looking for what I know must be here—a way down. The tourists' path is an easy walk, but no matter how lovely those formations are, I don't feel like chatting with strangers. If this town is so much like home in some ways, maybe it is in others.

It is: there's a stairway of sorts curving down the face, some of the steps natural, some hammered from the rock. I go down backwards, finding the chiselled handholds. Rock-walling was always my favourite workout at Tom's gym. Just before my head goes below the edge I look up at the hotel. A face is barely visible at one of the lower windows, half-hidden by light glinting off the glass. Sadie, I think. Maybe.

I cup my hands in the water and wash my face. When I look up again, I notice I'm under our room's window. I forgot to close it.

Tom died in the waters off Salianda. He and his friends had gone out in a small sailboat, thinking they could make it back before the clouds came up too dark. But you can't do that; they darken when they will. I went out by myself sometimes, often as not coming round to watch the young men diving off the end of The Wall.

That day one of them had stayed longer than his friends, unable to resist one more jump.

"Hey, Ross," I called, "are you waiting to grow wings?"

"Yes!"

We both laughed. "You need a ride in?"

"No, I'm all right."

We were both young enough to not be afraid, and old enough to know we should be. I turned for shore, racing the storm, admiring the sleek sailboat ahead of me. It was manned by people I didn't recognize. Tourists, they'd have to be. I saw the wave that lifted one of them out. His friends didn't. I went in after him, into my father's cold arms.

He was far down and limp when I finally grabbed him. I lost my boat, but got him to the shore, both of us staring too closely at the next world. He still wasn't breathing when Ross arrived. He'd gone deep into the Salamander's mouth.

I brought him back.

Waking in my grandmother's house, he said, "Where is she?"

"Who?"

"There was a woman in the water."

She gave him a mug of sugared tea to warm him. I thought she seemed pleased that he didn't much like it. "That was my granddaughter, Maya," she said, nodding at me.

"Your name is Maya?"

"Yes."

"Wexton?" I nodded. He introduced himself and said, "I came here to find you."

I knew *The Little Mermaid,* the story of a prince who falls in love with the woman who saved him from drowning. So did my grandmother, who pursed her lips with displeasure as we chattered on the couch. When I came to help prepare supper, she took me aside and said, "Just you remember, girl, our people don't shy away from doing what needs to be done."

The only thing I remembered at that moment was my mother once saying the same thing. Maybe she'd inherited her knack for strange proverbs.

Tom slept as I peeled the vegetables. I'd never met anyone like him. Even though his clothes were tattered, I could tell they'd been expensive. He was fair-skinned, and more handsome than any man I'd ever seen. I blushed as I recalled the feel of my mouth against his, giving him breath. His hands were smooth, not rough like a fisherman's, and, startled, I wondered how it would feel to have them on me.

The next day I found out.

When we went to the cottage his friends had rented, it was empty. They hadn't realized he'd fallen out until they beached; and by the time they called the police, my grandmother already had. Her conversation with the chief included the words *drunk* and *stupid* more than once.

Their carelessness didn't endear them to me, either, but Tom didn't seem surprised. They'd left him one of their cars, and when he drove out of Salianda I was in it with him.

"Don't do this," my grandmother said when I returned to pack my things.

"I love him."

"You love your *pride*," she spat.

"I'm going with him and you can't stop me!" I cried—and stepped back, shocked, as she took her sewing scissors in one hand and gathered up her hair with the other. Before I could speak it was on the floor.

The women of Eroth cut their hair to mourn the dead.

She locked the door behind me.

I never understood the cause of her anger. For choosing Tom, for disobeying her, I don't know. The memory still hurts.

And yet, I've seen incredible cities and exotic animals, mountains, canyons, unbelievable works of art. Tom showed me *away*, and it was as wonderful as I'd hoped.

As I turn back toward the cliff, a pile of white stones catches my eye. This, I realize, is where the bonfire is made. The stones are waiting to be set in a circle. I look at them for a long moment, remembering.

Then I head up the rock face to find Tom. Like always, if I want to go to him I have to turn my back on the sea.

"What did you do this morning?" he asks from behind the menu.

"Slept in. Did a little sight-seeing." I lie without thinking, sparing him from habit, giving him the kindness owed. He'd know what I did, if he cared to think about it.

The diner is sparse and clean. I order the chowder; Tom, a clubhouse sandwich. I steal one of his fries. His brief smile doesn't reach his eyes. The skin around them looks tight. He hates this place.

"Have you found anything interesting?" I ask.

"Like what?"

"I don't know—something in one of the craft shops? You're always on the lookout for a new painter, aren't you?"

"Sure." Then his cell rings, and he abandons his food. The man he's talking to, Ian, was among those who drove off and left him in Salianda.

Tom handles his phone the way he used to handle me. Naomi's photo is in its memory.

Much of modern technology is a mystery to me, mainly because so little of it interests me. I'm sure my indifference made them feel safe. But the one time I tried to use his phone I accidentally learned everything. She's lovely, younger than me, and married. She says her husband doesn't know about the affair. She writes fascinating texts. One of them makes a risqué reference to her new shoes.

And how eager she is to step into mine.

"And what are you doing this afternoon?" Tom asks when he's done. He orders coffee. They do espresso here. I could never get used to it—too much like eating the grounds out of the bottom of the pot.

"Shopping," I lie again. He relaxes visibly. He understands shopping. "Would you like to come with me?" He shakes his head like I knew he would. "Then we can meet here for dinner about . . . what, seven o'clock?"

"We close at seven," the waitress offers, setting down his cup.

"Thank you," he says shortly, nettled that one of the staff spoke without being spoken to. Her answering smile is sweet and understanding, and directed at me.

"I'll get some take-out and meet you back at the room," he says, and starts texting a new message.

"Okay, see you." He nods, but it might be at the phone.

The afternoon is warm, approaching thunder driving the heat ahead of it. I bypass the shops—there's nothing I need that I can buy, and I've never had much use for trinkets—but the museum draws me. I pause at the door, taking in the *No Cameras* sign, the soft light, the smell of wood polish. The blurred shadows of things that once watched us, and give the appearance of doing so still.

The few tourists ahead of me laugh furtively at the sepia photos of early Bormaine, at pictures of so-called sea monsters. One of them glances around, whipping out his cell phone to get a shot of the mutant squid, and sputters as the curator's hand blocks the screen.

"You saw the sign," he says amiably, and plucks the phone from the man's fingers. "I'll keep this at the front desk. You can pick it up on the way out."

The whispers that follow the incident try to be indignant, but are only embarrassed.

I trail after them, thinking they know nothing about the sea. If they did they wouldn't call its creatures monsters. Several glass cases contain the small remains of wrecked ships, and I offer a silent prayer for the sailors called home. Where life is given, life is owed, and sometimes Eroth collects.

The hand-written cards in the corner of the cases give only names and dates, but I can fill in the spaces. There were lives and families and dreams behind those names.

On the far side of the room is the last item for consideration: a giant squid in a cut-glass case. It would have been graceful in its element, tentacles drifting delicately. Deadly in the way of its kind, but only when necessary. Not one to shy away from what needs doing.

"Hello," the curator says behind me.

"Hello." My voice is rough with unexpected tears. "You have an impressive display here."

"Thank you."

"It's beautiful, beautiful. . . ."

"Oh, my father."

"Yes."

"I'm Max Kern."

"Sadie Kern--?"

"My sister-in-law. She described you to me, said you might drop by. You've made quite an impression on her."

"She's been very kind." The others have gone, leaving us alone. "What else do visitors do in Bormaine?"

"Leave, mostly. Almost all the gift shops close this weekend."

It's early for that, most places. But, like Salianda, Bormaine is far enough off the beaten track that there's no point waiting for the half-dozen travellers who still might pass through, but probably won't.

"However . . ." He lifts the round stone off the stack of brochures on his desk, and hands me one. "I think this might interest you."

And he's right.

Tom and I married six weeks after leaving Salianda. Lately I've been wondering why he married me when I was willing to be his mistress. Gratitude, perhaps. His idea of payment due. Maybe he thought he really loved me. I didn't know enough about love to know the difference.

I painted another dozen canvasses before I went dry. They paid for our house in Arizona.

More irony.

But here in Andrea Waylan's studio I don't have to work from memory. Like everywhere else in town, the sea is close. Three other women have signed up for her last art class of the year, and are chatting softly, self-consciously. I recognize one of them from the museum. She drops her cell into her pocket and mutters something about no service. The storm-to-come is interfering with the signal.

A few of Andrea's half-finished canvasses stand against the wall. Her style is nothing like mine, but a love of the water is clear in every stroke. All of them have faint grey bands along the top, a warning, to me at least, that there's a storm coming.

There most always is.

Andres waits until the appointed time, then, when no one else comes, asks, "How many of you have taken lessons before?" A couple of them raise their hands. "What did you paint?"

"Seascapes, mostly."

"You've come to the right place." She gets a few polite laughs. I try not to fidget. We've already paid for our canvasses and paint, and my fingers twitch in anticipation. "If you don't want to do a seascape, you can try this." She gestures to a still-life she's set up, a pretty arrangement of apples and flowers with a few crisp leaves.

I look out the big windows. The light is still good, but there's a line of grey along the top of the clouds. The Salamander's restless, too, I think, and finally pick up my brush.

I've always loved mixing the colours, the sharp smell of the oils, even the tiny *pat* of brush against canvas. But mostly I love the way time becomes irrelevant when I work, becomes fluid and ripples around me. In that timelessness is my niche.

I never did fit into Tom's world. In a world of haute couture and even more haute cuisine, there's not much use for a woman who can rebuild a small engine. Like the little mermaid, I was always dancing on pins and needles.

As I recall, she turned to foam and spread herself on the waves. Sometimes I've thought I could feel myself disintegrating, too.

But here in Bormaine I feel strong again. Back among people who know there are things in the deep sea that watch us go by, and wait; that we probably know more about outer space than the depths of the ocean; and that there are stars and whole worlds in both.

My grandmother knew all the constellations. She must have told me their names, but I don't remember: one more time I didn't listen.

The memory of her anger burns at unexpected moments. I hear the soft *shush* of her hair hitting the floor at my feet. The morning she counted me among the dead was an ordinary one, like this—the village going about its business, heavy rain just hours away, the sunlight on your skin like static. Like here, tourists were straggling out of town to find excitement, locals were gathering wood for the bonfire to celebrate . . .

. . . the equinox.

Like here.

Oh.

Oh, my father.

The last tourists out of town that day were Tom's friends.

He wasn't just an outsider in Salianda. He was the *last* outsider.

Oh, my father, I'm sorry. I'm so sorry I'm sorry I'm sorry I'm sorry—

"Maya? Maya!"

I startle back to Andrea's studio as she grabs my wrists. My hands are dripping blue paint, black, silver-grey. It take a moment for my voice to reroute to my mouth.

"What happened?"

"You threw your brush down and started slathering paint on with your hands."

What else, she doesn't say, but I must've been making some noise—the ladies are grabbing their coats and scurrying their paintings out the door. They look like young deer who've heard howling nearby.

"I didn't mean to chase away your students."

"Their time's up anyway," she says calmly, and studies my canvas. Dim eyes peer through great whorls of colour, but this painting isn't just of the ocean. There are bands of fire, streaks of lightning. There are ash angels flying out of the waves.

I know whose face they have.

"What do you want to do with this?" Andrea asks. Good question—I have no place to keep it, and it's too big to take if I have to move on. "Would you like me to see if I can sell it?"

"Yes, please. Um, is it okay if I clean up before I leave?" She points toward the bathroom and doesn't turn quite fast enough to hide her grin. The mirror explains: nothing will clean me up short of a garbage bag. My clothes are unsalvageable. But I scrub my hands anyway, and wipe the smears off my face.

She's waiting to lock up when I come out. It's almost six o'clock.

"Thanks, Andrea."

"You're welcome."

She doesn't hurry me out the door, but I know she has somewhere to be.

It's time to give the Salamander his due.

"Hello, Sadie."

"Hello, Maya." She comes down the stairs lightly, one hand holding a cloth bag, the other slipping something shiny into her dress pocket. "How was Andrea's class?"

"Good." I'm not surprised she knows where I've been. I know small towns well enough to realize that not only Eroth is watching.

I glance around. "It's awfully quiet. Have the others checked out?"

"Yes." Her eyes are very dark.

Oh, my father.

We pass on the stairs without speaking again.

"Maya, where have you been? Where have you *been*?" Tom pulls me through the door and locks it behind me. The room is cold. "Something seriously weird is going on here."

"What?" I didn't think I'd be hungry, but the containers of take-out on the bureau smell wonderful. He bought soup.

I take fresh jeans and a shirt from the closet. From where he's standing he can't see that his clothes and travel bag are gone.

"You don't have time for a bath. We have to get out of here. My cell phone's been stolen."

So now he's lost his voice, too. "Are you sure?"

"It was on the bed when I went in the bathroom just now, and gone when I came out. But that's not it, come on, I have to show you something."

I ball my clothes into the garbage can and dress quickly. He eases us down the stairs as if we were spies, and picks up the desk phone: static. I'd blame it on the storm coming, but I'm out of comforting lies.

"You have to see this."

The sky's black with waiting thunder. He pulls me toward the cliff—for him, an act of desperation. He leans over the fence and points. "You left the window up. I saw those when I closed it."

At first I can't imagine what's scared him so, then I remember—the skulls among the white stones, waiting to encircle the bonfire, are the reason Sadie doesn't put tourists in the back room. The Salamander takes the flesh and spits out the bones, and often they end up back where they were offered in the first place.

"We have to get out of here, Maya. You have no idea how strange these people are."

"Yes, I do." But he's not listening. He honestly doesn't know what he just said; it doesn't occur to him that I'm one of *these people*. Being this close to the sea, in a town so much like Salianda, terrifies him. The memories must be overwhelming.

But did he really think I *wouldn't* go down to the water?

"Do you see them?"

"Yes."

"Come on, let's head for the garage. Nate leaves the keys in the truck, remember? We can just go."

But, of course, we can't. Half the townsfolk are standing behind us when we turn.

"What the hell's happening?" he whispers.

Nothing. It's already done. I knew this might happen when Nate told him he'd have to order a fuel pump. There were two in his garage, either of them a good-enough fit for our car. He was hedging his bets, ensuring at least one outsider would still be in town come tonight. Once he'd decided that, there was no place to run.

I knew when Sadie didn't tell Tom about owning my painting. She didn't tell him anything he didn't have to know, treating him like outsider.

But I didn't tell him, either.

The last outsider come the equinox is always the sacrifice. The cold season is a lonely time, and the Salamander needs a companion until spring.

There's no credit card receipt to show we stayed in the hotel. I'm sure the register is already missing the page with our names. I expect Tom's phone is in the water by now, and, quite possibly, the car with it.

Sadly, I can't think of many people who'll miss him. Naomi might want to report his disappearance; but she's married, and, with him gone, will have to reconsider her options. She might come looking, or she may simply grieve as well as she can and move on.

His business contacts might have some questions, but these are the same people who abandoned him in Salianda. Moving on is second nature to them.

I expect it'll bother me for a while; but that won't stop me from, finally, doing what needs to be done. I've already rescued Tom from the sea once, my pride making me steal from the Salamander what it clearly wanted for itself. Even now, for a moment, I think we might be able to escape. But probably not, and I doubt these people would be as forgiving as my grandmother. I can't keep saving him, and I'm not willing to die for him again.

But I don't want to leave him for the fire.

I push him, hard.

He barely grabs the fence in time, staring up at me in horror, his gaze full of ghosts. Neither of us ever thought I'd do such a thing.

But today all kinds of lines get crossed.

Thunder cracks, and the ocean answers, spraying up into the rain. The Salamander waltzes with the storm. Tom wanted us to be unmarried. Tonight we will be.

But not yet.

I can at least give him a fast death. I scoop up one of the bricks and swing.

For this one last moment I'm still his wife, and I owe him kindness.

LOST
Amal El-Mohtar

I don't know where I am.
I close my eyes and there's a forest,
warm and dark, where I can reach out
and touch you. *I could get lost*
you say, from miles away,
in bed with you
right now
and I am already there, pine needles on the ground,
your body as near as the trees.

Your words make evening of my sheets,
a dim sky falling over woods
seeded in syllables, tangling
breath and branches together
behind the eyes I've shut to find you.
One can believe anything in the dark:
that I could turn and know
the heat of your back,
the curve of your shoulder,
the soft smell of your neck.

There is strange comfort in being lost,
in making a home of uncertainty—
a pillow of moss, a bed of leaves,
a presence out of absence.

But, equally,
one can believe anything in the dark.

I could tell myself stories. I could say

there once was a girl who made woods of words
and lay down in them to dream
lost her breadcrumbs to the birds
and her maps to a running stream

but in the dark, it's hard to know
middles from beginnings
or anything else.

It could be
that you, whose voice is an open door
that takes me no place twice—it could be
that you know exactly where you are,
keep a compass in your breastbone
and won't tell me where it points—
that when you say *I could*
get lost
you don't mean you will.

But, still,
anything is possible in the dark,
and everything is possible
in stories.

So:

it's warm beneath this blanket sky,
and she has been so cold,
his voice is still as close as sleep,
and still as sweet to hold.

So let him lead her into rest
be it here, or near, or far—
she's always loved the evening best,
the twilight, and the stars.

FIREBUGS
Craig Davidson

There are shapes that only live in fire.

Hunger. Fire's basic drive. The purest, most incarnate hunger you can imagine. Nothing mankind has ever assembled is impervious.

I've seen fire chew through lead girders: they soften and bend over backwards like a contortionist. I saw a column of flame ripple up a sheet of aluminum siding; it crinkled and contracted—the sound of ice cubes fracturing in a glass—as the metal curled up as if rolled by huge invisible hands.

Fire will grunt and growl and come at you with the soft slitherings of a snake. It'll howl around blind corners like wolves and gibber up from flame-eaten floorboards and reverberate in a million other strange ways besides: sounded like buzzard talons clawing across pebbled glass, this one time.

Other times it'll come for you silent as a ghost: a soft whisper of smoke curling back under a doorway, beckoning you to open it. That's when it's most dangerous—when it's hiding its true face.

Solid. That's one thing people don't get. There's a sturdiness to fire, which may seem odd seeing as it's flexible, too, happy to shape itself around its host. But I've seen it punch holes in walls and carry roofs off houses. I watched a rope of flame rip through a backyard elm quicker than a chainsaw. Neater, too. *Surgical*.

But most lethal are its shapes. Fire holds the most nimble, the most uncanny and breathtaking shapes. It strolls and eddies and curls over like tidal breakers. A man can stare into the shifting centre of a fire and see . . . well, everyone sees something different.

The shapes in fire echo those of familiar understanding. You believe you're watching creatures of smoke and char breathing themselves into existence. The shapes become more beguiling the closer you near to the flashpoint: when the heat is such that it'll steam the marrow in your bones.

Jerry Ullness, good friend of mine, a twenty-year vet on Ladder 11—saw him fall into a fire. He dropped his axe and raised his palms like a penitent evangelical welcoming the Lord into his heart.

It happened in a narrow staircase inside a firetrap off Morrison Street. The blaze had taken root in the basement and twined through the walls like ivy, crawling up the electrical wires with orange fingers. The flames licked up under the stairs and gnawed through the wood; the stairway toppled into a roaring pile of cinders directly in front of poor Jerry. He teetered on the precipice, peering down into drifts of glowing coals . . . he saw something. What, I couldn't say.

"No, Jerr . . ." I'd breathed.

But he was gone. Bewitched by the shapes. Like those demon-women in the old myths, calling from the jagged rocks, luring sailors to their doom. You get caught up in the shapes of fire, give yourself over to their authority, and by the time the flames reach out you'll go willingly enough.

I told Jerry's wife it was smoke inhalation. He'd passed out. Simplest explanation. Hell, maybe it even happened like that. She had him cremated. Truth told, Jerry was pretty much there already.

Part of me was jealous. A small part, but . . . I wanted to see what he'd seen.

I was born Blake Kennedy Jr., on a hazy July evening at the Cataract City General. It had been a humid season: *slut-hot*, people around here call that kind of heat.

A serial arsonist was at work that summer. The city was burning. My mother said I was born with old fires racing through my blood.

That summer's pyromaniac was a cagey bastard with a flair for the theatric: What he'd do was bust into a vacant home, crack open the Bakelite casing of the rotary phone, attach a wire to the ringer and thread it down to a jug of kerosene. He'd hightail it to a bank of payphones, hunt the number from the directory, put a nickel in the slot and place a call. The spark of the ringer traveled down the wire and set the kerosene aflame.

The local rag hired a headline writer with a tabloid background.
Dialling for Disaster! Calling for Conflagration!

When a local headshrinker postulated that the guy might've been setting fires to satisfy odd lusts, the headlines ran salacious:

Pervy Pyro's Phallic Phone Party!

Doc sez: Freaky Firebug is a Blaze-setting Bedwetter!

My mother said the locals stopped taking vacations: they didn't want to come home to a blackened shell. Investigators figured it was either a telephone repairman or a sneak thief, except nothing was ever stolen. They never did catch the guy.

A few of those fire-gutted houses stayed that way for years; as a kid I remember these whistling black skeletons dotting the city grid, charred plots where the sunlight went to die. Fire could re-shape any city—take away its profile, reduce and flatten it, rob the concrete memories of a place. The ultimate eraser.

I was a bit of a firebug myself. What boy isn't? I'd light rolls of paper caps with a magnifying glass. Make a homemade flamethrower by holding a lighter up to a spray-can of Pledge. Lord! Small wonder a lick of flame didn't travel back up the nozzle, ignite the pressurized contents and blow my face off. But I don't suppose I'm the first guy to have used up eight of his nine lives in boyhood.

Turns out I wasn't even the biggest firebug in our family.

That I'd become a fireman isn't exactly shocking; a lot of firefighters were fire-setters as boys. The polarity shifts: you want to stop fires rather than start them—but firemen end up setting a lot of fires, anyway, under the auspices of knowing thine enemy. You learn its tricks and tendencies in order to conquer it.

Which is a mistaken belief: you can't conquer fire any more than you can any classical element. Such forces are immortal and unfeeling. All you can hope is to divert them from humanity.

I was a firefighter—a Jake, as we call each other—right out of college, a job I held fifteen years. Then I snapped an ankle fighting an air-fed flashover in the Hot Box: a three-storey metal latticework where we staged controlled blazes. The sound of my ankle fracturing was like a pistol fired into wet sand. It healed bad. I couldn't meet the baseline physical competencies. Chief said: *Sorry, Blake, but you got to hand over your axe.*

So I don't fight fires. I investigate them. I'm the aftermath now, sifting the ashes for the hows and wherefores. The whys you may never know—that's something else you've got to make peace with.

Lately I've been busy. The city's burning again.

Detta Wilson. Name of the latest victim. *Odetta*'s the name on her birth certificate but she was Detta to her friends. Seventy-four years old. Cashiered for forty years at the Shopper's Drug Mart on Drummond. Devoted parishioner at First Evangelical. Widowed with two loving adult children. Black, but race didn't appear to have any bearing. Having a busted smoke detector and being a sound sleeper that did have bearing.

The incendiary rig was a plastic milk jug full of gasoline and a homemade wick. The pyro poked holes around the bottle-mouth to let some of the fumes escape.

It's a dead-simple device: light the wick, leave it on someone's doorstep and walk away. It won't ignite immediately—gasoline itself won't burn, you see; only its vapours do. The gas actually acts as a coolant, putting the brakes on the eventual combustion. That jug smolders away like a camp lantern until the flame dips inside, melts the plastic and lets that fuel escape.

The gas would have caught with a soft *whuumph* like the wind bellying a boat sail. Next the fire would have been chewing up the latticework to where Detta lay slumbering.

It pissed me off—all of it, but the *method* pissed me off the worst. Three liters of gas in a milk jug, an old rag for a wick. Punch some holes in the plastic like you would in a jar lid to keep an insect alive. Light it and leave. By the time it did its damage our boy would've calmed his wild eyes and sweated off the greasy stink of gasoline.

Three bucks' worth of material and a seventh grader's grasp of science. *Poof*—a good person gone to vapour.

Our boy was a dog who'd learned a very simple trick. A trick he'd performed eleven times in the past six months by my count.

"We got to ferret this firebug out," the Chief Inspector told us. "Every bug's got a routine. Suss out this nut's."

Problem being, our boy didn't hold to any pattern. Tenement rowhouses, brownstones, duplexes. Single-family dwellings, apartment foyers, warehouses that lay uninhabited but for the rats. Men and women, geriatrics and kids, black and white and red and yellow. I'd stuck pushpins into a map of the city for each site he'd torched: hopelessly random. He operated by no known logic—not even the herky-jerk logic of a pyro. Our boy seemed satisfied to see things go up in smoke; the "what" made no nevermind to him.

I returned to Detta's house the day after it burned. She'd made it out alive but succumbed to smoke inhalation a few hours later. It was midafternoon, wedges of terra-cotta sunlight burning between gaps in the city skyline.

The fire was slowly dying in the house: a thousand sly cracklings and crimpings as the heat seeped from scarred metal and wood. It had burnt the east- and south-facing walls off Detta's home. The brickwork had checked its progress in the other directions, so the fire had done what fire always does: it wormed its way between the floors, feeding on the dust and hair and seventy-odd years' worth of dead skin trapped under the boards—my old instructor told us that a human being sheds nine pounds of skin per year.

Old Man's Beard? he'd said. *Yellowed newspapers? Dry human skin has those beat all to hell. Skin's the ultimate tinder.*

What remained was a near-perfect cross-section of the interior: the kitchen and bathroom and master bedroom laid out, the contents smoke-damaged but intact. Detta's clawfoot tub tilted at an impossible angle from the charred second-storey floorboards. Her nightgown fluttered on a hook near the bedroom window, which firefighters had smashed to let smoke escape.

It reminded me of the Barbie Dreamhouse my sister had as a kid, the one that split open down the middle to present its guts.

I grabbed my kit and bent under the yellow police tape. The fire had trickled off the porch to ignite the dry lawn; my boots crunched over cooked grass. The branches of a mulberry bush hung in blackened spears, the ribs of a denuded umbrella.

The porch was ash. I braced my palms on the foundation and powered myself up to where the doorway once stood. The structure had been hosed off—water dripped off the scorched cornices and the obsidian-dark points of shattered glass—but the latent heat lay trapped in the brick. The fire turned Detta's house into a kiln.

Investigate enough arson cases and you'll realize just how reductive fire can be. All things, be they natural or forged by the hand of man, have colours and textures. Fire robs them of that. Objects either become light as ash or attain a shocking heaviness: after a restaurant blaze I'd found a stack of cast-iron skillets smelted into a solid mass, so heavy I couldn't lift it. A vulcanized sheen gets draped over everything: like it's all been dipped in a pool of rubber at a radial tire factory. That breed of blackness hurts your eyes. Your rods and cones get starved for colour.

I stepped over the floorboards to the wooden bannister railing, now just a jagged black spike. The carpeting on the stairs had melted and fused to the underlying wood. The billowing, circular smoke pattern on the walls indicated that the fire had carried itself swiftly up the staircase before its progress had been checked by the low ceiling, creating a dead zone of air circulation and denying it the oxygen it needed to thrive.

Detta had two means of escape: the upper-storey windows or the stairs. She hadn't jumped. But the staircase would have been consumed in flames by the time she'd woken up. . . .

I flipped open the kit and grabbed a few surgical pads. I blotted the ash-thickened water on the stairs. I sprinkled the staircase with flashing powder and let it settle. Then I switched on the hydrocarbon detector.

People believe a fire erases all signs of evidence. Not so. Sure, plenty of clues get incinerated—witnesses too, sadly—but inspectors have our ways and means. The hydrocarbon detector displayed trace amounts of carbonized natural matter on any surface. In most cases, that meant human skin.

The detector picked up footprints. Tiny, elegant footprints, one on each stair. Detta had run down them while they were on fire. I pictured her at the top of the staircase staring into the crackling glow. Her eyes would have been wide, the eyes of any creature facing such a killing element. I pictured her rushing down the stairs, taking them one at a time, trying to tiptoe maybe, the flames curling under her flannels, licking between her lips to blister her lungs. . . .

Twelve stairs. Twelve footprints. Twelve swathes of flesh in the exact shape of feet, like boot-prints in the snow, each one incrementally smaller than the last.

Detta's skin had fused to the stairs instantaneously—these are known as thermal fusion burns, when the trauma occurs deep in the subcutaneous skin tissues—and she'd have torn her burnt flesh away as she progressed. That raw skin would have hit the second stair, fused, torn free again. Her feet became smaller and smaller, the way a Russian Doll shrinks as you unpack it. Had the staircase been long enough, I suppose Detta would have run her feet clean off.

Did our boy even know what hell he was wreaking? He worshipped at the altar of Vulcan, and his god was a violent one. Vulcan would like nothing so dearly as to tear the world up in flames and stand by as it burns.

The next day I drove to the CAMH facility on Dorchester road. My baby sis, Franny, had been a resident for nearly twenty years. I wouldn't use the word *incarcerated*, but they didn't exactly throw the doors open and let her stroll around free-and-easy.

My sister's the sweetest, most trusting and gentle soul—but she's wrong upstairs. Soft in the attic, as people around here would say. Or fucked in the head—although I'd go to war with any man who said that of Franny, despite it being the literal truth.

Some people aren't built for the daily rigors of life, is all. Franny had this innate connection to the weak and the innocent. The beasts of the field. Starving orphans on TV. They wrecked her. She didn't understand that modern life . . . just to exist in it requires a certain hard-heartedness, right? You had to function within the awfulness surrounding you, divorcing your soul from the very worst of it. But if you kept your soul too distant—if it became a buoy tethered to your corporeal being—well, you became a sociopath just like our boy. Franny never achieved that necessary separation. Never formed a bulwark around her heart.

My shoes made no sound. The tiles were made from special rubber that cut down on the *tak-tak* of hardsole shoes, on account of some residents being peculiar about sharp noises. The TV in the dayroom was bolted to the wall too high for anyone to fiddle with the channels; the CBC was broadcasting an old episode of *Seeing Things*.

Two guys were playing Chinese Checkers. The one in the eyepatch kept putting the marbles in his mouth; his partner snorted like this was an everyday occurrence and said: "Stick them up your asshole, why don't you, and lay a fucking egg." His opponent seemed to be legitimately considering this prospect until the big bull orderly said: "Don't even *think* about it, Gene. If I have to go digging again I'm gonna stick a cork in you when I'm done."

Franny sat at a patio table draped in a big yellow parasol despite the fact we were indoors. Her face broke open in pure sunshine when she saw me. Franny was the most austerely beautiful woman—despite what she'd done to herself, she'd never lost her looks. With her hair swept back and halogens catching the crystalline blue of her eyes she had the wintery beauty of Grace Kelly in *Dial M for Murder*.

"Look at you," she said. "A million bucks."

"You look like a billion bucks."

"You look like a trillion, like—"

"*Infinity.*"

We'd spoken it at the same time. Jinx.

"So, Fran—, I—"

"You broke the peace, Blake," she said solemnly. "You owe me a Coke."

I paid for two sodas from the vending machine. Franny's hair was tied back today. My eyes oriented on the scar above her temple. My father's gopher gun had made it.

The day it happened we'd gone to the zoo. Franny wanted to see the polar bears and the naked mole rats. The animals were mostly lazing in the shade of their enclosures—all except the jaguar, who paced its pen as if committed to a ritual, patrolling the same circuit so doggedly that it had carved a ring in the grass.

"What's the matter with the big black cat?" Franny had asked our father.

"It's just on guard, dear. Protecting its cubs."

"I don't see any babies."

The jaguar bit into the marbled mass of its shoulder, fangs worrying right through its fur. Blood flowed over its black coat like oil. It left bloody pawprints in the dirt. Later I'd learn this kind of self-abuse was common amongst big cats in captivity. A reaction to the narrowing of their world and the bafflement of their primal instincts. The thrill of the hunt was gone, right? It drove them batshit.

Franny couldn't stand to see innocent creatures in anguish—because really, what had the jaguar ever done? It'd been sunning itself on the Serengeti plains, picking its teeth with a springbok antler, content in the elemental way of a creature who is perfectly in sync with the life it was meant to lead and then *wa-bow!* some Great White Asshole in a pith helmet shot a dart in its ass. Next thing it's 5,000 miles from its ancestral home eating boiled horsemeat at the end of a zookeeper's pole.

Franny could sense that animal's loss instinctually. It drove her batshit, too. And she was already halfway there to begin with.

On the drive home dad tried to comfort Franny but she was inconsolable. A wonder she didn't dry up like an old leaf, all the tears she shed. When we got back she snuck upstairs, got the rifle out of dad's closet, chambered a .22 shell, put it to the side of her head and pulled the trigger.

I recall hearing the *pop!* of the gun and next she'd wandered into my room with blood blurting out of the perfect little hole above her temple, smiled the sweetest smile you'd ever seen. Next she laid down like a girl falling softly asleep in a field of clover.

Once she'd been taken to the hospital and stabilized, I'd contemplated what she'd done. I couldn't even conceive of killing myself. I mean to say the act itself seemed impossible. At that age I was still wrapping my head around the notion of being *alive*, the hows and whys of that miracle. The word *suicide* was foreign to me. Our world was so wide-open—why would anyone want to cut themselves off from it with a bullet through the head?

But my twelve-year-old sister had done it. And so that knowledge became a particularity of my own existence.

What she'd done stunned doctors. The bullet travelled through her pituitary gland and cleaved the hypothalamus. About two tablespoons of grey matter had been pulped. A perfect lobotomy. She was instantly cured. Franny was left without a care on earth.

"Did you bring a book of matches?" she asked me.

"No, Franny. You know I didn't."

"You said you would."

"You know I couldn't in good conscience. Not after all that happened, sis."

"What happened?" she said, as if she really didn't know.

"You and matches don't agree."

She crossed her arms tight and said, "Oh, pooh."

She was sweating, which was another aftereffect of the bullet. She sweated slowly but continuously, like an aged cheese—most heavily when fire was involved.

The brain is a subtle organ and it breaks in subtle ways. By most yardsticks Franny was truly better off. The angst and existential dread fled. But after the bullet you could light a fire in front of her and she'd just watch it burn.

Before the accident—the whole family referred to it as such, even though it was like calling a state execution an accident—Franny was afraid of fire. The first time she'd caught me on the porch burning the edges of the White Pages with a magnifying glass, her hands had fluttered like startled birds.

"You're going to burn yourself," she said. "You'll need skin graphs like Michael Jackson!"

Jackson had recently burnt his hair off on the set of a Pepsi commercial. Franny—who was highly intelligent but very literal—envisioned a team of eggheads hovering over the immolated pop superstar, plotting graphs on his skin.

But after the accident her fascination with fire verged on obscene. A bizarre by-product of her brain circuits being so hastily rewired. She'd collect twigs fallen off the backyard maple and lit fires on the grass. She stole coins from my father's pockets to buy convenience store Bics. I'd find her on the porch with a Zippo, her nostrils dilated to inhale the perfume of lighter fluid, sparking the flywheel with her thumb but not quite hard enough to light the wick. When I got older I'd come to recognize the look on her face: pre-orgasmic.

She began disappearing at night. At about that same time, the reports had begun to surface.

"Can I ask you something, Franny?"

She traced her finger around the rim of the Coke can, dabbed her wet fingertip on her throat. "Of course, silly."

"Someone's been setting fires, Fran. A lot of them."

Franny's hands clutched the table's edge. Her knuckles whitened.

A rash of suspicious fires coincided with Franny's midnight forays. Nothing serious: dumpster fires, or a stack of pallets incinerated on a warehouse loading dock. But anyone with an understanding of pyromania could spot an escalating boldness.

One July night I awoke to the smell of smoke. I went to Franny's room and found her lying on top of the covers. Her nightgown was stained with sweat. The pads of her feet were black with ash.

"Don't tell," she said.

But I'd told, despite it feeling like a betrayal. I couldn't shake the image of Franny dashing down dark streets in the witching hours, her white nightgown fluttering around her bare ankles, a bottle of butane in one hand and her Zippo in the other. A beautiful wraith setting the city ablaze.

"Who's setting fires, Blake?"

"Well, Franny, if I knew who I'd stop him."

"Why?"

"What he's doing is dangerous. People have died."

Franny stared at her lap.

I said, "Has anyone here . . . have you talked to anyone about fires lately?"

She shook her head in a vicious side-to-side. Her gown slipped to one side to uncover the burn scar over her clavicle. The skin was the mottled pink of carnival taffy. She'd done it to herself in the facility's washroom, sprinkling hardware-store thermite on the toilet seat and lighting it. The reaction fused the plastic to the porcelain, sending up a cone of superheated gasses that burnt through muscle and fascia to scorch the wing-shaped bones next to her throat. The wall of her carotid artery had ruptured but the afterburn fused it shut; she'd only lost a few pints rather than the whole bottle.

After that, photos of Franny were distributed to area hardware stores, convenience stores and drugmarts with a warning: *Do not sell flammable materials to this individual.*

"You'd tell me if you heard anything, wouldn't you Franny? If you knew someone was playing with fire?"

"I don't know that I would."

"Why not?"

"Did you know that carbon is the chemical building block of all known life on the earth? There are only so many carbon atoms on our planet—no more today, right now, than when it all started."

"I didn't know that." I didn't like when she got this way.

"It's true. Things get born, they exist, expire, break down to their elements again. Carbon atoms don't die, they just get recycled–they go on to be part of new life. So you see, all of us are cobbled together out of carbon cells that were once other things entirely. You could have a trilobite's tail in your elbow, Blake, or a cell from Attila the Hun's moustache in your eye. Any creature to have taken on life, grown, crawled, run, learned, known, felt, loved or any of that. *Carbon.* Isn't that a wonderful idea?"

"It's not an idea. It's a fact."

Franny chewed her lip. I waited for the blood to come. "But you agree that it's wonderful?"

"Sure. I can agree."

"So you agree that when things burn, they get brought back to the beginning? The awfulness is gone. From that, something beautiful can spring up . . . because too much of what we have is ugly. I don't mean ugly on the eyes, brother. Ugly on the heart. Evil and cruelty and all those things that gut the soul. But when you burn them, just the potential is left. Just carbon, and carbon isn't inherently *anything.*"

"Oh, Fran . . . don't the creatures living right now, you and me and our family and friends—don't we deserve to go on living until nature decides?"

Franny had started to cry, which she did often and effortlessly. Her heart was an imperfect pearl, lacking the needed nacre.

"I wish it could be. Really, Blake, I do. But nature doesn't have its head screwed on tight. I wish the whole world would burn. You and me, too, even though I love you *so much*. I wish the earth was a black ball, all charred up. It could be that way for a few million years and then things would start to spring up. Things would be better."

Franny's tears ceased abruptly, like a sprinkler shutting off. She sipped her Coke and stared at me over the rim with her head cocked to one side.

"Oh, hello, Blake."

Cataract City kept on burning. Houses, schools, walk-in clinics. The Saint Ann church on Buchanan Avenue collapsed on itself; the church bell crashed through the narthex and melted into a pool of stannite.

My boss took a stress leave; there were rumblings he'd be fired. I believed he would accept a quiet shit-canning: almost overnight, his hair had gone white.

Nobody *saw* anything. For all anyone could tell the fires had kindled out of pure nothingness. The citizenry reacted with customary apathy: as if all this was the repayment of some well-earned debt.

The *Niagara Gazette* circulated a theory that we were under attack from militant anarchists—*What Are Your Demands?* one breathless headline read—until their printing press got torched. The overtly religious believed Our Boy (he'd earned the capitalization by then) was the Devil himself. Many were inclined to agree.

The other night a squat apartment block, the Portwood Arms, burnt to the ground. Our Boy managed to string fifteen jugs around the Portwood's perimeter. By the time the residents clued in, the fire had curled around the gas mains, which ruptured in gouts of blue flame and scattered the exterior brickwork over a three-block radius. Flames swept up the telephone poles to the transformers, which exploded in a cacophony of sparks, the creosote-inlaid wires catching like fuses as lines of gibbous whiteness—the distinct colour of an electrical fire—zipped from pole-to-pole across the city grid.

By the time the fire trucks arrived, residents were leaping from their balconies. Snapped ankles, spiderwebbed kneecaps. The firefighters did their best to catch the jumpers with the trampoline but some of the leapers were more ash than skin. The firemen were beat-to-hell, anyway; the stationhouse poles were getting more use than the ones at the strip clubs down Lundy's Lane—one of which had caught fire midway through the Saturday night disrobing: bucktoothed creeps and willowy half-naked women had spilled from the exits like solar flares released from a sun's glowing-hot corona.

I visited the burn ward. Gurneys strung down the hallways, air hung with the acrid tang of silver sufadiazine burn liniment.

Clifford Meggs, said the name on the chart clipped to the bed. Thirty-eight years old. Resided in suite 344 of the Portwood Arms. Junior partner at a local law firm. Drove a Saab—why the hell would *that* be on the chart?

Meggs was a WASP but parts of him were presently black. Joseph-Conrad-Heart-of-Darkness *black*, except without that beautiful Nubian shine. Meggs was more charcoal-briquette black. When silicite sand is heated to extreme temps it becomes obsidian: black glass. Human skin performs pretty much the same trick.

"Got a smoke?" Meggs asked.

His hands were swaddled in bandages. I lit one of mine, inhaled to get the ember aglow, set it between his lips. Meggs just let it burn.

I tapped the IV bag hung on a pole above his bed. "Methadone?"

Meggs said: "No pussyfooting around, bro. I told them to give me whole hog. Morphine. Self-administered."

"How?" I asked, nodding at his mummified hands.

"Button's between my toes."

Gingerly, I tented the sheet off his feet. Son of a gun. Meggs smiled—only an incremental lift at the edges of his mouth on account of the terrible burns on his neck.

"I'm a fire investigator, Mr. Meggs. I wanted to ask you about the other night."

For an instant I thought my request had surprised him. Then I realized he'd be wearing that same semi-shocked expression until his eyebrows grew back.

"I didn't leave my stove on, if that's what you're wondering."

"No, no, we're positive it was an outside instigator. What I'm interested in, Mr. Meggs, is what you might have seen."

Meggs' eyes closed. His eyeballs quivered behind vein-wormed lids. Without opening them he said, "Ash me, would you?"

I tapped the ash off. His eyes didn't open as his lips accepted it.

"Thanks. Now you're asking did I see anything. The answer is yes . . . but you're going to think I'm crazy."

"You seen the state of our city lately?"

"Point taken. Well, Mr. . . . ."

"Kennedy. Blake Kennedy."

"Well, Blake, I *believe* I saw a woman in a nightgown."

My heart gave a hard little kick—*ba-dum!*

"My kitchen window faces south over the Falls, right? I leave the window open at night to catch the rumble of the water over the rooftops. I was at the window nursing a beer when I saw, or *think* so anyway . . . yeah, a woman. In a nightdress. Some kind of gauzy material that you could *juuuust* about see through, but not quite . . ."

"Was she—?"

Meggs cracked one eye. "Carrying a torch? Yeah, although I can tell you weren't going to ask me that. A lit torch just like an Olympian. It left a contrail same as a jet leaves high in the sky. I've never seen anything move so fast . . . a heartbeat after she passed from sight, flames were climbing up to kiss me goodnight."

"Could you describe her?"

"Anymore than I just did?" Meggs rotated the cigarette from one side of his mouth to the other. "Not so that it'd stand up in court. But if you plunked her down in front of me?" He gnawed agitatedly at the filter. The blackness on his neck cracked open to reveal shocking veins of red. His drip must've been dialled sky-high. "But I don't think she's the one you're looking for."

"Come again?"

"You're looking for one person, right? A lone firebug."

"The assumption is—"

"What if it's a bunch of people, bro? A whole city?"

"I don't take your meaning."

Meggs swallowed. The working of his Adam's apple resembled the tunnelling of a beetle under crusted soil. "I'm going to tell you something, but if you hold me to it later I'll say it was the drugs I'm boated up on, right?"

"Go on."

"The other night I followed a stranger home. Yeah, I know. *Weird.* Didn't know the guy, just passed him on the street like I've passed ten thousand other guys . . . but something about this guy was different. Nothing you could put a finger on. I was just . . . curious. Wanted to see where he lived. What kind of car he drove. If he had a family. I followed him down Ancaster to his house on Harvard. He went inside. I was alone with myself again."

Meggs cadged another smoke off me. He hadn't smoked the first one, just let it go to ash between his lips.

"I walked back towards my own home. But I kept thinking about the guy. He had a pigeon-toed gait. That intrigued me. I wanted to see him again. But the only way I'd see him . . . this strangest thought entered my mind. The only way I'd see him again was through fire."

Meggs' face contorted. "I can't tell you what I was thinking. I can only tell you what I *did*, which was find myself at the PetroCan station off Harvard filling a jerrycan."

He shivered; the flesh split open across his forehead. I wanted to tell him to calm down but I needed to know.

"I had this . . . *fantasy*, is the only word for it. If I set his house on fire, he'd jump into my arms. I'd save him. He'd be grateful and we'd . . . the fantasy dissolved from there. I came to—like, from a dream—at the gas station. High-test was spilling over the lip of the jerrycan and soaking my shirtsleeve."

My hand groped under the sheets and found the button between his toes. I pushed it. I pushed it again. Again.

"What are you doing?"

"Nothing. It's okay."

"Jesus," Meggs rasped. "You can't . . ."

His voice trailed to a thin whisper then cut off entirely. I caught the cigarette as it slipped from his lips. I pinched off the ember between my thumb and forefinger.

I fixated on the black spots on Meggs. The skin underneath shone baby-pink. Fresh green shoots could push themselves up from that dark loam, right? A new version breathing itself into existence.

They burnt down the barber shops. The air hung with the reek of fricasseed hair.

They torched three firetrucks—half the city's fleet. They burnt in the firehouses while the firefighters slept upstairs. A parking lot full of police cruisers went off like chained firecrackers. Ambulances next. A city bus rolled down the street with flames licking from its blown-out windows, shedding passengers from its doors, the driver nothing but a blackened effigy heat-welded to the shotgun seat.

They. Had to be, you know? That kind of wide-ranging destruction . . . team effort, had to be.

The National Guard came in. They strung themselves down the Niagara river, bivouacking against the head of the Falls. What did soldiers know about fighting fires? Nothing, it turned out.

Someone lit up the whale tank at Land of Oceans. Floated a sheen of mineral oil on the show pool's surface and set it ablaze. The whale, Neeka, couldn't surface to take a breath through her blowhole; the ambient gasses would have roasted her lungs. She suffocated.

I called CAMH to speak to my sister.

"Were you out the other night?"

"No, Blake. They don't let me out unsupervised."

"That doesn't mean you weren't out, does it?"

"Don't talk to me like an infant, please."

"I'm sorry."

"What are you worried about?"

"Can't you see, Franny? The city's on fire."

"Of course I can see. I saw it all along."

"What the hell are you—?"

She hung up on me. She always did when I used curse words. A minute later the phone rang. "Franny?"

All I could hear were snakelike whisperings.

My job became redundant. I'd become an Armageddon Investigator— and really, what value was that at the end of times? Like a weatherman sticking his hand out the window to tell you it's raining.

Nobody left town. Oh, there was the odd short-timer with kin outside city limits who took a powder—but the locals, we all stayed. You'd see their haunted faces hovering behind their windows, scanning the night for blooms of flame. I stayed, too. Even considered buying a fiddle.

The forests banding the river went next. Silhouettes of flame danced upon the surface dark of the water. Afterwards the trees were nothing but charred pikes sticking out of the ground. The daggery teeth of some enormous subterranean monster.

The army went in to clean up the mess; when their utility shovels bit into the earth, fresh flames leapt up: the fire was still smoldering in the tree roots, waiting for the ground to open up and let it out again. Men died, though the Army never said just how many.

The gunner on a patrolling Humvee shot an old man in an alleyway. Apparently he'd snuck out to smoke his pipe—his wife refused to let him smoke indoors, figuring if her house was earmarked for ashes it oughtn't be her hubby who did it. The gunner was twenty-one years old and by all accounts flighty as a hummingbird. He opened up with the roof-mounted .50cal, pumping a belt of copperjacket rounds into the alley. There wasn't much left to bury.

The Army pulled up stakes. Ostensibly they were re-strategizing, generating a fresh tactical matrix, but they were abandoning us. They were fighting ghosts and losing badly. The city and those left in it were collateral damage.

In the end it was just the good people of Cataract City, and *them* . . . which might have been us all along.

Backdrafts form the backbone of any firefighter's nightmares.

Picture a room. One window, one door. Hardwood floor. One big overstuffed chair—a La-Z-Boy or like that.

Say that chair catches fire. It'll burn merrily, creating thick hot smoke that spreads across the ceiling. Embers will ignite the hardwood veneer, bubbling and pocking the laminate, burning between the slats.

The gasses will *evolve*—that's the scientific term: become saturated with heat, turn flammable.

A strange thing will happen: the flames will drop, like a gas range turned down low. All you'll see is the barest ripple: incandescent blue waves flickering over the floor. The fire has used up the oxygen, you see. It's starving. But at the same time it's intensifying, each molecule tightening. It's finding just enough air to survive: it'll pull it in from under the doorway and around the windowsill. The fire's a cockroach, doing anything to survive.

The fire becomes the equivalent of a man trapped underwater. If he stays under too long he'll die—and so it is with fire: in a few days you could open the door and all you'll get is a buffet of warm wind. But if you open it when the fire's desperate, let it take a big breath . . .

A backdraft is when a sleeping fire awakes. Its harbinger is a comical *whooooof*, like the bark of a Saint Bernard. Those evolved gasses ignite and expand: a quintillion superheated balloons bursting. Nobody can describe the experience of a backdraft: the first breath you take—a shock-inhalation—will broil your lungs. Backdrafts don't leave witnesses.

The horror of a backdraft is that you never see it coming—but it's been there a long time. Waiting for you. Primed. It waits in the places you've known all your life. Those rooms of fondest acquaintance. The places you've felt most safe.

I walked the shattered city to find her. The blackness of the earth leeched into the sky, a dark imprint on the undersides of the clouds. I knelt beside a little pile of sticks that someone—perhaps a child—had assembled before abandoning them.

I ran a strike-anywhere match along the sidewalk and touched flame to tinder. Idly I watched it burn.

Franny's facility was empty. The staff had deserted it. Rooms lay vacant. Beds had been torched down to the naked springs.

I found her on the roof. The city stretched down the alluvial slope to the Falls, which sparkled whitely in the twilight. It was the only place I'd ever known. Born at Niagara Gen, played Little League ball at the Lion's Club diamond, kissed Laura Crowchild on the bleachers behind Westlane High. All ashes now.

"Hello, Blake."

"Hello, Fran."

"Did you know," she said, "that we're all the same, chemically speaking? Everything starts as hydrogen. Every living thing on earth. Carbon and nitrogen and oxygen—the chemical building blocks of life."

"You've told me this already, Franny."

"No, that was different. *Listen.* Please. These chemicals came out of a fusion process that takes place in the centre of suns, where the heat is twenty-seven million degrees. This heat splits the hydrogen into carbon, into nitrogen, into oxygen. Humans are one of a trillion atomic byproducts of that intense heat. Think about it, Blake: we all hail from stardust."

"That's a nice thought."

"It is, isn't it? But we fuck it up. It's our nature."

When we were kids Franny used to pinch her skin hard enough to draw blood. When I asked why, Franny said she was waiting for it to shed off the way a snake's did. She hoped one night it would fall away and underneath would be a new face, not her own. I'd wondered: why would she ever wish to be something other than what she was?

She took my hand. The sleeve of her nightgown was frayed. Those threads would ignite without much trying at all.

"I've read about towns disappearing," she said. "It can happen overnight. No explanation. The fabric of a place dissolves. Entire families vanish. *Some awfulness gets visited upon the citizenry.* I remember reading that." Her fingers tightened around mine. "*Some awfulness* . . . but what if the people recognized the collective awfulness inside themselves?"

Flames nibbled at the periphery of my vision. The silky crackling of fire.

"Franny, we're not all bad."

"This part of us is."

"*What* part?"

Her arm made a vague sweep that took in the whole of the city. With one finger, she pointed through my skin at my beating heart.

"It wasn't anything you could have beaten, Blake. All this was bound to happen regardless."

Fire was always waiting, patient as a weed, to take us back to our base elements—back to stardust. On a long enough timeline everyone'll pay what they owe. Cities are no different. Fairness doesn't factor.

We stood on the roof, my sister and I, waiting for the payback.

FRANKENSTEIN'S MONSTER
James Arthur

I'm aging very slowly, because every part of me
is already dead. I spent years in the arctic, eating
seal fat and things better left unnamed, but now
I've got money, and a condo on the West Side.
I smell like formaldehyde, my teeth are grimy,

my limbs mismatched, but I'm happy in this place
where I'm one more person with panache
and an ugly face. I eat well. I can walk the bridge
Hart Crane walked, or get drunk, and not
conceal it. I'm not Boris Karloff, lurching
around, a mute—I hate that guy. I get laid.
Here, people suffer without believing

that every stranger should have to feel it.
The other day I walked from Cleopatra's Needle
to the far side of the Harlem Meer, thinking
about the Rockefeller Center, and the gigantic
armillary sphere balanced on the shoulders

of the Atlas statue there. My pants
are fitted. My beret advances everywhere
like a prow. My name isn't Frankenstein.
Frankenstein was my inventor.

CONDITIONAL SPHERE OF EVERYDAY HISTORICAL LIFE

Leon Rooke

In her younger days the woman who would become known as Old Mother had traipsed hither and yon, with never a home. She had come to pal with a gang of rover men, as most beings did at this time, since no other society was known or available to her.

In her ballooning the men shunned her and made her feel herself the outcast slave of them all. But one day a stranger arrived at their campsite. "Our time and being are at slip," he said, "and we must be done with our old split-headed gods who spit nothing but torment and rancour. We must offer our faith to the god of the one head and go forth in the founding of nations." Seated by their fire through the long evening, he endeavoured to set the rover men to thinking right on such issues.

It was at this point that the woman who would become known as Old Mother walked into the firelight, installing a cook-pot above the flames. The stranger teaching the religion of the one-headed god saw her swollen belly and knew then that fortune had steered him to a place of destiny. "Who has seeded this woman?" the man asked, and the men looked away from each other—in consternation at the naiveté of the question—inasmuch as they had as a community conspired in her taking.

"Are you members of the new order of humanity, then," the theologian said, "or shall you continue in the pathways of the alien?" The rovers in the encampment voiced "yea" to the former, for there was much about time and being and their existence under the stars which was disagreeable, as their split-headed gods slaughtered their numbers indiscriminately. They were anxious for something better.

The woman who would become known as Old Mother stirred the pot and fed them, and the stranger studied anew her high belly and the faces of the men who had seeded her.

"Tear off these slithers of tree-bark," he said to them, "and on each slither write your name's symbol, them that can. Them that cannot, then whisper same to me, and I will write down that name. We will put all these names in my hat, and stir the slithers about, and if you trust me I will blindly pluck one from the pot. Whichever slip it is, that will be the woman's name, and the name to be carried by the daughter or son born to her when she sojourns into the future to found our new nation of right and good thinking. "

But the rovers shied from putting their marks into the hat, and stomped and yelled as much as though their old gods of the split heads were again occupying their bodies. The "nations" idea was one foreign to their way of thinking, and how could such a fanciful configuration of beings be managed, and what was the time involved until such a whimsical condition might be realized? If their marks were to be in the hat as fathers of this brave initiative, then what was to be their personal liability if affairs did not go smoothly? Would the vengeful gods of the split heads return to smite or shackle them and drive them away into slavery?

"These are ancient questions unworthy of our release into modernity," the theologian said. "Look ye for the positive function in your existential angst."

The rover men then tried claiming some in their number had been with the woman more than the other and these parties should put their names into the hat by the twenty-fold. They argued on this matter endlessly, as the woman meanwhile swept the clearing for more wood and kept the fire going and bit her lips silent, as she had been compelled to do throughout her own long endurance of all matters pertaining to her time and being. It was a man's world, here among the rovers or elsewhere; fate had yet to decree that she could be in swing with her true and destined orbit.

It was a dreadful cold night, the sky rank and heaving, and the shrubs and tree-limbs nearby their enclosure at glittery freeze.

Eventually one of the rover men agreed he would put his name fifteen times into the hat, since that was his notion of times spent with her, and the others should do likewise, each according to his private reckoning. So they agreed on this method. But they bickered interminably when it came to the particularities of these reckonings, some remembering the one event but denying the other and all confused by those nights when the woman was made to trek from one straw patch to the next, on and on through the night, and by those nights, too, when they were all too wickedly under the influence of fermented juices even to consider with whom she lay or what had been done with her.

The woman busied herself with her tasks, and her opinion on these matters was not germane to anyone's time and being.

In the end the rover men agreed they would together enter forty slips of bark into the hat, plus the fifteen that had already been agreed upon. By this late hour in the proceedings they were all aswell with merriment and filled with self-importance, with food and drink in their gullets to the plenty; thus and so, it came to pass, at the religious fellow's urging, that they consented each to put one gold piece into the hat, for the woman to take away with her that she might provide her offspring with the proper refinements in this new nation of the one god with the one head and not the direful many.

The theologian collected these coins and dropped the mark of their names into his hat. But as he was stirring the names about, one of the men stopped him and said the stranger's mark should be in the hat as well, since he was a good fellow and regular to the bone, and one of them. The other rover men thought this a sound idea, and said furthermore they would make no call of the woman this evening themselves, for they were sick to their guts of her, and she could be his for the taking.

The theologian studied the woman a long time.

"Why have you been beating her?" he asked.

The men denied any whipping of her beyond the normal. They had done by her only what the flesh prescribed as their natural duty. They said she had stumbled upon them all gashed of skin, and that skin rusted, and her hair untamed, and her face swollen this very way he saw it. They reckoned it was how she had come from the harrowing, or how she had aged, or a result of what ill handling other rover gangs had perpetrated upon her, and none of it their doing beyond that which was ordinary and natural.

"How old are you?" the visitor asked the woman.

But he had to shake her by the shoulders and yank at her hair and pry open her mouth with a stick before she replied.

She did not know. And what did it avail her anyway to pursue such knowledge since each day and night of her life had been each day and night alike in its horror?

"Where is it you hail from?"

COPYRIGHT ACKNOWLEDGEMENTS

"The Book with No End" by Colleen Anderson. Copyright © 2013 Colleen Anderson. First published in *Bibliotheca Fantastica*, Dagan Books, 2013. Reprinted by permission of the author.

"Frankenstein's Monster" by James Arthur. Copyright © 2013 James Arthur. First published in *Little Star*, Issue 5. Reprinted by permission of the author.

"Social Services" by Madeline Ashby. Copyright © 2013 Madeline Ashby. First published in *An Aura of Familiarity: Visions from the Coming Age of Networked Matter*, Institute for the Future, 2013. Reprinted by permission of the author.

"The Correspondence between the Governess and the Attic" by Siobhan Carroll. Copyright © 2013 Siobhan Carroll. First published in *Lightspeed*, Issue 43, December 2013. Reprinted by permission of the author.

Red Doc> (excerpt) by Anne Carson. Copyright © 2013 Anne Carson. First published in *Red Doc>*, Knopf, 2013. Reprinted by permission of the author.

"Neanderthal Man, Theory and Practice" by Kate Cayley. Copyright © 2013 Kate Cayley. First published in *When This World Comes to an End*, Brick Books, 2013. Reprinted by permission of the author.

"Girls Watch in the Mirror at Midnight for a Vision of a Future Husband" by Kate Cayley. Copyright © 2013 Kate Cayley. First published in *When This World Comes to an End*, Brick Books, 2013. Reprinted by permission of the author.

"A Charm for Communing with Dead Pets During Surgery" by Peter Chiykowski. Copyright © 2013 Peter Chiykowski. First published in *Hamilton Arts and Letters*, 2013. Reprinted by permission of the author.

"Turing Tests" by Peter Chiykowski. Copyright © 2013 Peter Chiykowski. First published in *Asimov's*, August 2013. Reprinted by permission of the author.

"In the Year Two Thousand Eleven" by Jan Conn. Copyright © 2013 Jan Conn. First published in *Arc*, Volume 70. Reprinted by permission of the author.

"Jazzman/Puppet" by Joan Crate. Copyright © 2013 Joan Crate. First published in *Canadian Poetries*. Reprinted by permission of the author.

"The Runner of n-Vamana" by Indrapramit Das. Copyright © 2013 Indrapramit Das. First published in *Bloodchildren: Stories by the Octavia E. Butler Scholars*, The Carl Brandon Society, 2013. Reprinted by permission of the author.

"Firebugs" by Craig Davidson. Copyright © 2013 Craig Davidson. First published in *The Walrus*, June 2013. Reprinted by permission of the author.

"By His Things You Will Know Him" by Cory Doctorow. Copyright © 2013 Cory Doctorow. First published in *An Aura of Familiarity: Visions from the Coming Age of Networked Matter*, Institute for the Future, 2013. Reprinted by permission of the author.

"Lost" by Amal El-Mohtar. Copyright © 2013 Amal El-Mohtar. First published in *Strange Horizons*, February 2013. Reprinted by permission of the author.

":axiom: the calling" (excerpts) by Daniela Elza. Copyright © 2013 Daniela Elza. First published in *milk tooth bane bone*, Leaf Press, 2013. Reprinted by permission of the author.

"Trap-Weed" by Gemma Files. Copyright © 2013 Gemma Files. First published in *Clockwork Phoenix 4*, Mythic Delirium Books, 2013. Reprinted by permission of the author.

"Oubliette" by Gemma Files. Copyright © 2013 Gemma Files. First published in *The Grimscribe's Puppets*, Miskatonic River Press, 2013. Reprinted by permission of the author.

"Ushakiran" by Laura Friis. Copyright © 2013 Laura Friis. First published in *Lightspeed*, Issue 38, July 2013. Reprinted by permission of the author.

"A Cavern of Redbrick" by Richard Gavin. Copyright © 2013 Richard Gavin. First published in *Shadows and Tall Trees*, Issue 5. Reprinted by permission of the author.

"All My Princes are Gone" by Jennifer Giesbrecht. Copyright © 2013 Jennifer Giesbrecht. First published in *Nightmare Magazine*, Issue 11, August 2013. Reprinted by permission of the author.

"A Tall Girl" by Kim Goldberg. Copyright © 2013 Kim Goldberg. First published in *The New Quarterly*, 126. Reprinted by permission of the author.

"Ksampguiyaeps Woman-Out-to-Sea" by Neile Graham. Copyright © 2013 Neile Graham. First published in *Lady Churchill's Rosebud Wristlet*, 29. Reprinted by permission of the author.

"The Easthound" by Nalo Hopkinson. Copyright © 2013 Nalo Hopkinson. First published in *After*, Disney-Hyperion, 2013. Reprinted by permission of the author.

"Harvesting Lost Hearts" by Louisa Howerow. Copyright © 2013 Louisa Howerow. First published in *Ayris Arts and Literary Magazine*, 2013. Reprinted by permission of the author.

"Your Figure Will Assume Beautiful Outlines" by Claire Humphrey. Copyright © 2013 Claire Humphrey. First published in *Beneath Ceaseless Skies*, Issue 135. Reprinted by permission of the author.

"Salt and Iron Dialogues" by Matthew Johnson. Copyright © 2013 Matthew Johnson. First published in *Salt and Iron Dialogues*, Bundoran Press, 2013. Reprinted by permission of the author.

"The Salamander's Waltz" by Catherine MacLeod. Copyright © 2013 Catherine MacLeod. First published in *Chilling Tales: In Words Alas Drown I*, Edge Science Fiction & Fantasy Publishing, 2013. Reprinted by permission of the author.

"Said the Axe Man" by Tam MacNeil. Copyright © 2013 Tam MacNeil. First published in *Betwixt*, Autumn 2013. Reprinted by permission of the author.

"Nahuales" by Silvia Moreno-Garcia. Copyright © 2013 Silvia Moreno-Garcia. First published in *Bull Spec*, Issue 8+9, February 2013. Reprinted by permission of the author.

"The Fairy Godmother" by Kim Neville. Copyright © 2013 Kim Neville. First published in *Shimmer*, Issue 17. Reprinted by permission of the author.

"Black Hen à la Ford" by David Nickle. Copyright © 2013 David Nickle. First published in *Chilling Tales: In Words Alas Drown I*, Edge Science Fiction & Fantasy Publishing, 2013. Reprinted by permission of the author.

"Jinx" by Robert Priest. Copyright © 2013 Robert Priest. First published in *Previously Feared Darkness*, ECW Press, 2013. Reprinted by permission of the author.

"Knife Throwing Through Self-Hypnosis" by Robin Richardson. Copyright © 2013 Robin Richardson. First published in *Knife Throwing Through Self-Hypnosis*, ECW Press, 2013. Reprinted by permission of the author.

"How Gods Go on the Road" by Robin Richardson. Copyright © 2013 Robin Richardson. First published in *Knife Throwing Through Self-Hypnosis*, ECW Press, 2013. Reprinted by permission of the author.

"Conditional Sphere of Everyday Historical Life" by Leon Rooke. Copyright © 2013 Leon Rooke. First published in *CVC*, Volume 3, Exile Editions. Reprinted by permission of the author.

"Rosary and Goldenstar" by Geoff Ryman. Copyright © 2013 Geoff Ryman. First published in *Fantasy and Science Fiction*, Sep/Oct 2013. Reprinted by permission of the author.

"Stemming the Tide" by Simon Strantzas. Copyright © 2013 Simon Strantzas. First published in *Dead North*, Exile Editions, 2013. Reprinted by permission of the author.

"Book of Vole (Excerpts)" by Jane Tolmie. Copyright © 2013 Jane Tolmie. First published in *Strange Horizons*, May 2013. Reprinted by permission of the author.

"Fishfly Season" by Halli Villegas. Copyright © 2013 Halli Villegas. First published in *Chilling Tales: In Words Alas Drown I*, Edge Science Fiction & Fantasy Publishing, 2013. Reprinted by permission of the author.

"Lesser Creek: A Love Story, A Ghost Story" by A.C. Wise. Copyright © 2013 A.C. Wise. First published in *Clockwork Phoenix 4*, Mythic Delirium Books, 2013. Reprinted by permission of the author.

THE DEAD HAMLETS
PETER ROMAN

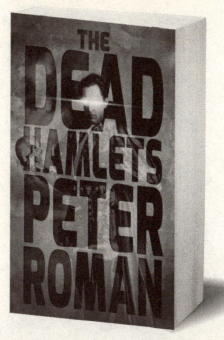

Something is rotten in the court of the faerie queen. A deadly spirit is killing off the faerie, and it has mysterious ties to Shakespeare's play, *Hamlet*. The only one who can stop it is the immortal Cross, a charming rogue who also happens to be a drunk, a thief, and an angel killer. He is no friend of the faerie since they stole his daughter and made her one of their own. He encounters an eccentric and deadly cast of characters along the way: the real Witches of Macbeth, the undead playwright/demon hunter Christopher Marlowe, an eerie Alice from the Alice in Wonderland books, a deranged and magical scholar—and a very supernatural William Shakespeare. When Cross discovers a startling secret about the origins of *Hamlet* itself, he finds himself trapped in a ghost story even he may not be able to escape alive.

AVAILABLE NOW
ISBN 978-1-77148-316-2

CHIZINEPUB.COM

ANGELS & EXILES
YVES MEYNARD

In these twelve sombre tales, ranging from baroque science fiction to bleak fantasy, Yves Meynard brings to life wonders and horrors. From space travellers who must rid themselves of the sins their souls accumulate in transit, to a young man whose love transcends time; from refugees in a frozen hold at the end of space, to a city drowning under the weight of its architectural prayer; from an alien Jerusalem that has corrupted the Earth, to a land still bleeding from the scars of a supernatural war; here are windows opened onto astonishing vistas, stories written with a scientist's laser focus alloyed with a poet's sensibilities.

AVAILABLE NOW
ISBN 978-1-77148-308-7

ALSO AVAILABLE FROM CHIZINE PUBLICATIONS

PROBABLY MONSTERS
RAY CLUELEY

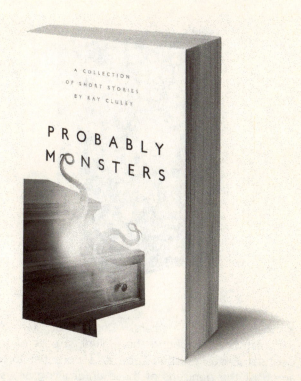

From British Fantasy Award-winning author Ray Cluley comes *Probably Monsters*—a collection of dark, weird, literary horror stories. Sometimes the monsters are bloodsucking fiends with fleshy wings. Sometimes they're shambling dead things that won't rest, or simply creatures red in tooth and claw. But often they're worse than any of these. They're the things that make us howl in the darkness, hoping no one hears. These are the monsters we make ourselves, and they can find us anywhere . . .

AVAILABLE NOW
ISBN 978-1-77148-316-2

CHIZINEPUB.COM

WHAT WE SALVAGE
DAVID BAILLIE

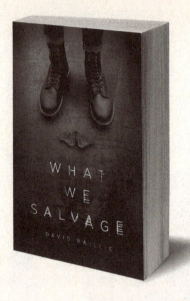

Skinheads. Drug dealers. Cops. For two brothers-of-circumstance navigating the violent streets of this industrial wasteland, every urban tribe is a potential threat. Yet it is amongst the denizens of these unforgiving alleys, dangerous squat houses, and underground nightclubs that the brothers—and the small street tribe to which they belong—forge the bonds that will see them through senseless minor cruelties, the slow and constant grind of poverty, and savage boot culture violence. Friendship. Understanding. Affinity. For two brothers, these fragile ties are the only hope they have for salvation in the wake of a mutual girlfriend's suicide, an event so devastating that it drives one to seek solace far from his steel city roots, and the other to a tragic—yet miraculous—transformation, a heartbreaking metamorphosis from poet and musician to street prophet, emerging from a self-imposed cocoon an urban shaman, mad-eyed shaper of (t)ruthless reality.

AVAILABLE NOW
ISBN 978-1-77148-322-3

ALSO AVAILABLE FROM CHIZINE PUBLICATIONS